EB

He has

HIS IRI

Bride

Three classic stories by three
wonderful Irish writers!

HIS IRISH

Bride

LYNNE GRAHAM

TRISH WYLIE

ABBY GREEN

*M&B™ and M&B™ with the Rose Device
are trademarks of the publisher.
Harlequin Mills & Boon Limited, Eton House,
18-24 Paradise Road, Richmond, Surrey TW9 1SR*

HIS IRISH BRIDE © by Harlequin Books S.A. 2009

The Stephanides Pregnancy © Lynne Graham 2004
White-Hot! © Trish Wylie 2006
The Brazilian's Blackmail Bargain © Abby Green 2007

ISBN: 978 0 263 87539 3

026-0709

*Harlequin Mills & Boon policy is to use papers that are
natural, renewable and recyclable products and made from
wood grown in sustainable forests. The logging and
manufacturing processes conform to the legal environmental
regulations of the country of origin.*

*Printed and bound in Spain
by Litografia Rosés S.A., Barcelona*

The Stephanides
Pregnancy

LYNNE GRAHAM

Dear Reader,

I'm thrilled to have the opportunity for one of my books to appear in a collection with other Irish writers. I'm proud to follow in the great tradition of Irish storytelling.

Telling a gripping story of romance and passion is my prime motivation and I fully believe that the country of my birth has provided me with a rich seam of inspiration. Although I love foreign travel, there is truly no place like home and the friendliness of the people here is legendary. History, which has always fascinated me, is ever present in Ireland in the ancient ring forts, abandoned towers and handsome mansions which act as tangible links to the past. The landscape ranges from the haunting beauty of frequently remote countryside to the grandeur of sheer cliffs, romantic Lakeland and deserted beaches that are often more windswept than sunlit. The forest behind my home and the peat bog along one side are wonderful wildlife havens and untamed scenery very much appeals to me.

On an autumn day when I look out of the window at the trees blowing in gale-force winds and driving rain, however, it is a delight to dream up a Mediterranean scene in which the sea sparkles and the sun shines, such as the deserted Greek island of Mos in *The Stephanides Pregnancy* where Cristos and Betsy fall in love. Writing that story I imagined the pure white sand of the beach crunching below my bare feet and the heat of the sun on my skin. If I can make those images come alive for you as they did for me, I will be satisfied that I have done my job well.

Lynne

CHAPTER ONE

CHRISTOS STEPHANIDES had never been into women in uniform. Had he been, the world would certainly have known about it for the tabloid press reported his every move. A startlingly handsome Greek tycoon with a legendary appetite for super fast cars, luxury homes and dazzlingly beautiful women, Cristos was hotter than hot in the gossip columns.

The young woman who had caught his attention, however, was not in his usual style. Nor was she even aware of his scrutiny because the tinted windows on his limousine shielded him from view. Tall and slender, she wore a dark green fitted jacket and tailored skirt that accentuated her tiny waist and delicate curves just as her plain shoes showed off her award-worthy legs.

'That woman in the peaked cap. Is that an army uniform?' Cristos enquired idly of his second cousin, Spyros Zolottas.

The portly older man peered out. 'She looks more like a flight attendant.'

At the exact moment that Cristos was about to look away, a gust of wind dislodged the woman's cap and sent it careening along the ground. Vibrant streamers of Titian hair flew out in an arc behind her as she sprinted off in pursuit. She caught up with the cap only a few feet from his car. Spring sunshine flamed over the glorious hair she was struggling to coil back into concealment. Surprised by the vivid beauty of her oval face, Cristos stared. Luminous eyes and a luscious cherry-pink mouth highlighted skin as fine and smooth as alabaster: she was knock-down stunning.

Timon, his PA, said quietly, 'I think she might be a chauffeur.'

Disconcertion pleated Cristos' ebony brows, for to his mind a chauffeur fell into the same prohibited category as a servant. Watching the redhead climb into the driving seat of a Bentley that bore the discreet but unmistakable logo of a hire company on the rear bumper, he quirked an ebony brow. 'A strange choice of career for a woman.'

Predictably, Spyros loosed a sleazy snigger. 'With a body like that she may well find it very lucrative.'

Distaste filled Cristos. Spyros had always given him the creeps but he was family and Cristos had been raised to rate blood ties higher than other more instinctive responses.

'Are you thinking of your betrothed?' Having mistaken the reason for the younger man's silence, Spyros released another suggestive laugh. 'Petrina is a well-brought-up girl who knows her place, and if she doesn't know it yet you're just the man to tell her!'

'We will not discuss my engagement,' Cristos murmured, his dark, deep drawl sounding a cool note of warning, which in no way reflected the level of his exasperation.

Cristos was a Stephanides and Petrina was a Rhodias. Their families had long been linked in business and marriage would forge even closer ties. Matrimony was for the preservation of wealth and power and the raising of the next generation. Nobody expected Cristos to be faithful but it would be tasteless to acknowledge that fact out loud. His cousin's vulgarity offended him.

In truth, Cristos had no time for the other man's laboured efforts to flatter and amuse him because he was already waiting for the usual punchline to come. After all, Spyros only ever approached him when he wanted money. Once Spyros had concocted elaborate tales of investments gone wrong and sure-fire business ventures that required capital. If those failed to impress, he would then turn the sob story screws by talking about how his family would suffer for his 'misfortunes'. A gambler and a waster, Spyros had once revelled in his reputation of never having had to work a day in his forty-odd years of life.

Six months ago, Cristos had destroyed the legend by putting Spyros to work in the London office of a freight company, one of the many subsidiary businesses that made up the vast Stephanides empire. He had hoped that, separated from familiar haunts and cronies, Spyros would make a fresh start. To aid that objective, Cristos had paid off all his cousin's debts. His own grandfather, Patras, had laughed like a hyena. In fact, when Cristos had given Spyros a job Patras had laughed so hard he had almost needed resuscitation.

'Spyros is a leech and a loser. There's one in every family and we're too rich to let his nearest and dearest starve. Pay him to keep him out of our hair. You won't change him.' Patras had laid a bet that within months Spyros would have reverted to his old habits.

Cristos had accepted the bet. He saw no reason why the Stephanides clan should fund the dissolute lifestyle that shamed and distressed Spyros' wife and daughters. Although he had every respect for his grandfather, it was his firm belief that someone should have made Spyros toe the line a long time ago. Now Cristos believed that he had lost that bet, for his keenly intelligent gaze had already noted that his late mother's cousin was betraying all the visible stress of a man striving to rise to the challenge of an awkward occasion.

'I know you have to be wondering why I came to meet you off your plane.' Spyros paused and breathed in deep. 'I wanted to thank you personally for the opportunity you gave me last year to turn my life around.'

Lean, strong face expressionless, Cristos stared steadily back at the older man, his surprise that his cousin should speak so freely in front of Timon concealed. 'If that has been the result, I am happy for you,' he murmured with his slow, devastating smile.

Cristos was enough of a cynic to be disconcerted but he was also genuinely pleased.

'You will join us for dinner this evening before you leave?' Spyros pressed with enthusiasm.

Cristos had had other plans. His current mistress would be waiting at the apartment. The perfect end to a long day of business meetings was sex on silk sheets with a woman who would meet his every expectation with unquestioning zeal. With regret he shelved that sensual image and cursed his powerful libido. His principles had spoken: the very least that Spyros deserved was recognition of his achievement.

Before she had even arrived at Gemma and Rory's apartment in the leafy city suburbs, Betsy had promised herself that she would not be over-sensitive to anything her sister said.

So when Gemma widened her china-blue eyes and tossed her pale blonde head and said, 'I think being very skinny is aging,' Betsy, who stuffed herself with biscuits in the forlorn hope that she would develop a larger bosom, just smiled and said nothing.

When Gemma exclaimed in horror over the nails that Betsy had broken tinkering with a temperamental car engine, Betsy said nothing and hid her hands below the table as much as she could. In the same way, she withstood the suggestion that her casual jeans and shirt made her look like a boy and even a later reference to her lack of material success in the world. Indeed she was proud of herself for not rising to the bait.

Rory shared the same table, both with them and not with them, his discomfiture at the atmosphere between his girlfriend and her older sister pronounced. Every so often he made a clumsy attempt to bring in a new conversational subject but no matter what it was it always seemed to provide Gemma with more grist for her mill. Betsy studied Rory in a quick stolen glance. He looked grim, tense and embarrassed. Like Betsy, he was in the dark as to why Gemma seemed to have a need to verbally attack Betsy in every way she could.

After all, on the face of things, Betsy rather than Gemma should have been the sister with the axe to grind and the chip on her shoulder. Three years earlier, Betsy and Rory had been on the brink of getting engaged when Gemma had announced that she was pregnant and that Rory was the father of the baby she was carrying. Their parents had urged Betsy to take the news on the chin. She had done so. She had been far too proud to show any sign of wanting to hang onto a man who had gone behind her back to sleep with

her very much prettier sister. She had also cared too
much for both Rory and Gemma to have made a truly
ghastly situation worse than it already had been and
tear her whole family apart. And unhappily for her,
Betsy reflected ruefully, she had never yet learned how
not to love Rory.

'Every other single girl I know is out partying seven
nights a week...I can't believe that you *still* haven't
found a bloke of your own!' Gemma commented
tartly.

For a split second angry pain gripped Betsy and she
pushed restive fingers through the feathery fringe of
dark red hair on her pale brow. She almost blurted out
that she had had a bloke of her own until Gemma had
stolen him and she only bit back that crack with difficulty. The cost of restraint made hot pink flare over
her cheekbones and she let her pride do her talking
for her and she lied. 'There's a guy at work...I'm seeing him.'

In open disconcertion, her younger sister stared at
her. 'What's his name?'

'Joe...' Betsy compressed her lips and looked down
at her meal without appetite. The same instant as the
untruth had left her lips she'd regretted it, for she realised that that one lie would only lead to further lies.
But Joe did exist, she reminded herself, and, while she
might not be actually dating him, he had at least asked
her out. 'He's new...he started at Imperial two weeks
ago—'

'What age is he? What does he look like?'
Interested questions flooded from Gemma.

'Late twenties. Tall, broad, fair.' Betsy shrugged,
thinking that if she did go out with Joe even once it
would magically transform her lie into the truth.

Gemma grinned. 'Well, it's about time—'

Rory was frowning. 'How much do you know about this guy? There are a lot of creeps out there. Be careful,' he urged Betsy.

Gemma's grin fell off her pretty face as though she had been slapped and Betsy could have groaned out loud. Gemma took offence if Rory showed the slightest interest in or concern for her sister. Bowing her head, Betsy got through the awkward silence that followed that comment by scooping up the pyjama-clad toddler who had crept into the room while the adults were talking. Snatched up into a cuddle by her fond aunt, the little girl giggled and turned up an entrancing face. An adorable mix of her parents' genes, Sophie had Rory's dark brown hair matched with Gemma's big blue eyes. Soon after the diversion supplied by her niece's entrance, Betsy announced that she 'really *had* to fly' because she had an early start in the morning.

She had only just got back to her cramped bedsit in Hounslow when her mother phoned her.

'Gemma's really upset…' Corinne Mitchell began, and although a sense of absolute frustration engulfed Betsy at those familiar words she still sat down to dutifully listen.

'I shouldn't have gone over for dinner.' Betsy sighed. 'It just causes friction.'

'There wouldn't be a problem if Rory would just *marry* your poor sister,' her mother lamented. 'There she is, the mother of a two-year-old, and there's still no sign of a wedding ring! Of course she's unhappy. They've got their nice apartment and Rory is doing well as a lawyer. What's he waiting for?'

Betsy drew in a slow, deep sustaining breathe. 'This isn't any of my business, Mum—'

'But you know Rory Bartram better than anyone!' Corinne protested vehemently. 'He's breaking Gemma's heart—'

'Lots of couples live together these days,' Betsy interposed gently.

'Rory wasn't planning to make you live in sin, though, was he?' Corinne snapped out that reminder with audible resentment on her younger daughter's behalf. 'Is it any wonder that Gemma feels terribly hurt when she sees the father of her child paying attention to you?'

'He *wasn't* paying attention to me,' Betsy stressed wearily, but she knew that the older woman was barely listening. All worked up by the spur of a doubtless emotional phone tirade from her younger daughter, Corinne Mitchell was set on having her say about the deficiencies of Gemma's relationship with Rory.

It was a familiar pattern and it hurt Betsy a lot that her mother should be so indifferent to her feelings. Why did she have to be upbraided with the tale of Gemma's problems with Rory? Why was she expected to endure her sister's shrewish comments in forgiving silence? Even less welcome was the wounding bitter note in her mother's voice that implied that it was somehow Betsy's fault that Gemma's world was not as rosy and perfect as she thought it should be.

More and more Betsy was learning that when Gemma was annoyed with her she would be shunned by the rest of her family as well. It would be quite a few weeks before she heard from her mother again. Gemma was very like her mother in looks and personality and Corinne identified closely with Gemma's interests. When she was a kid, Betsy had never questioned the reality that her sister two years her junior was the favoured child. As a baby, Gemma had had a heart murmur and everybody had fussed over her. By the time she'd received a clean bill of health, her parents had been so used to giving her the lion's share of their attention that nothing had changed. Betsy's parents simply idolised Gemma and Sophie was the jewel in her sister's crown.

In comparison, Betsy had always been a bit of a misfit in the Mitchell family circle. Her preferences in clothes and her interests had never been feminine enough to meet with her mother's approval. In fact her happiest childhood memories revolved round her late grandfather, who had restored classic cars in his spare time. As a teenager, she had been a sporty tomboy, obsessed with cars when other girls her age had been obsessed with the boys who drove them. On that front she had been a shy late developer and intimidated by the success of her kid sister in the same department. Boys had started chasing Gemma when she was only thirteen.

Betsy had met Rory at a sports club when she was eighteen. He had been a friend first, but she had known how she'd felt about him long before he'd got around to asking her out. At that point, Betsy killed her forbidden thoughts stone dead. That was the past, she reminded herself sharply. Nobody needed to tell her that no man could be 'stolen' by another woman against his will. Nor, she reflected, should she even have been surprised when Rory had fallen for Gemma, who was much livelier and sexier. That mental slap administered, Betsy got into bed.

The next morning when she arrived at work, Joe

Tyler was already putting a gleaming polish to the bonnet of the car he drove. He was a hard worker, she acknowledged grudgingly, and she questioned her own almost instinctive recoil from him. So he struck her as being a little arrogant and conceited, but he was young, attractive and single and she had met men smug about a great deal less. It was only two weeks since he had joined the staff at Imperial Limousines and he didn't join in with the usual grousing about the awkward hours, the low pay and the demanding and unappreciative customers. In fact, rather like herself, Joe was a loner and a man of few words. How long had it been since she had dated someone? *Too* long, she decided, strolling rather self-consciously closer to the blond man.

'You said you would get tickets for the racing at Silverstone…is the offer still open?'

Joe kept on polishing. 'Maybe…'

Her ready temper sparked her into embarrassed defensiveness. 'Well, when you've made your mind up, tell me. But then maybe *I'll* need—'

'No, you took me up wrong,' Joe protested, planting a large hand on her arm to prevent her walking away again. 'Offer's still open.'

He was built like a rock face and the unease that he had awakened in her before almost surfaced again. Mastering the urge to go into retreat, she managed to smile instead and told herself not to take offence at the smug satisfaction he could barely hide. If Joe Tyler thought she would be a pushover for his muscular charm, he would soon find out how wrong he was…

Six weeks after his previous visit, Cristos flew into London from the South of France.

Timon met him off his flight and handed him a sealed envelope.

Cristos raised a questioning brow. 'What's this?'

'Spyros Zolottas asked me to give it to you before you left the airport.'

Cristos pulled out a brash greetings card signed by his cousin. 'But it's not my birthday,' he said in bewilderment.

Timon looked tense and said nothing. Some minutes later, Cristos came to a halt twenty feet away from the limousine that his PA had indicated across the car park. His mystification came to a sudden end and was replaced by a raw leap of anticipation. He had a photographic memory. It was the same car that had been driven by the beautiful redhead he had admired while in his cousin's company more than a month earlier. He could not initially credit that Spyros could have come up with such a classy surprise.

Timon broke into an urgent explanation, 'Your cousin was determined to surprise you. He said that he would take responsibility for hiring this particular limo company for the weekend but I didn't feel—'

'No need to hyperventilate,' His employer advised in a husky undertone, his bold dark eyes glittering over the female figure already emerging from the driver's seat.

Not even the chauffeur's uniform could conceal her essential perfection. Slender as a reed with a waist that could not be larger than the span of his two hands, she moved with the liquid grace of a dancer. He pictured her in silk. Silk that would slide across her fine skin and feel smooth as satin beneath his hands. It did not cross his mind for even a moment that he might not be able to have her. Whenever he wanted a woman, she came to him. Whichever woman he wanted, he got. Once or twice the strength of his own magnetic pull with her sex had been a curse when the wives and partners of his friends had given him willing and eager signals. But he had never met with failure.

'I should warn you that your security team are very concerned by this last-minute change in your travel arrangements,' Timon continued anxiously. 'There has not even been time to check out this new company.'

'I am entirely content,' Cristos drawled, his whole attention on the young woman pacing round the limo in a last-minute inspection. He sensed her innate pride in the angle of her small head, the straightness of her spine and the upward tilt of her delicate jaw line. Would she be a challenge? He loved a challenge but he was practical too: he only had a weekend to spare.

'It is a much smaller firm…standards of service may not be what you are accustomed to—'

The beginnings of a wicked smile tugged at Cristos' wide, sensual mouth. 'On the other hand, standards of service might be beyond any I have previously received.'

At that point, Timon took the hint and surrendered to the inevitable.

'I'm afraid you'll have to find your own way back to the office today,' Cristos added without hesitation.

An involuntary grin chased the earnest aspect from the younger man's face.

Betsy was in a very prickly mood. Her boss had warned her that the new client was a mega-rich foreign VIP to be treated like a god in the hope of attracting further business. While amazed that an employer who gave all the best opportunities to the men on his staff had selected her as driver, she had been pleased as well. However, before she'd even left for the airport Imperial Limousines had received a visit from Cristos Stephanides' bodyguards. That had caused a stir. Their usual clients were not in the league that required hefty personal security. The bodyguards had not been impressed by the shabby premises that housed the limo firm. They had turned up their noses at the vehicle she was to use, queried her excellent driving credentials and warned her that they would be in close supervision at all times. A bunch of unredeemable sexist pigs, she thought bitterly, who had been busily engaged in patrolling the car park like the cast of a gangster movie ever since her arrival.

Sixth sense warned her that she was under scrutiny. Spinning round, she jerked still at the sight of the male striding towards her. It was as if someone somewhere turned the pace of time to slow motion. He was tall, lean and...and so beautiful that her chest went all tight and she couldn't breathe and couldn't stop looking. But then her brain stepped into the breach and forced her to grab a hold of herself and break free of her own shocking paralysis.

'Mr Stephanides...' Mercifully her voice emerged a little breathless round the edges but calm and quiet in tone.

'And you are...?'

'Betsy Mitchell,' she framed, holding open the door to the rear passenger seat.

'Betsy...' He said her name as if he were savouring something edible and he had a voice like no other she had ever heard before. His drawl had a dark, deep, masculine pitch, a sizzlingly sexy accented edge that sent a quiver down her taut spine. 'So that's what I call you.'

'Mitchell will do, sir,' she answered without expression, throwing up the barrier of their differing status with a strong sense of relief.

Unaccustomed to being contradicted, Cristos glanced down at her. She was not as tall as he had assumed she was from a distance: she was around five feet eight or nine. What was more, her façade of cool professionalism was a fake. He was a trained observer and he could see the almost undetectable tiny nervous tremors assailing her slight length.

'I prefer Betsy,' he murmured softly to make her look up at him.

Disconcerted, she tipped back her head to lift her gaze and met his brilliant dark eyes for the first time. Her mouth ran dry and her heartbeat took off at a sprint. His provocative appraisal dropped to linger on her soft full lips and then roamed on down to the pouting thrust of her breasts before flicking back up again to spell out a message of sexual interest as blatant as a speech.

Deeply shaken, she tore her gaze from his fiercely handsome features. He swung into the car and she closed the door on him. Her palms were damp on the steering wheel. How dared he look her over as if she were on offer to him? Perhaps he had noticed the way she looked at him, a snide little inner voice mocked and a wash of hot, guilty pink warmed her cheeks. What had come over her? He was the fanciable equivalent of a flying saucer. Of course she had stared. Any woman would have stared. Why was she beating herself up about a perfectly natural reaction? The guy was drop dead gorgeous. He was lucky she hadn't stuck a pin in him to check he was real and not an illusion.

Nervous laughter bubbling in her throat, she hit the communication button.

'Everything in order, sir?' she asked.

'There's no still water in the fridge,' he informed her.

And there she had been thinking he would be dazzled by the array of soft drinks available to him! He was supposed to be very rich, she reminded herself, and the rich were reputed to be picky about little details. There was the proof. His refined taste buds could not tolerate sparkling in place of still water. She pulled off the road at the first garage and was in the act of climbing out when he buzzed down the glass partition dividing them. 'Why have we stopped?' he demanded.

Betsy spun back in surprise and leant back into the limo to address him. 'You wanted still mineral water. My boss said your every wish should be my command…'

'I *wish*…' Cristos Stephanides murmured, smooth and soft as velvet.

Staring at him, she was entrapped by his sheer animal magnetism and exotic dark good looks. His luxuriant hair looked very dark against the pale backdrop of the leather head restraint. His bronzed skin was stretched taut over hard masculine cheekbones, an arrogant nose and a beautifully chiselled wide, sensual mouth. With an immense effort, she broke free of the scorching dark golden eyes that were making her tummy flip like a schoolgirl's.

She hurried into the garage shop. Her legs felt like cotton-wool supports. She was in a daze. So he was flirting a little—so what was new? Some guys thought you expected it. Some guys flirted with every woman they met. *I wish* he had said. Why was she suddenly acting and thinking like a ditzy teenager? He made her feel like one. She blinked in bemusement as she turned away from the checkout.

His senior bodyguard, a giant with shoulders the size of tree trunks, barred her passage. 'Who gave you permission to stop the limo without warning us?' he asked in an angry hiss. 'You have left Mr Stephanides in an unlocked vehicle without protection. How could you be so foolish?'

Betsy was astonished by the force of that verbal attack. 'Nobody told me I needed permission or that I should warn you—'

'How else can we do our job? Don't deviate from the agreed route again,' he admonished.

Pale with angry discomfiture, Betsy got back into the car. She passed the mineral water into the rear seat without turning her head and ignited the engine when she heard her passenger speak. She was annoyed at a telling off that she considered unjust. She drove people to functions like weddings and balls and had only once dealt with a minor celebrity. Imperial Limousines was a small firm that did not have a VIP client list. She was not accustomed to dealing with wealthy international businessmen and had not been trained to handle complex security requirements. The sooner she delivered him to his fancy country estate, the happier she would be.

'What happened back there?' Cristos enquired.

'I beg your pardon?' Betsy questioned in turn, face and voice deadpan.

'One of my bodyguards approached you...' Dolius, the head of his security team, whose abrasive personality would never fit him for a diplomatic career. Cristos had watched her green eyes flare with anger while her chin had tilted at a very feminine wounded but stubborn angle. He had been startled by his own urge to leap out of the car and tell Dolius to pick on someone his own size and sex if he wanted a fight.

'Oh, *that*…yes, he was just wondering why I'd pulled off the road,' she advanced with studied lightness.

Dolius had come down on her like a ton of bricks for that impulse, Cristos translated. 'He upset you.'

'No, of course he didn't!' No way was Betsy about to tell tales on another employee whom she had to deal with.

Cristos was furious that she was lying to him. That she was upset was painfully obvious. She was no good at hiding her feelings. She was also driving very, very slowly and making all kinds of restless, unnecessary adjustments to various switches and dials. He was even less pleased when she closed the partition.

Betsy was trying not to think about what a truly horrible week she had had. She had ignored her ESP when it came to Joe Tyler and she had paid the price. A cold shiver of remembrance ran through her. At the end of the first date he had parked the car down an entry and tried to treat her like some hooker he had picked up off the street. She had had to fight him off and he had been very abusive. It had been a seriously scary experience. In the light of that ordeal, she could only marvel at her own adolescent response to Cristos Stephanides. As she hadn't been remotely attracted to Joe, she should never have encouraged him. Cristos Stephanides? He was as safe a fantasy as a poster on a bedroom wall, she decided, and she accelerated down the motorway.

Cristos had never been so comprehensively ignored

by a woman. Having no intention of opening a conversation with the back of her head, he opted for the direct approach. He lifted the car phone to communicate with her. 'Take the next turn off. There's a hotel. We'll stop there for a break.'

'Is this a scheduled stop?' Betsy enquired.

'I don't have a schedule this weekend. I'm not working,' Cristos spelt out.

Betsy tried not to smile at the thought of the mayhem that had to be breaking out in the bodyguards' car when the limo was seen to deviate yet again from the agreed route. But she resisted any urge to glance into the back seat and catch another glimpse of her passenger. At twenty-five years of age, she was too old to be daydreaming like a schoolgirl over a guy she knew nothing about.

Her footsteps crunching over the gravel outside the gracious country hotel, she pulled open the passenger door.

'I hate being locked in a car for hours on end,' Cristos imparted in his rich, dark drawl. 'We'll have coffee.'

She forgot her embargo on looking at him and tipped her head back to encounter brilliant dark golden eyes fringed by black spiky lashes. 'Thank you, sir…but I'll stay with the limo.'

His gaze narrowed. 'That wasn't a request…it was an order.'

Off-balanced by that unhesitating contradiction, she stared at him for a split second too long and then hurriedly dropped her head, her colour fluctuating. Maybe he was keen to ensure that his driver remained alert by taking an adequate break. Fair enough. She locked the car and followed in his arrogant wake. His head bodyguard strode towards them. Cristos Stephanides addressed him in what she assumed to be his own language. Just a handful of brief, softly spoken words and the security man turned pale and backed off with what might have been a hasty apology.

Indoors, engulfed in the ticking-clock silence of the kind of luxury establishment set up to create the atmosphere of a private country house, she was hugely uncomfortable. But it made no impression whatsoever on her companion. He addressed the receptionist with the calm expectancy of a male who had been waited on hand and foot from the day of his birth.

'Sit with me…' With a lean brown hand he indicated an armchair beside the magnificent marble fireplace.

Betsy stared fixedly into the burning embers of the welcoming fire. 'It wouldn't be appropriate, sir.'

'Allow me to decide what's appropriate.'

'But not what I do with my free time. If this is an official break,' Betsy responded with flat clarity, 'I'm entitled to choose how I spend it.'

'Obviously the whip and chair approach is unwise with a woman of your strength of character,' Cristos Stephanides conceded lazily. 'I ask you in all humility…please join me for coffee.'

Involuntary amusement tugged at Betsy. *In all humility?* Was he serious? She almost laughed out loud. He had the extreme poise and arrogant assurance of a male who had never known what humility was. Why was he even making the invitation? What was in it for him?

'Why?' she asked baldly, tipping her head back, eyes as bright as emerald chips gleaming with suspicion.

Theos mou, why was she fighting him? Back at the car park in that very first visual exchange, Cristos had recognised her desire. She had not been able to hide the feverish longing that he had seen on so many female faces since he'd been a teenager. But he could not recall when he had last had to make so much effort. She was not encouraging him. She was making everything difficult. He had got lazy, he acknowledged. His women always did most of the running, but now he was dealing with a female who looked as if she would bolt at the first ill-chosen word or move.

'I feel like company,' he murmured with deliberate casualness, hitching back his powerful personality and swallowing the smarter comments hovering on the tip of his tongue.

Betsy was bemused. A client had never tried to cross the boundaries with her before. She saw no reason why he should be any different. Her uniform was old-fashioned and unflattering. In the course of her working day few men had given her a second glance.

'Are you married?' Cristos asked abruptly, belatedly wondering if there was a reason for her surprising hesitance. 'Living with someone?'

'No…but—'

Cristos curved a confident hand to her spine and urged her down onto the richly upholstered sofa. 'Then join me.'

Unyielding as a stone pillar, she sank down. He took her taut silence in his stride and filled it with the story of a society wedding he had recently attended at the hotel. He was very amusing. She sat there enthralled, unable to take her eyes from his lean, devastating features. Indeed the excuse to watch him was a conscious pleasure and a release from the deprivation of not being able to look. Everything about him fascinated her.

She drank her coffee without tasting it. At his request she took her cap off and coloured at the intensity of his scrutiny. She answered his few questions. She was twenty-five, single, had worked at Imperial for three years, had always wanted to work with cars. That he was not that interested in her answers was not something she judged him on for she initially assumed he was merely making polite conversation. Slowly, very slowly, for she had always held a very modest opinion of her own looks, she realised that Cristos Stephanides actually appeared to be attracted to her and was seeking a response.

At the point where she could no longer mistake his motives and without any hesitation whatsoever, Betsy lifted her cap, replaced it on her head and rose to her feet. 'I'm your driver,' she said bluntly. 'I'm not interested in anything else.'

In fierce disconcertion at that sudden bold assurance, Cristos sprang upright, brilliant dark eyes cool as black ice. 'That's a lie.'

Mortified colour stained her fair skin at that direct contradiction but Betsy still lifted her chin. 'I can admire a painting without wanting to buy it—'

'This situation may be unconventional—'

'There isn't a situation and if there were, it would be tacky.' Betsy was infuriated by his attempt to excuse his behaviour. 'This isn't a social occasion and I wouldn't risk my job for you. I drive limos for a living and you do whatever you do to afford to hire people like me…and that's it—'

'I'm not a snob—'

'No?' A delicate auburn brow rose, questioning that

assertion, green eyes scornful and furious. 'But then you don't need to be. You weren't asking me out on a date, were you? The only invite I was going to get was a sleazy sexual one. Well, no, thank you!'

Cristos wanted to rip the cap off her again and…? His lean brown hands coiled into savage fists. And then do all the sleazy sexual stuff until she was on her knees with gratitude that he had honoured her with his interest. Her attack on him was out of all proportion to anything he had said or done and he was outraged that she had chosen to spring such a scene on him in a public place where he could not freely respond. Across the room, Dolius and his second-in-command were studiously avoiding looking anywhere near him, which told Cristos that they had not missed a single second of the drama. Seething with injured pride and a fierce sense of injustice, Cristos Stephanides watched Betsy Mitchell stalk out of the hotel.

What a smooth, calculating, utterly ruthless bastard, Betsy thought tempestuously, slamming her way into the driver's seat of the limo and still shaking with fury. Had he really believed that he could sweet-talk her into going upstairs to a hotel room with him? For when he'd insisted she join him for coffee that had surely been his intent! Did she look stupid enough to make a mistake of that magnitude? Or so cheap and easy he had assumed she would be a pushover? Had he planned to reward her with an extra large tip? Or his magnificent body? When she saw him approaching in the wing mirror, she sat tight.

Hard jaw line at a stubborn angle, Cristos refused to open the door for himself. He stood there challenging her and, had it been necessary, he would have continued to stand there through thunder, lightning and

a force-ten gale to make his point. Clumsy with re-
sentful haste, Betsy finally scrambled out and
wrenched open the passenger door for him.

'Thank you,' Cristos breathed, smooth as glass.

She did not believe that she had ever hated another
human being so much as she did him at that instant.
She drove for an hour with a fierce concentration that
shut out every thought. The limo left the motorway
for quiet country roads and speed was no longer possible. With scant warning a tractor pulled out of a lane.
As the slow vehicle forced a passage out in front of
the bodyguards' car Betsy almost smiled at the thought
of the annoyance it would cause.

The partition between driver and passenger buzzed
down. 'For the record,' Cristos Stephanides breathed
with sardonic bite, 'I'm not into sleazy sex.'

'If you want an argument, come back and see me
when I'm no longer working for you and forced to be
polite,' Betsy snapped.

'Back at the hotel…that was you being *polite*?'
Cristos stressed in a derisive tone of wonderment that
made her want to stop the limo, leap into the back seat
and beat him up.

'You were out of line,' Betsy snapped at him furiously. 'What sort of a guy tries to pull his chauffeur?'

'One who has just become a convert to total snob-
bery,' Cristos spelt out with maddening assurance.

It was at that point that Betsy saw a male figure
crouched down by the side of the road just ahead. That
was the only warning she had before something that
gleamed metallic and grey in the sunlight was thrown
at the car. The wheels ran over it. A tyre blew out and
then another, sending the powerful vehicle out of her
control into a dangerous swerve. The limo hit the ditch

with a thunderous jolt that rattled every bone in her body. Almost simultaneously the door beside her was yanked noisily open.

In disbelief, Betsy saw Joe Tyler peering in at her and momentarily wondered if she was coming round after having been knocked out, for she could not understand how otherwise he could have been there on the spot. 'Joe...?' she framed uncertainly, still reeling from the impact of the crash.

'Have a nice sleep, Betsy.'

Too late she noticed that he had what looked like a gun clutched in his hand. She did not even have time to panic. A tingling pain hit her midriff and she gasped because without warning her limbs seemed to turn to jelly. Joe thrust her aside with no more care than he would have accorded a sack. Just before she passed out she heard him speak again, but what he said made little sense to her.

'Imagine a bloke like you fancying my girl-friend...well, you both deserve a surprise!'

The black claustrophobic cloud of oblivion rolled in over Betsy and her body slumped down on the seat. Within seconds her passenger was in the same condition.

CHAPTER TWO

CRISTOS recovered consciousness first.

Instantly he came alert and defied any awareness of physical discomfort to spring off the bed on which he had been lying. His keen dark eyes took on a dazed aspect as he struggled to get a handle on his unfamiliar surroundings. He studied the unconscious woman still on the bed with scorching intensity. The ubiquitous cap had gone and straying strands of bright Titian hair feathered her brow. Her skin was white as snow. Like Mary's little lamb in the nursery rhyme? A harsh laugh escaped Cristos but there was nothing of humour in it.

What a very dangerous distraction Betsy Mitchell had proved to be! There was nothing more galling to Cristos than the awareness that he had allowed a woman to lead him into a prearranged trap. It was poetic justice however that she had been double crossed by her partners in crime and abandoned to the tender mercies of their victim. No doubt she would learn the hard way that Cristos would choose death over victimhood any day.

Fierce thirst brought Betsy out of her stupor. Even before she opened her eyes, she knew she felt dreadful. Her limbs felt as heavy as leaden weights. She was also incredibly hot and it was that awareness that first roused her to register that something was wrong. She was wearing clothes and she never lay down fully dressed. In the same moment as she lifted her lashes on an unfamiliar room, she remembered Joe attacking

29

her. She pressed a hand to her midriff, felt a slight soreness there and tore off her uniform jacket to lift her shirt and touch the tiny red puncture wound. A sense of complete unbelief enveloped her. He must have shot her with some sort of tranquilliser dart because she had passed out. But why would Joe have done such a thing? *Cristos!* Cristos Stephanides. Where on earth was he?

In the grip of fear and horror that Joe was some kind of maniac who had kidnapped her because she had rejected him, Betsy scrambled upright. She was only wearing one shoe and there was no sign of the missing one. Kicking off the one that remained, she raced out of the bedroom and headed straight for the wide open door several feet beyond.

In that doorway, Betsy came to a breathless halt. She blinked. Her lower lip parted company from the upper in an inelegant expression of astonishment. Barely a hundred feet away a shimmering sea as crystal-blue as the sky above was washing a sandy beach. The beauty of the scene struck her as incongruous and she thought she had to be hallucinating. When she had lost control of the limo, it had been raining. It had been a typical English spring day: sunny and damp in turns with a breeze thrown in for good measure. But the heat of the golden sun above seemed Mediterranean.

Cristos strode into view from behind the rocks girding the northern edge of the beach. Her tummy flipped. Intense relief filled her. He was safe and, whether it was logical or not, his presence made her feel less afraid. As he drew closer she charted the changes in his once immaculate appearance. He had doffed his suit jacket and tie. A pearl-grey shirt open at his brown throat outlined his broad shoulders. His black hair was tousled and a heavy growth of dark stubble outlined his stubborn jaw line and wide, sensual mouth. He still looked spectacular. Her tummy performed another somersault. His hardcore sexuality had a powerful charge.

Seeing her, Cristos came to a halt. Glittering dark eyes zeroed in on her, his lean, handsome features clenching into formidable stillness. 'Where are we?' he asked roughly.

Her brow furrowed, for she could not understand why he should ask her that question in a tone that implied that she would have that information at her fingertips. 'I don't know…do you?'

'How the hell would I know? Don't play dumb with me,' Cristos warned her.

Her spine stiff with tension and forgetting that she was not wearing shoes, Betsy moved out onto the sun-warmed path. The surface was uncomfortably hot for soles encased only in nylon tights and she hurried into the sparse shade thrown by the gnarled tree that grew at the front of the house. 'Play dumb? I don't under-stand—'

'I know that you were involved in plotting my kid-napping—'

'You know…*what*?'

'You must've been shattered to wake up here and realise that your fellow conspirators had decided to ditch you—'

'My fellow conspirators? What on earth are you ac-cusing me of?' Betsy fired back at him in frank be-wilderment.

'You greeted the gorilla who shot us both full of knock-out drugs by name.'

Her brain, she discovered in frustration, was very reluctant to process thoughts with anything like its usual efficiency. Gorilla? Did he mean Joe? Of course Joe was involved in the kidnapping because he had attacked them both. 'Joe works for Imperial Limousines…I didn't appreciate what was happening when he first opened the car door—'

'You said his name quite happily,' Cristos Stephanides countered.

'I was in shock…I hadn't had enough time to appreciate that the crash hadn't been an accident.' She lifted an unsteady hand to her brow, which was damp as much with stress as with the unfamiliar heat. She pulled out the clip anchoring her hair and let it fall, massaging the back of her neck where the clip had left a tender spot. 'That was a stinger that was hurled in front of the car to puncture the tyres and force us to a stop, wasn't it?'

Cristos surveyed her with brooding intensity. 'If you're trying to convince me that you're innocent of any involvement, you're wasting your breath. You are also making me angry—'

Her anxiety growing, Betsy gazed back at him. 'You're serious, aren't you? But you can't decide that I'm a criminal just because I know Joe—'

'I don't think I'm quite that simplistic.' Cristos dealt her a derisive look.

'How could I not know him when he works in the same place?'

'Oh, I think the connection between you and Joe was a touch more intimate than that,' Cristos murmured with scathing softness.

Betsy was exceedingly reluctant to accept that he

might be implying a certain fact that she was in no hurry to tell him. 'What do you mean?'

'He referred to you as his girlfriend.'

The guilty colour ran up hot beneath her skin. Too late she recalled Joe making some crack in that line before she'd lost consciousness. 'I went out with him once...OK?'

'No, it's not OK. Nothing about this situation is OK.' His lean, hard-boned face was grim. 'You're involved in this filthy business right up to your throat—'

'Look, if you dated a serial killer once, would you be responsible for her crimes?' Betsy threw at him. He was being so unfair to her. She was ashamed and embarrassed that she had ever gone out with someone of Joe's evident propensities. But surely nothing she had said or done could possibly have contributed to the current situation?

'I haven't got time for this nonsense...' Cristos strode forward and closed lean hands to her forearms. 'I've been kidnapped. My life is at risk. I have no plans to sit around on a deserted island in the middle of an ocean waiting for the kidnappers' next move—'

'We're on an island?' Betsy interrupted in dismay, wincing a little at the strength of those long, tensile fingers, which were biting just a tad uncomfortably into her arms.

She had always considered herself to be a fair height. However, Cristos Stephanides had to be around six feet four inches tall. He towered over her to such an extent that she felt tiny. Indeed she was beginning to feel actively intimidated by him. He was very strong and he was very angry and he was not listening to her. Could she blame him for that? He *had* been kidnapped. His life probably was at risk. Whether she liked it or not she could understand why he should be highly suspicious of a woman who appeared to have been on terms of familiarity with one of his kidnappers.

'Where is this island?' Cristos demanded harshly. 'I need to know everything that you know so that I can work out what's coming next!'

'But I don't *know* anything…' In a sudden movement that took him by surprise, Betsy tore herself free and backed hurriedly away from him. 'You've got to believe me about that—'

Unafraid to turn up the pressure, Cristos advanced. 'I don't. You were the bait, and very effective bait. I went for it—'

Her slender length rigid, Betsy slowly increased the distance between them with quiet, cautious steps. Her nervous antenna was on a high state of alert. After all, what did she know about Cristos Stephanides and how violent he might be in such circumstances? He believed she had conspired with his kidnappers and might feel that his need for information was justification for getting rough. She found it bitterly ironic that just ten days earlier she would have stood her ground against Cristos, blithely confident that she could look after herself and that most men were essentially decent. It was Joe Tyler who had taught her to fear masculine strength. He had held her against her will long enough to teach her to be scared and had for ever stolen her peace of mind in male company.

'I wasn't the bait,' Betsy swore, fighting to put as much weight and sincerity into her voice as she could while at the same time wondering what the heck he was talking about. 'I had nothing to do with your kidnapping and I was as shocked by all this as you are.'

'Like hell you were,' Cristos growled, watching the sunlight pick up the deep coppery tints in the fantastic rippling coil of hair sliding across her shoulders with her every movement. He was convinced she had let her hair down in an effort to distract him. 'You were a part of it right up until your boyfriend decided to sacrifice you—'

'He isn't my boyfriend…he's a creep I went out with one time!' Betsy launched back at him in frustration.

'I won't accept your lies. I want answers from you and I want them fast.' Lean, strong face hard with determination, Cristos surveyed her with merciless dark eyes. 'You have put my life at risk and you owe me, so start talking…'

The menacing chill he exuded scared her. She felt that an unspoken threat hung in the air between them. The very tone of his dark, deep drawl sent a shiver licking down her taut spinal cord. In a sudden movement, she spun on her heel and took off across the beach. He shouted after her, called her name but she just ran even faster.

Cristos swore long and low. He had seen the stark fear blossoming at the back of her eyes and done nothing to assuage it. Was she used to men who lashed out with their fists? That concept shook him. He had never hurt a woman in his life. No woman had ever looked at him in that way before. No woman had ever had cause. He released his breath in a raw exhalation, acknowledging that he had been prepared to use her fear to his own advantage. His continuing health could well depend on what he could learn from Betsy Mitchell, but frightening her had been a wrong move.

Betsy cut up through the sand dunes and scattered

the clutch of small wiry sheep grazing there. 'Relax,' she told them apologetically, but they kept their distance.

Just as she would keep her distance from Cristos Stephanides until his temper had had time to cool, she decided. In spite of the heat she still felt cold when she thought about Joe Tyler. She doubted that that was even his real name, for he had only come to work at Imperial Limousines *after* the Stephanides booking had been made. No wonder Joe hadn't mixed with the other men. His objective must always have been the kidnapping of Cristos Stephanides. But she was mystified as to why Joe Tyler had shown such a keen interest in her from the outset and asked her out.

She sheltered from the sun under a clump of trees and tried not to think about how desperately thirsty she was. She could still see the terracotta roof of the stone house and beyond it another smaller building. A boathouse? A slipway ran between it and the jetty. In every direction she looked the views of sparkling turquoise sea, pale golden sand and lush green vegetation were incredibly beautiful. But she would have given them all up just for a drink. But how were the sheep surviving? Somewhere, she registered, there had to be fresh water.

Trees overhung the stream she found and the water ran so clear that she could see the colour of every pebble. Using her hand as a scoop, she drank deep and long and splashed her face into the bargain. Drowsiness overwhelmed her then and in the cool of the shaded bank she pillowed her head on her arms and let herself sleep.

Betsy wakened with a start, glanced at her watch and realised that she had been dead to the world for hours.

Dusk was beginning to roll in and she scrambled upright and headed back in the direction of the beach. On the way there she stumbled and cut her foot on a sharp stone. Peeling off her ruined tights, she examined the wound. It was bleeding freely and she grimaced and ripped up the tights to make an impromptu bandage. Someone had once told her that salt water could act like an antiseptic and she limped with difficulty across the sand and clambered onto the rocks that stretched out into the sea to find a place where she could safely bathe her foot.

Cristos was finishing his fifth complete circuit of the island. As the afternoon had worn on into evening and he could still find no trace of Betsy Mitchell his concern had grown in proportion. He had searched every possible hiding place and come up with nothing. When he saw her standing on the promontory his relief was immense. He strode across the beach towards her. She was standing on one slender leg like a heron but she lacked the bird's one-legged balance and she was swaying in apparent indifference to danger on the edge of the rocks washed by the surf.

'Betsy...come back from there!' Cristos launched at her in the command intonation that always extracted instant unquestioning obedience from his employees.

Betsy was startled by that formidable intervention when in the very act of dipping her throbbing foot into the rock pool she had discovered, and her head flew up. Her attempt to twist round and see him was her downfall because she lost her balance. Her toes had no grip on the slippery rock and she went flying backwards into the sea with a shriek of dismay. She panicked, for the water was deep and the current strong.

She was sinking below the surface for the second time, hands frantically beating at the surf, when Cristos, who had never moved so fast in his life, dived in.

She thought her lungs were going to burst. Strong arms grabbed her and buoyed her up out of the water again where she coughed and spluttered and struggled to suck in enough oxygen to satisfy herself. He swam back to the shore with her and heaved her up the beach.

'I'm OK...' she gasped.

He said something raw in Greek but the hands that held her were surprisingly gentle. The terror that had engulfed her in those frightening seconds when she had been in the water alone brought a shocked surge of tears to her eyes and, although she was struggling to hold them back, a stifled sob escaped her.

Recognising the depth of her distress, Cristos helped her back towards the house. 'What have you done to your foot?'

'I cut it...'

Lean, strong face taut, he bent down and scooped her up to carry her indoors. When he set her down in a bathroom, she was shaking. 'You're all right. Nothing is going to happen to you. Nobody is going to harm you,' Cristos asserted fiercely. 'You are safe with me...OK?'

She collided with lustrous dark golden eyes and her heartbeat limbered up as if she were about to go for a sprint. 'OK...'

'Let me look at your foot.' He sat her down on the cushioned wicker chair and turned up her sole, ebony brows drawing together when he saw the gash.

'I want a bath,' she whispered.

'You should stay out of the water with that cut.'

'I smell like seaweed...' Betsy pointed out.

'And look like a mermaid...' Cristos stared down at her. Drenched, her hair was more vibrant than ever but the sun had flushed her pale skin and her clear eyes were as bright and changeable a blue-green as the sea he loved.

'Something fishy about my legs?' she teased.

He looked. He knew he shouldn't because his body was already reacting to the mere presence of hers with a ferocious craving that not even his usual rock-solid discipline could kill. 'You have incredible legs,' he told her truthfully, for those slim thighs, elegant knees, narrow ankles and amazingly tiny feet of hers were in his far-from-humble opinion amazing works of art.

She went pink and, suddenly shy of him, she got up to run herself a bath. 'I'll be quick,' she muttered, belatedly recognising the reality that his clothes were wet as well.

He glanced back from the door, inky black lashes low over his brilliant incisive eyes. 'You can't swim. Don't go dancing on the rocks again,' he warned her drily.

'I wasn't dancing...I was trying to bathe that cut in salt water to prevent infection—'

'You were willing to risk blood-poisoning and drowning sooner than return here?' Cristos dealt her a stark look of impatience. 'Stop dramatising yourself—'

Betsy went brick-red with embarrassment. 'I don't dramatise myself—'

'What else were you doing when you ran away from me?' Cristos slung back with scorn. 'I don't abuse women. Have you got that straight, because I don't want to waste any more time chasing after you? I spent all afternoon searching high and low for you when I should have been concentrating on more important issues—'

'I didn't ask you to go looking for me. For goodness' sake, I was upset. I wake up feeling like hell and find myself in a totally strange place with a very angry guy...' Recalling the fact that that same guy had undoubtedly saved her life when he'd rescued her from the sea, she squirmed at the awareness that she had yet to thank him for that feat. 'Thanks for getting me out of the water,' she added in a small voice.

'No problem. I wouldn't dream of letting harm come to you,' Cristos contended silkily. 'If you *were* part of the kidnapping plot, I want you all in one piece to hand over to the police.'

Betsy sent him a furious look from eyes that flashed like emeralds. 'Get out of here!'

Wide shoulders thrown back, long, lean, powerful length fluid, Cristos sauntered out. On the other side of the door he smiled. It was very easy to get a rise out of her.

Betsy slid into the sunken bath that was embellished with water jets and set in a surround of exquisite multicoloured mosaic tiles. The floor was made of marble. No expense had been spared. The house might look delightfully rustic on the outside but from what little she had noted indoors the finish was more in the luxury millionaire class. Were kidnappers usually so generous to their victims?

Her hair rinsed and squeaky clean, Betsy wrapped herself in a big fleecy towel and padded back out to the bedroom. It rejoiced in Mediterranean-blue painted walls, a giant bed with a carved wood headboard and crisp white lace-edged linen bedding.

Cristos appeared in the doorway. Hair brushed back from his brow and clean-shaven, he was so incredibly attractive that just one look deprived her of the ability to breathe. 'I used the shower outside.'

In some disconcertion she studied his exquisitely tailored beige chinos and his short-sleeved black shirt. 'Where did you get the clean clothes?

'My weekend case travelled with us. Let me have a look at your foot. I found a first-aid kit in the kitchen.'

His hands were cool on her warm skin. His luxuriant black hair gleamed in the fading light arrowing through the window and she was horribly tempted to curve her fingers to his handsome head. Hands curling in on themselves to resist a level of temptation that was new to her, she sat very still while he demonstrated how extremely resourceful he could be with antiseptic and plasters.

'I'll loan you a shirt,' he murmured, vaulting upright again.

Finding that she was too self-conscious to look at him, she turned away, wondering why she got so embarrassed and tongue-tied around him. 'Nothing here is what you expect,' she muttered to fill the silence.

'Isn't it? I think this is an upmarket honeymooners' retreat that has been hired purely for our benefit. In the room next door there's a most incongruous arrangement of flowers and a bottle of celebration champagne awaiting us.'

'A honeymooners' retreat?' She grabbed at the shirt he tossed.

'The perfect place. Someone choosing to vacation on a tiny deserted island doesn't want company so whoever is in charge of this place won't visit. I imagine that there was a radio here for communication in the event of an emergency but that has naturally been removed.'

Betsy slid her arms into the blue shirt and began carefully to roll up the sleeves. Having buttoned the shirt, she gave the towel a discreet jerk to detach it. Watching her, watching her even when he knew he should not, possessed of the very knowledge that she was naked beneath his shirt; Cristos was endeavouring to get a grip on a powerful surge of rampant lust. His own weakness angered him. She was the gorilla's girl-friend. He was damned if he wanted a kidnapper's leavings. The cotton was so fine he could see the pale pink crests of her pert breasts, the faint hint of tantal-ising shadow below her belly. He was damned beyond all hope of reclaim. It was the weird situation, Cristos assured himself grimly. It was making him act out of character, it was making him behave like a testoster-one-charged teenager who had only had sex in his own imagination.

'Right now all I care about is eating.' Betsy stepped past him out into the spacious reception room beyond. 'Please tell me there's food.'

'Do you cook?'

Betsy entered the pristine kitchen. 'Abysmally… strong men have been known to weep at my table,' she lied, heading straight for the fridge.

'How did you comfort them?' Cristos enquired hus-kily.

Hot colour ran in revealing ribbons across her cheeks. 'I was joking.'

Colliding unwarily with scorching golden eyes, she felt dizzy but the invisible buzz in the air was wick-edly exhilarating. Her skin felt prickly, hot, tight. Her breasts felt full, the pointed tips taut and tender. At the heart of her, she *felt*…She burned with shame when she realised that just being around Cristos Stephanides excited her in a physical way. That had never happened to her before, not even with Rory. Tearing her troubled gaze from Cristos, she became a hive of cooking activity to give her thoughts a safer focus.

'How much food is there?' she asked, refusing to look in his direction lest that indecent sexual longing seize hold of her again and he somehow divine how she was reacting to him.

'Plenty…'

He watched while she made a stir-fry with staggering speed and efficiency. He was as impressed as a guy who had never even boiled a kettle for himself could be.

'How do you think they transported us here?' Betsy enquired when she sat down at the table to eat.

'My bet is that we were smuggled out as cargo from a private airfield and then brought the last stage of the journey by boat. An odd way to travel home,' Cristos quipped.

'*Home?*'

'This is a Greek island.'

'You can't know that for sure.'

Burnished golden eyes sought and challenged hers. 'I know. I am Greek and the very air here smells of my homeland.'

Betsy said nothing and ate her meal. He was the sort of guy who always set her back up. He was so full of himself, so arrogant. He knew everything. He even knew things he couldn't possibly know. Rising from the table, she said stiffly, 'I'm going to bed.'

'You should make the most of your rest,' Cristos murmured equably. 'We'll be up at dawn. We need to gather enough wood to light a bonfire and keep it burning. If the smoke is noticed hopefully someone will come to investigate.'

It was a good idea but she didn't say so because she had decided that he was already well aware of how clever he was. She slid into the cool of the bed, let her weary limbs sink into the comfortable mattress. Somewhere between closing her eyes and stretching out she fell asleep.

A dark male drawl that was already becoming familiar wakened Betsy again. She was deliciously warm and relaxed. 'We should get up...'

Her lashes lifted and she focused with drowsy admiration on the darkly handsome male face above hers. His black lashes were impossibly long and lush, unnecessary enhancements to eyes of lustrous gold. He was breathtakingly good-looking and devastatingly masculine, two traits that even she recognised were rarely found in one package.

'I want you to know this is a first,' Cristos informed her steadily. 'I've never slept with a woman before and not had sex.'

For a split second, Betsy lay there just staring up at him and then the implications of that sardonic assurance of his sank in. Eyes bright with accusation, a feverish flush on her cheeks, she hugged the sheet to her and sat up. 'You *shared* this bed with me last night?'

CHAPTER THREE

CRISTOS watched with a maddening air of scientific interest as Betsy lurched out of the bed in comical haste. It shook him that she looked so good first thing in the morning. Coppery red hair flying in tousled waves round her oval face and sheathed only in his crumpled shirt, she was very sexy.

'You don't need to act as if you've never shared a bed with a man before,' he said very drily.

'I haven't!' Betsy launched back at him. 'Nor is it something I can treat like a joke.'

Cristos had never felt less like laughing. 'Are you saying that you're...gay?'

Betsy froze and then shook her bright head in wonderment. 'You really don't know where I'm coming from, do you?'

Relaxing from his worst-case scenario, Cristos reclined back against the pillows. 'When you said you'd never shared a bed with a guy, you were obviously exaggerating.'

Betsy folded her arms. Furious as she was with him, she was beginning in a funny way to enjoy herself. 'And how do you make that out?'

'I very much doubt that you're telling me you're a virgin.'

'Why?' Betsy heard herself say defensively. 'Did you think I would be ashamed of the fact?'

Silence fell, a silence so thick and heavy it screamed at her. Cristos could not conceal his surprise. Her face burned with colour. Wishing she had kept her mouth firmly closed on the subject, she vanished into the bathroom. Why was she embarrassed by what she had just revealed? She had always been shy and Rory had been her only serious boyfriend. Two months after she had begun dating him, he had gone abroad to work for a year. Against the odds they had stayed together, but when Rory had finally returned to London Betsy had been reluctant to rush into intimacy with him. Even though he had asked her to marry him, she had felt that she needed more time to get to know him again and her caution had strained their relationship. Her sister had stepped into that breach.

A virgin. She was a virgin. Was that what was different about her? Cristos asked himself in bewilderment. His every expectation had been violently overthrown. He wondered why she should suddenly seem more desirable than ever. The strength of his own desire was beginning to exasperate him. She was just a woman like other women. Sexual hunger was simply an appetite to be satisfied. There was nothing special or different about her. But he *was* in dire need of another cold shower. Thrusting back the sheet, he told himself how fortunate he was that that was all that was available.

Betsy was astounded to find women's clothing hanging in one of the bedroom units. 'Whom do you think these belong to?' she asked when she heard Cristos behind her.

Cristos reached over her shoulder and drew out a woman's dress. 'This looks brand-new—'

'Tacky taste...' Betsy held the garment against her slim body, soft mouth down curving at the fact that it was strappy, low-necked and short. She swooped with delight on a pair of mules, hauled them out and dug her feet in. The mules were a good size too large but a great deal preferable to bare feet.

'It all seems to be beach wear…you might as well use it.' Cristos checked the size on an item and reckoned it would fit her like a glove. Coincidence? He didn't think so. Someone had put a great deal of planning into their reception on the island. He was not at all surprised to open the other unit and discover a selection of male apparel.

After checking that her injured foot was already well on the way to healing, Cristos went off to shave. Betsy donned a purple bikini and tied a sparkly blue sarong round her slender waist. The air was still cool before the build-up of the day's heat. The front door was wide and she hovered to drink in the beauty of the fresh dawn light filtering down over the sea and the pale sand while the sun rose in crimson splendour in the east. Finally tearing herself from the view, she noticed the champagne bottle still parked beside the flowers that Cristos had mentioned. Already the petals were dropping from the blooms. As she lifted the vase the sheet of paper that had been tucked between it and the champagne slid down flat on the table surface. Someone had typed several lines of a foreign language in large print on the paper.

'Cristos…' She went pink as she realised how easily his name came to her lips because she thought of him that way. 'What's this?' she asked, extending it to him as he appeared in the bedroom doorway.

An ebony brow lifted as he studied the sheet. 'This is in Greek…where did you get it from?'

'It was on the table…'

His brilliant dark gaze narrowed. 'It wasn't there yesterday.'

'But it must've been,' Betsy pointed out.

'If it had been there I would've seen it,' Cristos breathed with implacable assurance.

'I only saw it when I lifted the vase,' Betsy proffered in consolation. 'For goodness' sake, what does it say?'

Lean jaw line clenching, Cristos vented a harsh laugh. 'It's a load of rubbish. It says that we will not be harmed and that whether the ransom is paid or not, we'll be set free. As if you didn't know!'

Betsy stiffened, her bemusement complete. 'What are you talking about?'

'*This!*' Cristos crushed the notepaper in one powerful fist and let it drop at her feet again in a blatant gesture of contempt. 'It wasn't here yesterday. Therefore you must have planted it.'

'Me...plant it? Are you crazy?' Betsy countered in disbelief.

'If this is an attempt to persuade me to accept my imprisonment here, it's failed,' Cristos spelt out rawly. 'Right now the only person who concerns me is my grandfather, Patras. He's eighty-three and tough as they come. He's already buried my parents and my little sister. But he may not have the strength to survive the stress of my disappearance and the threat of another loss!'

Betsy was very tense. 'Do you think I'm not concerned about my own family? I don't know why you're so suspicious of me—'

'How can I be anything else? You presented me with that stupid note which doesn't make any sense. No more sense than anything else in this scenario,'

Cristos contended in unconcealed frustration. 'I've been kidnapped but, instead of being chained up in a cellar, I'm on a beach in reasonable comfort with a sexy redhead thrown in for good measure.'

'Count your blessings…next time I see a note around here, I'll just pretend not to see it. You haven't given me one good reason why you should still suspect me of having been involved with the kidnappers.'

'There's been too many coincidences,' Cristos delivered, lean, powerful face brooding. 'I saw you for the first time in my life six weeks ago—'

'Six weeks ago…*how*?' Betsy pressed in surprise.

'The wind blew your hat off and you were chasing it in a car park at the airport. You didn't see me. I thought you were gorgeous.' Dark golden eyes that seemed laden with condemnation rested on her.

Betsy had no memory of the occasion but her angry resentment was already starting to ebb away. He had noticed her six weeks back? Actually remembered her? Decided she was 'gorgeous'? She went positively pink with pleasure.

'But it never occurred to me that I'd see you again. I returned to London yesterday and, courtesy of my cousin, you'd been hired to drive me over the weekend.'

'What did your cousin have to do with it?'

'Spyros made the arrangements to bypass the usual limo company and use the one where you work instead. You were supposed to be my surprise.'

Her teeth gritted. No longer did the fact that he had found her instantly attractive seem like a compliment! No longer did she need to wonder why her boss had selected her for the plum job. The cousin would have specifically requested that she be the driver. Indeed the whole scenario that Cristos had depicted outraged her sense of decency.

'Your cousin thought that my services could be hired along with the car, did he?' Betsy fired a look at Cristos from stormy emerald eyes.

Faint colour scored his hard cheekbones. 'That is not what I said. My cousin's intervention simply gave me the chance to meet you. That's all.'

'That's very far from all,' Betsy contradicted, her hands knotting into furious fists as she rejected that much more mild interpretation of the facts. 'Speaking as the woman who was supposed to be your *"surprise"*, I have to admit that I've never heard anything more sexist or disgusting!'

Cristos stayed cool. 'That's your prerogative. I thought you were hot and I welcomed the opportunity to get to know you.'

'You waited less than two hours before you lured me into a hotel and tried to get off with me. Is that why you accused me of being bait? Your seedy cousin goes in search of me, sets me up and I get the blame for it because you have the misfortune to be kidnapped while I'm driving you?' Temper was leaping higher and higher inside Betsy.

'I took risks I would not normally take. I disregarded the advice of my staff. I paid no heed to my own personal security because I was more interested in you—'

'My goodness,' Betsy cut in as citrus-fresh and acidic in tone as a lemon. 'I even get blamed for your overactive libido.'

'Are you always this aggressive to guys who might try to separate you from your virginity?'

Betsy hit him a resounding slap and then fell back a step in shock at what she had done.

'Is that the best you can do?' Cristos asked in silken provocation. 'You'd have done more damage if you'd hit me with your fist—'

'I didn't want to damage you...I'm sorry I slapped you,' Betsy forced out that admission for the sake of form and averted her guilty gaze from the faint mark she had left across the proud angle of a bronzed cheekbone.

'Forgiveness has a price. You let me kiss you.'

Betsy lifted her head, green eyes bright and incredulous.

He shrugged a broad shoulder with immense cool. 'And if you hate it, I'll never do it again.'

Her cheeks warming, Betsy shifted off one foot to the other and back again. 'Of course I would hate it. Save yourself the embarrassment,' she advised him thinly. 'Not five minutes ago you were accusing me of having planted that daft note.'

Glittering dark-as-night eyes met hers and flamed gold. 'But intelligence doesn't come into this. I'm like a drunk who keeps falling off the wagon. I still want to taste you...'

Her breathing fractured in her throat. He was so close she could feel the heat of his male body warming the taut, bare skin of her midriff. A tiny little quiver started deep down inside her, fanning a spark in her pelvis. Her back arched a little. Her mouth ran dry. Slowly, more slowly than her nerves could bear, he lowered his handsome dark head. Common sense told her to back off but longing kept her still on a high of anticipation.

'I'm going to hate this,' she warned him, fighting

to the last ditch, willing herself to find all bodily contact with him revolting.

His wide, sensual mouth came down on hers and, on her terms, it was instant spontaneous combustion. It was like every kiss she had ever dreamt of in her teens and never received. Shell-shocked by the pleasure, she wrapped her arms round him to stay upright. He tasted divine. In fact everything about him might have been specially picked to please her. When he at last lifted his head to drag in some necessary oxygen, she subsided into his lean, powerful frame, losing herself with voluptuous delight in the heady masculine scent of his skin and the awesomely pleasurable feel of him against her. Scanning her feverishly flushed face with smouldering dark golden eyes, he crushed her even closer to him and went back for more of her luscious mouth.

In a fever, Betsy traded kiss for kiss. He employed his tongue with erotic expertise and she gasped, clung to him for support. Again and again she let her own craving rule her, unable to make the break that she knew she should. Her body was all heat and urgency and demand. That fierce hunger she had never felt before was winning the battle between control and restraint.

'Let's go to bed…' Cristos breathed with husky ferocity.

Striving to hide her disconcertion at how fast things had moved, not to mention her overpowering awareness of her own failure to resist him, Betsy looked up. Lean, hard-boned face taut, Cristos gazed down at her. Her knees were ready to buckle. The breathing space had changed nothing. She still wanted him regardless of pride, intelligence or self-respect. A wild, wicked wanting had been born inside her and had created a need so powerful it shocked her.

Cristos let lean brown fingers glide up from her waist to rest against her narrow ribcage. She was extraordinarily conscious of the swollen tenderness of her breasts, the sensation of forbidden warmth between her thighs. In fact she could hardly breathe for excitement and he knew it. In his stunning dark golden gaze burned all the unashamed expectation of a male accustomed to women who met his every demand without hesitation.

Betsy stiffened and fought her own weakness. With an effort, she parted her reddened lips and said hoarsely, 'The bonfire…we were going to build a bonfire…'

Disbelief flaring through him, Cristos watched her walk to the door. That she cannoned into a chair on her passage there was his only consolation.

Outside in the fresh air, Betsy lifted unsteady hands to her hot face and then dropped them hastily again in case he realised just how badly shaken up she was.

'Are you trying to tell me that you hated being touched by me?' Cristos demanded as he joined her, his Greek accent very strong.

She stole a glance at his bold bronzed profile and strove to suppress the inner quiver of response that sought to betray her. 'No but I don't want this to go any further…it's madness,' she told him gruffly.

'You may have a point,' Cristos murmured with a smooth acceptance that disconcerted her. 'I have no contraception here. I assume you're not protected—?'

'No, I'm not,' Betsy slotted in, reddening to the roots of her hair and hurriedly directing her attention elsewhere. He made her feel horribly immature. She was affronted by his assumption that a few kisses could have persuaded her straight into bed with him and his frank reference to the need for contraception embarrassed her. It infuriated her even more that he could switch off and be so cool and rational about the halt that she had called when she herself felt as a weak and stupid as an accident victim fighting shock.

And Betsy was in deep and genuine shock. Shock that she could be so passionate. But most of all shock that a man she barely knew could make her want him infinitely more than she had ever wanted Rory. Rory's kisses had not wiped out her brain cells or made her shiver with lust. She had never been at risk of losing control with Rory. She had honestly believed that she was not a very sexual person but Cristos had just taught her differently.

'The best place to build a fire as a beacon is on the headland at the northern end of the beach,' Cristos pronounced, digging hands balled into fists into the pockets of his tailored chinos in a determined effort to conceal how aroused he still was.

'I think we should scout around before picking a spot,' Betsy heard herself say, reacting to a barely understood urge to always disagree with him.

'Any passing shipping will be able to see a fire there.'

While she listened, Cristos produced another three excellent reasons why his site was the superior, indeed the only possible choice. When he began talking about shelter, wind speed and burn rates she knew herself to be utterly outclassed and subsided into her assigned role of being the willing worker directed by the mastermind.

There was a lot of driftwood scattered on the beach

below the headland and she gathered it piece by piece and carted it uphill to the designated area. Cristos, she learned, left nothing to chance. The fire was laid with geometric exactitude and the wood pile for feeding it was no exception.

'Your shoulders will burn in this heat. Go and put on a top,' Cristos instructed her as the flames smouldered.

'I'm fine,' Betsy framed tartly, temper on a thin leash after a lengthy period of hard physical labour in temperatures she was unaccustomed to working in. 'Why don't you just leave me to look after me?'

'How can I?' Cristos dealt her a glittering golden glance and elevated a derisive ebony brow. His shirt was hanging open to reveal a bronzed torso that rivalled the sculptured perfection of a marble statue. 'You're useless at it!'

Emerald eyes shimmering with rage, Betsy sucked in a great gush of air. 'And on what do you base that staggering assumption?'

'Where do you want me to begin?' Cristos sliced back with relish. 'When you got us kidnapped by not even locking the car door? When you cut your foot? Almost drowned? And you wonder why I should feel that it's my responsibility to ensure that you don't roast yourself alive?'

In a violent movement, Betsy chucked down the log she was dragging. 'You're just furious with me because I won't sleep with you!'

Cristos plunged down the sand bank towards her and scooped her right off her startled feet.

'What are you doing?' she screeched at him.

'I want you to look at yourself in the mirror and then tell me you're not going to cover up—'

'Put me down right now!' Betsy roared at him.

With exaggerated care, Cristos lowered her to the sand. 'I don't like being shouted at,' he warned her, smooth as silk.

'I don't like being lifted like I'm a toy doll! I don't like being ordered round all the time either—'

'Isn't it strange that you should have chosen to become a chauffeur?'

'I'm only filling in time until I start up my own business!' she yelled back at him.

'You'd be wise to get some professional advice before you venture into business on your own behalf,' Cristos pronounced in the most superior of tones.

Fit to be tied, Betsy studied him with outraged green eyes. 'You're a living, breathing miracle, Cristos.'

'Meaning?'

'How come you've survived to this age without being strangled? You're driving me crazy...you think you know everything and even if you do, there's no need to share it.' Betsy tilted up her chin. 'For your information, I have a degree in business and the only advice I will require in that field is my own.'

Having delivered that news, Betsy stalked across the sand into the house. She was in the bedroom when Cristos strode in. He stilled behind her and before she could even guess his intention he had skimmed down the bikini straps on her slight shoulders so that the amount of sunlight her skin had absorbed could be clearly seen in the contrast.

Betsy squirmed and groaned out loud in frustration as she sat down at the foot of the bed. 'Just because you're right...it doesn't make me like you any better.'

Cristos strode into the bathroom and reappeared thirty seconds later with a bottle of lotion. He dropped it on the bed beside her. 'Apply this now and maybe you won't be doing a lobster impression by this evening.'

Betsy collided with brilliant dark eyes and her tummy took a hop, skip and a jump like an over-excited child about to climb on a big dipper. She twisted her head round, denying herself temptation, and directed her attention at the mirror again. Cristos sank down on the bed behind her and infiltrated her reflection as well. He looked so devastatingly handsome that she just stared, soft lips parting, mouth running dry.

'Stop looking at me like that...' Cristos advised, reaching for the bottle.

'You've got to be used to it by now.'

At that crack, the faintest hint of colour accentuated his arrogant cheekbones and she was amused. Of course he was aware that he was drop-dead gorgeous. Nobody possessed of his looks, height and superb build could remain ignorant of his own immense appeal.

'In fact not only are you used to the effect you create, you use it shamelessly to get your own way,' Betsy added for good measure.

'I don't usually have much of a problem getting my own way,' Cristos admitted without an ounce of discomfiture. 'Lecture over yet?'

As Betsy stiffened cool fingers smoothed soothing liquid across the hot skin on her shoulders and a tiny startled moan of sound broke from between her lips.

'Am I hurting you?' Cristos asked lazily.

'No...' If anyone had told Betsy that some day the touch of a man's hand on her shoulder would set her alight like a match dropped on a bale of hay, she would have laughed out loud. But the confident caress of his lean fingers was somehow making her unbearably aware of her own body in a way that made it almost impossible for her to stay still.

'Should I stop?' he husked.

'No...' She could not bear the idea of denying herself that physical contact. A kernel of heat was unfurling low in her pelvis. She was tempted to lean back into the hard, masculine strength of his powerful body. Shaken by the very thought of such behaviour, she went rigid. Desire was in her like a secret agent programmed to seek out her vulnerability. She looked back in the mirror to see Cristos even though she knew she should not. Her heartbeat thudded heavily inside her tight chest.

She thought of all the safe choices she had made and so many of them had been mistakes. All her life she had erred on the side of caution. She had wanted to train as a mechanic but instead she had spent three years at university studying for a career she had no interest in. For a year after that she had worked endless overtime in an office job she'd loathed and her lucrative salary had been of no comfort. In the same way she had been protecting herself from potential hurt when she'd held back from sleeping with Rory. She had always selected the most sensible and least risky option available...and Cristos was a high-risk heartbreaker.

In her mind's eye she pictured herself swivelling round on the mattress and moulding her lips to that wide, sensual mouth of his. She was shattered by just how fiercely she longed for that image to be true.

Taking her by surprise, Cristos rose upright in a fluid motion. He strolled into the bathroom to rinse his hands and murmured levelly, 'Take a break. I'm a lot more used to this heat than you are.'

But very unused to suppressing his libido around a beautiful woman, he conceded inwardly. He raked long fingers roughly through his cropped black hair but still he could see the slender elegant sweep of her back, the fairness of her colouring against his own and the incredibly feminine silky feel of her soft skin. He was becoming obsessed, he told himself angrily. He fed the fire with fierce concentration and then stacked wood.

Betsy regarded sex as something serious and he had never regarded sex as serious. But in the back of his mind lurked a vague and unsettling recollection of the much more conservative views of his mother, Calliope, who had died when he was eleven years old. To combat the rampant sexism of the male contingent of the Stephanides family, his mother had even then been talking to her son about stuff like respect, fidelity and self-discipline. And love. His lean, handsome face clenched hard. Well, suffice it to say that Calliope, who had married her true love at eighteen, had been very naïve on that score.

Betsy was, however, in a class of her own. From the minute she had admitted that she was a virgin Cristos had been forced to reassess his attitude to her. No longer could he stick her in the same category as the countless forgettable women who were pretty much willing to spread their legs for any rich man. But her very exclusivity made her an even more potent symbol of desire to a male who had always regarded the best things in life as being his…

CHAPTER FOUR

WHEN Betsy wakened, she could hardly credit that it was after one in the afternoon. She felt hugely guilty about her sloth. From the window she could see that Cristos was still up on the headland working and what had she been doing? Sleeping!

Hot and sticky, she stripped off the bikini, freshened up and put on the colourful halter-neck beach dress instead. She wouldn't let herself glance in the mirror and get embarrassed about how noticeably tiny her breasts would look shorn of a bra and how very thin and giraffe like her legs appeared in too short a skirt. Instead she washed out the bikini, draped it on the rear terrace to dry and busied herself making lunch.

Were her family climbing the walls with worry about her? She winced. There was no point agonising over what could not be helped. But for how long were they likely to be living on the island? Earlier that day, Cristos had brought her up to speed on the food and fuel levels at the house, which typically he had already checked out and considered in depth. They had ample supplies. Although the fresh food would eventually run out, the freezer was packed. There was also plenty of fuel to keep the generator ticking over.

She would have liked to ask Cristos how his grandfather was likely to react to a ransom demand for his grandson's release. So far she had held her tongue on the topic because anything relating to the kidnapping seemed to send Cristos through the roof and awaken

all his dark suspicions about her having crime connections. In any case, how could Cristos really know
how his elderly grandfather might react?

She walked out to the front of the house to call
Cristos but there was no sign of him. Then she saw
the heap of clothes on the sand and his seal-wet dark
head gleaming as he cleaved through the sunlit waves
out in the bay. Even though he was a powerful swim-
mer, she could not stop thinking about scary stuff like
undertow. With considerable relief she watched him
heading for shore again and standing up to wade
through the last few feet of surf. At that point she
received her very first view of a naked adult male.

In dismay, Betsy retreated back into the house. But
that sight of Cristos unclothed was stamped in immoveable stone within her memory. He was magnificent: wide bronzed shoulders, powerful pectoral muscles accentuated by damp black curls, a sleek six pack
torso and the narrow hips and long, powerful hair-
roughened thighs of a male in the physical peak of
condition. She blacked out any recollection of the
more intimate part of him with puritanical thorough-
ness. After all, she was not a voyeur. She would give
him five minutes to get his clothes on.

But when she went back onto the beach, Cristos was
showering at the outside faucet and still naked as the
day he had been born. Thoroughly fed up with his
relaxed attitude to nudity, she backed off well out of
view and yelled at the top of her voice, 'Lunch!'

She was standing with folded arms under the tree
when Cristos finally came strolling towards her bare
chested and barefoot, his chinos riding low on his lean
hips, his shirt thrown over one shoulder. Dazzling dark
eyes sought hers and a slow, lethal smile began to tug

at the edges of his beautifully sculpted and highly expressive mouth.

That fast Betsy appreciated that he knew he had been seen and she turned a beetroot colour as far as her hairline. But, outraged as she was by his sheer insouciance, she still couldn't take her eyes off him. When he smiled her heartbeat went haywire and her mouth ran dry.

'You're so shy...it turns me on,' Cristos confided without shame.

'You must be hungry.' Betsy struggled to keep the lid on her responses to him by falling back on the prosaic.

'Right now...my only hunger is for you...' Smouldering golden eyes met hers with provocative force.

'You shouldn't be saying th-things like that to me,' she stammered, taken aback by his boldness.

Cristos helped himself to a glass of iced water from the table and drank thirstily. 'I want you, *pethi mou*. There's no shame in the truth.'

Entrapped, Betsy stared back at him and then painfully slowly she enforced her own will and disconnected from his stunning gaze to let her eyes drop. Only then did she notice what the taut fit of fabric straining over his groin could not conceal: he was fiercely aroused. Shock thrilled through her at that visible proof of his desire. Something that had repelled her in other men had a very different effect on her when it was Cristos in the starring role. She discovered that she was indecently fascinated and had to tear her attention from him.

'If you expect me to stop wanting you, go hide under a blanket,' Cristos advised.

'I am by no stretch of the imagination *that* fanciable!' Betsy shot back at him in angry embarrassment.

'You're so beautiful that I'm breaking my own rules and chasing a chauffeur,' Cristos informed her drily. 'You stopped *me* in my tracks and I don't mind admitting that when it comes to gorgeous women, I'm a connoisseur.'

Against her own will, she was captivated and madly curious. 'Have there been a lot of women in your life?'

Cristos nodded in silent confirmation.

'You *really* think I'm beautiful?'

Cristos read the anxious defensive look on her lovely face and wondered who was responsible for giving her such low self-esteem. 'You take my breath away,' he told her softly.

Her vulnerability touched him. She was so unlike the confident, conceited beauties that provided sexual entertainment in his leisure hours. Polished to the edges of their perfect nails, those women were as tough and cynical as he was. They traded their bodies for thrills, for status and for money. But neither his wealth nor his power had impressed Betsy. She was quite happy to shout at him and slap him and treat him as no other woman had ever dared. Was that why he found her such a distraction? Novelty value? Satisfied with that explanation, he closed the distance between them and pulled her into his arms with easy strength and unquestioning assurance.

In contact with the heat and solidarity of his big, powerful frame, Betsy trembled. *You take my breath away.* No man had ever said anything like that to her and it made her feel like a million dollars. She knew she ought to back off. She knew that she was dicing with danger and, in her mother's time-honoured phrase, asking for trouble. But when she looked up at Cristos and he held her close, she also knew that she would dig ditches and give at least ten years of her life to stay in his arms.

'You can kiss me…' she framed shakily.

A decent guy would walk away, Cristos reflected, forcing himself not to grab the opportunity with his usual immediacy. She was a virgin. He would be taking advantage. He did it in business all the time and never hesitated. What was the matter with him? He could make her first time special. Better him and his expertise than some drunken clumsy clod, who might string her a line and hurt her.

'I won't stop at kissing…' Cristos growled in hungry warning.

At that promise, a delicious little quiver shimmied down her spine, slivered through her belly and lodged low there in a burgeoning nest of warmth. She pushed her face into a powerful masculine shoulder, nostrils flaring on the sun warmed scent of him. She was utterly dizzy with longing and felt weak as a kitten. 'I feel all shaky,' she mumbled with a self-conscious laugh. 'What's wrong with me?'

He lifted her up into his arms and strode indoors. The shutters in the bedroom were half closed on the heat of the day. He laid her on the bed where an arrowing shaft of bright light flamed over her coppery mane of hair.

'Er…' Feeling hugely awkward and in shock in many ways at her own behaviour, Betsy cleared her throat. 'No-one in your life is going to be hurt by us getting together?' she queried, having belatedly appreciated that she had never actually asked if he was single.

'Nobody…' Cristos reached down to catch her hands in his and raise her up again.

Meshing long fingers into her wonderful hair, he brought his mouth down with passionate savagery on hers. His tongue darted in a searching foray between her readily parted lips and she jerked in eager response, locking her arms round his neck to imprison him. As he plundered her mouth with an erotic finesse that mimicked a much more sexual invasion, she shivered with response. When he lifted his handsome dark head again to let her breathe, being denied continuing contact with him was an actual pain.

'I was planning to teach you to swim this afternoon,' Cristos confided huskily. 'But now I'll teach you something infinitely more enjoyable.'

Barely able to credit that she had reached such a major decision without even thinking it through, Betsy wondered if there had always been a brazen hussy hiding inside her and waiting for her chance. 'I bet I'm useless at this…'

'But no way am I,' Cristos teased with bred-in-the-bone assurance.

Reaching behind her, he deftly undid the halter tie at the nape of her neck. She sucked in a dismayed breath and shut her eyes tight. The mere thought of baring her body for the first time froze her to the spot. She was *so* skinny. Her sister had had more of a bust at thirteen than Betsy had as a grown-up and Gemma still liked to show off her lush curves in tight tops and low necklines. He would be disappointed. Of course he would be.

'Open your eyes…' Cristos urged thickly. 'I wouldn't like you to get a fright when I throw you on the bed and ravish you.'

Her lashes shot up on startled green eyes.

His glorious smile slashing his lean dark features, Cristos sank down on the side of the bed and pulled her down onto his lap. He tugged the dress down inch by inch until it fell free of the weight of her long hair and tumbled. At the point of total exposure, she stopped breathing altogether. He prevented her from leaning forward in a concealing movement, brushed her hair out of his way and bent her back over one arm to get the full effect of the petite pouting swells adorned by delicate rosy nipples. He exhaled audibly.

'Exquisite…' he pronounced raggedly, his devouring appraisal and the roughened note in his rich, dark drawl convincing proof of his genuine appreciation.

He cupped one breast and toyed with the sweet, succulent crest until it was swollen and stiff. She squirmed on his thighs, the warm, achy feeling low in her belly making her restive. He employed his mouth on her tender nipples, tasting and teasing until she moaned out loud and dug impatient fingers into his luxuriant black hair to drag his head up and find his gorgeous mouth for herself again.

'Cristos…?'

'Let's get comfortable…' Pulling free, Cristos settled her back against the pillows. He closed his hands into the hem of her dress and whisked it from round her hips to toss it aside. Clad only in the rather daring cerise lace thong she had found in a drawer with other equally adventurous panties, Betsy felt horribly naked and exposed. Angling back from her in a lithe movement, Cristos sprang upright.

'I can't believe I'm doing this,' she confided jaggedly, green eyes bright with bemusement.

'You haven't done anything yet.' Cristos slid the

bedspread out from beneath her and cast it in a spill of silk across the padded seat at the foot of the bed.

But nor had she thought about what she was about to do, Betsy conceded shamefacedly. Going to bed with Cristos and surrendering her virginity had been concepts that took her by storm, not the reasoned calm decisions that were the norm for her. For goodness' sake, she was twenty-five years old and still keen on a man who belonged to her sister, she reminded herself guiltily. Why shouldn't she settle for a passionate affair? Cristos could turn her inside out with one smile and make her knees go weak with one kiss. He mesmerised her and it might be juvenile of her to get caught up in such a physical infatuation but at least she wasn't kidding herself that it was anything more.

Cristos ran down the zip on his chinos and then stilled, ebony brows drawing together in a frown. 'Are you willing to run the risk that I could get you pregnant?'

Betsy froze.

Cristos groaned out loud. 'I know…you forgot about that aspect. So did I. I can't believe that I almost overlooked an issue of that gravity but, for some crazy reason, I don't think straight around you.'

Betsy was very pale. She hugged her knees to her breasts. 'We can't do this…I would die if I got pregnant—'

Cristos winced. 'Don't be such a pessimist. I'll be careful…I'll withdraw.'

Betsy had turned very pink at that declaration and she was no longer meeting his brilliant dark gaze. 'It's too risky—'

'I'm a risk-taker—'

'I'm not, never have been.'

'If I get you pregnant I will be there for you every step of the way,' Cristos swore huskily. 'You don't need to worry. I don't think it's going to happen, but be assured that if it does I will take full responsibility and support you.'

Betsy stole a glance at his devastatingly handsome face. Was he really thinking things through? She could not help being impressed.

'Trust me, *pethi mou*...' Cristos added, doffing his chinos with a flourish.

His designer boxers interfered with her concentration. He shed those too with the natural grace that accompanied every supple movement of his lean, hard body. Involuntarily she stared at the rigid maleness of his bold shaft and hastily averted her eyes, thinking that she had just found another very good reason why they should not be getting together. In fact she was having very serious second thoughts.

'It's not that I don't trust you,' she began tremulously as the mattress sank beneath his weight. 'It's just that—'

'You're nervous and outrageously shy about displaying your fantastic figure.' Cristos parted her arms, spread them wide and rearranged her hair so that the tumbled strands no longer concealed her breasts. 'I'm your perfect match. I don't have a modest bone in my entire body.'

'I know that but...' Betsy looked up at him and met scorching golden eyes that sent her heartbeat into a sprint.

'All you have to do is lie back and enjoy being seduced,' Cristos told her lazily, tipping her back so that her mane of hair spread in a vibrant fan across the pillows. 'I had several wildly erotic dreams about you before we even met on Friday. Now I have you here on this bed I intend to live the fantasy.'

'I'm not a fantasy, though,' she whispered. 'I'm just an ordinary woman.'

'No ordinary woman could exercise this much sexual power over me...I'm a tough guy to pull,' Cristos asserted, holding her hands down beneath his and feeding from the sweetness of her already-reddened mouth with burning intensity.

It was as if every skin cell in her body were throbbing into new life. He let his teeth graze her throat and her pulses leapt with almost painful enthusiasm. Electric excitement had her in its grip. His thumbs flicked over her distended nipples, lingered to torment. Even more sensitive there than she had been minutes earlier, a whimper of sound escaped her. Her hips were shifting on the cool sheet below her. A barely understood hunger was tearing at her in waves of wanting. She was unprepared for the sharp bittersweet edge of sensation that bereft her of control, leaving her capable only of yearning for the next and the next. But, somehow, not the most passionate kiss or knowing caress could answer the fever burning inside her.

'I didn't know it would be like this...' she gasped, both exhilarated and scared by the sheer overwhelming force of her own longing.

'Layer on layer of the most perfect pleasure, *pethi mou*.'

He skimmed through the silken copper curls below her belly and lightly traced the thrumming heart of her. She was unbearably tender, hot and damp. She twisted. He held her still. He let his mouth trail a slow, soothing passage down over her quivering body. 'Relax...'

She was boneless with anticipation. Her hands fluttered over him, discovering the bunched muscles of his shoulders, the smooth hard strength of his back. The feel of his incredibly male body against hers held her rapt. The taste of his skin beneath her lips and her tongue enchanted her. She was in a world of discovery. He explored the slick wet heat of her. She twisted and turned, the fire of her desire racing higher and higher until it threatened to consume her.

He tilted her back and shifted over her to ease into her tight, moist entrance degree by degree. Her eyes opened wide in wonderment. Where she had ached he filled her to the hilt. The sudden stark flash of pain as he powered through the barrier of her resisting flesh took her by surprise and then he thrust into her some more.

Cristos looked down at her with hot golden eyes. 'You feel awesome.'

He eased his hands beneath her hips, arched her up to him and sank even deeper into her with a groan of very male satisfaction. She had no time to catch her breath. With slow, provocative deliberation, he set a sensual rhythm that made her heart pound like mad against her breastbone. He ground down into her and wild excitement seized her. The pace quickened. She moved against him with an abandon that became more and more frenzied. Any notion of control was long gone. She was reaching for the very zenith of pleasure when without any warning he suddenly yanked himself back from her.

'Cristos…?' she yelped in disbelief and she stretched up and hauled him back to her before he could complete his withdrawal.

He slammed back into her willing body with welcome fervour. She hit the heights in an explosion of ecstasy. He bit out something raw in his own language. His magnificent body shuddered over her and she clung to him as the shattering pagan surge of pleasure rocked them both.

In the aftermath, she hugged him close, revelling in that new intimacy and feeling incredibly content.

'As withdrawals go, that was a disaster,' Cristos muttered breathlessly, surveying her nonetheless with scorching golden eyes of appreciation and smoothing back her tousled hair to drop a kiss on her brow.

'Oh…' Too late, Betsy realised what she had done and she blamed her own mindless excitement for her lack of awareness. 'My fault.'

'But as an experience…it was the ultimate. I do hope this isn't going to be a one-night stand,' Cristos murmured teasingly, flipping over onto his back and scooping her up to arrange her back on top of him.

In rather a daze at the new state of play between them, Betsy gazed down at him. Feeling quite unlike herself and insanely happy, she smiled.

The softened light in her clear eyes disturbed Cristos. 'A word of warning,' he murmured lightly. 'Don't go falling in love with me. I'm not into all that.'

A deep inner chill banished her sunny mood. It took effort not to betray her disconcertion and her hurt. It took even more of an effort to produce an amused laugh. 'You don't need to worry,' she told him, affronted by the warning he had considered it necessary to give her. 'I'm in love with someone else.'

Astonished by that careless statement, Cristos went very still. He did not think about what he did next; he went with his gut reaction. Clamping two hands to her waist, he scooped her off him again and dumped her back on the bed beside him with a scant lack of ceremony. 'Then why did you go to bed with me?'

Taken aback by his flagrant anger, Betsy scrambled out of the bed. Only then did she recall that she was stark naked and an immediate need to drop to her knees in search of something to wear could not have been said to cool her temper. Below the bed she found the sarong she had discarded earlier and she dragged it round herself.

'I'm *waiting* for an answer…' Cristos stressed.

'Well, I don't see what you have to get all worked up about.' Betsy's ire was up and she had gone on the defensive. 'When you felt the need to tell me not to go falling for you, you should be grateful to hear that I'm in love with another man!'

'Who is he?' Cristos growled, furious with her, aghast at her lack of shame. To think that he had fondly imagined that she was vulnerable, naïve…

'None of your business.' Betsy tied the sarong in a knot over her breasts. Her hands were all fingers and thumbs. She was upset and she couldn't understand why she had had such a violent adverse response to what he had said to her.

'You made it mine when you got into bed with me,' Cristos framed in a raw undertone. 'Who is this guy? Your boyfriend?'

Her resistance gave in the surge of bitterness that that enquiry produced. 'He was once,' she admitted tightly. 'But now he lives with my sister and they have a child.'

At that admission, the savage edge to his anger blunted. The other guy was unavailable and not a rival. 'How long since you were with him?'

'Three years.'

Cristos treated her to a derisive appraisal. 'And you *still* haven't got over him?'

'You are one hateful, sarcastic bastard when you want to be!' Betsy yelled at him full throttle, high spots of colour burning over her cheeks.

A symphony of bronzed flesh and powerful masculinity, Cristos lounged back against the tumbled pillows, offensive in his studied relaxation. 'Three years after this guy shacks up with your sister, you're still in love with him...don't *you* think that's more than a little sad?'

Betsy was in such a rage she felt light-headed. 'You don't understand what you're talking about. Rory was my best friend, my soul mate—'

'But you never screwed him,' Cristos slotted in with a blunt lack of respect for such high-flown sentiments that sent her hot temper climbing even higher. 'So he must have been a non-starter between the sheets.'

'You're disgusting...you reduce everything to a sexual level!' Betsy slammed back at him.

'I'm also the guy you gave your virginity to.'

'So you've got sex appeal ...just as well, you've got nothing else!' Betsy slung at him between gritted teeth. 'You're insensitive, ignorant, vain—'

'Where the hell do you get off calling me vain?' Cristos roared at her.

Hands on her slender hips, Betsy treated him to an all-encompassing look of scorn such as he had never before received from a member of her sex. 'Suggesting that I would be thick enough to fall in love with a guy like you! And you don't think that's vain?'

Golden eyes flaming with fierce pride, Cristos sprang off the bed like a panther about to pounce on prey. 'Why wouldn't you fall in love with me?'

'It's nothing personal but you're not Rory,' Betsy told him brittly, horrified to recognise the prickling sensation behind her eyes and taking hurried refuge in the bathroom before she let herself down a bucketful.

Seething with frustration, incapable of letting the issue drop, Cristos knocked on the door. She ignored it. He opened the door. Tear-tracks marking her cheeks, she was wiping her eyes. His anger vanished. He closed his arms round her. 'This is insane. I don't even know what we're arguing about—'

'Your conviction that you're an intensely lovable person and fatally attractive to virgins,' Betsy countered somewhat snidely in punishment for his having caught her crying.

'It's the tension we're living with here...it had to find a vent somewhere,' Cristos asserted, disregarding that facetious comment.

Her rigidity gave and she collapsed into the sheltering warmth of his lean, powerful body. She didn't know why she had got so angry and distressed. She didn't know why he had a magical ability to make her so angry she was ready to explode. She didn't even know why she was ruder to him than she had ever been to anyone else. All she recognised at that instant was that she was confused, afraid of the disturbing strength of her own emotions and in dire need of comfort. She had not acknowledged that they were both stressed out and striving to make the best of a frightening situation they could not control. Cristos was like her. He didn't whinge.

Pulling her close, he scooped her up and carried her back to bed. 'You have three choices,' he murmured, stunning dark golden eyes entrapping her with charismatic ease. 'One...I give you some space.'

Betsy considered that and finally wrinkled her nose.
'Two...I give you your first swimming lesson.'

Betsy made a rather vulgar gagging sound, which
made him grin with startled appreciation.

'Three...I get out the champagne, which is probably
of vinegar vintage, and come back to bed.'

'Stuff the champagne,' she told him, but hot-
cheeked at her own nerve she opened her arms. She
wanted him. It was that simple. No need to make a
production out of it, she told herself staunchly.

Five days later, Betsy flopped on the sand and punched
a victory sign in the air. 'I can swim!'

'But you still don't go into the water on your own,'
Cristos delivered.

Laughing, green eyes shining with mischief, she
leant over him. 'Don't you ever get tired of ordering
me about?'

'No, I really get off on it...' Cristos curled his fingers into the wet coil of her bright hair and dragged
her down to him with the cool confidence of a male
who knew that his attentions were always welcome.
He captured her lips, conducted a sensual invasion that
reduced her to shivering compliancy. His beautiful
dark golden eyes flared over her with sensual intent
and then he sat up, carrying her with him. 'I want you
again, *pethi mou*.'

He took her into the cool of the bedroom. He had
barely touched her but already her body was ready for
him. She wanted him so badly she was trembling. He
unclipped her bikini bra, baring her pert breasts. His
roughened growl of pleasure broke the buzzing silence
and she leant back against him with a low moan of

encouragement while he stroked the distended pink nipples straining for his attention.

'You're so quiet with me now,' Cristos censured, pressing her back against the bed where she rested boneless, enslaved by him.

Her lashes lowered in concealment. What was there to say when she had to be careful not to betray herself? There was not a minute in the day when she did not think of him. Initial fascination and attraction had melded into a much more dangerous obsession. She had begun admiring the flip side of his arrogant temperament: his courage, his uncompromising strength of character and intelligence. Before she knew where she was, she had found herself lying in eager wait for his wonderful smile. In spite of all her proud assurances to the contrary, she had fallen headlong and hopelessly in love with Cristos Stephanides.

'But even your silence excites me,' Cristos confided, tugging up her shapely knees to remove her bikini pants. 'It gives me a high when you cry out with pleasure…'

He parted the damp petals of her womanhood to find the most sensitive spot of all and suddenly she was all heat and desperate need. But where she most ached for him, he touched her not at all. In a process of sensual torment he took her to a peak again and again, always denying her the fulfilment she craved. She writhed in frustration, whimpered in protest. Only when he was satisfied that she had reached the very edge of extreme arousal did he turn her over and plunge into the tender heart of her with a devastating expertise that sent her into an instantaneous and wildly exciting climax.

Afterwards, he curled her slender, exhausted body

up against him and surveyed her with immense satisfaction. Sex with her was incredible but he would not
have dreamt of telling her that. He could not get
enough of her. He would not have told her that even
under torture. He lifted her hand and planted a kiss in
the centre of her palm. He wrapped his arms round
her, submitted with only a very slight wince to being
hugged for the first time since his childhood. He knew
what she liked. He knew how to keep her happy. In
return for unlimited sex, and moreover the best sex he
had ever had, he made a very real effort to be affec-
tionate. Why? He had already decided that when they
got off the island he would keep her in his life as his
mistress. After all, he had moulded her into exactly
what he wanted.

When Betsy emerged from the bathroom towelling
her hair dry, she found herself alone again. Cristos
would be checking the fire on the headland. He was
impossibly energetic from dawn to midnight and she
struggled to keep up with him. The old boathouse was
piled high with junk and he was using it to keep the
signal fire alight. So far, the fire had failed to attract
attention. But then, since they had not even seen a
fishing boat, it was clear that the island did not lie
close to the shipping lanes. With stones they had
picked out a giant SOS on the beach that could be
seen from the air, but they had yet to see a single small
plane of the type that would fly low enough to read
their message.

It was very hot but Betsy was determined to do her
share of the heavy work. She padded into the shadowy
depths of the boathouse and swept up a dusty old card-
board box. Through the torn lid she could see maga-
zines. She would cart it up to feed the fire. It was a

steep climb and when she got there Cristos was nowhere to be seen. She espied him down on the beach.
The fire was low and she settled the box hurriedly on
top of it, reasoning that it would burn slower and last
longer as fuel that way.

She had reached the dunes below when a whistling,
hissing sound followed by an explosive bang brought
her to an astonished halt. The seeming equivalent of
a very violent firework torched through the clear blue
sky above and her jaw dropped.

'Why didn't you tell me you'd found a flare? Why
the hell did you just throw it on the fire?' Cristos
shouted at her from about thirty feet away, his lean,
darkly handsome face hard with incredulity.

Another flare shot up over the headland in a fierce
bright rocket of flame and a shower of sparks.
Paralysed to the spot, and it was a paralysis that
Cristos seemed to share, she watched in horror as a
pyrotechnic display of flares fired off in all directions.
In all six had exploded and of those only one failed
to make the ascent into the sky.

'I didn't know there were flares. I took the box out
of the boathouse. I thought it was full of maga-
zines…that was all I could see!' Betsy admitted in
consternation.

Glittering dark eyes pinned to her in angry condemnation, Cristos spread his lean brown hands wide.
'You put the box on the fire without checking the contents?'

Stiff with guilt, she nodded.

'Those flares would have had a much greater chance
of being noticed at night. Thanks to your carelessness,
they've been wasted!' Cristos derided.

'I thought you'd already searched through everything in the boathouse!' Betsy protested and, sidestepping him, she headed off, eyes stinging at the awful fear that she might have blown their best chance for getting off the island.

When Cristos was annoyed with her, a knot of pain formed inside Betsy and she started feeling as if she had lost a whole layer of protective skin. But in truth, she recognised ruefully, what she had lost was her independence and her peace of mind. She judged herself through his eyes. His opinions mattered. He had imposed his powerful personality on her whether she liked it or not. Her time with him had also taught her a lot about herself. The love she had honestly believed she still cherished for Rory had been composed of nothing more than fondness and her reluctance to let go of her sentimental links to the past.

Late afternoon, Cristos strode into the house and pulled her into his arms, impervious to the ice signals she was handing out. They were both hot-tempered. It was a scene that had occurred between them on several occasions. He would never discuss the argument. He would simply pretend it had not happened and even while she was soothed by the speed with which he always healed a breach that arrogant refusal to acknowledge their differences drove her crazy. But this time she had no opportunity to quibble about the silent terms of reconciliation. He kissed her with hard, hungry urgency.

Taken aback, she had no time even to catch her breath before Cristos, emanating tightly leashed emotions in a force field that she could feel, his dark eyes bright with satisfaction, turned her to the window so that she could see the blue and white fishing boat tied up at the jetty. 'We've been rescued...'

Everything from that point went at supersonic speed. The distress flares had brought the young fisherman to investigate. Within ten minutes, Betsy was being helped into the boat, still colourfully clothed in a sundress and bikini pants, her crumpled uniform stuffed in a carrier bag. While she watched the island recede into the purplish haze of ever greater distance, Cristos was talking in voluble Greek into the radio in the wheelhouse.

'Your family will be informed that you are safe,' Cristos assured her in an aside when she hovered nearby. 'My grandfather will organise everything.'

For all the fact that they had their freedom back, Betsy felt superfluous to requirements and oddly empty and scared. Even so she did not want to hang round Cristos like a limpet. When they were within sight of land again, she asked him if he had found out the name of the island they had been on.

'Why would you be interested?' he asked, his surprise palpable, but he spoke to the fisherman.

'Mos…it's called. We're in the Cyclades,' he added.

They landed on the island of Sifnos, which was as gloriously green in its spring splendour as Mos had been. Again she was left alone while Cristos went off to make use of the private phone offered to him. She did not like to ask if she could accompany him and it was thirty minutes before he reappeared, his bold bronzed features grave.

'Did the kidnappers ask for a ransom? Did you find out *anything* about them?' she prompted then, desperate for a little information. She was feeling shut out and excluded. Cristos was back in his own world, she conceded, and already he was acting cool and de-

tached. What they had shared on the island might as
well have taken place on another planet, she thought
fearfully.

His lean, strong face was expressionless. 'Nothing…but transport to take us back to the mainland
should be arriving very soon.'

'I have no passport…how am I going to travel
home?'

'Your embassy has been informed. They will take
care of that.'

'When are the police going to question us?'

Cristos shrugged. He did not know what to say to
her. He had been shattered by what he had just learned
from his grandfather and he was still in shock. Spyros,
his own cousin, had had him kidnapped. Cristos was
outraged but also ashamed that one of his own kin
could have sunk so low with only greed as an excuse.
And if Patras Stephanides had anything to do with it,
there would be no further investigation of his grandson's brief disappearance for it was not as though
charges could be brought against those responsible.

Five days ago, Spyros and his partners in crime, Joe
Tyler and two other men, had all been killed when the
helicopter that Spyros had been piloting had crashed
in the Aegean sea on the way back from Mos. Nothing
would be gained from revealing the truth to Betsy or
to anybody else. Indeed the honour of the Stephanides
name and Spyros' grieving family required the protection of silence.

As the silence stretched Betsy stiffened.

Dark eyes grim, Cristos breathed in deep. 'There is
something I should tell you…I'm engaged. My fiancée
will be waiting to greet me in Athens, so we will be
travelling separately.'

His words, for in no way could she have described that statement as either apologetic or confessional, hit her like a brick smashing through a window. In that moment everything changed and everything she had shared with him took on a far different aspect. She walked away a few steps to stare blindly out at the picturesque harbour. For long, timeless minutes she struggled to deal with the greatest pain she had ever known.

'You lied to me,' she said.

'I did not.'

'I asked you if anyone in your life would be hurt by us being together and you said no,' she reminded him in a shaking undertone while she fought not to lose her temper or cry or indeed do anything that might reveal to him just how badly she was hurting.

'I answered truthfully. Petrina does not interfere. She is not concerned by my fidelity but I respect her position and I am always discreet.'

Hatred and bitterness threatened to spread like a pool of poison inside Betsy. She hugged her arms round herself, striving to contain her tempestuous emotions.

'I want you to remain part of my life…'

An incredulous laugh empty of humour was wrenched from her and she moved away another step, terrified that she might break down into tears. 'You've got to be joking.'

'I won't give you up, *pethi mou*,' Cristos breathed, pale with tension beneath his olive skin, glittering dark eyes intently pinned to her every change of expression. 'Nothing is perfect. But you can still be with me.'

'You think I want you so much that I'd be prepared to share you?' Eyes witch-green with rampant loathing, Betsy rounded on him like a tigress. 'Go take a running jump, Cristos!'

CHAPTER FIVE

BETSY lifted the phone and heard the broken dialling tone that let her know that she had messages to collect on the answering service.

She listened to her messages. Cristos three times over: Cristos angry, angrier and even more angry. Cristos, who could not believe or accept that she would not speak to him. He was amazingly persistent and unbelievably stubborn in the face of repeated rejection. The guy whom she had believed was so special. The guy who had taken gross advantage of her naïve trust. She blamed herself more than she blamed him, though. Had ever a woman contributed more to her own downfall?

Cristos had only been interested in sex. Cristos had not even pretended that he was interested in anything else. A small example of that reality was that, in spite of spending virtually every waking hour with her for the best part of a week, Cristos had still never got around to asking her what sort of a business she hoped to start up. He had been careful to keep things unemotional and impersonal on his side of the fence, but she had got far, far too personal when she'd fallen in love with him.

It was only three weeks since she had returned from Greece. Her life had been turned upside down. She couldn't sleep, had lost interest in eating and had to drag herself out of bed in the morning. She felt like a fake person running round behind a plastic smile.

Inside herself she was hollow with misery and alone-
ness. But on the face of it, her life was virtually the
same as it had ever been.

The kidnapping had been hushed up. Why, she had
no idea, but she suspected that there might be a lot of
truth in that phrase, 'money talks.' A Stephanides lawyer had met her when she'd landed in Athens. He had
assisted her through the process of proving her identity
and getting herself home. He had also informed her of
the helicopter crash, which had taken the life of Joe
Tyler and the men with him. She had returned to work
to discover that the limo she had crashed had already
been repaired. Her boss had been advised to keep the
matter quiet and inform the curious that she had gone
off on a last-minute holiday. The Stephanides family
had gone to considerable lengths to cover up the evidence that a crime had been committed.

In an effort to distract herself from her unhappiness,
Betsy had decided it was time she took the plunge and
focused her energies on opening up a garage special-
ising in classic car restoration. It was two years now
since her grandfather had died and his estate had been
divided between Betsy and Gemma. With a healthy
savings account, Betsy knew the chances were good
that the bank would give her a loan.

Yet she had still not made that all-important appointment at the bank. Why? Her period was a few
days late and she was terrified that Cristos might have
got her pregnant. Yet she had still not worked up the
courage to go and buy a pregnancy test because she
was praying that fear was making her fanciful. After
all, Cristos had been reasonably careful. She blocked
out an uneasy recollection of the passion that had led
to one or two oversights. Furthermore, Cristos had

checked on the dates of her menstrual cycle and, while freely admitting that he had never made such calculations in his life, he had been of the opinion that they were really safe from repercussions...

Betsy was in the anxious act of wondering whether her vanished appetite might relate to more than a broken heart when a knock sounded on the door of her bedsit. It was Rory and she was really surprised: in all the years since they had broken up and he had set up home with her sister, he had never come to visit her. His blue eyes were red-rimmed with tiredness and his smart suit was crumpled. Once she had believed he was pretty attractive. Now, she registered that to her he just looked ordinary.

'What's up?' she asked. 'Is Gemma ill?'

'We've split up...'

Eyes rounding in disbelief, Betsy stilled. 'You're not serious?'

'I thought you'd be the last to know.' Rory grimaced. 'But *I* don't have anything to hide. I moved out yesterday.'

Betsy was shocked and could not think of how best to greet such an announcement from Rory. In truth, she just wanted him to disappear into thin air. His very presence on her doorstep meant trouble. Gemma would throw a fit if she found out that her boyfriend had gone to visit her sister and Betsy had no desire to get involved in the fallout. 'That's awful...I'm sorry,' she said stiltedly. 'But hopefully it's just a temporary blip—'

'It's no blip,' Rory informed her heavily. 'Your sister has another man. Aren't you going to invite me in?'

Trying to look more welcoming, Betsy stood back. 'There's got to have been a misunderstanding, Rory.'

'No, he's her boss and he's married. All the evenings that Gemma was supposed to be going to her fitness class she was actually with *him*. Do you know how I found out?' Rory prompted bitterly. 'The night your parents were told you'd been kidnapped they came round to our apartment and I rushed out to the college to fetch Gemma home early. The teacher hadn't seen her since last term!'

Betsy tried not to wince. 'Gemma would hate you telling me this stuff—' Her doorbell buzzed and, highly relieved by the interruption, she went to answer it, praying that Rory would take the hint and leave.

It was Cristos. The unexpected sight of him welded her to the spot. Sheathed in a caramel-coloured suit that shrieked designer tailoring, he was taller, broader, darker, and altogether more gorgeous than she had allowed herself to remember and, like a foodaholic on the edge of starvation, she couldn't stop staring. His stunning dark golden eyes met hers in an almost physical collision.

'I must talk to you…who's that behind you?' Cristos suddenly shot at her rawly, striding forward and setting her bodily out of his path to confront Rory. 'Who are you?'

Totally unprepared for his hostile behaviour, Betsy spun round in bewilderment. 'This is my sister's boyfriend, Rory.'

'What the hell are you doing here?' Cristos growled, hands clenching into fists, rage rolling up through him like volcanic lava seeking a vent. Rory, the guy she said she loved, here alone with her. While he was being treated like the plague for being engaged, Betsy was entertaining—in a room with a bed in it—the louse who had cheated on her with her own sister. Where was the justice in that?

Dwarfed by Cristos in size and never having been the physical type, Rory backed up against the wall. 'Betsy and I are good friends.'

Without the slightest warning of the aggression to come, Cristos closed two powerful hands into Rory's jacket and lifted him right off his feet. 'You're no friend. I saw the way you look at her and I'm a possessive man. I don't want you near her. Is that understood?'

'Have you gone mad?' Betsy screeched in horror at the scene before her and hauled unavailingly at Cristos' suit jacket. 'Let go of him!'

'Drop me...preferably all in one piece,' Rory advised drily, but his complexion was as colourless as the white-painted wall behind him.

'Cristos!' Betsy exclaimed fiercely.

Cristos lowered the smaller man to the floor again, backed off a step, twitched his cuffs straight while hoping that his target would do the manly thing and take a swing at him.

'I could have you charged with assault,' Rory informed him instead, straightening his tie.

Disappointed, Cristos thrust the door wider. 'Get out...'

Trembling, Betsy gulped in a sustaining breath. She was appalled by Cristos' conduct. Rory hovered, visibly keen to be gone but reluctant to back down in front of another man.

'I'll be fine...it'll be better if you leave.' She was quick to give Rory his escape clause.

Cristos stood at the window. He was thrown by his

own loss of control and shaken by his very sincere desire to hammer Rory to a pulp. He prided himself on his self-discipline. He could not understand what was wrong with him. Nothing had felt right since he'd returned home and all too many things roused him to impatience and annoyance.

His grandfather, Patras, had been blunt. 'You're like an angry bear looking for a fight. When you walk into a room, I feel I should take cover. What happened to you on that island?'

'I want you to leave...I'm not talking to you,' Betsy said doggedly, breaking into his ruminations.

Cristos devoured her in a long, lingering scrutiny. She had lost weight. Her eyes looked too big for her pale face. Her jeans and shirt were downright drab. But she was one of those rare women whose pure natural beauty would always outshine any frame and any physical flaw. Her unhappiness was also as apparent to him as his own seething frustration. 'What was Mr Sad doing here with you?'

An embarrassed flush lit Betsy's cheeks. On the island, Cristos had got chapter and verse on Rory's transfer of affections to Gemma out of her. It was, when she thought about it, the only personal topic he had pursued with the slightest interest.

'Rory and Gemma are having problems...he wanted someone to talk to—'

'I shouldn't think their problems will be solved by your personal intervention,' Cristos spelt out with contemptuous clarity.

'You're misjudging me,' Betsy murmured tightly, but ironically she was content for him to continue believing that she was still keen on Rory. While he believed that, he was unlikely to suspect the much more humiliating truth. 'And if you won't leave, I'm going out.'

'I want you to give me five minutes...that's all.' Cristos sought and held her evasive gaze and finally she jerked her chin in grudging agreement.

Restive as a jungle cat on the prowl, he paced across the room and, while he wasn't looking at her, she took the opportunity to feast her eyes on him. No matter how angry and bitter she was, she still craved him with every wretched fibre of her being.

Cristos spread fluid hands in a fatalistic arc. 'We're good together, *pethi mou*. I have missed you—'

'The sex...that's what you missed. You'll survive,' Betsy countered stonily.

'I miss your company almost as much. I have never said that to a woman before.' Cristos surveyed her as though he was expecting her to be so impressed she would pass out at his feet.

'You're engaged. You're not free to miss me.' Snatching up her fleece jacket and her keys, Betsy opened the door.

Cristos caught her hand in his. 'I won't quit...I *can't* quit. I want you. As my mistress, you would have everything.'

'Except the right to call you mine—'

'No woman has that privilege—'

'Except the right to walk down the street with you and be introduced to your friends as an equal.' Her voice had got thin and shrill and she was ashamed that she was actually answering him as if he had offered her a normal relationship.

What was normal about a guy who in all seriousness offered you the hallowed position of mistress in his life? And not in a tone of apology? He was spoilt rotten, she thought with fierce bitterness. So many women must have said yes to Cristos. His fiancée was equally to blame for giving him the freedom to do as he liked. He was rich, successful, breathtakingly handsome and fantastic in bed. Lots of women would bend the rules for him. A good few of those same women must have been as foolish as Betsy had been at the outset of their affair: quietly hopeful that his anti-love and -commitment warning was just defensive whitewash. She had learned the hard way that she was dealing with a cool and ruthless womaniser.

'Betsy…'

Betsy trailed her fingers free of his hold. 'Stop saying my name like it's something special because you treated me as if my feelings were of no account. I wasn't a person to you—'

Hard golden eyes challenged hers. 'That's untrue—'

'Then explain why you never even asked what type of business I was planning to set up? Classic car restoration, by the way! Or why I'm in the job I'm in. You cheated me too,' she condemned in fiery addition. 'I had the right to know that you were engaged to another woman. I would never have got mixed up with you if I'd known that—'

'*Theos mou…*' The merest hint of discomfited colour emphasising the sculpted slant of his superb cheekbones, Cristos vented an angry laugh of disagreement. 'Neither of us was able to fight the desire we felt for each other—'

'You didn't even *try*—'

'For your information, I walked away the first time I saw you,' Cristos reminded her furiously, lean, strong face taut. 'You were a chauffeur…do you really think I was keen to pull you when I realised that?'

'Oh, you patronising, snobbish jerk!' Enraged by that admission, Betsy stalked out onto the landing and headed down the stairs. 'Pull the door after you!' she called over her shoulder.

Above her the bedsit door slammed and Cristos strode in pursuit. 'I was not patronising you, I was being honest. Since when has it been a crime to be honest?' he demanded, following her out onto the street.

'It's a hanging offence when you've got no diplomacy and an exaggerated idea of your own importance!' Betsy launched back at full volume. 'And how dare you refer to yourself as honest? You were deliberately, sneakily, calculatingly secretive about the fact that you were engaged!'

Impervious to the fact that his bodyguards were open-mouthed with astonishment at the spectacle being acted out in front of them, Cristos drew level with Betsy. He was in a black fury that consumed all awareness of his surroundings. 'I won't phone you again,' he bit out.

'Promises…promises…' Betsy shot him a gleaming look of catlike provocation.

'I won't come here again either,' he gritted in a wrathful undertone. 'Next time you will come to me—'

'Only in your dreams!' she swore, stalking round the corner into the next street.

He was a step ahead of her. He splayed one hand against the wall to prevent her moving on and the other behind her. With an exaggerated sigh belied by the brightness of her gaze, she slumped back against the bricks. 'Haven't you had enough yet?' she asked, shamelessly, helplessly exhilarated by the cut and thrust of fighting with him.

'Nowhere near enough...' Scorching golden eyes assailed hers and the equivalent of an electric shock triggered inside her.

'Meaning?' Furious as she was with him, she was mesmerised.

Hands braced either side of her, he lowered his arrogant dark head and pried her lips apart in a kiss so hot she saw flames and sparks and inwardly burned.

Cristos lifted his head again, his stunning gaze radiating primal male satisfaction. 'I can wait, *pethi mou.* You'll come to me...'

Betsy walked on down the street on legs that were threatening to fold under her. She felt as if she were leaving part of herself behind. She also felt almost dizzy with rage. He was turning her into a split personality. She hated him but at the same time she craved him like an addictive drug. Furious tears prickled behind her eyes and she blinked them back, angry with herself for being so weak. She would get over him, she told herself. After all, she had managed to get over Rory without even noticing her achievement.

The following day, when Betsy finished work, she found Gemma waiting for her outside Imperial Limousines. Her sister had a tight defensive set to her pretty face that made Betsy's heart sink.

'Have you seen Rory?' Gemma asked stiffly.

Betsy very rarely told a lie but her backbone crumbled at the prospect of confessing that Rory had called round the night before. 'Why would I have?' she asked with what she hoped was a convincing show of surprise.

Gemma looked so relieved that Betsy knew that lying had been the right thing to do. Her sibling dragged her across the road into a bar and proceeded to tell all about her big bust-up with Rory. Unaccustomed to such a sisterly confessional, Betsy was nonetheless very pleased.

'I wanted to make him jealous because he's been taking me for granted. But of course I haven't been having an affair.' Gemma tossed her blonde head. 'I just wanted to light a fire under Rory.'

'Well, you've certainly done that.'

'He wasn't supposed to pack his bags and move out!' Gemma snapped. 'I got fed up with the evening class and started going off for a quick drink with a mate instead. Rory's had a thing about my boss ever since he saw me flirting with him at last year's Christmas do. We had a fight and I wanted to hurt him, so I let him think the worst.'

Betsy was feeling a little nauseous and preoccupied. 'Do you smell that perfume?' she whispered across the table. 'Isn't it overpowering? I swear it's making me feel sick.'

'It's not bothering me. But I was very sensitive to certain smells when I was carrying Sophie,' Gemma confided. 'Anyway, as I was saying, I was testing Rory—'

Betsy had paled at that casual reference to Gemma's pregnancy. 'Testing him?'

Gemma gave her a defiant look. 'He's never told me he loves me. But then he probably got fed up telling you and being treated like a doormat—'

Tired of being attacked, Betsy said, 'For goodness' sake—'

'You walked all over Rory! First you gave up that terrific job you had without even consulting him, then you signed up as a limo driver and then you told him you needed time to think about whether or not you wanted to marry him. You were much too bossy for him,' Gemma informed her smugly.

Betsy compressed her lips. It was an unfamiliar view of her relationship with Rory and, even if it did contain glimmerings of truth, Betsy was weary of the past being constantly rehashed. 'Haven't we moved on from all that yet?' she asked quietly. 'It is a long time ago.'

The rebuke made Gemma colour angrily. 'It's been no picnic for me following in your footsteps. Always feeling second-best, always wondering if he's only with me because of Sophie—'

'But Rory loves you,' Betsy countered levelly.

'He's never said so.'

'You can see it,' Betsy assured her.

'Honestly?' Her sister's face lit up and Betsy was surprised to appreciate just how insecure the younger woman still felt. Insecure and jealous, she saw for the first time. 'I think I'll ask him round to talk tonight...'

Soon after that, Gemma was about to take her leave when she began rustling in her handbag. 'I almost forgot. I thought you'd be interested in seeing this...'

'Seeing what?'

Gemma handed Betsy a magazine clipping that carried a photograph of Cristos dancing with a blonde woman. The blood drained from Betsy's face.

'I can't get over the fact that you never even *mentioned* that Cristos Stephanides is a mega-sexy hunk...' her sister was scolding.

Her stomach churning, Betsy read the inscription below the photo: 'Greek tycoon, Cristos Stephanides, with his fiancée, heiress Petrina Rhodias, opening the Stephanides charity ball in Athens.

'He's very good-looking—'

'Yeah,' Betsy cut in tightly, staring fixedly at Petrina, a stunning Nordic blonde in a fabulous white ballgown, diamonds sparkling at her throat. Talk about being outclassed! The photo really said it all! Petrina was Cristos' equal in looks, status and wealth. Betsy's throat closed over and she snatched in a great gulping breath in an effort to contain her agony.

'Are you…*Betsy*?' Gemma gasped.

'It's very warm in here,' Betsy mumbled and she hurried outside where the cold breeze cooled the perspiration beading her brow.

'I didn't know you and *he*…I swear I didn't!' her sister muttered uncomfortably. 'I'd never have given you that photo if I'd had the least idea—'

'I don't want to talk about this,' Betsy interposed flatly, mastering her tempestuous emotions.

'It's hard not to…I mean, you don't seem to have much luck with men,' Gemma pointed out. 'Rory and that thug, Joe…and *then*—'

'Rat of the century, Cristos Stephanides? Let's not go there either,' Betsy advised curtly and, for once, her sister was silenced.

On the way home to her bedsit, Betsy bought herself a pregnancy test. That evening the packet containing her purchase sat in solitary state on the table. It was the last thing she looked at before she switched out the light and the first thing she noticed in the morning. She did not sleep well. Telling herself to act like a grown-up instead of a scared teenager, Betsy did the test. It came up positive and the shock was so great she burst into floods of tears.

How on earth was she going to cope as an unmarried mother? She didn't earn enough to pay for full-time childcare. There was no way she could juggle a new baby and restore classic cars either. She would not be in a position to live on a shoestring and put in the long hours that any new business demanded. In short, her goose had been well and truly cooked and who had thrown her independent, perfectly free and happy life to the lions? Cristos Stephanides!

Why was it that the one time she had decided to take a risk on a guy she had been well and truly punished? It had taken Cristos little more than twenty-four hours to talk her into bed. She had been a very easy conquest. Shame made her squirm. At the time it had seemed so brave to throw away all caution and follow her feelings. Now she just felt plain stupid. She had acted like a slut, she thought painfully. Was it any wonder that Cristos had had no respect for her and the neck to offer her a place in his life as his mistress?

But what about all those fine promises he had made to her? About how he would be with her every step of the way if she fell pregnant? About how she could trust and depend on him…oh, yeah, and all the time he had been engaged to another woman! How could he have done that to her? From where had he got the nerve to approach her again? Had Cristos no sense of shame? Tears blinding her, she rocked back and forth on the side of her bed.

Why had she had to find Cristos so irresistibly attractive? Every time he'd smiled, she had carried on like a teenager. She had cooked for him and hand-washed his shirts. Without effort, he had turned her into a domestic slave. Poor Rory had been told that if they got married he would have to do his own washing and that it was about time he learned to cook so that he could take a turn. Had she made Cristos take a turn on the domestic front?

No, having fallen in love, she had been all sweetness and light. She had wanted everything to be perfect for him. Now she was going to have a baby, *his* baby. She imagined that that news would be one of the biggest shocks that Cristos had ever had. At their last meeting, he had been so blithely unconcerned by the possibility of consequences that he had not even bothered to ask her if she was all right. Cristos exuded the cool expectation and confidence of a male who had always led a charmed life. The kidnapping had been a major shock to his equilibrium. However, she thought it painfully typical of Cristos' charmed existence that when he was kidnapped he had been put on an idyllic island in luxury accommodation with good food and a willing bed partner thrown in.

On the other hand it seemed that his luck had ended there, Betsy conceded unhappily. Evidently her luck had been at its lowest ebb too. Cristos would not find it easy to handle her news. It would not be any easier for her to tell him. After all, how pleasant could it be to inform a guy who was engaged to someone else that you were carrying his baby? A baby he couldn't possibly want? A baby that would only be a source of annoyance and an embarrassment to him?

Betsy breathed in deep and scolded herself for getting so upset. After all, she could not afford to be oversensitive. Cristos would have to be told. She had to be sensible and consider the baby's needs and her own. Furthermore, it took two to make a baby, which meant that he was as much to blame as she was…

CHAPTER SIX

FEELING stiff and uncomfortable in the sober dark brown skirt suit she had dug out of the back of her wardrobe, Betsy sat down in the elegant waiting area on the executive floor of the Stephanides office block.

With an unsteady hand, she lifted an architectural digest adorned with a picture of the strikingly contemporary and comparatively new building. She opened it up, was confronted by a photo of Cristos smiling and hastily returned the magazine to the coffee-table.

'Miss Mitchell?' A svelte older woman approached her with a cordless phone. 'Mr Stephanides asked me to offer you his apologies. He's in an important meeting but he would like to speak to you.'

Bemused, Betsy accepted the proffered receiver.

'I'm so pleased you're here. We'll have lunch together,' Cristos murmured huskily and somewhere in the background she could hear the dulled drone of male voices talking.

Betsy tensed, for she had not viewed her visit as being in the light of a social occasion. 'But—'

'I'd love to chat but I can't. Listen, I've already arranged transport for you and Dolius will take you downstairs. I'll wrap up things here within the hour and join you.'

Before she could catch her breath, Cristos had terminated the call. She should have told him in advance that she was coming to see him or at least made an appointment, Betsy reflected uncomfortably. The bodyguard whom she had crossed swords with on the day of the kidnapping stepped out of the lift.

'Will you come this way, please?' Dolius enquired, his craggy features as expressionless as though he had never met her before.

For the first time in her life, Betsy travelled as a passenger in a luxurious limousine. But she could not relax enough to get anything out of the experience. Her nerves were as active as jumping beans. Where was she being taken? Some hotel? She could hardly announce that she was pregnant over lunch in a public restaurant. When Cristos arrived she would have to explain that she needed to speak to him in private.

Her every expectation was confounded when she was taken to an exclusive block of accommodation and ushered up to the penthouse. Assuming that the palatial apartment was where Cristos lived when he was over in London, Betsy paced the carpet in the magnificent drawing room. It was, however, a curiously impersonal room. It had neither photos nor books; indeed there was nothing on display that would have cast the smallest light on the nature, family connections or interests of the owner. At the other end of the apartment, the distant clatter of dishes and voices indicated that lunch was being prepared.

'Betsy…'

She whirled round.

Dark eyes flaming gold, Cristos stared across the room at her. 'So how do we celebrate this historic moment?' he drawled.

His business suit was a dark grey pinstripe tailored to an exquisite fit on his broad shoulders and long, powerful thighs. His slow, devastating smile slashed his darkly handsome features. For a shameful instant, her heart leapt inside her chest with excitement. A split second later, she remembered Petrina Rhodias and the pain of that humiliating recollection stiffened her backbone.

'What historic moment?' Betsy echoed, struggling to regain her concentration and say what had to be said. *'Celebrate?'*

'This apartment is yours. I bought it for you soon after we regained our freedom,' Cristos imparted, strolling forward. 'But if you don't like it, we'll find you somewhere more to your taste.'

It was only then that Betsy realised that Cristos had got completely the wrong idea about why she had come to see him. 'If you bought this apartment for me, you've made a really expensive mistake. I don't understand why you won't listen to what I say to you—'

'How can I?' Cristos demanded. 'I want you back. Why are you doing this to us? You look miserable—'

'Yes...' Betsy conceded tightly. 'You've got that right. But you've got everything else wrong. In fact we're talking at cross purposes. I wanted to see you today for one reason only—'

'Let's discuss it at our leisure over lunch,' Cristos cut in, smooth as silk.

'I don't feel sociable...look—' Betsy hesitated and then stabbed on '—I'm pregnant.'

Cristos went so still he might have been a statue. His expression did not alter but his superb bone structure tightened beneath his bronzed skin. The silence went on and on, nagging at her ragged nerves.

'Are you sure?' Cristos asked with pronounced clarity.

His dark eyes no longer flamed gold. His gaze had grown sombre. The care with which he spoke and the sudden definable edge of his Greek accent betrayed the level of the shock she had dealt him.

'Yes. I saw a doctor yesterday.' In the tense silence, Betsy dragged in a quivering breath. 'He confirmed what I already knew.'

His hard jaw line squared. 'And you chose my office as the ideal place to make such an announcement?'

A rueful little laugh fell from her lips. 'I don't know where you live when you're in London. Have you forgotten that? It really seems to say it all, doesn't it? Here I am, pregnant by a man whose address I don't even know!'

'I don't see the significance of my address.'

'I didn't think you would. You have the sensitivity of a concrete block.'

'Would you like a drink?' Cristos spoke as though she had not, his rich, dark drawl laced with excessive politeness.

Feeling cut off, Betsy reddened. 'Anything...'

'But not, of course, something alcoholic,' Cristos affixed with innate arrogance.

Rage shot through Betsy's slight frame like an adrenalin jag. Within ten seconds of learning that she was pregnant, Cristos was laying down the law with a galling air of superior authority. 'Know a lot...do you...about how to treat women in my condition?'

'Only what is common knowledge,' Cristos murmured with unimpeachable modesty.

'Well, let's hope you know more about the health issues of being pregnant than you knew about the risks of getting pregnant!' Betsy shot at him accusingly.

'So blame is to be apportioned.' Cristos raised an

infuriating winged dark brow. 'Is that what you call constructive?'

It was like a red rag to a bull. 'No, it's not constructive but it expresses how I feel and that is horribly bitter and angry!' Betsy admitted. 'When we were on Mos, I trusted you. You made loads of really impressive promises. You swore you would stand by me if anything went wrong—'

'Perhaps your unfortunate experiences with other men have misled you,' Cristos murmured flatly, pressing the bell on the wall.

'What's that supposed to mean?'

'You're not used to men you can rely on—'

'Don't you dare tell me that I can rely on you!' Betsy warned him, her incredulity at his sheer nerve unconcealed. 'Don't you *dare*!'

'Don't judge me without giving me a chance—'

'Don't throw Rory and one date with a kidnapper in my face!' Betsy traded fiercely. 'You do it one more time to me and I'll scream!'

'This is degenerating into a very unproductive confrontation.'

'After all, if you want to discuss my lack of judgement when it comes to men, please include yourself in that study,' Betsy slung back at him, refusing to back down. 'If you're honest, you will then see that you have caused me the most grief and the most damage. Being pregnant at this stage of my life will destroy all my future plans.'

Cristos said nothing. Her announcement had had a similar effect on him to watching a huge tidal wave wreak havoc while he stood powerless on the sidelines. Within seconds and with an immediacy that would have shaken her, for she had little faith in him, he had known what he must do and what would be the results. And the results even from a business and family point of view would be disastrous. The merger with the Rhodias clan would crash and burn at spectacular speed. The inevitable battle that would follow would be very bloody and very dirty. Share prices would fall, stockholders would get nervous, takeover bids would be launched. Job losses and restructuring would be inevitable. For the foreseeable future he would be working eighteen-hour days…

Tears stinging her eyes, Betsy spun away to stare blindly out the window. She was getting really emotional and she had tried so hard to stay calm. But her doctor had warned her about the often unsettling emotional effects of early pregnancy. Certainly she had never cried or shouted so much as she had in recent days. All she was doing, though, was making a bad situation worse. What was the point of hurling recriminations at Cristos? Where was the advantage in encouraging him to think she was a shrew? She was a grown woman and she had taken the same risk with him and should accept equal responsibility for the new life forming within her womb.

A light knock broke the silence and she spun back. An older man, who seemed to be an employee, was inclining his head to receive instructions from Cristos. Dully she watched the man open the drinks cabinet and proceed to pour brandy for Cristos and a soft drink that was presumably for her. She blinked, belatedly understanding the significance of the bell that Cristos had pressed. She mumbled thanks for the glass presented to her on a tray.

'Cristos…' she whispered shakily as the manservant withdrew. 'You just rang a bell and summoned another person to pour two drinks from a cabinet only ten feet away from you.'

His winged ebony brows pleated. 'What of it?'

'Oh...nothing,' she muttered.

His sublime lack of comprehension had penetrated. She went pink. He was accustomed to servants. Of course he was. He was not used to performing menial tasks on his own account. No wonder he had never seemed comfortable in the kitchen and had refused to eat there. No wonder he had gone into the dishwasher when she'd asked him to fetch her something out of the fridge. Domestically speaking, he was Stone Age man. When he had watched her ironing his shirt with apparent fascination and had commented about how much work it was, that had not been a back-handed way of thanking her but a sincere opinion of a task new to his experience.

Sipping at her drink, she watched him from below her lashes. Lean, strong face set, he looked as bleak as she felt. She could not bear to be responsible for that. For a moment she honestly thought her heart were breaking in two inside her. Certainly anything that had remained of her pride was swept away for ever in that instant. She still loved him and it seemed the final humiliation to know that right now he had to be deeply regretting ever laying eyes on her...wishing he hadn't noticed her that day in the airport car park.

His vibrantly handsome features grave, Cristos surveyed her. 'You're angry that you're pregnant and you're angry with me. I understand that. But I would like to know how you feel about this baby.'

Her vulnerable gaze widened and then veiled. It was like being asked to define the need for world peace in five seconds. How *did* she feel about the baby? She had not yet had time to consider the child she carried as a tiny person in its own right. But she did know that she felt guilty that she was not in a position to offer her baby more stable prospects and a father. She had a secret fear that she might turn out to be really hopeless in the parenting stakes. She also knew that she was genuinely afraid of the huge burden of responsibility that would fall on her shoulders. However, she was ashamed about all those feelings and could not bring herself to admit them to him.

'I am aware that this is a difficult time for you—' Cristos appeared to be picking his words with unusual care and she glanced up '—but decisions must be made and we need to be honest with each other.'

Betsy tensed. 'I don't want an abortion.'

'Is that what you thought I was asking?' His beautiful mouth quirked but his gaze was level. 'This is my child too. I was brought up to respect the ties of family beyond all others. This child will be my son or my daughter and the next generation in the Stephanides family. If you had wanted a termination, I would be trying to change your mind—'

'I don't think I can believe you when you say that,' Betsy muttered unhappily. 'What choice have you got?'

'There is always a choice. If I wanted nothing to do with this child, if I was prepared to walk away, I could make generous financial provision for you both. But I could not live with the option of never knowing my own flesh and blood,' Cristos confessed. 'My grandfather set me an example when my parents died.'

'How?' she whispered.

'When they died, Patras was about to embark on a fun-filled retirement and a second marriage with a much younger woman. I was eleven years old. For my benefit, Patras made sacrifices. He stayed at the helm of the Stephanides empire to conserve my inheritance. Even though he loved the woman, he gave her up because he knew that she wasn't stepmother material.'

Hurt tears prickled at the back of her nose. 'I really don't want to be your sacrifice, Cristos.'

'I'm not thinking about you...I'm thinking about our child,' Cristos pointed out drily. 'We're adults. We can sort ourselves out. This baby will only have us to depend on. I feel bound by my honour to offer our child a stable environment in which to live.'

'I don't drink or do drugs, so I don't believe that you need to speak as if I'm a totally unsuitable person to have the care of a child,' Betsy protested stiffly.

Cristos expelled his breath in an impatient hiss. 'You are determined to take offence. Can't you rise above your hostility and focus on the bigger picture? I didn't suggest that you would be an inadequate parent. But even you cannot deny that our child would benefit most from having two parents, who are married to each other.'

Her brow pleated in confusion. Her back was aching from the stress of standing rigid for so long. Surrendering to her discomfort, she sank down heavily on the sofa behind her. 'Run that by me again... married to each other?'

Brilliant dark eyes flashed gold over her. Cristos flung his arms wide in a volatile gesture of expressive frustration. 'Obviously we're going to have to get married!'

'Oh, no, we're not...go lay your sacrificial head on someone else's block!' Betsy advised, fighting to keep the lid on her absolute astonishment that he should even consider offering matrimony. 'I want to do the best I can for our baby as well, but wild horses wouldn't get me to the altar with a guy like you!'

'What do you mean…a guy like me?' Cristos demanded.

'You're engaged to another woman yet you've slept with me and you've asked me to be your mistress. With that evidence, I don't need to be bright to deduce that you would be the equivalent of the husband from hell!'

Outrage flamed through Cristos at that blunt response. 'I will be an excellent husband and father.'

Betsy tilted up her chin. 'But you won't be *my* husband.'

In the silence that spread like an oil slick waiting on a torch to ignite, the manservant crept in to announce that lunch was being served.

'I'm not hungry,' Betsy said thinly.

Cristos seared her with one glance. 'But possibly the baby is, so you can make an effort.'

In a room across the hall, a polished mahogany table had been laid with beautiful china. In any other mood, Betsy would have been impressed to death. However, she was still in too much shock from the revelation that Cristos was prepared to call off his engagement to do what had once been called, 'the decent thing' and give their child his name. Just as he had promised on the island, he was willing to support her through her pregnancy.

'You must not judge me on the basis of my relationship with Petrina,' Cristos drawled with supreme cool. 'Naturally you don't understand the bond that I have with her and it is not necessary that you should.

Some matters are private and not on the table for discussion—'

'Which is a very long-winded and patronising way of saying that you're the unfaithful type and not prepared to change,' Betsy filled in, her luscious pink mouth taking on a scornful curl.

Arrogant head high, lean, strong face hard, Cristos dealt her a steady appraisal that made her shift uneasily in her seat. 'I have asked you to marry me. Whatever else I may deserve, I don't believe that is an excuse for you to insult me.'

Mortified colour burned Betsy's skin. She felt like a child being rebuked for rudeness.

'I don't make idle promises. To the best of my ability, I would try to make our marriage work—'

'For the baby's sake,' she slotted in half under her breath, her throat aching.

'For *all* our sakes,' Cristos contradicted.

Mulling that over, striving to at least respect his good intentions even if she did not wish to be the charitable target of them, Betsy ate her fresh-fruit starter. 'Do you like children?'

'Very much…I may not have surviving siblings but I do have many cousins. Most of them have offspring.'

She had not been prepared for that wholehearted response. He liked kids. Then he would have expected to have children with Petrina Rhodias. Did he love Petrina? Love and fidelity did not always go hand in hand. Not everyone placed the same importance on physical fidelity. But Betsy placed huge importance on it. How could Petrina bear to know that Cristos slept with other women? Didn't she mind? Or didn't she know? Did Petrina love Cristos so much that she was

willing to share him? Her thoughts revolving in a mad,
frantic whirl, Betsy drew in a slow steadying breath.

'Talk about what you're thinking…raise your concerns.' Cristos leant back in his armchair, his glass of
wine cradled in one lean brown hand. His black hair
gleaming in the light from the window, bold bronzed
features intent, he looked incredibly handsome. He
also looked every inch what he was, she conceded
heavily. A Greek tycoon from a privileged world, an
intelligent, cultured and sophisticated male. Yet in her
opinion he was letting an old-fashioned sense of honour come between him and common sense.

'It wouldn't work,' she told him tightly. 'You and
I. We're chalk and cheese—'

'That's stimulating—'

'We fight all the time!'

His dark eyes glittered, his wide, sensual mouth
curving to reveal a glimmer of even white teeth. 'And
then we forget our differences in bed. We have passion. Respect it, *pethi mou*.'

'It would never be enough for either of us,' Betsy
told him flatly, pain infiltrating her.

Would he ever recognise how lucky he was that she
was turning him down? He drove her crazy but she
loved him. It would be so easy to be selfish. And she
was convinced that it would be selfish to let him marry
her. If he cared for anyone, she was convinced it
would be Petrina with whom he had so much more in
common. Betsy was sure that he would be willing to
help her financially. Just a little practical help would
enable her to remain pretty much independent and he
would be free to go on with his life and marry his
beautiful heiress.

After all, Petrina was the innocent party, Betsy conceded guiltily. When she remembered the unhappiness that Rory's infidelity with Gemma had caused her personally, she knew that she could not do the same thing to another woman. Yes, maybe it would cost Cristos to have to live with the awareness that he had a child he did not see. But no compromise was perfect.

'You're not being honest with me.' Glittering dark eyes raked her pale, taut, guilty face with condemnation. 'You're in love with your sister's boyfriend and their relationship is on the rocks. I think you're hoping to get him back—'

'That's absolute nonsense!' Betsy was seriously affronted that he could deem her capable of such calculating and low behaviour.

'I doubt very much that he will want you with my child inside you and with me *very* much on the scene,' Cristos forecast with burning derision.

Thrusting back her chair in a temper, Betsy threw herself upright. Without warning she was assailed by a powerful wave of giddiness and nausea. Swaying, she had time only to utter a faint moan of protest before she folded down into the claustrophobic darkness of a faint.

'Lie still…' Cristos urged when she began to regain consciousness.

For once she did not argue. She still felt sick. It was bad enough having fainted but there were even more embarrassing scenarios. She concentrated on controlling the nausea and kept her eyes closed. Cristos was talking to someone in low, urgent tones. She heard him replace a phone and she breathed in slowly to try and ward off the lingering sensation of being light-headed.

He curved his arms round her very gently and lifted

her. Unexpectedly her eyes filled with tears and she kept her eyes tight shut, willing them back. But when he settled her down on a bed, she began sitting up. 'I'm OK—'

'You're *not*,' Cristos delivered. 'It's my fault you collapsed. I upset you. I shouldn't have been arguing with you—'

'Pregnant women get dizzy…goes with the territory,' she muttered chokily, feeling horribly sorry for herself.

Cristos looked unconvinced. 'At least take it easy until the doctor arrives.'

'Why did you call a doctor?' she groaned. 'There was no need for that.'

In due course a suave older man from the private sector arrived. He was cheerful and brisk but he told her that she was exhausted and needed to take more care of herself. Cristos made no attempt to conceal his concern. She was almost willing to admit that she was so tired she could hardly lift her head from the pillow. 'I'll have a nap,' she finally conceded.

Cristos watched her from the foot of the bed, his spiky black lashes low over his incisive dark golden eyes. 'I should warn you that I haven't changed my mind, *pethi mou*. I still intend to marry you. I want the right to look after you and my proper place in my child's life. You will never convince me that there is a better option.'

'Right now I'm too sleepy to try.' Her softened green eyes lingered on his heartbreakingly handsome features and then, with a self-conscious flush, she turned her head away. 'I'm sorry I didn't believe you'd stick to the promises you made,' she muttered unevenly. 'I know you think you've come up with the

best solution and I respect that. But women don't have
to marry these days just to raise a child.'

'A Stephanides woman does.'

He was immoveable as a rock and she was amused.
She drifted off into a heavy sleep with a faint curve
to her weary mouth and slept for several hours. She
had wakened and sat up, feeling very much refreshed
by her nap when Cristos came in and extended a phone
to her. 'For you…your parents want to speak to
you…'

'My parents?' she mouthed in disbelief back at him,
but the door was already closing on his exit.

'Betsy…' Corinne Mitchell said chirpily. 'Your father and I just couldn't wait a minute longer to phone
you. While you were resting, Cristos called us and
introduced himself—'

'Cristos did…*what*?' Betsy prompted weakly.

'He's really worried about you doing too
much…and he's dying to meet us—'

Betsy had gone rigid. 'Is he really?'

'I have to confess that we are *very* taken with him.
I know he's so handsome and he has lovely manners
when you talk to him. And he seems to be terribly
well off. I know you think money shouldn't be important but I like a man to be a good provider—'

'Cristos is insisting that he will pay for the wedding,' Betsy's father chimed in, evidently on an ex-
tension line.

'Yes, he's so generous and considerate,' Corinne
Mitchell enthused. 'Mind you, I would normally be a
little upset about your being pregnant—'

'Cristos told you?' Betsy yelped in appalled embarrassment.

'But you'll be married soon enough and at least he's

not expecting you to be happy about being an unmarried mother like Rory does Gemma.'

'No, I must say you can't fault Cristos there,' her father pronounced with hearty approval. 'He can't wait to put a ring on your finger.'

'Where did you get the idea that Cristos and I might be getting married?' Betsy asked rather shrilly.

'When he suggested we draw up a full list of the guests we want to invite,' Corinne explained with palpable excitement. 'He said we could ask as many people as we like. Don't tease me, Betsy. We're just over the moon for you. I've already phoned half of our relatives to tell them our good news. Maybe a big wedding will put Rory in the notion.'

'It's a relief that your sister has made up with Rory,' her father commented. 'You'll be able to have Gemma as a bridesmaid—'

'No, she won't!' his wife interrupted in dismay. 'Gemma wants to be a bride too much to act as Betsy's bridesmaid. Much better just to have little Sophie.'

Those frank opinions having been exchanged, Betsy managed to finish the call by promising to ring back later. She was filled with shaken disbelief at the trap that Cristos had sprung on her without conscience. How could he have sunk so low? She could not credit that he had chosen to use her unsuspecting parents to put pressure on her. Her poor mother had started telling people that her eldest daughter was getting hitched, and if no wedding came off Corinne Mitchell would be devastated and humiliated.

Betsy found Cristos in the drawing room, talking on a phone in Greek. Brilliant dark eyes met hers with stubborn cool. He set the phone aside.

'How *could* you?' she pressed.

'Some day you'll look back on this and appreciate that I had your best interests at heart,' Cristos asserted smoothly.

'All you had at heart was your usual determination to do exactly what you want to do because you always think you're right!'

'You could have a point.' Cristos seemed determined to maintain a low profile in the aggression stakes.

'How am I supposed to tell my mum and dad that I don't want to marry you? Especially now they know I'm expecting a baby!' Betsy demanded in reproachful appeal.

'I can see you might have a problem.'

'I just can't believe you've done this to me…going calling my family and announcing that we're getting married when you know I've said no. You had no right to do that and involve them when they have no idea what's going on between us. I feel like I'm being blackmailed.'

'How do you feel otherwise?' Cristos enquired as if such accusations as she had made came his way every day and were unworthy of comment.

'Well, I feel just wonderful, Cristos!' Betsy slammed back at him. 'You're set on wrecking both our lives by forcing me in a direction I don't want to go. You can't do this to Petrina…it's so cruel—'

His hard bone structure clenched. 'Allow me to worry about Petrina—'

'I can't bear to hurt another woman the way I was hurt by Rory!' Betsy confided in distress.

His golden eyes shimmered, his lean, powerful face taut. 'The baby must have first claim on your loyalty and mine.'

Her slight shoulders slumped. He reached out to close his hands over hers and draw her close. She refused to look at him because she knew she could not trust herself.

'Stop tying yourself up in knots, *pethi mou*,' Cristos urged, the low-pitched timbre of his deep voice already achingly familiar to her. 'Why upset yourself over what can't be altered? I intervened with your parents because I want us to marry quickly. I see no reason why we should publicise the fact that we're getting married now because you're carrying our first child.'

Her fingers trembled in his. He knew how to press the right emotional buttons. Our *first* child. He was inviting her to look into a future that contained a real marriage in which other children would be welcomed as well. Her throat thickened and it was an effort for her to swallow. She really, really wanted to marry him.

'But wouldn't you feel trapped?' she prompted half under her breath. 'Wouldn't you resent me?'

Cristos closed one hand into the thick tumbling fall of her Titian hair to tug her head up. Stunning dark golden eyes met her troubled gaze in a direct onslaught. 'Never. I want you. I want our child as well.'

She braced a hand against his shoulder, let her fingers splay there in the shy but feeling touch of a woman longing to make physical contact. 'You'd have to be faithful…no excuses, no slips. I'd help you…I'd watch you like a hawk,' she warned him. 'You won't get away with anything, not even a flirtation if you marry me. Could you live like that?'

'Is there a choice?' Cristos dared.

Her green eyes fired up. 'No, and one strike and you're out too.'

'But you'll marry me.'

Today if you can fix it, she almost said. Fortunately she was too worked up to find her voice and it was only possible to nod, and she tried to nod with cool as if it were no big deal.

CHAPTER SEVEN

IT WAS Betsy's wedding day and she had never been happier.

A diamond tiara sparkling on her head, she studied her reflection in the cheval-mirror. Having fallen in love with the emerald silk bustier on sight, she had teamed it with a flowing ivory skirt that enhanced the elegance of her tall, slender figure. As an outfit, it just screamed Cristos at her. Green was his favourite colour. He liked her hair loose too, and her vibrant coppery-red mane hung as waterfall-straight down her narrow back as a sheet of silk.

From the minute she had agreed to marry Cristos two weeks earlier, she had entered another world. But undoubtedly the toughest challenge, she reflected ruefully, had been barely seeing Cristos since then. He had had to return to Greece and after that there had been a business trip to New York. On the single occasion when they had been together, there had been a crowd present. Two members of his staff had dealt most efficiently with the wedding arrangements while still allowing Corinne Mitchell to feel that her input was highly important. In truth, though, Betsy's parents stood in total awe of their future son-in-law and had deemed the organisation of a social event for hundreds of wealthy important people to be way out of their league.

At Cristos' instigation, Betsy had given up her job and moved into the apartment, and for convenience her parents had been staying there with her. She had been amazed not just at the cloak of secrecy that Cristos seemed determined to cast over their big day but also at the elaborate security plans that he had insisted were necessary. He had suggested that the press might be tempted to make what he had termed, 'a nuisance of themselves' and that, in that event, she and her family would be safe from annoyance at the apartment. Betsy still could not credit that newspaper reporters would be even remotely interested in her.

'How do you think you'll fit in with Cristos' rich friends?' Gemma remarked. 'Do you think they'll like you?'

Betsy turned her dreamy gaze slowly from the mirror. 'I hope so. People are people whether they're rich or not—'

'Well, his grandfather's obviously not too pleased about the switch in brides. I notice he hasn't made any special effort to welcome you into the family.'

Betsy was becoming tense. 'Why should he have done? He's eighty-three years old and I expect he's quite happy to wait until he meets me today. Let's not make assumptions—'

'I just suspect that your wonderful new life in Greece may not be a bed of roses. Cristos seems to go abroad a lot on business too.' Gemma sighed, somehow contriving to vocalise Betsy's every secret concern about her future as a wife. 'With a hunk as good-looking as Cristos, that'll be a real worry for you.'

'Why should it be a worry for me?' Betsy demanded for, while she ignored gibes angled at her, she could not bear to hear a word spoken against Cristos.

'Oh, come on...' Her sister vented a suggestive

laugh. 'Loads of girls would do *anything* to pull a guy like Cristos. He'll have to be a saint not to take advantage of the offers he must get. You're pregnant too and, let's face it, there's nothing sexy about a big tummy!'

If Corinne Mitchell had not popped her head round the door at that instant to tell Gemma that the bridesmaids' car had arrived, Betsy honestly thought she might have screamed. She looked down at her still-flat mid-section and grimaced. Would Cristos find her unattractive when she lost her waist? If he did, he was hardly likely to admit the fact.

The phone buzzed and she swept it up. 'Did she bitch at you?' Cristos asked, smooth as silk.

'I'm not answering that.' Involuntarily, however, a reluctant grin began chasing the strain from Betsy's raspberry-tinted mouth.

'I warned you not to have your sister as a bridesmaid,' Cristos reminded her softly. 'I only had to spend five minutes in the same room to see that she's a jealous little cat who can't stand not to be the centre of attention.'

'Don't be unkind,' Betsy scolded him. 'Gemma is just going through a rough patch right now.'

'Before I forget,' Cristos murmured then with studied casualness, 'there's a very large press contingent encamped outside the church. Ignore them. Dolius has arranged extra security cover—'

'But why should they be that interested in our wedding?' Betsy frowned. 'Are you so important?'

'No, I suspect they've heard a rumour about how very, very beautiful my bride is,' Cristos said, deadpan.

Thirty minutes later, climbing into the wedding car

with her proud father in tow, Betsy was still smiling. Although Cristos had warned her that the press was besieging the church, Betsy was still aghast at the sheer number of people waving cameras and shouting. Crash barriers were being employed and security men were standing shoulder to shoulder.

'Good grief…the television cameras will be along next!' her astonished father quipped.

Flash bulbs went off. Betsy kept her head down while Dolius strong-armed a passage into the church porch where he slammed shut the heavy wooden door. The calm and peace enfolded her, soothing her nerves. She was about to marry the man she loved, she reminded herself: it was going to be a fantastic day.

At the altar, formally garbed in a superb light grey suit, Cristos looked so spectacular, her tummy flipped. During the ceremony, he made his responses in a clear, crisp voice. She stumbled badly over his middle name, which she had never heard until that moment, and blushed in severe embarrassment. He was still smiling when he put the ring on her finger. They went to sign the register and she whispered, 'How on earth do you pronounce that name?'

'Xanthos.'

'I needed coaching for that one.'

As they walked down the aisle there was standing room only in the packed church. Cristos had a light arm curved to her spine. Her head was high and her eyes shone because he leant close to tell her how fantastic she looked.

'Now…you are a Stephanides and you must learn how to deal with the paparazzi,' Cristos informed her in calm continuance.

'How?'

'You ignore them,' he instructed her. 'No matter what you are asked, you don't listen, you don't answer, you don't look at them and you don't ever let your face reveal any response.'

'In other words, I am to stick my nose in the air and act like the press are absolutely beneath my notice,' Betsy paraphrased with bubbling amusement because she was in such a happy mood she could not be serious.

His arm tightened round her. 'The press can be cruel. Be warned, *yineka mou.*'

They walked out onto the church steps. The cameras went into a frenzy of flashing and clicking and requests to look this way and that flew from all directions and in more than one language. At the same time questions were being shouted. Cristos was urging her towards the limo when a raucous voice from quite close at hand yelled clear as a bell, 'Betsy…when's the baby due?'

Almost imperceptibly, she flinched but kept moving.

'Being kidnapped with Cristos has really paid off for you!' A dirty laugh punctuated that statement. 'Care to comment?' someone else bawled.

'Are you sure the kid wasn't fathered by your lover, Joe Tyler?'

When she fell abruptly still, white with shock and horror, Cristos let go of her and launched himself at the man who had hurled that final insulting question. Dolius practically lifted Betsy to get her into the shelter of the limo and then went back in haste to bodily retrieve Cristos from the fistfight breaking out. Hands braced to steady herself on the seat, her face stiff with humiliation, Betsy was trembling in disbelief.

Her pregnancy was no longer a secret known only to her family. The press knew she was expecting Cristos' baby. How could that have happened? The paparazzi also knew about the kidnapping and about Joe as well. She felt stripped naked and exposed. Her wedding day was absolutely destroyed.

Cristos swung into the car with athletic ease. He met her anguished gaze and shrugged. 'I knew they were on to us before I arrived at the church. I didn't want it to spoil your day—'

'It's a nightmare...' Betsy mumbled.

Temper back under control, Cristos flexed bruised knuckles with very male cool and acceptance. 'If it's any consolation, I hit the bastard who made that filthy comment.'

It wasn't. The guy who had told her how *not* to behave around journalists had just broken all his own rules because of something that had been said to her. She had become a source of embarrassment to Cristos. The whole world was now acquainted with the lowering fact that he had made a shotgun marriage. Even worse, nasty rumours about her relationship with the late Joe Tyler were doing the rounds. And, to top it all, Betsy reflected in positive anguish, absolutely everybody would be thinking what a slut she had to be to have gone to bed with Cristos when she hardly knew him!

'How did all the stuff about the kidnapping come out?' she pressed.

'It most probably came from more than one source. We did what we could to keep it quiet but perhaps too many people knew too much for it to remain buried,' Cristos breathed in a tone of regret.

Betsy could not really see why the kidnapping had

had to be hushed up to such an extent. She was a great deal more concerned by the much more personal nature of the revelations that had been thrown in her face in front of an audience. 'But who told them I was pregnant...who told them I'd ever even been out with Joe Tyler?' she gasped. 'I'd swear nobody at work knew about that one date!'

'I suspect that only a woman would time the revelations in the hope of wrecking our wedding day. No doubt tomorrow's papers will educate us as to the source of the leaks.' Cristos dealt her a bracing appraisal. 'Today, however, we have a wedding to celebrate and we must put this unpleasantness back out of our minds again.'

'But all your friends and family know that I'm pregnant now!' Betsy wailed.

'So we're fertile...' Cristos shrugged a broad shoulder with a magnificent disregard for her mortification. 'People love to gossip. Our guests will revel in all this controversy. Most weddings are rather boring.'

'Any day of the week, I'd choose to be bored rather than humiliated!'

'How does having my baby inside you humiliate you?' Cristos enquired, pulling her up against him and without warning splaying a bold hand across her stomach, lean brown fingers striking warmth and intimacy through the fabric that separated him from her skin.

Betsy found herself backtracking. 'I didn't mean it precisely that way. But I think it's really embarrassing that people should know that I slept with you so soon after meeting you...they'll all think I'm a slut,' she pointed out in a stifled undertone.

Cristos flipped her round and gave her a wholly unrepentant grin that radiated his natural charisma.

That grin made her want to hit him but it also sent her heart racing in a dual response that was becoming all too familiar to her in his radius.

'I'll take out full-page ads in all the major newspapers announcing that you were a virgin when we first shared a bed,' Cristos suggested levelly. 'Would that make you feel better?'

Thrusting herself free of him, Betsy studied him aghast. 'You're not serious?'

Glittering dark eyes gazed steadily back at her. 'I'm rather proud of the fact I was your first lover...I'd need very little encouragement to go public with the news. If you truly feel *so* humiliated—'

Betsy was pink to the roots of her hair. 'I don't feel *that* humiliated...you don't tell people stuff like that!'

Cristos closed an assured hand over hers, flung back his darkly handsome head and laughed with rich enjoyment.

Betsy launched herself back up against him and looked at him with a combination of chagrin, relief and grudging respect. 'You were teasing me!' she gasped, mortified that he had succeeded in fooling her.

Cristos folded an arm back round her and suddenly she twisted round and pressed into him to wind her arms tight round his neck. The feel of his lean, muscular body and the wonderfully familiar scent of his skin made her weak with longing. 'Sorry, I've been acting the diva,' she muttered guiltily. 'You're right...nothing should be allowed to cloud our day.'

In response, hard fingers tipped up her face. He drove her soft lips apart in a sensually savage kiss that brought her body alive with almost painful enthusiasm. 'I'm burning for you, *pethi mou*,' he growled with roughened urgency.

They had arrived at the hotel where the reception was to be held. The passenger door opened. Dolius' craggy face split into a smile at finding the bridal couple in each other's arms and then went poker-straight again.

Betsy had never met so many people in her entire life as she met at the wedding reception. Her head whirled with names and snatches of conversation. She was seated with Cristos before it dawned on her that she had yet to meet her bridegroom's closest relative, Patras Stephanides.

'Where's your grandfather?' Betsy asked in an urgent whisper. 'Didn't he want to sit at this table?'

'It may have passed your notice but my grandfather is not among our guests,' Cristos said stonily.

Betsy flushed. 'He's not here...why? Is he ill?'

'He chose not to attend.'

'For goodness' sake, why didn't you tell me?' Betsy whispered back in dismay. 'What an awful thing to do to you when you're so close! I'm so sorry—'

'It was my grandfather's right to choose not to be here. I won't have him criticised for it.' Grim dark eyes reproved her. 'His decision does not lessen my respect for him in any way.'

Betsy had lost colour. She tried not to feel hurt because she knew that she had touched a raw wound. Cristos was very attached to the older man. Naturally he was feeling the sting of his grandfather's decision to absent himself from so important a milestone in his grandson's life. At the same time Betsy could only feel as though she had been tried and found wanting. In opting out of their wedding, Patras Stephanides was expressing his uncompromising disapproval of the woman whom Cristos had decided to marry. Her heart sank because his grandfather's refusal to accept her was anything but a promising start to their marriage.

Later, after they had eaten and done a lot of socialising, which made any personal conversation impossible, Cristos drew her onto the dance floor. 'Stop brooding about Patras,' he instructed, demonstrating a dismaying ability to read her thoughts. 'He's as set in his ways as most men of his age and, in time, he'll come round.'

'Was he terribly fond of Petrina?' Betsy asked in a rush.

Cristos released his breath in a slow, measured hiss. 'It's not that simple. An engagement is a serious commitment in Greece. Having given my word that I would marry Petrina, I then asked to be released from it. Patras was devastated. The Rhodias family are outraged and Patras believes that I have dishonoured him.'

'And I bet he's blaming me for it.' Betsy sighed into his jacket, feeling more responsible than ever.

'There *was* no easy solution to our predicament,' Cristos murmured wryly, lean, strong face reflective. 'We have to be realistic. When you injure other people, there is always a price to pay.'

'But I don't want you to have to pay a price...' Betsy confided, disturbed that he had yet to make even the smallest reference to his own feelings regarding his broken engagement.

But then what on earth would be the point of Cristos confessing that he still cared about Petrina? It would change nothing and only make Betsy feel like an albatross round his neck. Having married her for the sake of their child, Cristos was the sort of guy who would make the best of their marriage. In fact he had already begun to act like a husband. He had tried to protect her from the hurtful intrusion of the press into their private lives. In a similar vein, he had not rushed to inform her that his grandfather was boycotting their wedding because he had known that that news would only upset her.

'I hope that a year from now you'll be able to look back and think that all this was worth it,' Betsy whispered earnestly.

'A year from now I'll be a father…I have no regrets now and I will have none then.' His beautifully shaped mouth quirked. 'Don't look for problems that aren't there.'

It was an excellent piece of advice but hard to follow. If he had loved her, she would have felt much stronger. It took two to make a baby, she thought unhappily. He had kept his promises to her because he was standing by her. For her sake, he had ended his engagement and as a result he was now estranged from his grandfather. He seemed to be the only one of them paying that price he had mentioned. After all, she loved Cristos and could hardly look on becoming his wife as being in any way a punishment.

Early evening, Cristos told her that they would soon have to leave. She went off to get changed in the hotel room set aside for that purpose and wondered where they were going on their honeymoon. Garbed in a funky pale blue tweed jacket teamed with a matching short skirt that was hemmed with a fringe, she was heading back towards the stairs when Rory accosted her.

'Can I have a word?' her former boyfriend asked earnestly.

'I've barely had a chance even to speak to you today.' Forced to move out of the path of a chambermaid and her trolley, Betsy backed round the corner and then shifted across into the more private seating area there.

'If you had taken the chance, Gemma would have thrown a fit.' Rory sighed. 'But I'm coming to the conclusion that that may be my fault. I haven't been fair to Gemma or you. The more she made it plain that she expected me to marry her, the more I dug my heels in. Now I'm going to make up for it...'

Betsy was hanging on his every word, a big smile building on her face.

'I've bought a ring,' he confided.

'Make sure you set the scene right...dinner out, Mum babysitting Sophie,' Betsy warned him chokily, her eyes overbright with happy tears. 'Gemma likes everything perfect. Don't just bung the ring at her and act like her acceptance is a foregone conclusion.'

'I've learned since I did that to you,' Rory confided with gentle irony.

She flung her arms round him and sniffed and laughed almost simultaneously. 'Just promise me one thing...'

'What?' Smiling down at her, he closed his arms round her and gave her a hug.

'Tell her that you care far more about her than you ever did about me,' she urged, wiping at her damp eyes with her fingers as she fell back from him again. 'I'd better get back downstairs...'

Rory only a step behind her, she walked round the corner and cannoned straight into Cristos. All three of them stopped dead. There was one of those horrid awkward silences.

Inclining his head with perfect civility to Rory, Cristos murmured silkily to his bride, 'Are you ready?'

Their departure was swift rather than lingering. Within seconds of getting into the car, Betsy was smothering a yawn. It had been an incredibly exhausting day. 'I'm so tired,' she muttered apologetically.

'Then close your eyes and sleep…' Cristos said it as if it was the most reasonable thing in the world.

'Where are we going?'

'We're spending the night at my country house. Tomorrow, we'll fly to Greece.'

'It was a beautiful wedding,' she told him drowsily.

'Was it?'

Something in his tone made her tense. 'Are you teasing me again?'

'Yes…forgive my cruel sense of humour.' Lounging back into his corner of the limousine, Cristos tugged her back against him, encouraging her into a more relaxed and comfortable position. Kicking off her shoes, she curled up against him with a grateful sigh and that was the last thing she remembered for a long time.

When she opened her eyes again, she was in a beautiful bedroom furnished with timeless antiques and lit with gracious lamps. According to her watch, it was almost eleven at night and Betsy groaned in dismay. It certainly promised to be a wedding night to remember. Cristos had to be really fed up with her for sleeping for so long! Catching a glimpse of her tousled and crumpled reflection in the dresser mirror, she winced in even greater consternation. Her cases were sitting just inside the door.

Forty minutes later, breathless from the speed with which she had showered, reapplied a little make-up and donned her slinky midnight-blue silk nightdress, Betsy descended the sweeping staircase.

She found Cristos in the library. Jacket and tie discarded, white silk shirt open at his strong brown throat, he was staring down into the fire, a brandy goblet curled in one hand.

Her attention welded to his classic bronze profile, she hovered on the threshold. 'Cristos...'

He straightened, brooding dark golden eyes narrowing. 'What are you doing out of bed?'

It was not quite the welcome Betsy had been hoping for. 'It's our wedding night...'

'*Theos mou*...is that an invitation?' Cristos drawled in apparent wonderment, his intent gaze dropping from her softly parted lips down to the pouting thrust of breasts defined by the silky material of her nightdress.

'I suppose it is...' Betsy dragged in a quick shallow breath to steady herself. She felt very self-conscious. Her body was already reacting with enthusiastic awareness to his appraisal. The rosy crests of her nipples stirred behind the lace bodice, the swollen tips tender. Her heart was thumping an upscale beat. The atmosphere had grown thick and heavy.

'A duty screw...?' Cristos lifted an ebony brow, his lean, darkly handsome features stamped with derision. 'Is that what you're offering me?'

Her mouth fell open. 'A...what kind of a thing is that to say to me?'

'That if you're only offering me your body because I married you today, I can get by without it.' Cristos drained his brandy and set down the empty glass with a decisive snap. 'I'm not that desperate.'

Betsy stared back at him in shaken disbelief. 'Are

you drunk? Is that why you're speaking to me like this?'

'I saw you weeping over Rory at our wedding. All that chummy hugging and pawing was a rather nauseating turn-off.'

Her troubled brow began to clear as she realised that he had misinterpreted what he had seen. 'I wasn't exactly weeping over him—'

Hard dark eyes rested on her. 'You *were*—'

'But not in the way you seem to mean. At the minute, a sad story could make me cry buckets. If my emotions are stirred at all, my eyes start flooding with tears. It's embarrassing but according to the doctor it's just my hormones.' While noting that Cristos was looking deeply unimpressed, Betsy was eager to explain. 'Rory was telling me that he's about to ask Gemma to marry him—'

Cristos vented a roughened laugh. 'Which is why the pair of you were tucked into a hidden dark corner in each other's arms, was it? Next you'll be telling me you were crying with happiness!'

'Why didn't you tackle me about this earlier?' Betsy prompted worriedly. 'Why did you pretend everything was OK?'

'Let me see…' Cristos murmured flatly. 'How many reasons would you like? Five hundred wedding guests? The fact that you're carrying my baby and shouldn't be subjected to stressful scenes? Or the simple reality that you told me you loved Rory on Mos? It's not very fair to castigate you for it now, is it?'

While he'd spoken, Betsy's colour had fluctuated, and by the time he made that last statement she was embarrassed enough to instinctively turn away. What an idiot she had been ever to claim that she loved

Rory! Words employed to conserve her pride had come back to haunt her. She saw that she had no choice but to explain herself and with as much frankness as possible.

'That stuff about me loving Rory,' Betsy confided, cheeks hot, green eyes only contriving to meet his for an instant. 'It was a total fabrication. I just didn't want you getting the idea that I might be getting too keen on you, so I told what I saw as a harmless fib at the time.'

'A total fabrication...' Cristos repeated rather thickly, brilliant dark-as-midnight eyes locked to her guilty face.

'Yes...maybe it sounds a bit strange to you but you're a guy...at the time it seemed a good idea to lie,' Betsy completed awkwardly.

'I don't believe you,' Cristos asserted without the smallest hesitation.

Betsy winced, her smooth brow furrowing. She was very aware that she was not telling him the whole truth. On the other hand, she was highly reluctant to confide that at any stage of her relationship with Cristos she had genuinely believed that she was still in love with Rory. 'All right...I'll tell you the truth—'

'Wasn't that what I got a minute ago?' Cristos asked with dangerous quietness.

'It was a harmless, slightly doctored version,' Betsy muttered, horribly aware that, for someone stuck in a literal hot seat, she was not doing very well. 'The truth is that I remained very fond of Rory for quite a while after he and I broke up because I didn't get close to anyone else.'

The silence stretched.

'Is that it?' Cristos queried.

Betsy nodded jerkily, studying him with desperate intensity in an effort to read his thoughts. Right now the last thing their marriage required was his conviction that she was madly in love with another man.

'I thought there might be a version three in the pipeline...' Infuriatingly, Cristos elevated a questioning brow. 'No?'

Feeling like a child caught out in a shameful act, Betsy compressed her lips. 'No.'

'So why did you come looking for me?'

Her face flamed.

'I'm only teasing...' But there was no lightening flare of gold in his stunning gaze, no amused curve to the sculpted line of his beautifully shaped mouth. He could not even summon up a smile at the sure knowledge that he was married to a woman who lied so badly she embarrassed him.

'You do believe me, don't you? About Rory, I mean,' Betsy checked anxiously. 'It's so important that you do...I really want our marriage to work.'

His incisive gaze veiled. 'I believe you.'

Betsy tensed when it finally dawned on her that she was practically begging him to come upstairs and make love to her! Mortified by that conviction, she walked to the door, a tall, slender figure with a mane of copper hair that was a vibrant splash of colour against her pale skin and the dark blue of her nightdress. 'Goodnight, then,' she told him rather stiffly.

On the way up the stairs, she was thinking fast and furiously. This was the same guy who had hardly been able to keep his hands off her on the island. Why was he so uninterested? Did pregnancy make her seem less attractive to him? She might not have the big tummy yet but was he already looking at her and mentally endowing her with an imaginary one? Or was it possible that he mistakenly believed that sexual intimacy might endanger her pregnancy? Who knew what strange old-fashioned ideas he might be harbouring?

Shedding her nightdress, because there was not the smallest sign that Cristos had ever had any intention of even sharing the same room as her, she got into bed. She was reaching out to switch off the lights when her bridegroom entered. Cristos sent her a winging golden glance, kicked the door shut with an air of purpose and began to undress. Her hand fell back nerveless from the light.

'I need a shower…give me five minutes, *pethi mou*.'

He stripped where he stood. Out of the corner of her vision, she was maddeningly conscious of him. She listened to the shower running and wondered what had kept him from her earlier. Would she ever understand Cristos Stephanides? Would she ever learn to penetrate that tough facade that could keep her as much in the dark as a stone wall?

When Cristos returned to the bedroom, crystalline drops of water were still shimmering on the curling dark hair that accentuated his powerful pectoral muscles. 'You stayed awake for me…' he murmured lazily.

And that fast the atmosphere switched to electrifying. Her tummy tensed and flipped. Meeting his shimmering golden eyes, she was suddenly extraordinarily short of breath. 'I thought you weren't even going to sleep here,' she confided, relief making her chatter.

'Sleep is the last thing on my mind, *yineka mou*.' With a rueful laugh that sent a sizzle of awareness travelling down her backbone, Cristos flicked back the sheet and lounged beside her.

His first kiss sent fire slivering through her tautness and made her melt from the outside in. Her hands coiled tight in on themselves. The silky touch of his tongue flicked the roof of her mouth. She gasped and he shifted against her, acquainting her with the bold potency of his arousal.

He let his lips travel hungrily down to the delicate skin of her throat and she rubbed against him with helpless encouragement, reacting to the tormenting pressure of his mouth in certain places. He toyed with her urgently sensitive nipples, suckled the straining pink buds until she was clutching at him and crying out helpless in the grip of her own excitement.

'It's time you stopped being so shy and learned how to please me…' Cristos breathed thickly, guiding her down to his hard male heat with an unconcealed urgency that had the most wickedly erotic effect on her.

Touching him, she trembled. The very scent of his bronzed skin was an aphrodisiac to her. She was eager to please and even keener to learn because his response to her was hot and sensual and undeniable.

Tangling long fingers in her Titian hair, he drew her back up to him. 'Fast learner…' he acknowledged raggedly, claiming her reddened mouth in a fierce, drugging kiss. 'We've been apart too long. I remember the island in my dreams…I could devour you.'

His skilful fingers found the liquid heat pulsing between her thighs. She squirmed, her hips rising in helpless supplication. Her body was tight and aching with readiness and she moaned out loud, controlled by the bittersweet intensity of the pleasure. 'Cristos…'

His smouldering golden gaze connected with the

plea in her passion-glazed eyes. In one lithe, powerful movement, he came over her and into her. In the throbbing agony of need, she was gripped by the headiest and wildest excitement. Lifting to him, she clung, intoxicated by the exquisite power of his dominant rhythm and the frantic urgency of her own need. The intolerable pleasure reached a crescendo and hurled her into an ecstatic release. She was full of joy and love and gratitude in the aftermath, hugging him close, dabbing kisses on an angular cheekbone, a smooth brown shoulder, indeed any part of him within reach.

'I gather I was good, *yineka mou...*' Resting his angular chin on the heel of one hand, he inspected her with slumberous golden eyes. He rolled back against the pillows and carried her with him, clamping her to his warm, damp body with a possessiveness that turned her heart over inside her.

'I can only compare you and you. But I just think everything's fantastic with you.' By the time she had finished telling him that, her voice had sunk so low with self-consciousness he had to angle his proud dark head down to catch her final words.

'You never will get to compare me with anyone else between the sheets,' Cristos murmured. 'Does that bother you?'

She was delighting in their closeness, thinking back in dismay to the trouble that had been caused when he'd suspected her of hiding out in dark corners with Rory and grateful that she had managed to sort that out. It was a lesson to her, she thought with an inner shiver, a lesson about how easily misunderstandings could occur. Saving face just wasn't worth the risk.

'No...why should it?' she countered softly. 'In fact

I wouldn't be surprised if I fell madly in love with you.'

Lean, strong face hardening, Cristos regarded her with glittering dark eyes. 'Good sex is not love. I found that out as a teenager when the target of my romantic affections invited her best friend to join us in bed.'

Shock shrilled through Betsy. 'Good grief...but *why*?'

'She thought I might be getting bored with just her and decided to surprise me.'

'She was a slut,' Betsy told him in disgust.

'But honest about what she was,' Cristos traded, cool as ice. 'She didn't pretend to love me. I should add that I'm not looking for love from you.'

Long after he slept, Betsy lay awake watching the thread of moonlight that pierced between the curtains dancing across the ceiling. She felt hollow and hurt. She would not be confessing to true love in an effort to get closer to Cristos. Even though they were married, he had rejected that emotional bond most conclusively. In fact the icy note in his rich dark voice had chilled her. Was it possible that he already suspected her feelings for him? Look at the way she had behaved after he had made love to her! She'd been all over him like a rash. Did he found that kind of enthusiasm a big turn-off?

In the morning she wakened alone but a white rose and a jewellery box sat in a prominent position on the pillow beside hers. She pulled back the curtains and opened the box. Sunlight illuminated the creamy perfection of the pearl necklace, which was brought bang up to date with a glittering diamond pendant in the shape of a daisy.

'Wow...' she breathed, fastening it round her neck and pausing only briefly to admire herself.

Hauling on the towelling robe on the back of the bathroom door, she sped off in search of Cristos to thank him. If she lived to be a thousand years old, she would never work the guy out! One minute he was telling her that he wasn't looking for love from her and the next he was giving her a rose and a fabulous necklace to wake up to on the very first day of their married life.

Her bare feet made no sound on the antique rug in the elegant flagstoned hall. She could hear Cristos speaking in his own language and his voice was coming from the room next door to the library. Catching a glimpse of him through the ajar door, she suppressed a loving sigh. Had he been born with a phone in his hand?

'Petrina...' he was saying with low-pitched urgency.

Betsy fell still, her skin turning clammy. She heard every word he said after that but understood nothing because it was all in Greek. What she did grasp was that Cristos sounded concerned and strained and that he was definitely trying to soothe and comfort the woman at the other end of the line. How selfish and blind she had been, Betsy thought then in a sick daze of shock.

All along she had been ridiculously reluctant to contemplate the personal dimension to his broken engagement. She had not even wanted to think about Petrina Rhodias. Why? She had been too jealous. She had never wanted to credit that Cristos might genuinely care for the Greek woman. Now that she was being forced to accept that Cristos did have feelings for the gorgeous blonde, she could finally understand why he didn't want his shotgun bride to love him. He knew that there was not the slightest possibility of his returning her feelings…

CHAPTER EIGHT

Elegant in a short sleeveless dress that had a tiny flower print on a yellow background, Betsy came down to breakfast.

'Thanks for the pearls...' she said woodenly, taking a seat at the dining table.

Cristos waited while the manservant tried to attend to her needs before she attended to them on her own account and then dismissed his employee with a nod. 'I think it would be a good idea if you didn't read any newspapers today,' he imparted.

Betsy was no great fan of reading newspapers but in one sentence he had ensured that she would spend the whole of the day perusing the printed word. 'Why?'

'I've always attracted a lot of press coverage. I'm used to it. It doesn't bother me.' Concerned dark golden eyes rested on her delicate profile. 'But you have no experience of how the tabloids sensationalise personalities and events. I don't want you to be distressed.'

Chin at an angle, Betsy was already standing up. 'Where are the newspapers?'

'Betsy—'

'Don't try to tell me that I can't read what's been written about us!' she exclaimed. 'I'm not a little kid!'

'OK...but first I have to explain something about the kidnapping. A member of my own family was behind it,' Cristos delivered grimly.

That did grab her attention. 'You're joking me…a relative of yours?'

'I wish I were joking.' Cristos told her about Spyros Zolottas, who had, she now learned, been one of the men who had died in the helicopter crash with Joe Tyler. 'Unlike my grandfather, I believed that the leopard could change his spots. I was wrong. Spyros decided to use his knowledge of my movements to stage a kidnapping and extract money from Patras. He was with me the first time I saw you. Obviously he realised how he could use my interest in you to his advantage.'

'He's the man you said arranged for me to pick you up that weekend as a surprise,' Betsy recalled.

'To meet you, I was prepared to overlook my security team's concerns and expose myself to a degree of vulnerability that made the kidnapping more likely to succeed.'

'So it was your cousin who was responsible for it all…' For a wordless moment she sat there slowly shaking her head, but deep down inside more turbulent reactions were being born. 'But you're only telling me this now because the newspapers have got a hold of it…am I right? When did you find out that Spyros whatever-you-call-him was behind it all?'

'When I made my first phone call to Patras after we had escaped.'

'But you didn't tell me. We had spent almost a week living together. We were lovers facing the same fears and challenges…and yet you didn't think that I had the right to know *who* had put us on that island?' she demanded shakily, her temper and her hurt rising by equal degrees.

'It was a family matter,' Cristos countered with

measured care. 'When Spyros was killed, my grand-father felt that his family had suffered enough. He saw no advantage and neither did I in publicly exposing Spyros' wife and daughters to the disgrace of his crim-inal behaviour.'

Betsy was barely listening. Her mind was hopping like a rabbit from mortified peak to peak. 'Was Petrina excluded from the same information?'

'No.'

A bitter laugh fell from her lips. 'That says it all.'

'*Theos mou*...it says what?' Cristos demanded, plunging upright in an expression of mounting frustra-tion.

'Even though I went through that kidnapping with you, I was nobody on your terms. I really was just the silly slapper you seduced to amuse yourself!' Betsy vented painfully.

'That is not how I thought of you...'

'How you behaved tells me exactly how you thought of me!' Tempestuous emotions were pulling at Betsy and a wounded sense of rejection and inad-equacy lay at the heart of her agony. 'When I think of how you dared to accuse me of being involved with the kidnappers and all the time one of your own blasted relations had organised the whole thing!'

'I know it looks and sounds bad—'

'And you have never yet apologised for misjudging me!'

'I thought we had gone beyond that level.'

Rising to her feet, Betsy settled furious green eyes on him. 'Where are the newspapers?'

'The library,' Cristos advanced, darkly handsome face taut. 'I won't apologise for believing that it's my

duty to protect you from anything that might upset you—'

'Go lock yourself up behind bars, then!'

In the library, Betsy sat down to study the papers.
She was shattered to realise that her whole family had
come under scrutiny with her. One of her parents'
neighbours had used their anonymity to make cruelly
cutting comments about Corinne Mitchell. Betsy's
eyes filled with tears for she knew how her mother
would writhe to see herself castigated in print for all
their friends and relatives to see. That Gemma was an
unwed mother was also pointed out with a glee that
could almost be felt. Stories were angled at presenting
Betsy as an ambitious young woman who could only
have taken a job as a chauffeur in the hope of meeting
and marrying a rich man. Salacious stabs were made
as to what must have occurred on the island. Never
had she felt more humiliated.

However, at the turn of a page, Betsy learnt that
there were still greater depths for her to plummet to
in the humiliation stakes. There was more than one
two-page spread on Cristos' long and colourful reign
as a womaniser.

'I don't want you looking at rubbish like that,'
Cristos ground out from behind her.

'I'm sure you don't...' Her tummy churning, Betsy
was studying a photo of Cristos getting into a brawl
on her behalf at their wedding. She was trying not to
feel hideously responsible for what the gossip col-
umnist asserted was a very rare loss of temper for
Cristos and 'very revealing of his state of mind on the
day he married his pregnant bride'. That was followed
by a quote purporting to be direct from Petrina
Rhodias in which the Greek heiress referred to Cristos

as 'a man of honour shamelessly entrapped by his own decent values'.

'Did Petrina phone you to commiserate with you?' Betsy launched at him, quivering with pain and humiliation.

His jaw line squared. 'What kind of a question is that to ask me?'

'I heard you on the phone to her this morning!'

'As I haven't spoken to Petrina today, that is an impossibility—'

'I heard you *say* her name!' Betsy practically sobbed in her distress.

His ebony brows had pleated and then the light of comprehension flashed through his lustrous dark eyes. 'I did speak to Spyros' eldest daughter before breakfast. She is called...Petrine. Petrina and Petrine. Could you have misheard me?'

Betsy flushed. The difference between the two names was almost indistinguishable and she felt foolish. At the same time she was intensely relieved that she had jumped to the wrong conclusion. 'Yes, obviously I did mishear you,' she conceded almost cheerfully. 'Sorry, my mistake.'

'Spyros' wife and daughters have only just learned that he was responsible for the kidnapping. They are extremely upset and wished to express their regret for what he did to us both.'

'I hope you assured his family that I don't consider them in any way to blame for what happened.'

'Of course. That is generous of you,' he responded approvingly. 'Will you eat some breakfast now?'

'I'm not hungry.' Betsy gathered up the necklace she had removed in a hurried movement. 'I really ought to be ringing Mum and Gemma—'

'Later…' Cristos advised, removing the pearls from her fingers and turning her round so that he could deftly fasten the necklace back into place. 'You've had a rough morning and we're leaving for the airport soon—'

'But it's my fault that poor Mum and Gemma have been lampooned in print along—'

Stunning golden eyes lodged to her, Cristos had pressed a silencing fingertip to her tremulous mouth. 'No, it is *not* your fault. You did nothing to ask for that coverage. Take my advice. Let the dust settle first.'

At his behest she ate a light breakfast.

They were travelling to the airport when she began mulling over what he had said to her earlier. 'What did you mean when you said you hadn't spoken to Petrina Rhodias…*today*?' she suddenly queried.

His brilliant gaze narrowed, superb bone structure taut.

Betsy had lost colour. 'When did you last speak to her?'

'Yesterday. She phoned me before our wedding,' Cristos admitted flatly.

The silence was as taut as elastic stretched to the edge of endurance.

'I've got no right to ask…I know that, but I'm not going to give you a moment's peace until you tell me what she said,' Betsy confided in a driven rush of unsparing honesty.

His devastatingly handsome features set. 'She asked me not to marry you. May we drop the subject now?'

Betsy stared out the window but she was quite unaware of the scenery beyond the tinted glass. So now she knew. On the day of her wedding, Petrina had waved a come-home-and-all-will-be-forgiven flag. And why not? Petrina had been engaged to Cristos. Betsy had been the other woman. Cristos had only married her because she had fallen pregnant by him. *A man of honour, shamelessly entrapped by his decent values.* Since men did not have the ability to conceive that was rather an unfair assessment, Betsy thought wretchedly. But was that secretly how he felt as well?

Cristos closed a hand over hers. 'You're my wife now. Stop dwelling on the past.'

'I can't help it...one minute I'm feeling guilty about your ex-fiancée and the next I'm feeling sorry for me.'

'I suspect she was the source who tipped off the press about Spyros having me kidnapped and also about your pregnancy. Only Petrina knew the score on both those counts.'

As a device to ease her conscience that revelation worked; Betsy started feeling a lot less guilty. Had Petrina Rhodias deliberately set out to destroy their wedding day? Betsy suppressed a shiver, for such calculated malice was foreign and very threatening to her. At the same time, however, she was also carefully thinking over what Cristos had revealed. Clearly, he had not staged a diplomatic cover-up for Betsy's benefit. He had not gone to Petrina and simply said that he was sorry but he must break off the engagement because he was in love with someone else. No, it seemed that he had told the beautiful blonde the truth and nothing but the brutal, unlovely truth: that he felt he had to marry Betsy because she was carrying his child. Betsy very much wished he had lied.

'We have our whole lives ahead of us, *yineka mou*,' Cristos drawled, level dark golden eyes resting on her tense face with a degree of censure. 'Even more importantly, we have the birth of our child to look forward to.'

Her fingers flexed in his. 'Are you really looking forward to the baby?'

His slow, charismatic smile curved his wide, sensual mouth and her mouth ran dry and her heartbeat quickened because he looked so spectacularly attractive. 'Of course I am. I don't care if it's a boy or a girl either.'

Her tension evaporated. She had had so little time to think about the baby. First she had been afraid that she was pregnant, then had come the confirmation and the fear of how she would cope, finally the guilt that she should be happy that Cristos, who didn't love her, should be willing to marry her. Now she found herself wondering whether she would be blessed with a boy or a girl. Whichever, she would be content. In the same way, she swore to herself with determination, she would appreciate what she did have with Cristos rather than brood about what she did not have.

Cristos received a couple of what appeared to be important phone calls soon after the Stephanides private jet landed in Athens. Lean powerful face grave, he settled himself into the limousine beside her and regarded her with veiled dark eyes. 'I'm about to take you back to my home, give you a brief tour and then head straight into the office, *yineka mou.*'

Very much taken aback at the thought of just being abandoned in a strange house in a strange country virtually the minute she had arrived there, Betsy breathed in deep. 'No problem,' she told him, reminding herself that she was not a wimp.

Respect banished the wary aspect from his keenly intelligent gaze. 'As you may have gathered there's no room in my schedule right now for a honeymoon.'

'You never said there would be.' Betsy pinned on a smile, working hard at hiding her disappointment. If anything she felt distinctly foolish for having assumed that he would at least spend a few days with her before he returned to running his business empire. It had become obvious even before the wedding that Cristos worked pretty long hours.

'When I'm less busy, I promise I'll take you away somewhere special and do all that newly married stuff with you.' Cristos was still watching her like a hawk. 'You do realise that you're reacting to all this bad news like a woman in a million.'

'Yes…' Her ready sense of humour sparkled in her green eyes. 'Saintliness is much more likely to induce guilt than recriminations,' she pointed out sweetly.

After a startled pause, he laughed with true appreciation and tugged her across the seat into the strong circle of his arms. After that response she would have braved the Amazon jungle on her own and she snuggled back into him warm with love. A little voice in her subconscious whispered that surely he would have made the effort to find time for a honeymoon with Petrina Rhodias. She jumped on that dangerous inner voice and snuffed it out like a flame threatening a destructive blaze.

His shore-front estate on the Greek mainland took her breath away. She knew Cristos. She had expected an impressive house and was not at all surprised that it overlooked the sea he loved. But she had not been prepared for an historic mansion, the thickly wooded acres of grounds and the private beach or even the two dozen staff lined up to greet her. He made a special point of introducing her to Omphale, an apple-cheeked middle-aged lady with a big cheery smile, who had been his nurse when he was a child.

'Did you tell Omphale I was expecting?' Betsy whispered suspiciously as they crossed a big echoing hall full of light.

Cristos said nothing.

Betsy realised that there was nothing tactful he could say. So many stories about their marriage had appeared in the English newspapers that it was highly unlikely that her condition could still be a secret in Greece. 'It's OK…I'm not being silly—'

'I would have wanted the staff to know anyway, *thespinis mou*,' Cristos confided abruptly. 'How else can they look after you properly? We need to get you signed up with an obstetrician here too. I'll ask around the family for a personal recommendation. It also occurs to me that Greek lessons might be a good idea.'

'I love it when you get bossy…it makes me feel like I'm starring in a madly exciting costume drama where some big tough man talks down to some twittering little woman. Yes, sir, no, sir, three bags full, sir!' For good measure, Betsy raised a hand in what she hoped was a fair stab at an army salute.

Cristos clamped her to him and kissed her breathless. Framing her lovely face with long, spread fingers, he finally drew back from her with pronounced reluctance. His mobile phone was buzzing again.

'I don't need a tour of the house…' Hot pink stained her cheekbones. Almost imperceptibly she was leaning forward, vulnerable green eyes meeting his smouldering appraisal. 'Well…you could show me the bedroom,' she managed, framing that invitation as boldly as she dared.

He groaned out loud. 'I *can't*…don't tempt me.'

He answered his mobile phone, paced away a few feet to speak in low, urgent Greek. He swung back. 'I must go.'

'Trouble at the ranch?' she quipped tightly, striving not to reveal how desperately cut off she felt by his rejection.

He frowned in incomprehension.

'Problems at the office?' she rephrased, feeling very superfluous to his requirements, for he was so obviously mental miles away already.

Stunning golden eyes collided with hers with unexpected force and he laughed and shook his handsome dark head in seeming wonderment. 'No, of course not. What an imagination you have!'

'I'll see you tonight then...'

'It may be late...'

'Then kiss me again,' she heard herself say.

He obliged.

'It may be *very* late,' he confessed when she was holding onto him to stay upright and his own voice had developed a husky edge.

'You'd better kiss me again...to keep me going,' she mumbled.

'If I do it again, it will hurt even more to walk away. You are so beautiful, *yineka mou.*'

'I'll sit up for you,' she promised, watching him back slowly towards the entrance.

Both of them had been so intent on each other that they had not noticed the silver-haired elderly man who was standing there watching them. Cristos cannoned into him and swung round with an exclamation of surprise.

Betsy was welded to the spot. One look at the tall visitor with his spare, sculpted bone structure and deep-set eyes and she knew exactly where Cristos had inherited his good looks from, for the family resemblance was pronounced.

'Betsy...allow me to introduce my grandfather, Patras Stephanides,' Cristos proclaimed with warm pride and affection.

Patras Stephanides walked towards Betsy and stretched out both his hands in an expansive invitation to her. 'Will you forgive a foolish man for his prejudice?' he asked in a voice roughened by emotion.

'Of course.' With a misty smile she grasped his hands and stood while he kissed her with solemn care on either cheek. 'But there's a price,' she warned him. 'There's hours and hours of film on our wedding and I shall make you sit through every minute of it.'

The old man's poker-straight carriage relaxed a little and his appreciative smile lightened his serious expression. 'I shall look forward to my punishment.' He skimmed a wry glance back at his restive grandson. 'Don't let me keep you late, Cristos. I am aware that you are exceptionally busy at present—'

'*Ne*...yes,' Cristos breathed, his attention on Betsy. 'But—'

'A young woman who can tease me within thirty seconds of meeting me is not in the least afraid of me,' Patras quipped with unconcealed approval. 'Stop worrying about your wife. I will look after her. That is what family is for. Good times and bad times must be shared. I'm afraid that for the space of two weeks I forgot that most basic principle.'

Betsy already knew that she was going to like Patras. She always felt most at home with people who were blunt and open in expressing their views. Cristos was more subtle, more sophisticated and much harder to read. His grandfather, on the other hand, was making no bones about his regret at having missed their wedding and his eagerness to heal the breach with his grandson and his bride. She was more than willing to meet the old man halfway. She would have made as much effort even if she had not liked Patras Stephanides. Cristos had been troubled by that breach and for his sake, much more than her own, she was overjoyed that his grandfather had had a change of heart.

'Where do I take you in this house to offer you tea or coffee?' she asked Patras with a rueful grin. 'Cristos didn't get time to show me round.'

'Later, if you will permit me, I will act as guide. I was born here, as was Cristos.' He took her out to a shaded loggia where a slight breeze cooled the air. 'At this hour this is the best place.'

Refreshments were served. Patras answered her questions about the house, which had been in the family for generations. He told her about his collection of classic cars and promised to invite her over to his home for lunch and a tour of inspection.

Just before he departed, Patras studied her with wry acceptance. 'One look was enough to tell me what attracted my grandson to you. You're his Helen of Troy.'

After a startled pause, Betsy laughed. 'Hopefully nobody is about to start a war over me!'

'Don't underestimate Cristos.' Patras looked pensive and rather sombre. 'I'm glad you love him, though. That is as it should be.'

She went bright pink.

The old man awarded her discomfited face an

amused glance. 'I saw how you look at him...it relieved all my concerns.'

Three weeks later, Betsy sat on the top step of the stairs and watched Cristos walk into the dimly lit hall. It was two in the morning.

'And what time of day do you call this to come home?' Betsy enquired with pretend annoyance.

His proud dark head came up, the aura of weariness cast off when he saw her perched on the stairs waiting for him. A softer line eased the hard set of his mouth. 'A time when you should be in bed, Mrs Stephanides.'

Betsy padded down the staircase, a slender figure in a simple white wrap. 'I'm not planning on staying out of bed for very long,' she confided, pink washing her cheeks because she was trying to give him a saucy look of invitation.

He grinned.

'For the baby...' He tossed her the package in his hand.

She unwrapped a brightly coloured toy and a faraway look came into in her eyes: she was imagining a little boy thumping the life out of the drum. It had become a ritual. Every couple of days, Cristos brought back something for the nursery. The drum would join a mobile, a boy toy train set that would require a room of its own, a cute stuffed dog and a little board book that had reminded Cristos of one that he had had as a child.

'Are you hungry?' she asked him.

'I could be tempted...' Dropping a powerful arm round her slight shoulders, Cristos headed her back up the stairs.

Betsy wondered if he was ever going to stop playing

macho man and confide in her. Was he convinced that he had to protect her from all stress simply because she was pregnant? Or was it a Greek male thing? This silent, steely refusal to admit that anything was amiss on the work front? She needed no crystal ball to know that the Stephanides empire was facing challenging times. But Cristos had ignored her every subtle invitation to share his concerns and had denied that there even was a problem.

At the same time he continued to work eighteen-hour days. Only when he was at home after midnight was the phone silent but within a few hours his relentless punishing schedule would begin again. Around eight, his personal staff would arrive to brief him before he even left the house. He would have a working breakfast and walk out to the limousine, dictating orders, listening to bulletins read off sheets. The tension in the air betrayed how serious were the issues at stake and the reality of the crisis.

Crossing the threshold into their bedroom, Cristos rested back against the door, pulled her close and released a low, slow sigh of satisfaction. 'I shouldn't say it...but I love it when you sit up waiting for me. It makes coming home special.'

'That's the point...I aim to make myself indispensable.'

He tipped her head back. His brilliant dark golden eyes inspected her lovely face and the crackling energy of the coppery-red mane flowing round her shoulders. 'You're the most amazing woman...you haven't complained once.'

'I'm running a book,' she teased.

Long fingers knotted slowly into strands of her bright hair. 'I didn't have you picked as the restful, sympathetic type. I underestimated you. I'll never for-get how unselfish you've been—'

'Do you think all women are as spoilt and demand-ing as little kids no matter what the situation?'

'Your predecessors were...' With a slumberous sigh, Cristos bowed his brow down briefly on top of her head and then straightened again. 'I'll go and get a shower.'

The instant he departed, Betsy sped across the vast room to spread wide the French doors and light the candles waiting in readiness out on the balcony. Dragging in the giant floor cushions she had assem-bled, she tossed a couple of throws over them to create a relaxed atmosphere. Last of all, she brought in the capacious hamper, poured some wine for him and ar-ranged the mouth-watering spread of dishes.

Shedding her wrap, she curled up on the cushions and thought about how ridiculously, incredibly happy she had been since her arrival in Greece. The business emergency that was responsible for forcing Cristos to work such impossible hours had made remarkably lit-tle impression on their relationship. But then they had both made a huge effort to make the most out of every minute they could spend together.

There had been early morning swims, midnight bar-becues on the beach listening to the surf and snatched snack lunches in his office where sometimes they ditched eating for kissing because they were so des-perate to be together. If he had one minute free, he called her and they talked on the phone.

During her very first week in Greece she had been engulfed by the warm and generous hospitality of Cristos' large extended family. There was not a day of the week when she needed to be lonely, for there was always someone wanting to entertain her by taking her out shopping, sightseeing or simply visiting. Perhaps she had learned to appreciate Cristos most when she'd realised just how popular he was with his own relations. For his sake, she had been given the benefit of the doubt and wholeheartedly accepted into his family.

She got on with Patras like a house on fire and he had already developed the habit of dropping in to see her most days. He had assumed responsibility for squiring her about to events where she might have felt a little self-conscious shorn of a male escort. So, she had dined out several evenings in high style and was indeed a little giddy at the amount of socialising she had done.

Cristos emerged from the bathroom, a white towel knotted round his lean hips. Scorching dark golden eyes took in the effect of Betsy, her porcelain perfect skin and stunning shape enhanced by a strappy gold satin nightdress, sprawled among the cushions, and glittered with raw male appreciation. '*Theos mou*…you could seduce a saint with one smile, *thespinis mou.*'

'No saints round here that I know of…'

Cristos groaned. 'Agreed. Are you going to make me eat first?'

Betsy nodded very seriously. 'You know the rules.'

'Do I get a massage later?' Cristos shot her a gleaming look of pure devilment that had the same effect as a megawatt charge on her susceptible heart.

'Forget it,' Betsy advised, her colour heightening, her pride still stinging from the recollection of his response to her very first massage attempt a couple of nights earlier. 'I do not massage people who laugh themselves sick in the middle of my best efforts.'

Eyes bright with unholy amusement, Cristos flung himself down on a cushion opposite and reached for a piece of barbecued chicken. 'It was that very strange New Age music that really sent me off the edge. You do do a very good line in a sexy picnic,' he pointed out in teasing consolation.

She watched him eat. He was truly the most important thing in her world. She wondered how she had ever imagined that she loved Rory because she would not have compromised an inch for Rory or gone out of her way to smooth his path. Whereas Cristos, she just adored, and he might not love her but he did make her feel hugely important to him and hugely appreciated. Around him, she was really beginning to believe that she was a stunningly beautiful, rampantly sexy woman. He told her she was and he made her feel good about herself.

When he had finished eating he reached for her and peeled off the golden scrap of silk and carried her to bed.

'There's just one thing I want to say...about this stuff going on at work that you don't want to talk about,' she framed in a rush.

Superb bone structure tautening, Cristos looked blank. 'What are you referring to?'

'All I wanted to say was...I can live without this big house and all the staff and the luxury—'

'I couldn't,' Cristos slotted in with feeling.

'Yes, you could. At the end of the day, things like that aren't what is most important.'

'Betsy...' Cristos surveyed her with a deeply pained expression. 'I very much appreciate the message that you are trying to give me but there is nothing for you to worry about. I am very wealthy and I have every intention of staying that way, *pethi mou*.'

'But—'

The hard, hungry onslaught of his mouth silenced her. He buried his mouth in the delicate bluish hollow below her collar-bone where a tiny pulse beat and slivers of delicious awareness awakened her body to the animal attraction of his.

'You're so sweet…' Cristos said raggedly, tugging her back against his lean, powerful length to mould the pouting tenderness of her breasts.

The pleasure was a hot and insidious seduction as powerful as an invasion force. She did not and could not resist him. Afterwards, he held her close and murmured her name and she revelled in their closeness.

'Promise me I can meet you for lunch tomorrow. I know dinner's out because you'll be working late but I want to do something to mark my birthday.'

Cristos tensed. 'If I admit I haven't got you anything yet, are you likely to string me up?'

'No…it would be too quick and clean for you. Don't be daft,' she whispered snuggling up to him forgivingly, for when he was frequently so preoccupied he barely knew what day it was she saw no reason why he should have thought to look up her birthday. 'Worry about a pressie next week…tomorrow I just want you and I to get together somewhere other than your office for lunch.'

'I'll arrange it. It's the least you deserve,' he assured her.

The next morning a member of his staff called to inform her that Cristos would meet her at a restaurant at one. Betsy took real care getting dressed up. Her linen dress was the rich colour of amber and the shade looked amazing against her skin and her hair. She was the first to arrive at the restaurant and it was so up-market an establishment that she felt desperately self-conscious seated at her table in what felt like the most prominent spot in the room.

Cristos was late. Surreptitiously, she tried to raise him on his mobile phone but it seemed to be switched off. She rang his office, only to be told that he was out and had not left word of his whereabouts. Believing that he had deliberately chosen to do that so that they could eat without interruptions, she assumed he was already on his way. Time passed painfully slowly. He was late but he would come. For goodness' sake, it was her birthday! She began to rehearse witty but rather stinging comments with which to greet him. She tried his mobile again without success. She did not try his office again because she did not like advertising the reality that she was still sitting waiting for him. It was after two when she left the restaurant, cut to the bone, tears closing up her throat in a painful knot.

The limousine got stuck in traffic. She switched on the television, desperate for something, *anything* to take her mind off her angry, hurt mortification. She was trying to think herself into a more reasonable frame of mind. Presumably some crisis had blown up and he had simply forgotten about her. Was she so self-important she could not accept an oversight?

The news was on, a background buzz in a language she didn't yet understand. She wasn't really looking at it until she saw that it was Cristos on camera. She sat forward then, intent on the screen. He was entering a large modern building, lots of people all around him.

The crowd waiting in the foyer parted and a female figure sped towards him. It was Petrina Rhodias and she flung herself in Cristos's arms. The camera work became positively frenzied, zooming in to show that not a paper width separated the former engaged couple. Petrina looked shockingly beautiful in spite of the tears on her face. She also looked ecstatically happy and Cristos was not fighting her off, imposing a touch of married-man-decent distance or pushing her away.

Betsy hit the off button on the remote control. The car phone was ringing. She stared at it. She just knew it was Cristos calling her but she couldn't face speaking to him. She used the override button on the rear passenger door lock just to climb out into the midst of the bumper-to-bumper traffic and lose herself in the throng of shoppers in the busy street.

Cristos had stood her up on her birthday to stage a public reconciliation with Petrina. A month ago that would have struck her as being as strange as the presence of cameras at the event. She would have been ignorant of how things had once been for Cristos and Petrina. But by asking the right questions of his chattering cousins she had learned a good deal. He and Petrina had once been the leading couple in Athenian high society, two young, beautiful and very rich people from socially and commercially prominent families. Their breakup had been equally big news. The public had once paired the Stephanides heir and the Rhodias heiress like salt and pepper and Betsy had become uncomfortably aware that some people believed that regardless of his marriage Cristos would somehow end up back with Petrina.

Was he back with Petrina? Or was what she had seen on television just a staging post on the path to that ultimate end? How did she know that Cristos had told her the truth three weeks ago when he'd sworn that he had been speaking to Spyros' daughter, Petrine, and not his former fiancée, Petrina? The truth was that Betsy had wanted to believe the explanation he had given her. When you were head over heels in love with a guy, Betsy reflected wretchedly, the last thing you wanted to do was doubt his honesty and his level of commitment.

If she even began to count the number of things that Cristos must have in common with Petrina Rhodias, she would run out of fingers. Petrina appeared to be his perfect match. But they had not been quite Adam and Eve. The fatal flaw had been Petrina's reluctance to attach the strings of fidelity to Cristos. When Betsy had conceived, the perfectly matched couple had been destroyed because Cristos could not bring himself to walk away from his own child.

But before Betsy had married Cristos, she had warned him that she did not want to be his sacrifice. Now her pride was warning her not to make a complete fool of herself. How could she fight to hang onto a guy who didn't love her? If he wanted Petrina back, there was nothing Betsy could do to change that unless she was prepared to use guilt as a weapon to keep him with her. However, she didn't want Cristos on those demeaning terms. What was the point of confronting him about Petrina? Of condemning and crying? She couldn't *make* Cristos love her, could she? Her only option was to surrender with dignity and go back home to London.

Betsy sat on a bench in a busy square striving to talk herself into the dignified option. But there were problems. One, she couldn't bear the idea of Petrina having Cristos. Two, she hated both of them with a vengeful passion that had nothing forgiving or dignified about it. Three, underneath the hatred, she still loved him and walking away from him was easier to think about than actually do.

Tiny shooting pains were tensing her tummy muscles. She had had those same little stabs on a couple of occasions in recent days but, as they had caused her only the most brief and minor discomfort, she had ignored them. She would mention them at her next visit to the obstetrician. A sharper stab made her draw in a surprised breath.

At that point, she emerged from the distancing fog of her unhappy, circuitous thoughts. Fear for her baby seized a hold of her and blanked out everything else. When she stood up the pain got worse and she staggered, doubling over. Suddenly arms came out of nowhere to support her and she registered that she had not contrived to shake off her bodyguards.

'Hospital…' she said jerkily and then she began to pray.

CHAPTER NINE

CRISTOS was waiting to see Betsy when she emerged from surgery.

He looked shattered: ashen pale beneath his bronzed skin, stunning bone structure rigid, gorgeous eyes bleak with shock and regret. Betsy learned that she could hate him almost as much as she loved him for caring to that extent. He had sincerely wanted their child and he was sincerely devastated when she miscarried. But at the end of the day when all the drama was over what was his disappointment and sympathy worth? Not very much, in her opinion. Cristos would have other children…only she was convinced that they would not be with her.

'I don't want to talk about it…I just want to be on my own and sleep,' she told him numbly when he tried to talk to her in her private room.

He closed his lean brown hand over hers, engulfing her smaller fingers. 'Did you see me on the news with Petrina?' he asked tautly.

Betsy yanked her hand free of his in instantaneous rejection.

'I take it that that's a yes. Please listen to what I have to say, *pethi mou*.'

'I don't want to talk to you!' she ground out.

His forceful energy laced the atmosphere. She could feel him willing her to hear him out. 'You have every right to be furious with me and to feel that I've let you down. But things aren't always what they seem—'

'Do you really think I care right now? Do you really think that after what's happened I'm sulking about you not turning up for lunch?' Betsy hurled in tempestuous condemnation. 'Why can't you go away and leave me alone?'

'I won't speak. I'll just sit here with you.'

'I want to be on my own,' she reiterated tightly.

'Right now, we should be together. I may not know what to say…I may be afraid of saying the wrong thing, but I do know that I want and need to share this with you,' Cristos drawled with dogged determination.

She turned her back on him to stare at the wall. She could not look anywhere near him without recalling Petrina Rhodias clinging to him as if she had every right in the world to do so. There was a clenched fist inside her where her heart had once been. She wanted to cry but her eyes burned and stayed dry.

'Please just go home and go to bed,' she urged a couple of hours later, unable to bear even his silent presence in the same room for it was a comfort to have him there and she would not surrender to her own weakness. There was no point needing Cristos when he was not going to be part of her life for much longer.

'Don't shut me out like this, *agape mou*,' Cristos breathed in a roughened undertone. 'It's making me feel as though I have lost both of you.'

And he waited and waited with a phenomenal patience that was quite unlike him for some sign of response from her and received nothing. Finally the door slid softly shut on his departure and she wept then, painful noiseless tears that inched down her cheeks like stinging rain. She wept because she loved a truly decent guy, who was still so busy doing what he felt he ought to do for his wife's benefit that he could not yet allow himself to contemplate the fact that there was no longer any reason for their marriage to continue.

When Betsy wakened the next morning, she lay very still and faced how much had changed in the past twenty-four hours. In some respects she was still in shock. She had got so used to being pregnant. Without her even appreciating the fact, the very condition of being pregnant had become a central theme in her life. She had been so careful about what she ate and drank and even more keen to ensure that she took the right amount of exercise and rest. She had read books about pregnancy. She had toured baby shops with enthusiasm, looked at maternity clothes and made plans for decorating a nursery. And now, without warning, all that was at an end. She was no longer an expectant mother and she had not yet come to terms with that cruel reality.

'One of those things,' the obstetrician had told her the day before, giving her statistics that made it clear that early miscarriages were quite common. There was no need for special investigation into the reasons why she had lost her child. Even had she rushed to a doctor when she'd first felt those trifling pangs, she had been assured that it was highly unlikely that anything could have been done to alter the eventual outcome.

Kindly meant platitudes that seemed to take no account of her anguish had followed. She was young. She was healthy. She should try again soon and put this experience behind her. There was absolutely no reason why her next pregnancy shouldn't be successful. It seemed that nobody had the slightest suspicion that in certain circumstances a miscarriage could sound the death knell for a marriage as well.

She had just finished breakfast when Cristos reappeared.

'I saw the tray…you have scarcely eaten enough to keep a bird alive.' He sighed on the threshold, lustrous dark golden eyes sombre and concerned.

'I wasn't hungry. I'll be glad when I can get out of here—'

'If you like you can leave as soon as the doctor has given permission,' Cristos was quick to interpose, his approval of that course unconcealed. 'I'd like to have you home again.'

Suddenly evasive, Betsy bent her bright head. 'I'm not just ready yet,' she muttered hurriedly.

Silence lay while he computed her change of heart.

'You have to let me explain what happened yesterday…and to do it effectively I have to go back a few more weeks in history,' Cristos advanced.

He would give her no peace until she heard him out. She let her head rest back against the banked-up pillows, her hair as vibrant as a fire against the pale linen.

'When I broke off my engagement to Petrina, there was a business as well as a personal dimension to be considered. The Stephanides holdings were on the brink of merging with her father's companies. When we parted, the merger plans went up in smoke. Since then we've been at war in the market-place.'

Betsy was no longer aping relaxation. Stiff with tension, she had sat up. Cristos was telling her that his decision to marry her rather than Petrina had resulted in serious consequences on the business front and she was appalled.

'Why didn't you tell me?'

'What would have been the point? I didn't want you worrying about the situation.'

'That's why you've been working night and day,' Betsy registered with a sinking heart. She was thinking how complex it must have been to pull two such large businesses back from the edge of a merger. By that stage both parties would have been well aware of the strengths and weaknesses of the other and the resulting battle for supremacy would have been even tougher.

'So who's winning?' Betsy enquired tautly.

'I was but it was not a fight I ever wanted. I have a great respect for Petrina's father, Orestes. He is one of my grandfather's oldest friends.'

'Oh, no...is there anything that isn't my fault?' Very pale, Betsy slowly shook her head. She felt so horribly responsible. Nothing but trouble had resulted from her pregnancy. An engagement had been broken and two families and two businesses had been torn apart. Even Patras, it seemed, had suffered as the same divisions affected even his friendship with Orestes Rhodias.

'How is it *your* fault? None of this is your fault!' Cristos exclaimed with fierce feeling. 'I was engaged and playing away. All the responsibility for every wrong thing that has happened since then is mine!'

The sound of such an admission from Cristos twisted like a knife inside Betsy. He had finally got back to basics and acknowledged his own mistake. But what had brought about that miraculous transformation? His loss of Petrina.

'You must not blame yourself for any of this, *yineka mou*,' Cristos asserted with raw conviction. 'It's all over now. Yesterday, Orestes Rhodias had what he believed was a heart attack. I was on the way to meet you for lunch when I received word that Orestes had been rushed into hospital. Although we had not been on good terms, I still wished to pay my respects. I asked one of my staff to contact you and I'm afraid the wrong restaurant was contacted...'

It felt to Betsy as though a hundred years had passed since she had been stood up on that lunch date. 'It doesn't matter.'

'It matters to me, especially with what happened afterwards,' Cristos revealed tautly, reluctant to be any more specific lest he upset her. 'I should have called you myself. I intended to. I believed I would only be twenty minutes late.'

'So what happened?' She did not wish to talk about anything personal.

'Orestes was told that he was suffering from stress and he was so relieved that his heart was all right that he made peace with me. The battle between us is at an end.' Cristos hesitated. 'Petrina arrived at the hospital not knowing whether her father was alive or dead and she broke down when she discovered that it was a false alarm...'

'And, of course, you knowing each other so well, she just naturally fell on you for support,' Betsy filled in, affecting more interest in her nails than in all the hugging and so forth that had gone on at that hospital the day before.

'I didn't like to reject her in front of the television cameras. She was a bit hysterical,' Cristos proffered. 'There was nothing in it.'

Betsy doubted that Petrina would have looked quite so ecstatic without encouragement. She had seen him on camera too and he had not acted as though he were enduring an attack by a hysterical woman. He had been smiling that very special smile of his, that smile that Betsy had come to think of as being uniquely hers.

'It's important that you believe that there was nothing personal about her getting all touchy-feely. I haven't looked at Petrina since I married you...'

Literally! He had not had the opportunity. She would not let herself look at him. She felt explosive and bitter and terribly sad. He didn't love her and without love she should never have married him. In particular she should have been careful not to marry a guy who had been engaged to someone else. That had been asking for trouble.

'I don't know you when you're quiet like this...' Cristos confided tautly. 'I'm not used to doing all the talking.'

If she talked she was afraid that she would start crying. She loved him so much. Walking away would be the hardest thing she had ever done and yet, now that there was no longer to be a baby, she owed him his freedom back. He had stood by her just as he'd promised. The costs of doing so, she had just learned, had been even higher than she had realised. Ever since he had married her he had been fighting to keep his business empire afloat. Now thankfully that crisis was over, but it was time for her to move on.

Cristos sank down on the side of her bed and entrapped her restive hands in both of his. Stunning dark golden eyes framed by spiky black lashes assailed hers. 'I want to make everything all right for you again and I can't...I feel helpless,' he confided roughly under his breath.

He seemed so sincere, so caring. She wanted to wrap both arms round him and hug him tight. He was upset about the baby. Was it possible that she had

misjudged him? Reacted to an overdose of jealous in-
security?

'I've wrecked so many things in your life,' she muttered shakily.

'That's rubbish.' His hands tightened on hers. 'You
haven't wrecked anything.'

Then why did he not mention the possibility of their
having another baby? Why the heck could he not offer
her the one option that would be a consolation and
persuade her that he still saw them as having a marriage that had a future? For goodness' sake, why was
she so pathetically weak? All he had to do was be
kind and sympathetic and she was willing to keep him
tied to her for the rest of his days! Did he deserve
that? Did he deserve to have to stay married to a
woman he didn't love just because she had fallen in-
conveniently pregnant? After all, there wasn't going
to be a baby now.

Hauling her hands back from his, she flipped away
from him, no longer trusting herself that close. 'I need
time to think about things—'

'What things?'

'About stuff like how I feel,' she mumbled tearfully.

Cristos gathered her up and crushed her against him.
'You're miserable right now…you shouldn't be thinking about anything!'

She wanted to sneak her arms round him but she
wouldn't let herself. He was very good at doing the
supportive thing but it wouldn't do to read too much
into it. She was in no hurry to remember it but Cristos,
she reminded herself, was still the guy who had told
her that he wasn't looking for love from her. Pulling
herself back together again, she told him she was tired
and eventually he took the hint and left. He had only

been gone five minutes when the phone by her bed rang.

'This is Petrina Rhodias...may I visit you?'

Betsy tried and failed to swallow. 'When?'

'Now...' The voice was cold, imperious, feminine.

Betsy acceded and wondered whether that had been wise. What could Petrina possibly have to say to her? Was there any point in putting herself through a potentially upsetting meeting? But the truth was that Betsy was curious, very curious about the other woman.

By the time, Petrina entered the room, Betsy was seated in the chair by the bed, clad in a white wrap. Petrina was very much the kind of woman who turned male heads, Betsy noted uneasily. Slim and curvaceous with big blue eyes and a wealth of blonde hair, she was as dainty as an elegant doll.

Petrina studied Betsy with unhidden dislike. 'I won't waste your time or mine. When are you planning to let Cristos have his life back?'

'Meaning?'

'Let him have a divorce.'

'If Cristos wants a divorce he only has to ask,' Betsy countered, tilting up her chin.

'He's not going to request a divorce the instant you lose your baby! Naturally he feels sorry for you.'

Betsy lost colour and compressed her lips.

'Woman to woman,' Petrina said snidely, 'Don't you think Cristos has paid enough yet for the mistake of getting you pregnant?'

Petrina was not a nice person. Betsy felt oddly relieved by that discovery even as she flinched. She wondered if Cristos had ever seen this nasty side of Petrina and knew he would not like it at all. But maybe he loved Petrina. Lovers did not demand perfection. And Petrina had yet to utter any lies. Cristos did feel sorry for his wife and even if he did want a divorce, she too was pretty sure that he would not ask for one while she was still grieving for the child she had lost. Furthermore, Cristos *had* suffered for his decision to marry Betsy. He had suffered both in his business and in his personal life and had even endured differences with his grandfather.

'Have you nothing to say?' Petrina derided, her scorn palpable.

'I just want Cristos to be happy,' Betsy muttered, and she wasn't entirely sure about what she was saying. She believed that she ought to mean every syllable of the sentiment she had uttered. But when it came to picturing Cristos with Petrina, she felt gutted and desperate.

'He will be happy with me. He loves me,' Petrina asserted without hesitation.

'And yet you didn't mind that he wasn't faithful?' Betsy pressed half under her breath.

The Greek woman settled scornful eyes on her. 'Why should it bother me when he amuses himself with a little slut like you?'

Betsy walked over to the door to spread it wide. 'I think it's time you clambered back on your broomstick.'

But, although Petrina departed, Betsy's mind had been made up for her. If Cristos loved Petrina, he deserved the freedom to choose to be with the other woman and Betsy ought to remove herself from his path as tactfully as she could.

'I think I should go home for a while,' she informed Cristos when he came in to visit her that afternoon.

His lean, strong face set in taut lines. 'I don't think that's a good idea at present. You need to convalesce.'

'I can do that in London. I'd like to see my family.'

'Then we'll go together.'

'I'd prefer to go on my own.'

'We've only been married a few weeks,' Cristos reminded her.

'And a very eventful few weeks they've been,' Betsy pointed out tightly.

Cristos lodged at the window and she watched his lean, powerful hands curl into fists and flex loose again. 'I still believe that we should stay together and work through this. We can go away…anywhere in the world that you like, *yineka mou*.'

Her throat thickened and she would not allow herself to meet his intent gaze.

'Will you stay at our country house in England?' he asked abruptly.

'OK.'

'If you are there I can at least be sure that you're being properly looked after.' Suddenly, Cristos sounded as weary as she felt. 'That matters to me.'

'I know…' Her voice was going all wobbly and gruff.

'If I let you go, you have to promise to come back to Greece again.'

Her blood ran cold when she tried to imagine making a final visit to discuss the end of their marriage. 'No problem.'

'I'll give you two weeks—'

'That's not long enough,' she muttered. 'I need a month.'

'A month is a long time,' Cristos gritted.

Yes, long enough for him to tire of the role of being

a supportive husband with no wife around. A month in which they could both heal and he could start considering the futility of resurrecting a marriage in which they were already living apart. When she came back to Greece it would be to agree to the official separation he was almost certain to request. And she would make it easy for him. She would be bright and breezy and he would never ever guess that her heart was breaking...

'I'll phone you every day,' he murmured flatly.

Betsy breathed in slow and deep and suppressed her anguish. 'I think we both need more space than that...I think it would be better if you didn't call.'

CHAPTER TEN

IN THIRTY minutes, the private jet would be landing on Greek soil.

Betsy went off to tidy herself. She wondered if her black shift dress and jacket looked a little funereal. She had put her hair up in an effort to look cool and restrained and now she decided it made her look plain. Cristos might not want her back, but she didn't fancy the idea of him looking at her and wondering what he had ever seen in her.

For the whole month, she had stayed at Ashstead, the Stephanides country house in Devon. The first week she had done nothing but cry and sleep. At the start of the second week she had dutifully gone to London to visit her family, accept their commiserations over her miscarriage and admire Gemma's engagement ring. When she returned to Devon, she began going out for long country walks. Her appetite came back and a sparkle returned to her eyes. Patras came to stay for two days and, although she had to ban him from trying to behave like a heavy-handed marriage guidance counsellor, she really enjoyed his company and absolutely adored all the stories he told her about Cristos as a boy. By the end of the fourth week, when Cristos had his PA call her to relay her travel arrangements, she was feeling thoroughly rested.

But while she had come to terms with her grief, she found it quite impossible to come to terms with the prospect of losing Cristos. Even worse the concept of surrendering Cristos to Petrina, who she was convinced was wholly undeserving of him, kept her awake at night. She missed him every hour of every day. A hundred times over, she almost lifted the phone to ring him just to hear the sound of his voice. Only the question of how she would explain herself prevented her from succumbing to temptation.

After the jet landed at Athens, Betsy was ferried across the airport to board a helicopter. When the flight winged out across the Aegean Sea she wondered where on earth she was being taken, yet in another sense she didn't care enough to try and ask. If journey's end meant politely accepting that her marriage was over, she would just as soon remain an eternal traveller. As she'd left London her spirits had been buoyed up by the knowledge that she would soon be seeing Cristos again. Fear of what he would be telling her had plunged her into the downward descent of misery.

So preoccupied was she that when the helicopter landed she scrambled out without the smallest idea of where she was. A few hundred feet away the turquoise sea shimmered in the late afternoon sunlight and the golden beach bore not a single footprint. Disbelieving the evidence of her own eyes, she discounted the strong sense of recognition that was trying to persuade her that she was back on the island of Mos again. In that mood, she hurried round the helicopter and there, nestling below the headland, sat the little villa with the terracotta roof.

Kicking off her shoes, which were sinking into the sand, and discarding her jacket, Betsy sped on towards the house. A figure appeared in the doorway and her steps faltered and started to slow. Shock slivered through her: it *was* Cristos. Sheathed in tailored beige chinos and a black shirt, he looked drop-dead gorgeous. He stayed where he was, waiting for her to come to him. To a woman starved of the sight of him, he was the equivalent of a feast after a famine.

Several feet from him, Betsy froze in her tracks. She was bewildered by the shock of finding herself back on the island and she hated the fact that she'd been taken by surprise. 'What is this set-up? What on earth is going on?'

'You're going to be angry with me,' Cristos imparted.

'Don't tell me what you think I'm going to do…tell me why I would be angry.' Suddenly she stalked forward and pushed past him to peer indoors with suspicious eyes. 'Do you have Petrina in there?' she demanded.

His astonishment was unfeigned. 'Is that a joke? Petrina wouldn't dream of gracing a place as primitive as this with her presence.'

Still very much on the defensive, Betsy folded her arms. 'I don't think it's primitive but I do think it's extremely tasteless to bring me back here.'

The deafening roar of the helicopter taking off again drowned out all possible exchanges for a couple of minutes. Betsy threw her bright head back and pursed her lush mouth. 'How am I supposed to get back to Athens?'

'You're not…at least not without me,' Cristos informed her. 'I'm afraid you've been kidnapped for the second time in your life.'

'Kidnapped?' Betsy parroted.

'When you and I were last here, things were very

simple. I thought it would be a good idea to take our marriage back to basics too.'

Betsy could not believe her ears. 'Are you telling me…that you lured me out here with the intention of keeping me on this island against my will?'

Cristos nodded.

Betsy had fallen very still. 'To save our marriage?'

'I appreciate that it would be more ideal if I gave you a choice, but I want the chance to do some tough negotiating and if you can't walk away from the table, it gives me an advantage.'

'True…on the other hand, I might not want to walk away,' Betsy pointed out a little unevenly. 'Hasn't that occurred to you?'

'That's not how you've been behaving. No visits, no phone calls, an enforced separation,' he reminded her bleakly.

Betsy stopped hiding behind her pride. 'I didn't want you to stay with me just because we were married. I wanted to give you the chance to choose…and I really did think that you might choose Petrina.'

'Even after all you and I have been to each other?' Cristos framed in apparent amazement.

'She told me you loved her—'

'You've met Petrina…but *when*?' Cristos demanded, taken aback.

Betsy explained about the visit she had received at the hospital.

Cristos swore under his breath in his own language. '*Theos mou*…if I had known I would not have been responsible for my actions. How could she be that cruel? You had only just lost our child. You were so vulnerable then.' His clear dark golden eyes were bitterly angry. 'There was no love in my relationship with her—respect, familiarity, and tolerance perhaps. I thought that that was all there was. I honestly believed I wasn't missing anything...and then I met you.'

And then I met you! Betsy savoured that admission, for, if Petrina had only qualified for respect and tolerance, he was making it sound as though Betsy herself had made much more of an impression. He had never loved Petrina. The relief of learning that fact made her feel dizzy. He had set her worst fear to rest.

'Everything got so complicated with you.' Cristos raked long fingers through his cropped black hair. 'You told me you loved Rory. When I saw you together at our wedding, I believed you *still* loved him—'

'No...no!' Words of eager disagreement tumbled from Betsy. She closed her hands over his. 'I grew out of Rory a long time before I even realised it. That's all over and done with—'

Rueful golden eyes flared over her anxious face. 'I was so angry and jealous on our wedding day that I almost wrecked our marriage before it even began!'

'But you said you believed me when I explained about Rory.'

'Wasn't that also the evening that you gave me multiple-choice answers on that subject?'

At that reminder, Betsy reddened. 'It's been a very long time since I thought I loved him. I was trying to save face. You put me on the spot but you weren't giving me any answers about how you felt about Petrina,' she reminded him. 'I needed reassurance too.'

'Once I knew you were pregnant, I didn't have to think about how I felt about you,' Cristos acknowledged, tugging her gently indoors and out of the strong sunlight that he could see was making her uncomfortable. 'I knew I wanted to marry you. I didn't have a moment's doubt. It was that simple—'

'But it wasn't simple for me,' she protested.

'It was only simple for me because I loved you. I didn't appreciate it then, but that was *why* marrying you was such a simple decision for me.'

'You love me...' Betsy blinked in bemusement, not certain she was hearing him right. 'When did you decide you loved me?'

'At our wedding. I saw you with Rory and I wanted to rip him apart. But I realised that if I didn't want to lose you, I would have to try and pretend that I hadn't seen anything that bothered me.' His dark eyes momentarily reflected the bleakness of that recollection. 'That was a major challenge, *pethi mou*. But it was also the moment when I appreciated that there was virtually nothing I would not do to keep you and that I loved you.'

Betsy's eyes were stinging like mad. 'You love me...honestly?'

His slow, devastating smile slashed his darkly handsome features. 'Do you think I'd kidnap just anybody?'

Betsy surprised both herself and him by bursting into floods of tears.

In consternation, Cristos hauled her into his arms. '*Theos mou*...what's wrong? What did I say?'

'You said you loved me...and I've been so miserable the last few weeks and I needn't have been!' she sobbed helplessly.

He bent down and swept her off her feet to carry her into the air-conditioned cool of the bedroom. 'The last month has been hell for me too,' he admitted rawly, 'but I didn't want to be unreasonable and crowd you. I wanted to be with you but you didn't seem to want to be with me—'

'That's not how I felt. But we only got married because I'd fallen pregnant,' Betsy reminded him jaggedly, her breath catching in her throat. 'When I lost the baby, I thought there was no reason for you to want to stay with me any more and that our marriage was over—'

'You crazy woman...how could you have been so blind?' Cristos demanded incredulously. 'We were really happy together. It was insane. I was living through the most stressful time of my entire life at the office and coming home to paradise with you. I've never been so happy in my life...in fact I didn't know it was possible for one person to make such a difference. Yes, it was devastating when you had the miscarriage but we still had each other—'

'But we *didn't*...I went back to England. You're probably going to find it hard to believe but I love you too!' Betsy gasped apologetically.

Cristos vented a startled laugh and shook his handsome dark head in amazement. 'Patras said no woman could be interested in hearing what a smart-mouthed kid I had been unless she loved me. I didn't believe him.'

'He was right...he had me hanging on his every word. When he came to stay, I was just missing you so much...' Betsy squeezed out tearfully.

'You love me!' Without warning Cristos lifted her up in the air like a doll and spun her round and back against him.

'Oh, that was so uncool...' Betsy whispered with

immense appreciation, stretching up to frame his face with her spread fingers and survey him with loving pleasure. 'But now I finally believe you're mine.'

His stunning dark golden eyes clung to hers. 'Always, *agape mou*.'

'So what happened to that…you weren't looking for me to love you stuff?' Betsy enquired saucily.

'That was my pride talking.'

She wound her arms round his neck and pushed into the hard, muscular heat of his big, powerful body. He answered her encouragement by kissing her breathless. Crushing her to him, he muttered thickly, 'I'd love it if we tried for another baby some time—'

Inspired by a project that had such immediate appeal to her own heart, Betsy leant back from him to say, 'Would right now be too soon?'

The strain etched in his lean, powerful face evaporated. 'I was afraid that I was going to upset you and that maybe you wouldn't want to risk a second pregnancy—'

'We just had bad luck. Oh, I do wish that you'd told me how you felt when I was in hospital,' Betsy admitted unsteadily, her emotions very close to the surface.

'That I'd like us to try again? One of my female cousins warned me on no account to mention anything like that in case you felt I wasn't showing proper respect for the child we had just lost,' Cristos confided in a taut undertone. 'I didn't want to risk hurting you.'

'I wouldn't have felt like that…I was just desperate for some sign from you that you still saw us and our marriage as having a future,' Betsy explained.

'Our future is together, *pethi mou*. I went through hell when you went back to England,' Cristos admitted raggedly, gazing down at her with adoring intensity. 'Never again do I want to go through the agony of wondering if I've lost you—'

'From now on, you won't have that worry,' Betsy assured him with sunny good humour and newly learned confidence. 'You won't even get time off for good behaviour.'

Cristos threw back his handsome dark head and laughed with true appreciation. 'I love you,' he intoned then with smouldering intensity and she dragged him down to her and found his sensual mouth for herself.

Almost a year later, Betsy gave birth to their daughter, Karisa. Karisa was followed eighteen months afterwards by the arrival of a son, Darian.

Overjoyed with his two great-grandchildren, Patras Stephanides bought the island of Mos and gave it to Cristos and Betsy to mark their fourth wedding anniversary.

* * * *

Looking for more Lynne Graham? Don't miss
The Greek Tycoon's Blackmailed Mistress,
available this month from Modern™ romance.

White-Hot!

TRISH WYLIE

Trish Wylie tried various careers before eventually fulfilling her dream of writing. Years spent working in the music industry, in promotions, and teaching little kids about ponies gave her plenty of opportunity to study life and the people around her. Which, in Trish's opinion, is a pretty good study course for writing! Living in Ireland, Trish balances her time between writing and horses. If you get to spend your days doing things you love, then she thinks that's not doing too badly. You can contact Trish at www.trishwylie. com.

Available this month from Romance, travel to Los Angeles with Trish Wylie in *His L.A. Cinderella.*

Dear Reader,

The Irish have a long history of storytelling. It's in our blood. Long before books there were rambling houses; places where people would gather around the fireside to listen to tales that more than likely were never quite the same when told more than once. As we travelled around the world those stories were taken with us, passed on from generation to generation. I think we're natural optimists at heart too, but then having survived so much in our history we have cause to be. And what is more optimistic than the belief in love?

So add a history of storytelling to a healthy dose of optimism, the sense of humour we're famous for and the romantic surroundings of the island of Ireland and it's not hard to figure out why I do what I do. I can only hope people enjoy reading it as much as I enjoy writing it.

Hugs and kisses,

Trish

CHAPTER ONE

'I HAVE new carpet coming next week.'

Shane laughed. 'Not any more you don't.'

'It's cappuccino.'

'You bought coffee?'

'No, the carpet colour.' Finn nudged him hard in the ribs. 'It's cappuccino. That's what it's called.'

'I'm sure it'll be lovely on the lawn.'

There wasn't anywhere else left to put it.

'We might have stood a chance of catching it if you hadn't thrown vodka on it.'

Finn grimaced. 'I thought it was water.'

'Water would have been better. Though to be honest it would have taken more than a glass of the stuff.'

'All right, wise ass. But if you didn't have all that expensive training that I, as a tax-payer, *paid for* then you might have thrown the first thing that came to hand at it too.'

'I might have remembered what I was drinking before I went to bed.'

'*I* wasn't drinking it.'

Shane's dark eyebrows rose. 'Oh, really? Do tell.'

There were times when Shane Dwyer's way of asking a question accompanied with a mischievous sparkle in his blue eyes just bugged the hell out of Finn. Standing freezing to death in her pyjamas on a wintry December evening while her house was on fire was one of them. The fact that to answer him would involve a foray into her disastrous love life didn't help any.

She smirked at him.

After a brief burst of deep laughter, he inclined his head. 'C'mon, babe, move back a wee bit more.'

She stood statue-still on the pavement for another second as she looked at her house, eyes wide and blinking.

After all, a moment like this one deserved a little reflection, didn't it? She should be thinking deep and meaningful thoughts, contemplating twists of fate and the flammable quality of racks of underwear set to dry in front of a fireplace. Even *with* a fireguard.

Though, in hindsight, throwing the burnt-out candle ends on the open fire before she went to bed probably hadn't been a Mensa moment.

If only she'd forked out for a tumble dryer. But it had been a choice between a tumble dryer and nice carpet. And carpet had won...

'Finn?'

She found herself curious about the stupidest things. Had she put away her ironing? Had the DVD recorder taped the show she'd set it for before she'd left on her date? If she'd thought to have a selection of mixers available for her date would there even have been a glass of neat vodka for her to throw at the flames?

'*Finn.*' The deep voice became more demanding of her attention. 'C'mon, look at me a minute.'

Turning her head, she had to tilt her chin up to look into his familiar blue eyes. She could see many things there when she searched. She could see concern, warmth, sincerity. Obviously her taxes hadn't been wasted on his training in the customer service department.

She scowled at him. 'I'm having a moment here.'

He grinned down at her, white teeth glinting in his dirt-smeared face. Then he reached a gloved hand out to touch her arm. 'You go right on and take that moment. Don't let the chance of smoke inhalation ruin it for you.' He winked. 'Eddie is on his way; he'll be here any minute.'

He'd called Eddie already? That was nice of him, considerate even. Not to mention above and beyond the call of duty. But then it wasn't everybody whose house was burning down that had connections to the local fire brigade as Fionoula McNeill did.

Her brother Eddie was third generation after all.

Technically she'd now broken new ground by being the first generation to actually *start* a fire, so it would be sad if her brother missed it, right?

Shane continued to grin. 'It's almost all done here anyway. Then we'll get you home to our place, babe.'

Babe. He kept calling her *babe*, didn't he? Somewhere in her addled brain she allowed the endearment to slip through where it rattled around in her skull for a while and then seeped down into her chest. She'd have paid good money to hear him call her that in that tone before.

It was an awful shame it had taken her house to burn down for him to use it, *on her*. He never had trouble using the word on any other female on the island they called home. Finn *knew*.

It was a throwaway word for him, thrown mostly at skinny blondes with skirts so short they probably had permanent kidney infections, as it happened.

Knowing that meant it shouldn't have had any effect on Finn. But it did, it made her feel as if she had his full and undivided attention. Which didn't suck. Though the smoothing of his hand on her arm should have been more than enough to tell her she did even without the sexy sparks in his eyes.

If she'd just known all it would take was for her to burn her own house down…well, *damn*. Mentally she clicked her fingers at the missed opportunity.

Apparently sarcasm was her way of coping in a crisis. She sighed. Oh, well, it had always worked for everything else, why would this be any different?

Her eyes focused on his hand as she cleared her throat and managed an eloquent, 'Thanks.'

'No problem. I keep tellin' you I'm one hell of a guy, don't I?'

'That you do. But I'm wearing entirely too much for you to waste time flirting with me.'

'Oh, I dunno.' He lifted the hand from her arm and tilted his helmet back on his head. 'It's kinda sexy.'

Folding his arms across his wide chest, he let his eyes drop to stare openly at her breasts. Finn's chin dropped and then she looked upwards and rolled her eyes.

Shane lifted a hand and rubbed his chin. 'The hedgehog knows that's a brush, it's—'

'That's the whole joke, so, yes.' Well, if she'd known there would be a half-dozen guys to look at what she wore in bed most nights she'd maybe have planned better. Maybe. 'If it was another hedgehog it was doing it to it wouldn't be as funny, would it?'

'Still, you gotta wonder if it's not—' he paused for a second and then smiled his beautiful lazy smile '—a little *uncomfortable* for hedgehogs.'

Her eyes focused on his smile and then his lips and where they'd be if she took a step forward. *Tempting*. But it would be a bad case of any port in a storm. This was Shane Dwyer; they'd been dancing around each other for a while. So long as it never became a horizontal mambo she'd be just fine.

With a lift of her chin and a quirk of her head she

smiled sweetly. 'They manage. And thanks so much for helping put out the fire and all. Another day at the office all wrapped up.'

Something flickered across his eyes when she looked back at him. 'Mmm.' His voice dropped an octave as he stepped closer, inclining his head towards her ear, 'Just don't go tryin' to burn down any more houses, babe. I don't like thinkin' someone that matters to me might be hurt.'

Huh? Her eyes widened.

Oh, well, this was just great. Her house, her first ever house as a home-owner, the one she'd made less than flipping seven mortgage repayments on, was burnt to a crisp in front of her by her own hands. And now she was reading between lines.

If her brother didn't get here soon she'd no doubt be imagining Shane professing undying love, throwing her over one of his broad shoulders and taking her back to his cave somewhere to distract her from her woes with hours of wanton—

'*Finn*!' Another voice sounded behind her. 'Finn, are you all right?'

Shane stepped back as Eddie grabbed her and pulled her into a bear hug that knocked her held breath from her lungs.

'I'll be fine so long as you don't crush me to death.'

'What the hell happened? Shane said someone made the call from a mobile?'

'I called it in.' She looked up into eyes the same green shade as her own. 'It happened very fast.'

'Where *were* you?' He stepped back and placed his large hands on her shoulders, shaking her gently. 'What the hell happened? Did you leave those damn straighteners plugged in again?'

'No! I didn't leave the damn straighteners plugged in again.' She shrugged free from his hold, her chin rising indignantly that he felt the need to give out to her when *her house had just been on fire*!

Then she glanced at Shane and saw his shoulders shuddering in barely suppressed laughter. Damn him! If she didn't tell her brother then he would, wouldn't he?

She looked back at Eddie's face and fluttered her eyelashes at him, pouting. It was worth a try. '*Anyone* could have made the same mistake.'

'You set fire to your own house?' Eddie glanced across at Shane as he hid his mouth behind a glove. But his eyes told the tale. 'Bloody hell, Finn.'

Her temper sparked. 'It's not like I planned on it! It was an accident. Why would I want to see my own house on fire? I ordered carpet, for crying out loud!'

'Yeah, espresso.'

'Cappuccino!' She glared at Shane.

'How many times have I told you about being careful?'

Finn scowled at her brother and opened her mouth to speak.

But as Shane stepped forward and placed a friendly arm around Eddie's shoulders he beat her to it. 'Hey, ease up. She did try to put it out.'

Son-of-a—

'You tried to put it *out*?' Eddie's face was incredulous. 'You stupid—'

He paused and took a breath. 'What did you do— throw a pan of water on it?'

'Not exactly.'

Shane lowered his voice and choked out the words, 'Think smaller.'

'Shut up, Shane.'

He laughed out loud, 'Oh, c'mon! You think the lads at the station aren't gonna pull his leg about this one for years? The least you can do is give him the heads up.'

'What did you do?'

With a scowl at Shane and a purse of her lips she jumped on in. 'It was the first thing that came to hand.'

'What was?'

'A glass of vodka.'

Eddie's mouth gaped at Shane's words. But before he could gather up a head of steam Finn added, 'It *looked* like water. Kevin must have left it on the side before we went out for dinner.'

'Who's Kevin?'

'My date.'

'What'd you do, send him out for a can of petrol?' Eddie pointed down the street.

'Don't be ridiculous!' She glared at them both one final time and started to march past them, her head held high.

They turned and fell into step on either side of her.

'How was the date, then?' Shane's deep voice sounded to her left.

She stopped, gaped at him for a second and then decided he was making with the funnies, so she stormed onwards. 'Ha, ha.'

She cleared her throat. 'Just tell the guys I appreciate what *they* did, will you, Shane?'

'No problem.' He glanced across at the rest of the crew as they began rolling up hoses and packing away equipment. 'I better go anyway.'

Eddie nodded across at him as they stopped by his Jeep. 'I'll take her on back to the house.'

'Probably best; she's too calm about this.'

'Probably shock.'

Shane nodded. 'Probably.'

'Could you two stop talking about me like I'm not here?' She glared at them in turn. 'I hate it when you do that.'

'We know.'

She glared harder when they answered in unison. 'Well, knock it on the head, then.'

'We're just concerned about you, is all.' Eddie smiled. 'Would you prefer it if we yanked out some marshmallows on sticks?'

'Yeah, we keep bags of them on the truck, you know that.' Shane's face was deadpan but his eyes sparkled.

'You're both hilarious.'

'Babe, we're only trying to take your mind off it.' He reached out a large gloved hand again and squeezed her upper arm, his eyes focused on hers. 'This is a big thing that's happened here and you're gonna need a little time to deal with it. All joking aside, you've lost a lot.'

They could be too protective when they wanted to be. She knew how big a deal what had happened was. She gave a little laugh, but a chill suddenly radiated through every inch of her body at the thought of what could have been. 'There's not much to deal with that I can see. I have no home, no clothes, in fact everything I own bar what I have on and what's in the car is now a great smoking pile of ash. Seems pretty straightforward to me.'

It was the wobble on the last few words that brought her sarcasm to a halt and she knew Shane had caught them too when a small scowl appeared on his forehead.

He released her arm and stepped back, his voice firm as he glanced at Eddie. 'Take her home. I'll be back before you go on shift in the morning and I'll look out for her.'

Oh, yeah, that would help no end. Stuck inside four walls with Shane 'looking out for her'. Her throat threatened to close over and she could feel tears prickling at the back of her eyes as hysteria rose in her chest.

This was a disaster. It really was.

When she spoke her voice was brittle. 'I don't need looking after and I have *work* in the morning.'

'The hell you do.'

'You're not going to work.'

She scowled when they spoke in unison again. 'Yes, I am! I need to earn a wage to pay for wee things like clothes, seeing as I don't have any any more.'

'We'll lend you some.'

While Shane nodded in agreement with Eddie's statement Finn quietly fumed. It felt better to be angry with them than to focus on what had just happened and the repercussions of it on her calm and organized world. Typical macho men—it just wouldn't occur to them that she might see anything hurtful in the fact that they believed their clothes would *fit* her!

Add that to talking over her, joking about marsh-mallows and the fact that she now had to go stay in Shane's house…

Well, hell, why didn't they just give her a nice paper cut and some lemon juice?

'C'mon, Finn, let's get you back home and I'll make you some sweet tea. You'll feel better then.'

Sure she would. Tea was the cure for all ills, after all. As her brother cupped her elbow and guided her away from the burnt ruin of her house she glanced back over her shoulder. She couldn't help herself.

But her eyes didn't stray to the house for long. Without thought, they sought out Shane where he stood watching them walk away. And the bubble of hysteria returned.

She didn't want to be stuck under the same roof as him. She really didn't. Why was someone somewhere punishing her for the loss of her house? She really hadn't burned it down on purpose, even if she had truly hated the carpet and bright yellow doors gave her migraine.

Staying with Shane had the possibility of being an even worse disaster than her house burning down.

CHAPTER TWO

A YELLING voice woke Shane up.

When he'd got back home after his shift he'd only had a few moments to get an update from Eddie on how Finn was.

'Still too calm if you ask me,' Eddie stated. 'I gave her a good dose of whiskey in some tea before she went to bed and she's been fairly sound since she drifted off. But I don't think it's hit yet.'

Shane smiled, 'So long as she didn't try to throw it on any flames, eh?'

Eddie laughed. 'It could only happen to Finn, you know. When disaster strikes her it's as subtle as an elephant in a tutu.' His smile faded. 'She has to be cut up, though.'

Shane stared his best friend straight in the eye. 'She's not made of stone and she worked her ass off for that house.'

'Yeah, well, I rang her work and they know she'll not be in for a while. Keep an eye out.'

So he'd settled himself on the sofa, reckoning that way he would hear when she woke up and started moving around. If he knew Finn she'd try to sneak out to work.

The next thing he was aware of was the sound of her voice calling out, pulling him from the depths of slumber.

It got louder as he ran upstairs two steps at a time. 'No!'

He was at her door in a few more steps.

'It's too hot. Get out! Out of the fire!'

'Finn.' He sat down beside her, his weight dipping the mattress and rolling her body towards him. 'Finn, wake up.'

When he reached a hand to her arm she stirred and her eyes shot open, widening at the sight of him, 'Shane! What the hell—?'

'You were yelling.'

'No, I wasn't.' She struggled into a sitting position, instinctively drawing the duvet up with her like a protective shield. 'I was asleep.'

'Then you were dreaming.' His hand smoothed along her arm until it met her hand and squeezed gently. 'You were calling to get out of the fire.'

The touch of his hand had momentarily drawn her attention but his words drained the colour from her face. 'No, I wasn't.'

'Yeah, you were.'

The soft tone in his deep voice made her heart

twist nearly as painfully as her dream had. There was no use denying it; if Shane said she'd called out about a fire, then she had. Thing was, she hadn't had the dream in years. Not since she'd been a kid.

She took a moment to compose herself, determined not to go all weepy and girly when he smiled a gentle smile at her. It was just a natural reaction to her house burning down, was all. She was overly sensitive. Understandably. But damned if she would show it in front of *him*.

His hand tightened on hers. 'You okay?'

'I'm fine.' She tugged her hand free before the warmth his touch created could work its way up her arm, then shuffled ungracefully off the other side of the bed. 'What time is it? I can't be late for work.'

'Eddie already rang in for you.' His eyes followed her movement around the room, drawn of their own accord to the long length of naked leg beneath the over-sized T-shirt she wore. Well, it couldn't be helped really, he was a legs man, after all. Old habits and all that.

When she swung to face him she caught him looking and a flush crept up her neck. Her hands lowered in a reflex action to the hem of the T-shirt where she tugged. As if the action would somehow make it floor-length. Suddenly she wished she'd kept on the pyjamas that had stunk of smoke. 'What do you mean he rang in for me? I'm not twelve years old. And I can't miss a day at work. We're busy, for crying out loud. It's December; we do a third of a—'

'Year's business in one month.' He nodded, continuing to look at her legs from shapely ankles upwards. 'You tell us that every year. We nearly know the music distribution business as well as you do now.'

'Well, it's true. This is just about the worst time of year for me to be off.' Her eyes dragged away from his face as she searched frantically for something to cover her legs with. Then she stopped looking and scowled. This was supposedly *her* room while she stayed in his house. Who was *he* to come in uninvited, to hear things he had no right hearing, that would no doubt need an explanation she wasn't ready to give, and to then openly ogle her? And even more to the point how dared he raise her pulse rate doing it?

'Could you kindly leave now?'

His eyes rose slowly to meet hers. 'I only came up 'cos you sounded upset. I was being a gentleman.'

Finn snorted gracefully. 'Well, I'm not upset, I'm fine. And you're not being a gentleman; you're staring at my legs is what you're doing.'

He smiled. 'What can I say? There's a lot of leg to look at.'

And with that his eyes flickered back down. Finn felt her flush working its way up off her neck onto her cheeks, felt her pulse beating harder in the base of her throat. It was ridiculous. It wasn't as if Shane Dwyer hadn't ever looked at her before. It was just she hadn't been semi-naked, *sans* underwear at the time. Or alone in a bedroom with him. Which hadn't happened *ever.*

'So is this what you do to look out for someone when they've been through a traumatic experience? Ogle them?'

The smile was slow and sensual, accompanied by a twinkle in the blue of his eyes as he looked back at her face. 'Only when they have legs like yours, babe.'

Finn stared in blatant disbelief.

'Taken your mind off your bad dream, though, hasn't it?'

Brute. But he was right. The dream had sneaked into her mind in that period of sleep between deep, dreamless slumber and wakening and she knew the memory of it would stay with her even now that she was completely awake. If she wasn't being distracted by other things.

Even mentioning it brought it back. And it still ached. An ache on top of an ache of old unless she was very much mistaken. Which was all she needed! His quiet study of her had taken that ache from her chest and moved it in a more southerly direction, that much was true. But it didn't stop her from being ticked at him.

Because now that he'd pointed out how it had been a purposeful distraction ploy, the ache moved into her mind like a dull headache, where the recent memory was still as clear as a picture on a cinema screen.

'Right then, seeing as you're wide awake now and *fine*—' Shane stood up and walked towards the doorway, his naked feet silent on the carpeted floor

'—throw something on and we'll go take a look at your house.'

Finn's eyes widened. 'What would we do that for? There's not much point seeing as it's gone.'

'You still need to see it, though.'

'I don't think I do.'

'Well, *I* do—' he turned at the doorway and looked her right in the eyes, his own silently determined '—and I've been doing this kind of thing longer than you have. So get dressed and I'll take you shopping afterwards for being a good girl. Get you some clothes.'

The shopping was certainly a necessity. But she didn't need him to take her, she could take herself. The independent woman in her rebelled at his bossy, patronizing attitude. Up until a few hours ago she'd had no one to answer to. No one who felt she needed babysitting in case she dissolved into a crumpled heap of despair.

But then a few hours ago she'd had pyjama bottoms, and plenty of underwear that wasn't used to burn her own house down…

As his eyes swept again to her legs and a dimple appeared in his cheek to accompany a roguish lopsided smile she decided she'd let herself be led, just this once. Out of necessity.

Then she would find somewhere else to live. Where she couldn't be ogled by six feet two of dangerously distracting male.

* * *

It was a mess. With Shane at her side she picked her way tentatively through the sodden heaps that made up all of her earthly possessions.

Then it started to hit her, the stark reality of what had happened. She was picking her way through her life. Her own carelessness had destroyed everything. She could have died drying practical cotton underwear on a rack by the fire. Not even nice underwear, though G-strings might not have caught fire so easily, but honest to goodness large flammable pants could have killed her.

Put that one on a gravestone…

Leaning down, she pulled a blackened picture frame from the floor, her trembling fingers brushing dirt back from the glass to reveal the faces of her family. The first stroke revealed her brother Niall's face, then Conor, then Eddie, then a small ponytailed version of herself. Then she could see her mother's smile before her fingers finally revealed her father's beaming face.

Her throat closed over and she had to blink hard to hold hot tears at bay. Damn it. Damned stupid fires.

Shane had been looking around at the structure itself, while he stood a few feet away from her. The house was old, and the interior had taken a beating in the fire. But the structure still looked pretty sound to him, the walls all still in place. He would never have asked permission to bring them in otherwise. But it would cost a fortune to rebuild. Finn would probably be better cutting her losses on it. 'You have house insurance, right?'

She cleared her throat. 'Yes, and contents.'

He continued to survey the room. 'Good. You'll be all right, then. It wasn't like you did this on purpose. We'll go get the paperwork started this afternoon and then that'll be one less thing for you to worry about.'

When his eyes found Finn again she had her back turned to him, her head slumped forward. He stepped closer, his voice softening. 'You okay?'

She lifted a hand and swiped at the tears that had escaped from her eyes before he could see them. 'I'm fine.'

Another photograph caught her eye, the glass shattered inside the frame. Hunching down, she shook the glass out and looked at the singed picture. It was one that had sat on a wide window sill, had had pride of place, of Eddie and Shane on the day they had become fully fledged firefighters.

Between their equally large frames was Finn, a huge grin on her face as they all hammed it up for the camera.

The air displaced behind her as Shane got close and she shivered involuntarily as he spoke over her shoulder. 'That was a grand day. We all went out on the tear after, remember?'

Finn nodded, her voice low. 'Then after a few

drinks you both spent the evening demonstrating your fireman's lifts with single women in the bar.'

'Before Eddie got that twinge in his back.'

'And you told him his career was over before it had even started.'

'I was wrong there; he's saved dozens of cats since then.' His eyes studied the back of her head as she stood up, then he reached a hand to her shoulder and turned her to face him. His gaze narrowed briefly. 'This is tough, babe, I know, but there might be a few other things you can save. Take your time.'

She couldn't look up at him, her focus remaining on the picture. 'I'm f—'

'I swear, Finn, if you say "fine" one more time I'm gonna have to kick you.' One long finger tilted her chin up and he studied her face with a small smile. 'It's okay to not be fine when it's something this big.'

'No, it's not.' The smile she gave him was unconvincing. 'I'm a firefighter's daughter, a firefighter's sister, and I just set fire to my own house.'

He kept smiling. 'It's not like you're planning on taking up a career as an arsonist, though, is it? It was an accident, that's all. Give yourself a break.'

'I know that. I do. No one got hurt and I hadn't bought a cat yet so it's not that big a deal really.'

'This house was a big deal when you got word you'd bought it. It was a big deal when we all helped you move in. It was such a big deal when you had your first dinner party that we even used napkins.' He reached his free hand to the smears she probably didn't even know she'd made on her cheek and rubbed at them with a roughened thumb. 'You worked hard for this place and everyone was proud of what you'd achieved. You should go right on ahead and be sorry it happened; you just shouldn't blame yourself. That's all.'

It was quite a speech for Shane, and they both knew it.

'You've owned a house for years—' she managed a smile '—and you've not set fire to it. So you're way ahead of me.'

Yeah, but he hadn't had to work to buy his house. It had been a final gift from his mother. Finn had worked for hers, he had watched her do it and could never remember being so proud of anyone before.

He studied her face for a long moment, then tugged her roughly into his arms and held her against his broad chest as she gave in to silent tears. 'I'm fully versed in the dangers of underwear.' He chuckled. 'It could have happened to anyone who wasn't trained. You were unlucky, is all. Just unlucky.'

She allowed the warmth of his body to seep through to her chilled bones. Felt a sense of safety being held by him that she couldn't remember having felt in a long time and she let her fears slip out in response. 'If someone had got hurt I don't know what I'd have—'

He interrupted her again, accompanying the words with a tightening of his arms. 'Quit it now; no one got hurt. So there's not much point torturing yourself over it. You're okay and that's what matters.'

'Thank you.' She didn't know what else to say to him. He was right, so matter-of-fact and practical about it, but still understanding how much owning the house had meant to her, yellow doors and flowery carpet and all; buying it had been her first major achievement. She *had* worked hard for it, damn hard. And even though she knew the insurance would take care of everything it still didn't make up for all the things she'd lost. Things that might have seemed trivial to someone else but had held memories for her. Like pictures of her dad that couldn't be replaced.

That was probably what her dream had been about.

But even though she appreciated what Shane was trying to do for her, and how being held in his arms made her feel cared for, she had to pull herself together and step away from him. She couldn't go getting all gooey around him or allowing herself to get used to being held. That would be bad.

Because she had found it difficult enough to mentally keep him at arm's length for the last while, had discovered a new-found fascination for him that wasn't exactly platonic. Which was *b-a-d*.

He allowed her to get as far as half an arm's length. 'You want to look around for some more pictures and stuff?'

'Yeah, that would be good.'

'We'll salvage what we can and then we'll go get you some new clothes.'

'When these are so attractive?' She used it as an excuse to pull free, looking down at the oversize sweater and jogging pants that Eddie had left out for her. She laughed wryly, trying to ease the tension she felt. 'I feel like someone on the end of a massive weight loss diet.'

'Well they're not as sexy as the hedgehog was, right enough.' He grinned when she pulled a face. 'But I bet we can do better. Think of it as an opportunity to revamp your wardrobe.'

Finn arched an eyebrow. 'There was something wrong with my wardrobe before?'

'No-o, not exactly.' He turned and began to look around at the crowded floor again, leaning down to push aside some sodden cushions. 'But you could be a bit too strait-laced, y'know. You should loosen up some.'

Strait-laced? He thought she was *strait-laced?* That kind of a statement would have been enough to make her want to prove him wrong, if he'd been anyone else. 'So I should take this opportunity to buy things a little more *slutty*?'

He glanced up at her from beneath long dark lashes, his eyes glinting dangerously. 'Well, hell, Finn, now I *really* want to go shopping.'

'Oh, I'll bet. You'll have me in miniskirts and fishnet stockings before I can blink an eye.'

'You run around my place wearing miniskirts and fishnets and I might not be held accountable for my actions. I'm only human.'

Finn gaped. He was flirting with her? Shane Dwyer superhero, was *only human*?

Not that he hadn't turned on the charm around her before. But he'd never been so brazen about it. She shook her head. *Nah.* He was just trying to distract her again, that was all.

Proving very good at it, as it happened.

'Very funny, Dwyer.' She pointed across the room. 'You can just go over there and look for more photos and I'll stay over here where I won't bump into your ego.'

The laughter was deep and melodious, filling the silent wreck of her house as he moved away.

After a moment she smiled too. She couldn't help herself. It was nice of him to try distracting her, even if his method was so outrageous. And for a split second she even wondered what would happen if she flirted back.

Ah, well. Every girl had to have an imagination. It was healthy, right?

Half an hour later they both had armfuls of photos, a few ornaments that had survived, and Finn turned to him, feeling a little easier. 'You don't have to come shopping. We can go back to the house and I'll get my car. You're bound to be tired after being on night shift.'

She looked across at the dark shadow of stubble

on his cheeks and the lazy blink of his eyes. He *was* tired; she could see it. His being so easy to look at meant she could read his face pretty well after years of intensive study.

Green eyes continued their study as he moved across to her side again, picking his way over piles of wet furniture and burnt curtains with confident steps. She'd always been aware of how he looked; it wouldn't have taken her house to have burned down for her to have noticed. But she'd never really spent any time alone in his company to allow herself the luxury of studying him closely enough to see beneath the surface.

He took up a large space on the planet, which would have drawn any woman's gaze in his direction. At a rock concert he would never have any difficulties seeing the band on stage. Mind you, neither would Finn. It was probably the first reason she'd had for looking at him. At five eight, she wasn't exactly a leprechaun herself. Which meant taller guys caught her attention.

Then add to the height a devastating combination of black hair and startling blue eyes, dimples and disgustingly white, straight teeth and, *well*…

She wondered for the gazillionth time just how in God's name someone who looked like him managed to stay single. Women certainly had never had any problems falling at his feet. Finn could even guess at how many. Not that she'd kept a score card or anything.

Watching his approach she wondered if he could actually be that guy who kept notches on his bedpost. While she was in his house she could take a look. For curiosity's sake, not because she wanted to see the inside of his bedroom. Well, okay, she wouldn't mind seeing if he had black silk sheets and a leopard-skin printed throw on a water-bed. That would be evidence enough.

He stopped right in front of her and winked. 'I wouldn't miss this shopping trip for the world.'

'Oh, I'll bet.' She leaned her head a little closer. 'Though if you insist on going, you should know: *I'll* be picking the clothes. You can carry bags. That's what guys are for on shopping trips.'

Shane grinned when she smirked at him. 'I think you'll find we're for way more than that.' He laughed as she narrowed her eyes. 'Think of it as an opportunity to get a male perspective on what you wear.'

'Yeah, right.'

'Where's your sense of adventure? You've been hiding under business suits and rugby shirts for as long as I've known you.'

Hiding was right. She wasn't exactly a perfect size ten, after all, and she certainly didn't want to encourage him to look at anything other than her bare legs. But the last thing she needed was Shane helping her pick out a new wardrobe. Not if he was going to spend the whole afternoon flirting with her as he did it. 'I wear clothes that are appropriate for the things

I do and, seeing as how most of the time I'm either working or hanging around with you losers, then what I normally wear is just fine.'

Shane leaned in so that his nose almost touched hers, his warm breath fanning out across her face. '*Chicken.*'

She had to resist the urge to step away from him. But she was damned if she'd let him see she was affected by how close his face was to hers. How all it would take would be a small tilt and a tiny lean forward and she could kiss the sensual curve of his mouth to shut him up. *If she'd been someone else.*

But she would *not* be intimidated and she would *not* be called a chicken. He had advantage enough by the very fact that she kept looking at him and thinking the way she was. 'One outfit.'

His eyes blinked slowly as he continued to smile. 'One?'

'You can help pick out one outfit that won't get me arrested and that's it. Then you'll never criticize my wardrobe again. Deal?'

The challenge in her voice and the raise of her chin brought his dimples out in force. He leaned back and reached a hand forward, waiting for her to add hers for a shake to seal the deal. With her hand enclosed in his he dropped his voice an intimate octave. 'Deal.' But when she smiled smugly and tried to tug her hand away he held on for another second to add, 'And underwear.' He laughed as she gaped in outrage. 'It's not like you have any left, after all. And if you're gonna live in my house you should have some, don't you think?'

When she continued to gape he shrugged. 'Consider it an early Christmas present. Otherwise you'll end up wandering around with me looking at more than just your legs.'

CHAPTER THREE

WELL, if it was Shane's way of continuing to distract her, it was certainly working. House fire? *What* house fire, *where*?

Though Finn wasn't overly keen on her reaction to the female sales assistants that radiated to him in the middle of the exclusive underwear store he found in Dublin city centre. In fact, any shop they visited that had female assistants under the age of eighty seemed to end up with the same result. As if it weren't *Finn* that was shopping.

Talk about bees round honey! The minute the bell over the door jingled they all looked his way. And Finn might as well have been invisible.

She scowled across at him. It was the most ridiculous shopping trip she'd ever been on in her entire life. Trust a man to ruin *shopping*!

'Can I help you?'

Oh, Finn would just bet she'd love to *help* him!

No doubt hanging naked from a chandelier if he asked her to.

Stepping between them she smiled a sugary-sweet smile. 'We're just browsing.'

'No, we're not.' Shane placed an arm around her waist and squeezed in warning. 'We're shopping.'

'No, *we're* not.' She smiled through gritted teeth. '*I* am. He's just here to carry bags.'

'Not in here I'm not, babe.'

The 'babe' thing was really starting to grate on her nerves. Especially when he accompanied the word meant for her with a winning smile aimed at the assistants. She had managed to grit her teeth through three stores so far but the underwear thing was where she was determined to draw the line. No matter what he thought.

Extricating herself from his hold, she aimed a sickly sweet smile in his direction. 'Yes, you are. You can stand here and talk to these nice ladies while I pick up the basic essentials and then we're outta here.'

'She gets all embarrassed when I pick underwear for her.'

'Surely not,' one svelte blonde purred across at him. 'Women love it when good-looking men like yourself pick out something special for them.'

Something that would no doubt be stupidly uncomfortable and designed to be worn in a bedroom for thirty seconds, and not all day underneath one of the new business suits she'd just bought.

How exactly had she been conned into this again?

'You'd have thought so, wouldn't you?' Shane continued to smile at the assistants. 'But Finn is a little shy when it comes to this kind of thing.'

Because Finn had never actually thought about wearing '*this* kind of thing'. Her eyes widened as he pointed at a dummy displaying a teeny garment that seemed to be made of lace and dental floss.

'This one is nice.' He stepped closer and ran his finger under a strap, his eyes moving over the head of the assistant to clash with Finn's. 'Don't you think, babe?'

The tone was seduction itself and Finn felt her body respond with an immediate surge of heat while her eyes focused on the finger playing with the strap. For a brief moment her imagination painted a picture of the finger caught between the strap and her skin. Then the finger would gently slip the strap from her shoulder, the material would whisper down over her breasts.

He smiled a knowing smile as she blew out a puff of air. So she answered with a scowl.

He was a dead man. That was what she thought.

'I prefer this.' She nonchalantly dangled something more practical above her head.

'Now, remember we talked about your sense of adventure?'

'Yes, and remember we also promised that we would buy you something to wear the same as I get only in red?'

She leaned closer to the only assistant still beside her and hissed, 'I swear he has more heels at home than I do.'

The blonde assistant took a visible step back from him while Shane's eyes narrowed. 'We'll take this one.'

'In what size?' the blonde asked with a cool voice and Finn had to swallow a bubble of laughter.

The laughter then froze when he rhymed off her size after a flicker of his eyes down over her body. How could he *do* that?

He then raised a single eyebrow in challenge and began to walk amongst the displays, lifting items and running his fingers over their textures. 'And this, and one of these and two pairs of these and—'

'Whoa one minute, buster. We agreed one outfit.'

'C'mon, it's nearly Christmas and, anyway, you can't walk around half naked all the time.'

She had not been half naked! Not entirely. Pretty much naked, yes, but Eddie's T-shirt had covered everything that mattered, hadn't it? Except the legs Shane had been so interested in. The fact that he might have known she was all but naked kicked her imagination into gear again. Just what had he thought of that idea? What would he have done if he'd known for sure and taken it as an invitation? Just exactly how many moves had he picked up over the years? How long could he have kept them occupied?

She had a few moves of her own, after all…

All right-y, this *had* to stop. And she really had to get back to the house so she could ring all her friends and beg for a place to stay. A sofa would do.

Lifting a handful of less X-rated bras and knickers, she added them to the pile he'd been making and then pushed him back from the counter. '*Enough* already.'

His arm snaked around her waist and held her tightly in place at his side as he swung his credit card at the blonde with a cavalier sweep. 'On me.'

'No, I've got it.' She fumbled in her bag, which rubbed her rear a tad too deliciously against his hard frame. 'You're not buying all this underwear for me, Shane.'

'Yes, I am. It's worth every penny to see you so *hot* and bothered.'

The words were whispered close to her ear and the already rising warmth in her body hit boiling point. But when she tried to pull away from him he merely held on tighter. Strong as she was, she couldn't get away without making a massive scene. So she smiled through gritted teeth and turned to whisper back, 'I *owe* you.'

Shane's eyes danced. 'Just model some of this lot some time and we'll be even.'

'That's not what I meant I owed you for.'

The minute they left the store she swung the bag at him, hitting the centre of his chest.

He laughed and made a mock grunt of pain.

'Careful, now; you'll bruise me with all that heavy underwear.'

'You deserve a good bruising for that performance in there. You can just quit it now; you've done your job,' She raised her chin and walked with a determined stride along the wide pavement. 'I've been well and truly distracted from my arson problems all afternoon. So you can knock it on the head now.'

Shane had no problem keeping up with her fast pace, but the minute she finished speaking he caught her arm and tugged her round to face him. 'You think that's what I'm doing? *Distracting* you?'

The sudden change in direction had swung her hair into her face and the auburn ends caught in her mouth. With her free hand she plucked the ends free, frowning into his smiling face. 'You didn't think I'd figure it out? I may be many things, Shane Dwyer, but dumb isn't one of them.'

'I wouldn't have said so until now.' He cocked his head to one side, his bright blue eyes focused on her mouth as she cleared the last strands of hair. 'I'm not trying to distract you, Finn. If all this is taking your mind off other things, then that's great. But I hadn't thought about it that deeply. Sure as hell not since we started looking at underwear, anyway.'

Finn frowned in confusion. He wasn't trying to distract her? Then why was he flirting with her? Her eyes widened. He wouldn't dare…

The dimples flashed at her before he released her

arm and sauntered ahead of her down the street. Whistling.

Whistling, for crying out loud!

After a full afternoon in Shane's company, one-entirely-too-closely-on-one, she was more than grateful to get a call from her best friend, Mel. After a half-hour's conversation on her mobile about the fire, Mel decided that sweet tea sucked and what she needed was to drown her sorrows in a more traditional Irish manner.

And at least at O'Malley's she was out of the house and away from Shane.

'So, what does Mr Sex-on-a-stick look like first thing in the morning?'

Too damn good, as it happened. 'Can we talk about something else?'

'Wow, that good, huh?' Mel waggled her eyebrows as she raised her glass. 'Figures.'

'I keep telling you, if you think he's so hot then you should just go for it.'

Her friend knew her too well. 'Yes, and I can tell from that tone that you'd be chuffed to bits by that.'

Finn sighed. 'He can date whoever he wants, it's nothing to do with me.'

'Mmm.'

'Don't do that.'

'What?' She blinked innocently.

Finn smiled at her amateur dramatics, 'You know what. I've told you before, I'm not interested.'

'Uh-huh.' Mel's fingers swirled the plastic stirrer around in her glass, tinkling ice cubes against the edges. 'But that'd be a teeny bit of a fib, wouldn't it? Sometimes you look at him like a choc-a-holic looks at a plate full of Death By Chocolate.'

'Looking is one thing.'

Mel nodded wisely. 'So you have no problem when chesty women throw themselves at him?'

Finn laughed. 'Oh, honey, you're not chesty. We've talked about this loads and we've always said there was no danger of you getting black eyes if you took up jogging.'

'I wasn't talking about *me...*'

With a sinking feeling in the pit of her stomach, Finn turned on her tall stool and looked at the bar. Sure enough, Shane and Eddie were there and Shane had already attracted a chesty woman. His dimples still present from something she had said to him, his eyes rose and met hers.

Her breath caught as his eyes twinkled across at her. He really bloody did have the charm of the devil, didn't he?

With a scowl she turned back round to face her grinning friend. 'Don't say a word. Not one, y'hear?'

Mel held both hands up in front of her body. 'Silent as the grave over here.'

Finn downed a large mouthful of the concoction Mel had got her from the bar, her eyes watering slightly as she swallowed.

When she looked back at Mel she saw her eyes move upwards. Immediately she sat taller on her chair, her spine stiff as she waited for the air behind her to tingle as it had all afternoon.

A beer bottle appeared on the table in front of her. 'Drowning your sorrows?'

Exhaling the breath she was holding, she looked up at her brother. 'Don't you think I'd have good reason to?'

'Well, of all the lame excuses you two have used on a night out before I guess this would be one of the better ones.' He winked across at Mel. 'Hey, gorgeous.'

'Hey, Eddie. Kathy let you out on your own? She must reckon she has you well pinned down.'

'I'm not on my own; I'm with Shane.'

'And if ever there was a mate who could find you a woman to get you in trouble, it would be *him.*'

Eddie laughed. 'He's always been a babe magnet. Beats me how he does it.'

Finn could write him a list if he asked. She sat silently fuming for no apparent reason. 'Well, there better not be a string of them at the house while *I'm* there.'

'String of what?' Shane plunked himself onto the stool next to her. 'Hi, Mel.'

Mel practically batted her eyelashes at him. 'Hi, Shane.'

Eddie laughed as he lifted his beer bottle and Shane turned his body towards Finn, leaning his elbows on the table, which rocked it and had both women rescuing their glasses. 'String of what at the house while you're there?'

Finn searched her mind frantically for a suitable reply. But her brother beat her to it. 'She's afraid you're gonna bring a string of babes back to the house while she's there. Doesn't want you showing her how sad her own love life is.'

Shane's eyes had strayed to Eddie as he spoke but then his gaze slid slowly to her face. Lifting his elbows, he reclaimed his bottle and examined her above the rim for a long moment. 'Is your love life sad, Finn?'

'None of your business.' She smiled sweetly as she sipped her drink again. Forcing herself not to pull a face as the liquid seared her throat.

'Didn't you have a date before you had a late Halloween bonfire?'

Glaring at her brother, she sniped back, 'Thanks *so* much for bringing that up.'

'Oh, yeah, what's-his-name, the librarian. How'd that go?' Mel rattled her ice cubes again as her eyes sparkled.

'He's not a librarian; he's a clerical officer.'

'Same thing, isn't it?' Shane queried with a wink at Eddie.

Finn smirked. 'Not everyone suits the cape-and-tights look.'

Eddie laughed. 'At least if we got a ladder in our tights it could be put to some use.'

After simultaneous groans Mel quipped, 'Stuns me why you bother with all those librarians when you have a dating agency for a brother.'

'Finn doesn't date firefighters.'

'Too hot for you, Finn?'

Finn avoided looking into Shane's blue eyes again as he asked the question in a voice steeped in innuendo. She was suddenly more aware of the nuances in his voice than she had been before. She could chalk that one down to his flirting with her all afternoon, she guessed.

All right, so his use of the word 'hot' twice in one day had helped. He had a way of saying that word that went straight to the part of her body that then squirmed on her stool.

Lifting her glass to hide behind its rim, she glanced at Mel and her brother to see if they'd caught it too. Flirting with her when they were alone was one thing. A bad enough thing. But flirting openly in front of friends and family and getting her *squirmy* in public was worse.

'They'd have to get past me first,' Eddie said in a grim voice. 'I have to look out for my baby sister.'

Finn snorted into her glass. 'I feel *much* safer now.'

'You could always have your librarian fend them off with a good hard-backed book.'

The various defensive weapons available to a librarian were discussed for a while as the bar began to fill up. Someone somewhere put dance music on the jukebox so their voices all rose accordingly and they had to lean their heads closer to hear. And all the while Finn was totally aware of where Shane was, of how his throat would convulse as he swallowed a mouthful of beer, of how his long fingers curled around the bottle.

At one point she even chanced a look at him while his head was turned towards Mel. She looked at the way he sat so easily on the tall stool, one foot resting on the floor, legs wide, his broad frame tall and lean. Any bit of wonder women in bars gravitated toward him!

Her eyes were on the broad column of his neck at the V of his polo shirt when she realized he had turned his face back towards her. She glanced upwards into eyes that looked black in the dim light of the bar. And he looked back at her with several lazy blinks of thick dark lashes.

Her throat went dry. With a small wave of panic her eyes flew to Mel, who smiled at her with a knowing look.

'Anyone want another drink?' Eddie's voice rose at her side. 'Mel, you'll take one. Shane, need I ask?'

'I'm grand.' Finn couldn't face another drink. She needed her wits about her.

'I'll come with you, Eddie.'

Finn glared at her soon to be 'ex' friend as she smiled on her way past.

'So...'

She took a deep breath as Shane's deep voice

rumbled close to her ear. Leaning back a little on her chair, she turned her face towards him, blinking calmly. 'So?'

'Maybe we should have a chat about bringing people back to the house while you're staying there.'

'I'll not be staying all that long.'

'Still, if you're *bothered* about it, maybe we should discuss it. Set the boundaries.'

Jealousy swept through her chest like a hot knife through butter. It was one thing witnessing him surrounded by women on a night out, but she'd never had to think of him sleeping with someone under the same roof as her. It was none of her business. And it was *his* house. She had no right to dictate to a grown man what he could and couldn't do, did she? And it really shouldn't matter. But—

Lying in the dark listening to them? Oh, 'cos there'd *be* noise, she'd bet—

'Do what you want. It's nothing to do with me.'

She knew his eyes were still on her as she turned her face away and squirmed again.

'I have no intention of bringing anyone home.'

Oh, no. Now, y'see, *that* was worse. With a groan she looked back at him, determined to tell him it really didn't matter a damn to her only to have him add, 'And if you even think of it I'll probably break his neck and chuck him out on the street.'

Her mouth dropped open.

Shane shrugged, a small smile twitching the corners of his mouth as he lifted his bottle again. 'Just so you know.'

Not that she would have. Not that she actually had any candidates or had done in a long, long while. The very fact that he thought he could just say something like that and get away with it…

'Like I said, I won't be there all that long.'

He seemed to think for a while as he swallowed and set his bottle back down, folding his arms across his chest in a way that highlighted the muscles in his upper arms. 'Don't know that it would make a difference even if you moved out. Not now that we've bought underwear together.'

'Why, you—' She found herself lost for words, again. Then did the only thing she could think of and reached an arm out to shove him.

The stool wobbled; he had to set his other foot on the floor to balance himself. And as he did he swiftly unfolded his arms and caught her hand in his.

She laughed at the momentary panic that had crossed his face. 'You deserved that.'

Turning her hand in his, he tangled his long fingers with hers and held on, leaning closer with dangerously glittering eyes. 'You know one of the first things a boy learns in the playground is that when a girl hits him it means she likes him?'

Finn shook her head, a smile still on her lips while he guided their joined hands below the table. 'Jeez, and you actually get laid with these chat-up lines?'

It was Shane's turn to laugh. 'It's worked before.'

'You really need to date women with an IQ above fifty, you know.'

His eyes flickered to one side, then back to hers. Then he nodded. 'Oh, don't worry, babe, I'm thinking about it. I've been thinking about it *plenty*.'

He released her hand a second before Eddie placed drinks on the table. 'What did I miss?'

CHAPTER FOUR

THE damn dream came again just before dawn.

Clearer and more real than it had been the night before. This time Finn could feel the thick smoke burning the back of her throat and making her eyes sting.

She felt the heat against her face, heard the crashing close by as bits of ceiling fell down. But it was too dark for her to see the figure clearly.

She pushed a door open and flames jumped out at her and then she could see the shadow of him as he pushed through the room, an oxygen mask covering his face.

'Get out of there. You have to get out.' She could barely call the words out, her throat burned so badly.

'It's too hot!' She held her arm above her face as another flame rushed at her. Opening her eyes again, she could just see the roof cave above his head. 'No!'

And then she was awake. Sat bolt upright in her

bed with her new nightdress soaked in perspiration and clinging to her body.

She sat in the dark room, holding her breath in case Shane appeared beside her again. Then she exhaled. This was getting ridiculous. Maybe if she'd had clearer thoughts when she'd gone to bed in the first place. Maybe if she'd not been so worried about when she could find herself somewhere new to live. Maybe…

Ah, heck, who was she kidding? Maybe if she hadn't already been *hotter than hell* going to bed she wouldn't have had the dream about heat of a different kind.

Whatever the fixation she had with Shane was, it had to go. There was no way she could allow herself to get involved with him. There were a million different reasons why she shouldn't.

To pass the time until light came through the window she silently listed them all. Brother's best friend, well-known outrageous flirt, the kind of guy who to her knowledge never stayed with anyone longer than five minutes. Firefighter.

The last one was the clincher really. Eddie was right. She didn't date firefighters. Had bloody good reason not to. Her childhood dream was reminding her all too clearly of that.

Nope. There was just no way. She'd have to weather whatever fad it was he was going through while she was under his roof. And then it would fade away and he could find another of his usual vacuous females to buy underwear for. He wouldn't be alone for long.

And she'd just go right on out and find someone who could get her just as hot. That shouldn't be a problem; she lived in the city, for cryin' out loud!

She had her own way in the morning and went to work. Though she did take the coward's route and leave before Shane got up to leave for the station.

Well, a girl had to do what a girl had to do.

At least work took her mind off things for a while. It was the busiest time of the year for a music distribution company, after all, thousands of discs making their way in and out of the door every day. And Lord knew she needed distraction from Shane now, as much as she did from her homeless state and the night-time meanderings of her overactive imagination.

The only thing that ruined her day was that no one seemed to have a sofa they could spare for a few weeks. That was what she got for being one of the last single ones in her group of friends. She was a year away from thirty and they were dropping like dominoes.

If Eddie had just lived alone instead of sharing with Shane there wouldn't have been a problem. Stupid brothers!

She would just have to avoid Shane. Heaven knew she'd managed it for this long. Well, avoided as in not given in to falling at his size elevens like every other single woman with a pulse, that was. He truly was almost as well known for his lack of commitment as he was for his looks, which helped.

Finn might not have been making an active search for a long-term partner, but she did believe in something more lasting than a few weeks' fun indoors, or outdoors, or hanging naked from a chandelier. And even if that kind of fun was *mighty* tempting, there was still the matter of his being her brother's best friend and a firefighter. She recited her morning list over and over to keep reminding herself. Brother's best friend, flirt, firefighter. Brother's best friend, flirt, firefighter…

She could get past basic carnal lust. She *could*.

But the minute she dragged her exhausted behind in through the door that evening and bravely sneaked upstairs, Shane was right in front of her, in the hallway, where she couldn't avoid him.

Coming out of the bathroom after his shower, wearing what looked like a hand towel…

She gasped and then forgot to breathe.

His head turned and he blinked slowly at her for a few seconds, studying her as if she were transparent. Then he grinned. 'Tough day at the office, babe?'

She swallowed hard and willed herself to focus on his blue eyes and not on the killer six-pack and the dark hair peeking along the towel edge. She could do it; she could hold a normal conversation with a pretty-much-naked Shane. She *could*.

'Erm…' She licked her lips. 'Great. Thanks.' She tilted her head and looked past his right ear. '*Busy*.'

Shane's grin grew and he stepped closer, leaning an

arm out so he could rest his palm on the wall. 'Third of a year's business in one month and all that...'

'Uh-huh.' Oh, wow, did he smell good up close. He smelt of soap and shampoo and *testosterone*. Her mouth watered. But the fact he was so tempting and the fact that she couldn't string a sentence together started to get to her, so she turned her frustration at herself onto him. 'If you're into some weird natural-ist thing you can bin it while I'm here.'

'There's nothing unnatural about doin' the things that come natural.'

She rolled her eyes at his words. 'It's stunning to me that you've stayed single.'

Shane's eyes seemed to glow at her. 'Maybe there's a reason for that. Maybe I need the right gal to pin me down. You have a think about it sure, and let me know if you can think of anyone who might keep me occupied long enough.' He pushed off the wall and turned around, turning his head to add, 'Bathroom's free.'

Her damn traitorous eyes watched as he walked down the hallway. She watched the muscles in his back move, watched his taut thighs as he walked away. Even hoped, for a small second, that the hand bunching the corners of the tiny towel together might slip.

There was a hint of laughter in his voice as he rounded the corner. 'I think there's another one of these towels left.'

Oh, yeah. Because having just watched Mr. Eye

Candy wandering around she was likely to squeeze her figure under anything less than a flipping beach towel! And with her hair in a turban and no make up on she'd just look great, wouldn't she? He'd really want to continue flirting with her then.

The smile started as a twitch at the corner of her mouth. Then it grew and grew until a bubble of laughter escaped. She clamped a hand over her mouth to stifle it.

If she was going to spend time in Shane's company, then he would have to learn that he couldn't wander around throwing his big sexy self in front of her every minute.

She would show him that she was just one of the guys. And yet gross him out with girly stuff at the same time.

The sooner he went back to treating her the way he always had, the sooner she could start doing the same thing with him. Because there wasn't really any point their being any other way.

Shane had spent a good portion of a nine-hour day shift thinking about Finn.

It really couldn't be helped. It was the underwear's fault. He might have been curious about her before, but now he was moving rapidly into the region of 'need to know'.

Especially after the fun he'd had flirting with her in the bar the night before.

He needed to know what she would look like in the underwear they had bought. He needed to know whether the slow looks he kept catching her giving him meant what he thought they meant. He needed to know why it was he needed to know with *her.* Why couldn't he have been so damn interested in someone less complicated?

And he really wanted to know what would happen if he went ahead and *made* things complicated.

He needed to know.

So he'd come up with a plan. In the last few hours of his shift he had formulated a detailed plan to take advantage of the twist of fate that had thrown her under his roof. Into the land where curiosity lived.

And, of course, he could keep her mind off her house at the same time. Which was a considerate and thoughtful thing to do, he reckoned. Even if he still laughed out loud daily at what she'd done.

Planning was comfortable territory. It was a guy thing. Shane had always felt comfortable with a good, well-thought-out plan. Part of his training as a firefighter, he'd guessed. In the service a guy knew how things worked, where everyone should be and how each person's actions could affect the overall picture. Guys stuck to the plan, to a method of doing things to get results.

And, after all, if nothing else it would be a chance to get to know her better, one on one. Something that he really hadn't had much of a chance to do, seeing as he only ever saw her when they had others around. One on one would be good for a change.

Though where his night-time thoughts of one on one had taken him recently had kind of veered off the path of no involvement with his mate's sister. It had broken rules. Which kinda made it even sexier.

He could hear her moving around the house when he went to his room. But by the time he was dressed he could hear running water in the bathroom. Which gave him time. Women didn't see baths as a way of getting clean. It was some kind of religious event to them.

So, with Eddie out for the evening with his girl-friend, he had time for step one of his plan: get her to relax and talk some. See if there were any more long looks to be had so he knew it wasn't just his furtive imagination. Though her reaction to him up close and almost naked in the hall had been encouraging.

While he'd walked away he'd even been tempted to throw his towel over one shoulder…

He started throwing together a supper and making the large open room 'comfortable'. He then lit a couple of candles that Eddie's girl had left behind. Women liked that kind of stuff.

In the half hour she took to reappear he had every-thing just about right: soft lighting, soft background music. He had even gone to the bother of setting places at the table in the kitchen rather than the usual balancing of plates on knees in front of the TV set that Eddie and he favoured when alone.

Pouring wine into two glasses as he heard her coming down the hallway, he turned with one in his hand and a smile on his face.

A smile that faded when he looked at her. 'What the—?'

'No wine for me thanks. A beer will be fine.' She walked past him and dug in the fridge for a bottle of her brother's favorite brand of beer, not bothering to look for a glass as she opened it. 'Bottoms up.'

Shane stared at her as she saluted him with the bottle, then set it to her lips and drank a long gulp of the amber liquid. She raised an eyebrow at him. 'What?'

'What in hell is that stuff on your face?'

'Mashed-up avocado and honey, why?'

His eyes moved up for a second to the giant mussed-up ball of hair on her head, down over her green face to an oversized T-shirt with a lewd suggestion on the front that he recognized as Eddie's. Even the legs he liked so much were shrouded in beat-up sweat pants that Eddie would have worn to paint walls in and probably had, judging from the stains on them.

He blinked. 'No reason. I made us something to eat. But it can wait if you want to take that stuff off.'

Her shoulders shrugged beneath the voluminous shirt. 'It's good for the skin. I'm gonna go sit on the sofa and do my toes, so just yell when the food's ready, sure.'

Shane refused to shudder at the thought of what

she might be doing with her toes. Instead he swallowed the contents of one redundant wineglass before turning around to find trays from the cupboard. His great plan wasn't going so good.

When he appeared with a tray she was hunched over her feet, giant wads of cotton wool separating her toes as she applied polish to each nail.

She glanced up at him, her eyes sparkling in the lamplight. 'You should have yelled.'

'You can walk with your feet like that?'

She smiled. 'Just about.'

As he set the tray on the coffee-table beside her his attention was momentarily caught by the TV screen. '*What* are you watching?'

'It's a makeover show where they show you all the surgery.'

He grimaced. 'Do we have to watch that while we eat?'

'You got a weak stomach?'

'I didn't used to, but that could do it.'

As he turned around he just caught the spark in her eyes before she turned her attention back to her feet. He knew that spark.

It was *mischief.*

She was up to something, wasn't she? And with a light-bulb moment he suddenly knew what it might be. It was a nice try. He'd give her that much.

She continued the charade. 'I think it's fascinating.'

'Do you now?'

She nodded. 'I'd have that done in a flash if I had the money.'

'You don't need it.'

'Sure I do; everyone has something they don't like about themselves.' She continued to focus on her toes.

'Like what?' Shane crossed his arms across his broad chest and raised a dark eyebrow at her, 'Show me and I'll let you know what I think.'

Yeah, right! Like she'd show him! That wasn't the point of this game at all. 'The whole thing about having parts of yourself you don't like is that you don't want them on display in the first place.'

'Okay, then.' He kept his expression deadpan even when he heard the edge to her voice. He was heading in a direction she'd been looking to avoid, unless he was very much mistaken. Directly into the kingdom of intimate information.

If that was the case, then she damn well deserved whatever she got. Because she should have known better. It was *him* she was dealing with here. And she was messing up a plan he'd taken hours formulating, which meant there would be *consequences*.

'What would you change?'

Carefully taking her time to screw the lid firmly in place on the polish bottle, she then tilted her head to look up at him. 'Apart from losing about twenty pounds, you mean?'

'You're fine the way you are.'

'Yeah, right.'

'Not everyone likes the anorexic look.'

'Sure they don't, that's why every guy on the planet turns round to look at them as they walk past.'

He moved a little closer, unfolding his arms. 'Doesn't do it for me.'

She almost asked him what did, but wasn't sure she wanted to hear the answer. 'Well, you must get real hot at the thought of cellulite, then.'

'Haven't had much experience with it, I must say—' he smiled a slow, lazy smile '—but I'm always open to new experiences. So why don't you show me?'

Her eyes widened. This wasn't working the way she'd thought it would. In fact it was pretty much having the opposite effect. With a swift rethink she swung her legs off the sofa and pushed up onto her feet. 'I'm going to take this stuff off my face.'

'What about your food?' He stepped into her path.

'I just told you that losing weight isn't a bad idea. So skipping a meal or two might be a good place to start.'

'You don't need to lose weight.' His eyes made a slow study of her green face, then moved equally slowly down over her body. 'You curve in all the places a woman should curve. In *and* out.'

His eyes eventually locked with hers and gut instinct told her she'd been caught. Her voice dropped a husky octave as she warned him, 'Don't.'

'Don't what?'

'You know what.'

'Oh.' His eyes sparkled down at her, his mouth quirking. 'You mean this.'

Her traitorous feet froze to the ground as he encircled her waist with his arms and pulled her body hard against the length of his. She gulped, her voice barely a whisper. 'Please, Shane, be reasonable—'

'Well, since you asked so nicely…' He lowered his head, and, regardless of the sticky avocado that smeared onto his face, pressed his warm mouth to hers.

Her knees gave for a brief second. Oh, *c'mon*, this just wasn't fair! No one had ever made her knees wobble before. She had rugby players' knees, for crying out loud! Nice sturdy knees that had held her upright perfectly well for twenty-nine years.

He moved his mouth back and forth, adjusting to the shape of her, discovering where they fitted best. Then, confidently, he deepened the kiss, running the tip of his tongue over avocado at the edge of her mouth before pushing against her lips and forcing her to taste the sweet concoction with him. *Payback time.*

An anguished moan escaped from deep in her throat. Avocado had never tasted so good. Who knew it was an aphrodisiac?

Large, competent hands moved against the material of her huge shirt, smoothing it in against the small of her back, moving around to shape the inward curve of her waist.

Her blood boiled, her abdomen twisting up almost painfully as spirals of desire had her squirming against him. Heat thrummed through her veins,

gathered at the apex of her thighs. Her body screaming: oh, yeah, *bring it on.*

She had to stop this, had to try and fight him off
or, at the very least, struggle a little. She certainly
needed to stop her traitorous mouth from joining in.
Any second soon would be good.

Large hands moved again, slid down the outside of
her thighs, around them, and then back up to curve her
buttocks. Then his long fingers moved in a kneading
motion before he drew her hard against his pelvis.

Her eyes shot open when she felt his hardening
length push against the soft curve of her stomach.
And she continued to stare, his face slowly coming
into focus as he lifted his mouth from hers and gazed
down at her with smoldering eyes.

He smiled slowly, stepped back, releasing her
completely as one hand wiped avocado off his face.
As he then carefully sucked each finger clean he
looked her directly in the eye, his voice husky.

'You don't need to lose any weight, Finn. You fit
me just fine.'

Well, hell. As he turned and walked calmly away she
couldn't bring herself to say anything. She couldn't
think beyond the fact that, having just had the hard
length of him pressed so intimately against her, she
wasn't convinced she could say the same thing to him.

Apparently the rumor about the size of men's feet
wasn't entirely wrong.

CHAPTER FIVE

FINN spent most of the rest of the night tossing back and forth between cool sheets in a warm room. When she did catch any sleep it wasn't the deep, restful kind that would prepare her for another hectic day at work. Oh, no. It was that half-asleep, half-awake kind of time-wasting that allowed her troubled mind to make weird dreams out of her confused reality.

At least her dreams weren't about a man in a fire.

How dared Shane go and kiss her? Making things even more complicated than they were before!

How dared he make it a kiss that curled her toes and woke every nerve that had been asleep in her body.

Why couldn't he have had bad breath or been allergic to avocados? And why had he felt the need to make a pass at her when she'd done everything in her feminine handbook to appear unattractive?

But most of all damn the enormous lump of a man for making her furtive nocturnal imagination play with the idea of having worn avocado and honey *all over,* with having him smear it on slowly, and lick it off even slower. Did whipped cream go with avocado and honey?

By the time light was shining through the curtains she was completely infuriated and mad at him. And by the time she came down for breakfast with her ultra-soft facial skin she was ready with a much-rehearsed put-down for *Mr* Shane Dwyer.

He didn't even have the courtesy to look up from his newspaper when she walked in.

'You're never doing that again; you hear me, you moron?'

'Doing what?'

'Oh, you know what.'

'If that's your attempt at predicting the future then you're way out.' He glanced up for a brief second. 'Whereas your horoscope for today says "red hot passion is headed your way".'

He smirked as he bit into his toast and continued with his mouth full. 'I'd say that was closer to the mark myself.'

'You…you…' she spluttered at him, angry heat rising on her cheeks '…you really are the most arrogant—'

'Now, Finn, *language.* Eddie said you weren't much of a morning person.'

She spoke aloud a word her mother probably didn't even know she knew. Would slap her silly for saying, even at *her* age. Irish mothers were famous that way.

He coughed as his toast went down the wrong way, then laughed. 'Man, did you ever get out of bed the wrong side this mornin'. Have some coffee, babe. Chill.'

'You just think this is hilarious, don't you?'

He continued smiling as he looked up at her stunned expression. Oh, she was angry all right. Angry, and, little did she know it, sexy as anything with it. Flushed cheeks, sparkling eyes, the rapid rise and fall of her breasts beneath her strait-laced jacket.

She'd be worth riling up every now and again.

For a brief second he wondered what she was wearing underneath her jacket. Was it something he'd picked, something lacy and brief and made to be removed?

His body was harder than a brick wall after one avocado-flavoured kiss. So hard that there'd barely be time to take that underwear off.

What was with that, then? What had happened to those rules down at the station? The rules he knew better than to break… In theory.

The very least he could have done, after years of playing the field, was choose to get all fired up with someone who wasn't going to fight him off tooth and nail or earn him a few black eyes along the way from his best mate.

Thing was, the chase was as erotic as hell.

'I think if you get this annoyed after one wee kiss then you're going to be fun to live with when we—'

'We *won't*! So you can just get that into your thick skull right this minute.'

'I think we will—' he nodded '—and I think you know we will too.'

'No, *we won't.*' She planted her hands on her hips and glared at him from the space between the kitchen and living room. 'Trust me.'

He took his time folding the newspaper before calmly setting it down on the table. Then, with his steady gaze fixed on her fiercely determined face, he stood up and took a step towards her.

When she moved back a step he merely quirked an eyebrow. 'We will, Finn. It's just a matter of when. This thing that's going on with us has been brewing a while and I think you know that as well as I do.' He took a step towards her, she took a step back. 'I wasn't the only one doing the kissing last night.'

She fired an answer back at him. 'Reflex.'

His eyebrows quirked in unison. 'What?'

Swinging a hand back and forth in front of her body, she avoided his eyes and explained, 'It was a knee-jerk thing, that's all.'

Dimples creased his cheeks as he laughed. 'Now, you see, a lesser guy would take that as an insult.'

'Well, thank goodness for your ego, then.'

'Maybe I should kiss you again to see who's right.'

'I already told you, you are *not* kissing me again!'

'All right.' He shrugged as her eyes shot to his in surprise. 'Next time you can kiss me. I like it when a woman takes the initiative. And not just at the kissing part, just so you know.'

'Shane—' She couldn't actually think what to say in reply to that while her mind painted some very dirty pictures of taking the initiative. There were several to pick from in her nocturnal imagination's personal version of *Nine and a Half Weeks*.

She glanced briefly at the fridge. 'Will you see some sense here? This really wouldn't be a good idea.'

'Is that you trying to convince me or you?'

'It's me talking sense!'

'Okay, then. Why not?'

Finn stared in astonishment as he crossed his arms across his chest. 'What do you mean, "why not"?'

'Why wouldn't it be a good idea?'

'Because.'

'Oh, well, *because*. I get it. That's that, then. Clear as mud when you put it that way.'

She swore again. 'Why is it I can't string a proper sentence together when you get like this?'

Shane shrugged again. 'Because I'm right?'

'I am not getting horizontally involved with you, Shane, so just deal with it. There are a million reasons why it wouldn't be the best plan in the world, and you know that.'

'I know you can date as many librarians, or whatever it is the guys you've been dating recently do, as you want to avoid me. But what we have here isn't going away. There's only one solution.'

'You think I've been dating—' she scowled when she almost said 'librarians' herself '—those guys to avoid *you*?'

'Haven't you?'

Her green eyes widened at the question. Had she? Was that what she'd been doing, avoiding Shane by dating the 'safer' options? Or someone just like Shane, someone hot and addictive?

Finn wouldn't allow herself to think that, even silently. Because if it was true it meant she had to think long and hard about the reasons *why* she would do that. And that was way more therapy than she had money to spend on.

Her chin rose. 'You're wrong.'

'Am I?' For the briefest moment he wondered if maybe he was. She seemed to have the ability to make him doubt his own powers of perception. Even with his vast experience.

But then his eyes dropped again to the rise and fall of her breasts, the flush at the base of her neck. And he smiled a slow smile. *Nah.* She wasn't this affected by him for no reason. 'I don't think so.'

He stepped forward again, she stepped back. Her feet moved swiftly from tiled floor to wooden. Many more steps of retreat and they'd be talking next door.

'If you're so immune to me, then how come you're so freaked out that I might touch you again?'

She stopped dead and raised her chin. 'I am not.'

It was getting tiring, especially after a night

without much sleep. All that mental strain during the day planning a detailed plan of seduction and then a night spent making tents…

Shane sighed, running his hand back through his hair and searching the kitchen with his eyes for inspiration. When none appeared he looked back into green eyes filled with determination, taking in the stubborn rise of her chin along the way.

'There's no point in pretending this isn't here. It is. And we can argue about it all you like but it's not gonna change it.'

The truth of the words, so calmly spoken, made an angry retort die a death somewhere in the region of her throat. But there was one other truth that wouldn't change. 'I won't let myself fall for you.'

'You're taking this too seriously. I haven't asked you to marry me.'

The words were like a slap in the face. 'So we just roll about 'til one or the other of us gets bored? Is that how you see this going?'

'No!' His voice rose at her interpretation. 'Damn it, Finn, that's not what I meant.'

'But you see us doing something about—' she waved her hand back and forth between them '—this *thing* that's going on. You just don't see it as being anything too important? That's romantic. You're a real charmer.'

Ignoring the main part of what she was saying, he picked up on the one part that had come through clearly. 'At least you're admitting there *is* something going on.'

She flushed a fiery red. 'Answer the question, Shane.'

'Which was what?' He focused hard on forcing himself not to step forwards and shut her up the best way he knew how. She was shooting his great plan to win her over to hell in a handbag and all it did was add to his frustration.

He was a guy, for crying out loud. A guys' guy at that. He wasn't supposed to be good with words. And what did she expect from him so early on— wasn't just taking a chance to begin with a big enough step for her?

'You see me as some quick thrill, some sort of a challenge to you? Is that it?'

'No. That's not how I see you.' And it wasn't. He already cared about her. Something he didn't feel as if he had to tell her, as she should know by now! Hadn't he made it obvious?

'Then what is it you want?'

You. He knew the answer was just that simple. In his mind, anyway. And to him that was enough. Because he knew Finn McNeill. Had liked her more every time he'd met her or talked with her or played the verbal sparring game they were so good at. Then the liking had turned to curiosity and then to fascination.

It had only been a matter of time before the fascination had turned into something more. Anything more than that was a bigger step than he was ready to take. Never mind discuss.

He shook his head. 'How about we talk about this when you're in a better mood?'

'My mood is just fine, thanks.' Her eyes narrowed, 'You're the one that doesn't want to talk about this. Your solution is to just get physical and forget about the consequences.'

Shane could feel his temper rising. She was pushing harder than he'd ever let any woman push him before. And the worst part was, to a certain extent, she was right. It would be the easier option for him, had been before. To just give in to need and then walk away if he couldn't find it in himself to give anything more.

And with Finn it would all have to happen under cover of secrecy from their friends and family.

But that almost made it sordid. And she was worth more than that, wasn't she?

He tried to find a simpler solution. A starting point. 'Okay, then. Let's say I ask you out on a date. Just the two of us. Would you go?'

'No.' She stared him straight in the eye.

'Why not?'

'I don't have to give you a reason.'

He shook his head and sighed. 'No, you don't have to, you're right. But I think we've pretty much established that it wouldn't be because you don't fancy me.'

'If I do then it'll wear off.'

'You think?'

'I *know*.'

He shook his head again, 'Well, I hope you have better luck than I have. 'Cos wanting you would seem to be something I have no control over. And I have no idea what I'm supposed to do about findin' out what that means when you're being so bloody-minded.'

Finn gaped at him. It was quite a confession. And for a split second she actually considered thinking about it. Seriously considering an affair that would lead to major trouble all round. Was she insane?

Her first attempt at speaking failed on a croak that brought his gaze back to hers. So she cleared her throat and tried again.

'You want me that bad, Shane, then there's only one thing you'd have to do to change my mind about seeing what might happen.'

'And that would be?'

'Quit the service. Quit the fire brigade and, I swear, we won't leave your room for a week. Then we'll just see what happens.'

'Now you're being ridiculous.'

She ignored the scowl on his face and ploughed on, frustration forcing the words out. 'If you were anyone else we wouldn't even be having this conversation. Eddie already told you that I don't date firefighters. *Full stop*.'

Eddie had. But Shane hadn't really paid much attention. Mainly because, at the time, it hadn't occurred to him that it was that important a detail. But now was a different matter.

Now he needed to know why. 'Why?'

'Because I won't end up like my mum did. That's why.'

The simple statement was said with wide eyes and flushed cheeks. Almost as if she hadn't really meant to say it out loud.

Then she gathered herself together, smoothing the front of her jacket with calm hands before she added with a short smirk, 'So that's the deal. Take it or leave it.'

Watching her leave, Shane knew she'd got him. Because she knew he wouldn't quit what he loved doing, wouldn't quit on the family.

Not for any woman.

CHAPTER SIX

EDDIE seemed oblivious to the tension in the house when he met Shane that evening.

'Hey, Shane, where's Finn at?'

She was hiding upstairs somewhere, he assumed. He'd heard the door slam on her return and had heard bath water running, but since then she'd been as silent as the grave.

And he didn't feel much like running up there to see what she was at. She could have drowned for all he knew.

Quit the fire brigade his ass!

'Upstairs somewhere.'

Eddie threw himself down on an armchair, one long leg swinging off an arm. 'How's she doing?'

'Fine.' He focused all his attention on the football match playing on the widescreen T.V. After a moment of silence he glanced over at Eddie's face. 'She seems to be coping just fine.'

Eddie nodded. 'She's a trooper.'

Oh yeah, she was *something*.

'You two getting on all right?'

The beer bottle in his hand froze halfway to his mouth. But Shane recovered quickly and raised it the rest of the way with barely a heartbeat of pause. 'Just dandy.'

Eddie laughed. 'You have a row already?'

'Not a row.' He shrugged. 'More of a difference of opinion.'

'That's my little sister, all right. She has differences of opinion with me all the time.'

Yeah, but Shane bet she'd never told him to leave his job before. It was on the tip of his tongue to open his mouth and say as much. But he knew it wasn't worth going there.

Thing was, under different circumstances Eddie would have been the one he'd have chatted to about it. Eddie would have understood how ridiculous her demand was, he would have laughed with him over a beer about women who tried to change men and why they felt they needed to do that. Eddie would have got it.

Whereas Finn evidently didn't.

She should have, though, coming from the background she came from. Not that that had helped her with fire safety of late.

Eddie bounded on in when his words were met with silence. 'What was it about?'

'Makeover shows.' It was the first answer that

jumped into his head under pressure. 'She thinks she needs to go under the knife to fix her flaws.'

There was a burst of laughter from the chair. 'She'd better take that one up with Mum. It's her fault we all ended up the way we are. Hers and Dad's. Finn was always paranoid about her size. It's not easy being her height, and, *you know*, curvy.'

Shane tried to concentrate his gaze on the screen, though he had to blink a few times to get his mind off the word 'curvy'. Instead he focused his thoughts on something less sexual, attempting to keep his tone nonchalant. 'How *is* your mum?'

'Grand. She's been seeing some bank manager for a while. I think she likes the company.'

'She's happy, then?'

Eddie's eyes focused on Shane's profile. 'Course she is. Why the sudden concern?'

Turning his head towards his friend, he smiled. 'Can't I ask about my favourite girl?'

There was a burst of laughter. 'Yeah, twenty years younger and she says she could *be* your girl all right.'

Shane's eyes softened at the statement. Moira McNeill was a sweetheart who had 'adopted' him from the first day he'd been invited down with Eddie. He in turn flirted outrageously with her at every meeting. 'I could have been your stepdaddy.'

Eddie shuddered. 'Thanks for that image.'

'You're welcome, *sonny*.'

They fell into a companiable silence as the match

reached half-time, then Shane stretched his long legs out in front of him and savoured another long mouthful of beer.

He mulled over the best way to broach the subject that had had him curious all day long, when he hadn't been mad enough to spit nails. Eventually he decided to just go for it.

'It must have been rough for her after your dad died.'

Eddie was silent for a few moments, his voice low when he answered. 'Yeah.'

'She's a gutsy lady.'

'Yes, she is.'

It was like getting blood from a stone. And Shane knew with a certainty borne of familiarity that he was flogging a dead donkey. He knew that Eddie and Finn had lost their dad when they were quite young. He knew that the man had been a fellow firefighter, but beyond that he didn't know a lot.

From Eddie's reaction to the questions, the answers weren't going to be found with him. Which meant he had no choice but to try finding out from Finn.

Which made Shane wish he didn't want to know.

'I'm gonna move in with Kathy.'

The words brought him out of his sombre thoughts. 'What?'

Avoiding the surprised eyes that looked in his direction, Eddie swung his leg off the side of the chair and sat with his elbows on his knees. 'Yeah. I've been thinkin' about it for a while but I didn't want to leave you in the lurch. What with Callum getting his own place and all.'

When Shane had bought his house it had been a little more than he'd planned on spending in month by month expenses. But with two mates from the station sharing the bills it had been a breeze. Callum had been the first to move on, buying his own place further outside the city. Which was why there'd been room for Finn lately.

'Don't worry about that. Moving in with Kathy is serious, though. You're sure?'

Eddie's face warmed. 'Yeah. Sure as I can be. We talked it over and it just feels right, you know?'

Actually he didn't. He'd never met anyone who had made him feel he could be with her twenty-four seven. But then he'd never spent time with a woman who got under his skin like—

He frowned.

Eddie misinterpreted the frown. 'I'm really sorry, Shane. I could leave a month's rent if it helps any.'

Shane schooled his features, grinned across at Eddie. 'Shut up. You don't need to leave anything; it's fine. I'll put a note on the board at work and someone will need a room. One would do. It's no big deal.'

Eddie seemed to relax. 'End of an era, though, isn't it?'

'Yeah, that it is. But it's not like you're planning on living under the thumb, is it?'

'Hell no.'

'Then nothing's changed beyond the fact I get complete control of the remote.' He waved the object back and forth between them with a wink.

There was a burst of laughter. 'Yeah, if you can wrestle it off Finn.'

A very vivid mental image of wrestling with Finn entered his head. Oh, they'd wrestle all right, he had enough information from their differences of opinion lately to know they could spark off each other. And after the few days she'd put him through he had every intention of torturing her long and slow.

'Hey, you should speak to her about staying on here for a while. All that insurance stuff can take months and you two get along most of the time.'

Now Eddie thought they should live together? That would be a new experience. One that, while he wrestled with her some, mightn't be all that bad. But if she really was serious about him quitting the service, they wouldn't exactly be perfect house-mates. 'I don't think that would work out.'

Eddie laughed. 'She'd cramp your style right enough.'

When Shane simply cocked a dark brow at him in response, he shrugged and continued, 'Anyway. Since I'm settling down I thought me and Kathy would throw a party to celebrate.'

'Good plan.' That was what the doctor ordered. A night of drunken pranks and the chance to bump into uncomplicated single women. 'You havin' it here?'

'No, over at Kathy's. She wants to play hostess.'

So much for drunken pranks. He grimaced. 'You mean a dinner party.'

'That was *her* plan. I have different ideas.' He pushed himself off the chair with a wicked grin. 'I even have a theme like we used to do when we had parties here. So I'm gonna skip upstairs here and invite Finn along too. She used to think those parties were a hoot.'

Shane reached his beer bottle to his lips as Eddie bounded upstairs. There was just no escaping from Finn, was there?

The bottle froze in mid-air for a second time. Hang on. Eddie was moving out. That meant he was going to be alone in the house with Finn. All alone.

There was no way he was quitting the fire brigade for her. But that didn't mean he couldn't work on her some more, wrestle with her until she saw he was right and she was wrong.

A slow smile worked its way across his mouth as he leaned back on the sofa and lifted his legs to cross them on the coffee-table in front of him. Shane Dwyer had never lost a fight before.

Finn McNeill had a heap of trouble headed her way.

If he kept looking at her like that she was going to scream. In the house she'd had to do major ducking and diving to avoid him, knowing it would take something miraculous to get them back to where they'd been before she'd given him her 'ultimatum'.

It had been a completely ridiculous suggestion. One she'd known there wasn't a bat's chance of him taking up. Because after all, Shane loved what he did and it wasn't as if Finn was known for being an irresistible sex goddess.

Not that she couldn't give as good as she got with the right partner. If he had any idea the way her mind had been working of late…

But she *was* really missing the way they'd been before. The way they had been easy in each other's company, could have shared a few jokes and more than a little teasing. It had just been—simpler.

Now, every time she talked to someone or laughed along at a joke she could feel his eyes on her. The couple of times she attempted a sideways glance at him he would simply smile a slow smile and look her straight in the eye. And that simple glance was enough to run her blood faster through her veins, to have her heart stop for a beat and then quicken to compensate.

And the amount of effort she was putting into having a good time in front of him was getting exhausting.

'Finn, you're up,' Eddie's voice called from the sofa as he waved the slip of paper at her. 'Your name just came out of the tub.'

Great. Of all the adolescent ideas her brother had ever had for a party, this one was the most childish. Literally. She'd always hated his dumb themed parties.

'C'mon, Finn, don't go letting the family name

down. Unless you'd prefer some nice dry paper and a match…'

With a scowl she made her way to the edge of the game mat. 'I hate you.'

'Nah, you love me really.' He put his hand back into the tub and drew another piece of paper, then laughed. 'Oh, this should be good.'

Finn glared at him as he laughed. There were at least a dozen names in that tub. There was just no way—

'Shane, my man!'

Aw, c'mon!

He walked slowly across the room, grinning as if he had known it would happen. 'This should be fun.'

Finn's chin rose. 'You're toast.'

He lifted his index finger and beckoned her forward, his eyes sparkling. 'Come on, then. Give it your best shot.'

Fine. He wanted to play, she'd play.

Ten minutes later she really didn't want to play any more. 'Watch it with the hands.'

'Oh, I'm watching, don't you worry.' Deep blue eyes gazed into hers up close and personal and then one of them closed in a lazy wink. 'I'm watching *really* closely.'

Finn aimed one of her patented 'drop dead' looks at him while he made his move. It was obviously in need of a battery change, though, because Shane just continued to grin at her, his face inches from her own.

He was just too damn close and the proximity

was doing things to her it had no business doing. Boy, did she ever need to get out and find someone else who could do this to her. She was wound tight enough to commit murder.

In fact there was a likely candidate right in front of her. Did considering it make it premeditated?

'Finn, right foot green.'

She dragged her gaze away from his sparkling eyes and tried to twist her head around enough to find wherever green was. When she located a free circle she sighed. *Great.*

Shane's head dropped until he could see between his legs and then he laughed. The sound rumbled from low in his chest, vibrated the air in the small space between them, went straight down her neck and warmed her breasts, which went heavy and ached.

His head rose again and he looked into green eyes filled with resignation. 'Go for it, McNeill.'

'I look like a contortionist to you now?'

'I heard you'd started that yoga thing a while back and you *know* I'm ready for any of your hidden talents.' He tilted his head and added, 'But I'll bet you're thankful now that we didn't follow Eddie's suggestion of naked Twister…'

Finn blushed. Yet again. Damn it. This was so Eddie's fault. It had been *his* stroke of genius to run with the 'kids' games' themed party and it therefore followed that playing Twister was *his* fault too. They'd only just avoided any sort of nakedness because Finn had insisted that that didn't make it a 'kids' game' any more.

And now she was about to try and twist her body underneath Shane's, with an audience to boot. When she'd spent all of her efforts recently trying to avoid ending up in that exact position, *without* an audience.

Not that there wasn't enough room under there, even for her Rubenesque figure. He really did cast enough of a shadow to block out light over small European countries.

She ran her tongue along her lips as she tried to figure the best way of managing the move without quitting. Fionoula McNeill was no quitter, after all. She couldn't let him get the better of her. No way. She'd win this game if it killed her. Even if she was killed when Shane fell on her and crushed her to death.

All she had to do was focus on the game and less on his body so close to hers. Less on the familiar scent she was breathing in with each breath. And especially less on how every nerve ending in her body seemed to be boiling hot with the same awareness as standing next to open flames.

Simple really. She just needed to focus.

Shane felt a bolt of pure unadulterated heat run through him, blood running south, as the end of her pink tongue appeared. She even had the gall to curl it up slightly against her upper lip before she left it held between two rows of straight white teeth.

Her eyes narrowed in concentration, she swooshed

her long hair to one side to see better, she made several slow blinks of her long lashes.

She knew how to entice without even trying. Could make the simplest of movements an invitation. And the urge to kiss her was so strong it almost floored him.

'I have somewhere to be next week, so are you moving or what?'

Finn caught the tense edge to his voice. Her head tilted and she batted her lashes at him. 'What's wrong—you feelin' a little shaky over there?' She pouted a bottom lip at him. '*Aw*, you wanna quit, big guy?'

Shane's eyes glittered and he moved his face an inch closer, his breath fanning across her cheeks. 'Bring it on, babe. I can take it.'

Both their heads dropped as Finn made her move. She swung her right leg out in a half-circle over the edge of the slippery mat and then carefully rebalanced herself before slipping her bare foot under firstly her fingers, a careful swapping of fingers and thumb, and then under her thumb. Finally she stretched out and twisted her back so that her foot could reach the green circle underneath Shane.

With a triumphant smile she looked up into his face. 'Your move.'

She was practically underneath him, exactly where he'd wanted her of late. If there hadn't been an audience...

With his head tilted down, his eyes were within

close viewing of her well-rounded breasts. Very close. And for a long while he just allowed himself to look. If they'd been playing naked Twister he would only have had to lean forward an inch and he could have placed his mouth right around—

'Ahem!' Eddie's voice sounded from beside them. 'That's my sister's assets you're ogling, pal.'

Shane glanced up at the audience on the long sofa, a thick wave of dark hair falling across his forehead. Deciding to brazen his way out of what had the potential to be a very dangerous place, he grinned. 'Can't say I'd noticed.'

'How can you miss them?'

'Well—'

'Would you two knock it off?'

They both looked back at Finn, Eddie lifting his shoulders and asking, 'What?'

'I'd prefer it if my breasts didn't become the subject of conversation tonight.'

Shane saw the colour rise in her cheeks and wondered if it was embarrassment or the exertion of staying 'in the game'. She was one hell of an opponent.

But she should have been used to ribbing about her 'attributes'; she'd certainly been getting it for years from Eddie and his friends, Shane included.

But now was different. There was an element of sexual tension that had never been acknowledged before and Shane knew it. It gave him a real kick, as it happened.

As to wondering why it was that way with Finn and never before with anyone else? Well, he wasn't so sure it mattered any more. The fact was it was there. And it was amazing.

His eyes skimmed down to her cleavage again. He'd never liked skinny women, maybe partly due to his own size. Nah, he didn't need some female who looked as if she might break in a brisk breeze. Someone a little sturdier, well rounded in all the right places, a woman who would fill his arms and occupy a more equal space in his bed. That was more to his liking. And Finn certainly filled all those criteria.

A glimpse of lace caught his eye. Was she wearing—?

'And *you* can just knock it on the head.'

Her voice brought his focus back to her face. Her flushed face, her wide eyes, the large dark pupils. He was looking desire straight in the eye. Oh, she might think she was putting up a fight. But she was *losing*.

He stared for a long moment and then smiled a slow, lazy smile. 'I believe you said it was my move.'

The dial was spun beside them. 'Left hand red, Shane.'

The smile remained as he craned his neck to look over her shoulder. With a dip of his head that brought his cheek to hers, he whispered, 'You just stay still, now; no fancy yoga moves to distract me. Let me do *all* the work.'

Finn swallowed hard to damp her dry mouth. She

forced herself to breathe normally as he reached over her, stretching his hand towards the red circle. And then his groin brushed against her hip and her eyes widened.

He was getting *turned on* by this? Was there anything he didn't get turned on by?

Blue eyes rose again and she could see he knew. He knew she could feel him hard against her hip. He knew she knew he was turned on, knew that she knew it was because of her he was turned on. And he just went right on looking at her, almost challenging her with the slow blinking of his thick lashes.

Finn's fingers wobbled on the mat and his dimples deepened. 'Your move. *Babe.*'

CHAPTER SEVEN

FINN'S eyes narrowed at Shane's words, the sexual suggestiveness in his voice.

Her move?

Well, he'd already given her the advantage in the latest round of their game, hadn't he?

So she played her ace.

First of all she arched upwards, her shirt stretching at the deep 'V' of her neckline. She saw his eyes drop, saw a pulse beat against his temples before he looked back in her eyes. Saw from his expression that he knew she was wearing one of the concoctions of lace and dental floss he had favoured.

Then with a single blink of her eyes and a deliberately slow licking of her lips she simply raised an eyebrow and smiled. 'Indeed it is.'

She moved her hip up, then down, against his groin, just the one time. And the result was swift. She heard his sharp intake of breath and watched triumphantly as he wobbled.

Her smile grew as she watched him trying to exert some self control. She watched a bead of perspiration appear on his upper lip, the pupils in his eyes enlarging.

His voice dropped to a husky grumble, close to her face. 'You play dirty.'

'You'll never know…' Her mouth formed the whispered words with alluring deliberation.

That did it.

Those three simple words sent him over the edge and the muscles in his legs started to twitch. He wobbled, his feet began to slip on the mat. Hell, even he had his limits.

With a little swift thinking he managed to shift the bulk of his weight a split second before he landed on her, their bodies a tangle of limbs on the ground.

There was loud cheering and clapping in the background as Finn looked up into Shane's face with pure glee. '*Loser.*'

With her lush body entangled with his and his chest cushioned against her breasts he wasn't entirely sure that was true. In fact it was so close to his many night-time fantasies of late that it was almost a reward.

Though they were wearing less in his imagination.

'We really would have had more fun if we'd played it Eddie's way.'

'In your dreams.' She giggled the words at him, revelling in her victory.

Oh, yes, indeed.

Eddie called for the next names to be drawn from the Tupperware bowl, while Finn waited for Shane to be a gentleman and move so she could get up.

Yep, any second now he would move, leap to his feet and offer her a hand. That was what he would do. He had to know now he couldn't rule the roost with her, couldn't bully her into submission. And he had to know they still had an audience.

Any minute now.

He propped his elbow on the floor and rested his head on his hand. Then he studied her with an intense gaze.

Thinking about how to get up without hurting her. Obviously.

'You okay?'

Aha. Concern. The first step in ensuring she'd be fine when she stood up.

'I'm fine. Thanks.' She smiled.

A nod. 'Good.'

Finn blinked at him from the floor. He'd move now.

He blinked back.

She raised an eyebrow. It would be polite to return the favour and check he was okay she supposed. After all, it would be better to know he was capable of getting up on his own, mainly because she doubted she would be able to remove his sheer bulk alone.

'You?'

'Huh?' He smiled a small smile.

'You okay?'

'Oh, yeah. A hundred percent. Better than that, I'd say.'

She frowned when he said the words with an almost smug tone. She'd just won, for crying out loud! What did he have to be so pleased about? Her voice rose. 'Well could you move, then?'

'Yeah, move, Dwyer; we need the mat.'

She smiled smugly. 'See, they need the mat.'

'They can have it when the new players are here.'

Finn wanted badly to slap him. Instead she wriggled hard and pushed against his chest with her one free hand. 'Get off, you oaf.'

Shane stayed still, his voice dropping. 'You think you've won something here, don't you?'

'I know it comes as a big shock to you to lose at anything—' she wriggled harder, her eyes sparkling dangerously at him as she did so '—and this would be the second time in a few days for you, wouldn't it? Poor you.'

Shane nodded wisely. 'You may think I've lost—' he moved a tiny amount, so that his lower leg held her more firmly in place '—but I don't see it that way myself.'

She glared up at him, her breasts rising and falling rapidly. 'Oh, really.'

'Yes, really.'

'And how do you figure that one, then, genius?'

Lowering his head towards her, he whispered in a low grumble, 'Because firstly you wore the underwear I bought you.'

Finn felt a shiver run down her spine again, her breasts suddenly *very* confined within the lacy garment.

'And, secondly, payback for what you just did is going to be a heap of fun.'

When he moved back an inch to glance over his shoulder at their audience, Finn thought fast. She used his momentary lack of focus to kick hard and free herself. Then with a roll and a decidedly ungraceful scramble on the slippery mat she was on her feet and glaring down at him.

She raised her trembling hands to straighten first her hair and then her clothes, before letting his look of surprise lift a smile onto her face.

With a quick upward glance she put her acting skills into motion again, laughing loudly for the benefit of the masses. 'You're a jerk.'

He placed two large hands over his chest and flumped back onto the floor in mock pain. 'Ow.'

With another quick upward glance, this time directly into her brother's suspicious eyes, Finn rolled her own. 'He's such a jerk.'

'Yeah, well, we all know that.'

'I'm gonna get my stuff. I have work in the morning.' She smirked back at Shane. 'No, really, don't get up.'

'You're leaving?'

She glanced over at Eddie. 'I have work tomorrow. I'm gonna leave you boys to your games.'

Eddie glanced at Kathy beside him, leaned over to whisper something in her ear and then untangled his arm from around her shoulders before standing up. He jerked his head towards the hallway as he got closer to Finn. 'Could I have a quick word?'

Finn followed him through the crowd to the hall. 'Eddie, honestly, I have to go. We're hectic in work at the—'

'Yeah, yeah, third of a year. I know. It's just I needed to tell you something.'

'What's wrong?' She folded her arms across her breasts, her eyes narrowing in suspicion when he couldn't look her in the eye. 'What dumb stunt have you pulled this time?'

'You have so little faith in me.'

'No, I know you, that's all.'

He smiled back when she smiled affectionately at him, 'I'm gonna stay here from tonight.'

Finn's eyes widened. 'Right now this minute? I thought when you said you were moving that it would take a while.'

Eddie shrugged. 'Now that we've made the decision it seems stupid to wait. Life's too short.'

It was something they both understood only too well. Had known from earlier in life than had seemed fair at the time.

So Finn understood.

But it didn't make her feel any better about the fact that she was now stuck in Shane's house alone with Shane.

The look of uncertainty in her brother's eyes made her see sense, though. She was being selfish, thinking only of herself and that just wasn't like her. Normally.

She reached a hand out for one of his and tangled their fingers before squeezing reassuringly. 'I'm happy for you; you know that, don't you?'

Eddie squeezed her hand in reply. Then he leaned down a little and looked her in the eye. 'You okay?'

'I'm fine.' She forced a bright smile for his benefit. 'Why wouldn't I be?'

'It can't be easy, what with losing the house and all.'

She smiled when he managed to mention her house without making a joke about how it had happened. 'No, that bit's not easy. But I'm fine, really.'

'Look, I just wanted to tell you not to worry. I know you do.' He lowered his head, gazing up into her eyes. 'I'm still gonna call after every shift like I always do.'

Her heart warmed, and it showed in her eyes. 'Thanks.'

'No problem.' Then his eyes narrowed. 'Will you be okay at Shane's?'

The question, coming from Eddie, caught her off guard. Just how much had he seen in the game they'd been playing not five minutes beforehand? The last thing she wanted to happen was for the situation she had with Shane to flow over into his relationship with Eddie. They'd been friends for ever. Like brothers almost.

Even if she herself had never quite managed to see him in the same light.

She was going to have to deal with her Shane problems alone. There was no way in hell she'd be held responsible for screwing up anything else.

Bright smile back in place, she squeezed the hand she held one last time before letting it go. 'I'll be fine, really. It's only 'til after Christmas and then I'll have time to look for a place of my own again.'

Eddie leaned in and planted a kiss on her cheek. 'Well, if you ever need me to kick his butt, you just yell.'

'Oh, I will.' But she knew she never would. What was going on between them was between them, full stop.

All she had to do was decide exactly what she was going to do about dealing with Shane. A stark truth was forming in the front of her confused mind: he wasn't giving up.

He was on the sofa when she came down for a glass of water.

'Bad dream again?'

The sound of his deep voice in the dark room made her jump. 'You scared the life outta me! What are you doing down here in the dark?'

'Thinking.' He reached a hand out for the closest

lamp and sent an arc of soft light around the room. 'I heard you calling out. Another five minutes and I was coming up.'

She was glad he hadn't. It had been worse this time and she had woken sobbing, had lain in the dark until the tears had subsided. To have woken like that with Shane beside her would have been too much. She didn't want to have to explain it to him, to have to try and psychoanalyse the dream to death on his insistence.

She pointed a limp arm in the direction of the kitchen. 'I just came down for a glass of water.'

'You want to talk about it?'

The soft tone accompanied with the warmth in blue eyes that looked like black pools in the dim light made her heart melt momentarily. He really could be a pretty damned tempting guy when he put his mind to it. 'Thanks. But I'm—'

'Fine?' His mouth quirked.

Finn smiled in response. 'Yeah.'

The clock on the kitchen wall ticked loudly, the noise magnified by the silence. Finn suddenly was conscious of her breathing, of how it had become more laboured and how her heart was beating erratically.

She shook her head. It was ridiculous to suddenly feel as shy as a teenager in his presence. She wasn't exactly a virgin who wouldn't know what to do with him when they finally…

Terrific. Now she'd mentally made the leap from 'never happen' to 'when'.

'What?'

She avoided his dark eyes, glancing around the room, 'Nothing.'

He continued watching as she turned on her heel and walked towards the kitchen. Then he took a breath. 'You can't avoid me for ever. We're alone in this house now.'

'I'm not avoiding you.'

There was a short burst of deep laughter. 'Liar.'

'I'm just giving you some space.'

'I don't need any space from you.'

'You need some time to get past all this…' she paused '…stuff.'

'You think that's all it would take?' He shook his head in frustration. 'You really don't get it, do you?'

Finn stood still while she heard him move off the sofa behind her. She should have had a sarcastic retort to his question, but she didn't. She should have turned round and gone back to her room, away from him. But she didn't.

She just stood still and waited until the air moved behind her and his voice sounded close to her ear. 'This isn't some flash fire. It's been slow burning for a while.'

Her heart thudded painfully against her ribcage as a tingle of sensual awareness shuddered through her body. 'I can't get involved with you, Shane.'

'You've said. But I think it's not a case of can't.' His large hands rose and ran a whisper-like touch along the length of her bare arms, from elbows to wrists. 'It's

more like won't, even though you know you want to.
But all you're doing is delaying the inevitable.'

'You've decided to leave the service, then?'

The hands stilled, the fingers tightening round her
wrists. 'You know I won't do that. You also know me
well enough to know I won't quit that easy.'

She tried to wrench her arms free but he held on—
not so tight a hold that it was painful. But tight
enough to let her know he wasn't letting go. 'Stop it.'

With a tug he brought her body back against his.
He spread his feet a little wider so he could support
her weight, used his nose to push her hair back from
her ear. He nuzzled against the curve of her lobe, and
lowered his voice to a husky whisper when she didn't
struggle. 'You don't want me to stop.'

Finn sighed, let her head fall back against his
shoulder. She was too tired to fight him, hadn't had
a deep, dreamless night's sleep since her pants had
caught fire.

She'd just give in for a little minute and then she'd
make him see sense. That there was nothing to be
gained in a physical relationship with him and everything to lose.

The first touch of his heated mouth against her ear
sent another shiver along her spine, sent heat to her
core and waves of moisture below.

His tongue curved along the shell, traced the shape
and then made a line along the sensitive line of her
neck. It was heaven.

'You *really* don't want me to stop.'

Lord help her, she *really* didn't. She didn't pull away when he let her wrists go and splayed his hands over her hips. She didn't move when he kissed the curve between her neck and her shoulder or when he grazed his teeth in a light nip.

She did let out a low moan, though. And immediately his mouth curved into a smile against her skin.

He raised his head a half-inch as he moved splayed hands from her hips to her stomach, his fingers moving back and forth. 'That's it. You know you want this as much as I do. Quit fighting me, Finn.'

And she did know she wanted it. She was one great big walking hormone. All the signs were there: the muscles in her abdomen tensing while his hands moved up her ribcage, the heavy weight of her breasts begging for his touch, aching to be cupped by his long fingers.

There was no denying any of it.

The problem didn't lie with her body. It knew rightly what it wanted.

But thankfully her head was still in charge.

Finally finding the strength to move, she raised her hands and placed them over his, stilling the movement. Stopping the torture long enough for her to lift her head. 'I may want to. But, you're right, I won't.'

Shane froze behind her and she tensed, waiting for his anger. But it didn't come.

When he spoke, the words were still soft, still

close enough to her ear for him to speak in a husky whisper. 'Explain why.'

The words froze in her throat and the inner battle between body, heart and mind was more painful than any physical pain she had ever experienced. Even the one time when she'd broken her arm as a kid.

The deep rumble came again. 'Tell me.'

'If I slept with you—' the deep breath she forced herself to take shuddered through her frame '—I'd be tied to you. That's what most women do, you see, they make the act an emotional thing.'

'Would that be so very bad?'

'Yes, it would—' her voice shook '—because if anything ever happened to you in your work, as a friend I'd feel pain. But bonded to you as a lover I might not survive it. I can't let myself get attached to you any more than I already am.'

His hands tightened, pressed in against her stomach, 'Nothing's going to happen to me.'

'You don't know that.'

'Finn—'

'You don't know—' she used her hands on his to prise them off her body '—and I just can't take that chance.'

She knew he would probably think she was being ridiculous, that she was overreacting to something that might never happen. But he hadn't been there before.

He hadn't been there when the car had pulled up at their front door. And the men in their dress uniforms had come to tell her mother that her husband was gone.

To tell all of them that Daddy would never walk through the door again or swing his small daughter up into his strong arms, holding her tight against his broad chest as he circled and circled until she was dizzy.

Shane hadn't been there when they had been told the most important man in their lives would never come back. Because a fire had taken him away.

Finn could never put herself through that again. And she'd had childhood dreams to remind her.

With slow steps she turned and found the guts to look up at his face. She could see the confusion in his eyes, the frown of disagreement between his dark brows, the tense set of his mouth.

In a shaky voice she made the biggest confession of all. In an attempt to make him understand. 'You see, the thing is I already care about you too much, Shane. I have for a long time. I can't take a chance on maybe falling in love with you. And I don't think you'd want to take that chance either. Because you don't like that kind of involvement.'

She made it halfway up the stairs before he spoke. 'I get it better now. I don't agree with it all but I get it.'

Her steps faltered. 'Thank you.'

'Don't thank me, Finn. I didn't say I was giving up. I just understand better your reason for fighting so hard.'

'I won't change my mind.'

'And I won't go away. You can pretend that this will just fade out if you ignore it, but it won't. We're already different. You just need to remember I'm still here. *I'm still here.* And I'm not going to stop trying.'

CHAPTER EIGHT

'WHAT does that *mean* exactly?' Mel took a bite out of her sandwich and then deepened her voice. '*I'm still here…*'

'Would I ask you what you thought if I knew?'

'Sounds like a line from a movie.'

Finn was at a loss what to do next about Shane and talking to someone outside of it all had seemed like a good idea. So she had asked for a second opinion of sorts, feeling a weight was lifted that she could talk it out with *someone*.

Though her initial confession had been met with a good ten minutes of gloating…

'So?' She bit into her roll and rescued coleslaw from her chin with a napkin. 'You think I'm just being overly dramatic?'

'I think the dramatic part comes in when you think that getting down and dirty with him automatically means he's going to come to harm.' A shrug. 'Unless you're into some kinky stuff that might *do* him harm? Which might be fun, you must admit.'

Finn glared at her. 'You're supposed to be helping.'

'I am helping. You're just resisting my help.'

'You know I can't get involved with Shane and why. It just wouldn't work. Not with my luck. I'd spend the whole time waiting for something bad to happen to him and what kind of way is that to live? Even if it only lasted five minutes.'

'Oh, I bet it'd last way longer than five minutes. He's probably got enough moves to—' The warning glare stopped her. '*Okay*. But you're already involved with him, and that's the real problem here.'

Finn continued glaring. 'Still not helping.'

'Well, he's obviously not giving up without a fight and that should tell you something. Most guys who are knocked back that many times and are as successful with women as Shane Dwyer would just move on to the next in line. It's not like he would be lonely for long.'

Finn felt a flash of jealousy at the thought. Which brought a scowl to her face. She would not allow herself to be one of those women who played the 'if I can't have him no one can' game. Damn it.

She pushed her roll away, her appetite waning.

Mel leaned closer and patted her hand. 'Honey, don't beat yourself up so bad about this. I imagine he'd be pretty hard to resist. Why don't you just allow yourself a bit of a fling and get it out of both your systems? There's nothing to say it'll go any further than that.'

Finn laughed. 'Yeah, right. A bit of a fling. That'll help no end. Scratching an itch may work for him but it won't for me. I just want us back to where we were before.'

As if. Having had so much time to mull over the dilemma she knew all the facts. And one major fact was that he would never be just a fling for her.

Shane Dwyer was the kind of guy women went weak at the knees over; his very profession immediately transformed him into hero material in an age where it was tough to find the shiny-clothed guys on horses. Certainly in the city anyway. Finn knew. She'd dated a few of the less shiny ones. And dozens of rusty ones.

Add to that the fact that Shane was strong, in character as well as body, that he cared, probably felt things deeper than he ever showed. All things pointed to the kind of guy that a female with half a brain would want for a long, long time. Not just a few weeks of mind-blowing sensual pleasure.

And Finn just knew, low down in the places *where* a grown woman's body knew, there *would* be satisfaction. Deep, rippling, toe-curling, crying-out-loud—

'Finn?'

'Sorry.' She shook her head to clear the images and checked her watch to hide her flushed cheeks. 'I gotta get back.'

Mel looked at her own watch. 'You've only had a half-hour.'

'We're manic. You know the music business and Christmas…'

'Yeah, you've mentioned it every year since you went to work there. Third of a year's business in one month, yada, yada, yada…' She tilted her head from side to side with each 'yada', then stopped to waggle a finger. 'But I still think that geek of a boss of yours could have given you time off since your house *burned down*!'

Finn sighed. 'I can hardly say much when it was me that caused it, can I? And, anyway, I need this job more than ever now. And at least while I'm flat out at work I'm not having to sit on a sofa watching TV with flipping Shane.'

'Or doing anything else with him, for that matter.'

She rolled her eyes. 'It's more exhausting being there than it is being in work.' After folding her roll back into its wrapping, she pushed it into her large bag for later. 'I just need to get through the next two and a half weeks and then I can try and find some-where else to live.'

Mel grimaced. 'Have I mentioned in the last five minutes how bad I feel about there not being any space where I am now? We're on top of each other in that flat as it is. Are you quite sure you can't just go home to your mum's?'

Finn shook her head. 'It's a two-hour commute

either way, and that's four hours I just don't have at this time of year.' One hand reached out and patted Mel's sleeve as she stood up. 'It's not your fault, hon, don't worry about it. I'll be home for Christmas soon anyway.'

Her friend smiled, a twinkle in her eyes. 'And safe?'

'Ha, ha.' She flung the strap of her bag over her shoulder, planted a kiss on Mel's cheek and turned to leave.

'Finn.'

The hand on her arm stopped her. 'What?'

'Just have a wee think about why he's chasing you so hard? It might be he sees you as more than an itch.'

Finn laughed a short burst of laughter. 'Mr Love-'em-an'-leave-'em? I think not.'

She squeezed Mel's hand and then turned to leave again.

She got as far as the door before her name sounded once more. 'Hey, Finn?'

'Yes?' She looked over her shoulder as her hand pushed open the glass door of the sandwich bar. 'What?'

'Just remember—' Mel winked across at her and added in a 'Terminator' voice '—he'll still be there.'

Laughing despite the fact it really wasn't funny, she pushed out into the crowded street and drew the lapels of her coat up against her face.

The early December wind was crisp and whistling, stinging against her cheeks and tossing her hair into her eyes. So it took several brisk steps with her face tucked into her coat before she could hear her mobile ringing.

Jostling past a couple of Christmas shoppers, she leaned against a shop window and fished it out of her coat pocket, glancing briefly at the name on screen before she answered with a frown. It was too early for an end of shift call. 'Hi, Eddie. What's up?'

She could barely hear him. 'You'll have to speak louder, I'm in the middle of town.'

'Just wanted to let you know we were okay before you heard any news.'

'What news?' Her half eaten sandwich churned in her stomach. 'What happened?'

'There was a house fire early in our shift. We got the call out.'

'What happened, Eddie?' It was Eddie calling so she knew he was okay. But she also knew that it was one of the days when Shane and Eddie worked a shift together. 'Was someone hurt?'

'It was hairy. But everyone's okay.'

'Shane—?' She tried to control the edge of panic in her voice. 'Is he with you?'

'No. But he's fine.'

Fine? Finn knew only too well how useless the word could be in describing how a person really was. '*What* happened?'

'It was a family. Couple of them had close calls. I just didn't want you to worry in case it made the news.'

The call was currently worrying her more than the news would have done.

Eddie paused, his voice more serious than usual. 'Look, sis, when we get a call out like this one, me and Shane normally talk it through that night. But I don't live there any more. You do, and I just wanted to give you the heads up. Just in case. Though you know he's not much of a talker usually.'

'You want *me* to talk him through it?'

'You're the right kind of person. You get it, Finn. You know better than most.' He paused again. 'And, like I said, it was hairy for a bit.'

'Busy day?' Shane didn't turn round when she got home late that evening after another hectic day in work. A day when she'd made more mistakes than usual with orders, distracted by what was to come.

She didn't know if she would find him a depressed, slumped heap, drinking his day into oblivion, or a cheery figure trying to pretend he hadn't had a tougher day than most of the population.

But he was neither.

His voice was steady and he just kept on making dinner at a bench in the kitchen, slicing vegetables with even knife strokes. To anyone else it would have seemed nothing was out of the ordinary.

Finn wasn't anyone else. She knew him well enough to see tension in the set of his shoulders, to recognize the overly calm tone to his voice as false.

'Not as busy as yours.'

'Just some more evidence for your reason not to get involved with me, I s'pose.'

She ignored the jibe, even though for a brief second she wanted to say, 'Fine, then,' and leave him to it. It would have been the easier option. But Finn had always been a bit too bloody-minded for 'easy'.

'Eddie said it was hairy.'

'There were moments.'

'You want to tell me about it?'

His burst of laughter was harsh. 'Not so much.'

'Maybe it would help to talk.'

'You're a therapist now?' He glanced over his shoulder, then slowly turned around and faced her.

She stared with wide eyes. 'Oh, my God.'

Wide shoulders merely shrugged in response to her gasp. 'It's just a few bruises.'

It was way more than a few bruises. He looked as if he'd been run over by a bus.

His face. His gorgeous face was covered down one side with cuts and angry swelling, his right eye half closed over, his cheekbone red and angry. Only his mouth seemed to have escaped.

Forcing her feet forwards, she asked in a small voice, 'What happened?'

His shoulders shrugged again. 'Some stuff fell.'

The words made her heavy feet stop while an overplayed scene from her dreams flashed in front of her. 'Did the roof fall in?'

Shane frowned in confusion. 'No, the roof didn't fall in. Who said it did?'

She shook her head. 'No one.'

'That overactive imagination of yours again.'

Maybe so. But she didn't stop to think it over because she couldn't stop looking at his face, her eyes moving over every scrape.

He managed a small smile. 'I'm not scarred for life.'

Finn blinked and swallowed hard. Then she looked away. It didn't matter what had fallen, didn't matter to her whether the bruising would be gone in a day or a week. Because the damage was already done. She'd already been forced to look her fears in the face.

But if she had thought holding herself back from sleeping with him would make it any less painful to her if he got hurt, then she'd been wrong. Very wrong.

The only thing she wanted to do was step forwards and fling herself into his arms. To have him hold her tight, to reassure her that he was still there, that he was safe.

Anger rose inside her, burning in her stomach like acid. *Son-of-a—*

She spun on her heel and ran back through the living room and up the stairs, his voice sounding out behind her.

'*Finn*! Finn, wait a minute!'

His heavier feet sounded on the stairs, giving chase. 'Stop, would you?'

She was almost in the safety of her room when

his hand grasped her shoulder and swung her round. He then pushed her hard, her back hitting the wall. 'Look at me.'

Her eyes stayed fixed on the rise and fall of his broad chest, on the heavy breathing that was so real and reassuring.

'*Look at me!*'

With slow blinking she gradually raised her eyes. It was when she could see his face again that tears came. Hot, angry, frustrated tears, blurring the view of what she already knew was there.

'No, don't do that.' He raised his free hand and brushed her hair back from her cheek with tenderness that only made her cry more. 'I'm fine.'

She jerked her face from his touch. 'Don't say fine. You're not *fine*.'

He scowled at her. 'Yeah, I am.'

Green eyes locked with blue. Finn was angry. So, so angry. He'd just given her all the proof she needed that she was right not to get any more involved with him. But he'd also just shown her that she already cared what happened to him, that, no matter how she tried avoiding him, he was already entangled in her life.

And the fact that one thing was so conflicted with another made her mad. Mad at *him*. Mad that he had made her cry in front of him so that he knew she cared without her even having to say so out loud.

Thick, dark lashes blinked slowly at her, his hand rising again, this time to her neck where his fingers curled into her hair, cupping the back of her head. He stared, a steady gaze that felt as if it could see through to her soul. And there was a tenderness there that made her mind up for her.

Without thinking any further, she grasped handfuls of his shirt and pulled herself forwards, forced her mouth onto his.

The last tears rolled silently off her lashes as she felt him tense against her, then he groaned and matched her move for move, their heads moving frantically from side to side. His long fingers moved against the back of her neck, his other hand snaking around her waist to hold her so tight she could barely breathe.

Somewhere in the back of her mind there was a momentary sense of panic. A 'what am I doing?' But while she had her fists tangled into his shirt and her tongue tangling with his it was tough to think much beyond wanting his weight on her, wanting to feel his skin on hers.

Releasing the tight grip she had on the material and overwhelmed by the combined heat of their mouths, she let her hands drop to the bottom of his shirt. Her knuckles grazed against the bulge of his erection beneath the shirt edge and she smiled against his mouth. This was all the reality she was interested in.

Tomorrow and its repercussions could wait.

Her fingertips found where the shirt edges met at the first button and she gripped again. Gripped and then tugged with all her strength, popping buttons that pinged off the wall behind her and clattered onto the wooden floor. It took two tugs. And then he was hers to touch. So she did, savouring the sensation of taut, warm skin.

Flattening her hands against the flatness of his abdomen, she smoothed her palms up while her fingertips dipped and rose over each of his ribs, turning her wrists as she swept over his nipples to his broad shoulders where she pushed the shirt back, then down along his arms.

Shane dropped his hands from her long enough to give his arms one shake so the shirt hit the ground at his feet. Then his hands were on her, undoing the buttons on her jacket with infinitely more finesse than she'd used on him. Finesse that he then used on the tiny buttons of her blouse, each one undone with a deliberate slowness that drove her insane.

So she helped him. Tore her hands from his skin to struggle out of her clothes, pushed off the wall to reach for the clasp of her lace bra, kicked her heels off her feet so that she had to rise up on her toes to keep kissing him.

His hands closed over hers behind her back. Squeezed once, removed them from the clasp. Then he tore his mouth from hers and looked into her eyes, his head still tilted. He didn't speak, didn't say a single word as he undid the clasp, smoothed his roughened fingertips up along her shoulder blades to slide the lace straps slowly from her arms. As he eased his body back an inch, eyes steady, the wisp of material slithered off her breasts and whispered against her stomach before it joined his shirt.

Then he leaned his head back, looked down at her full breasts, raised his thick lashes to look at her. And she knew instinctively he was giving her a second to think about what was happening.

A second that, had it been any longer, she might sensibly have used to step away.

But when his hands were on her breasts, cupping their weight and teasing her taut nipples with his fingers, there wasn't any room for thinking sensibly.

Finn flopped back against the wall, her head tilting back, lips parting as she surrendered to sensation. Her hand fumbled for the door handle beside her, almost of its own accord. But when she found it and opened the door to her room her eyes opened and she looked at him as he looked through the gap.

He looked back at her again.

Her eyes flickered over his face, from the thick dark wave of hair that fell across his forehead, past equally dark eyebrows to the sparkling blue of his eyes. Past the cuts and bruising on one side to the smooth flushed skin on the other. To the sensual sweep of his mouth with its fuller lower lip. There was no going back.

While she had studied him it was almost as if time had slowed. But by the time they were moving into her room everything sped up. Clothes hit the ground, mouths touched and seared and parted. Then Finn's knees hit the back of the bed and they tumbled back.

It occurred to her that he was wearing more than her. His hard length pushing against her thigh beneath the soft layer of his cotton boxers. She rolled over, straddling his hips, her breasts crushing against the coarse hair on his chest as she asked in a husky voice, 'Protection?'

Shane laughed a deep, purely sexual laugh that teased the hair that fell against her nipples and sent waves of wet warmth to her core. 'Across the hall.'

Finn froze, her eyes widening as she looked down at him. 'You're kidding me.'

'Nope.' He shook his head.

She blinked at him for several long moments. But when he smiled, his dimples flashing, then grimaced slightly at the pain it caused his cheek, she couldn't help but laugh too. 'I s'pose I have to go get it?'

'We'll both go. Sit up.' He continued smiling when her eyebrows rose. 'Sit up.'

So she did, sighing breathily as his erect penis settled between her legs.

Shane groaned. 'If we don't get a move on I'm not going to last 'til we get across the hall.'

And with that he pushed up on his elbows, wrapped his arms around her waist and pushed their bodies to the end of the bed.

Finn gasped when he pushed upwards. 'What do you think you're doing? You'll break your back.'

'Shut up and wrap your legs around me.'

'You can't—'

He was already on his feet so she had no choice but to do as she was bid. She wrapped her legs around his waist, gasping again as he hoisted her up so that her breasts were once again grazed over his chest hair. It was too, too good and she'd honestly never been so turned on in her entire life. But then she'd never had anyone carry her to their bed before. She'd never actually believed that anyone would be strong enough to do that. And it was the sexiest thing in the world.

They were in his room fast. He deposited her unceremoniously on his bed, yanked open his dresser drawer, tore open the foil packet with his teeth while his free hand pulled his boxers off and then he was on her.

She opened her legs with barely a hint of a touch from his hand on her knee; her eyes flickered closed again.

'Look at me.'

Her eyes opened and she looked up at his face, his body poised above her. 'Don't close your eyes. I want to see what you're feeling.'

It was the most difficult thing anyone had ever asked of her. More intimate than anything she'd ever experienced and for a moment it was the most frightening.

What was she doing?

But as the thick length of him slid into her with one smooth, practised stroke, all thinking stopped.

Finn's breasts rose and fell in deep staggering breaths. There were no words. Nothing beyond the sensation of being so completely filled, nothing beyond the ache low in her abdomen.

Then he moved, slid out until he almost left her, pushed back in to fill her again. His eyes locked on hers.

Her breathing got faster, the knot in her abdomen got tighter, his smooth strokes got faster and harder. And the urge to close her eyes and get lost in sensation was overwhelming.

'Don't-close-your-eyes.'

Her body arched up to his, the knot bunched her stomach muscles tight and then her release came, shattering her nerves and rippling out in spirals across her body. And her cries echoed around the room.

Through the haze of her pleasure she saw his brow crease, saw the dark pupils in his eyes enlarge until she could barely see the blue. Then he moaned—his body spent in ecstacy.

Finn stared up at him in wonder as he smiled a slow, sensual smile down at her.

Oh, *now* she'd gone and done it, hadn't she?

CHAPTER NINE

SHANE wasn't sure how he knew something had changed. But he knew.

At one point, when they'd been in the hall, it had crossed his mind that he should have stopped what was happening. For Finn to have changed her mind so suddenly should have shouted a warning note to him. He should have taken a moment to slow down and get her to talk things through. Even though talking things through wasn't really his forte.

But he'd wanted her for so long, had fanatisized so much, that having his desires presented to him had been too damn hard to resist.

It had been when he'd been buried deep inside her for the first time that the magnitude of what had been happening had hit him.

He'd never felt so connected to someone in his entire life. Not physically, not emotionally and most certainly not so strong a combination of the two that it had rocked him to his core.

He couldn't ever remember having felt so deep a sense of fear. Even when fire had been burning around him or when he'd known that lives were at risk.

The only thing that had kept that fear at bay had been his body's need for completion. And even that had been way more than he'd ever experienced.

But before he could take the time to think it all through he knew something changed in her.

Then her expressive eyes closed before he could search them for answers.

Their bodies still joined, he leaned down and brushed a light kiss across her swollen lips, his voice a whisper. 'Don't shut me out.'

Her breasts rose and fell in a shuddering breath. 'I didn't exactly plan for this to happen.'

'I know you didn't. But it did.'

'Boy, did it.'

He laughed a low laugh. 'Yeah.'

Her eyes flickered open and she studied his face for a long moment. 'It doesn't change anything.'

It didn't? How did it not? He'd just had the most mind-shattering sensual experience of his life and she was telling him it didn't change anything? What was it, then—sympathy sex?

'Oh, really?'

'It can't.'

Maybe not from where she lay. 'We just made love. I'd say that changes things plenty.'

Her tongue ran nervously over her lips. 'I guess

you were right—this was going to happen at some point. And it was—'

'Yes, *it was.*'

'But you got hurt today.'

'And that confirms your reasons for not getting involved with me.'

'Yes.' The expression on her face seemed to soften, probably because she believed that his under-standing meant he agreed with her. 'It does.'

Shane studied her for a long moment, then moved, breaking the bond their bodies had to adjust his weight so that his legs stayed tangled with hers. With one hand he reached for the edge of the bedcovers and drew them over their torsos.

Then he propped his hand on an elbow so his face was still close to hers and raised a hand to brush damp tendrils of hair from her cheek. 'And the first thing you felt you had to do when you had your fears confirmed was to get closer to me. You say one thing but your body says another.'

Finn didn't look at him, her gaze fixed on the ceiling. 'What happened today wasn't that big a deal. Really.'

He waited while she carefully considered what he'd just said. Then her face turned towards his. 'So what fell?'

Shane shook his head. 'You don't need to know that.'

'I want to know.'

'I already said it wasn't a big deal.'

But Finn refused to be deterred. 'You talk to Eddie about this kind of thing after it happens.'

'I'm not lying naked in bed with Eddie.'

'Why don't you want to talk about it if it was no big deal?'

The question made him think some. He could make an excuse or just try showing her again what kind of a connection they already had. But he felt she needed a little honesty if they were ever going to head in the direction he would like them to try heading.

'I guess I'm a wee bit worried that if I talk to you, you might use it as evidence for the prosecution in the case of McNeill v. Dwyer.'

From the flash of guilt that crossed her eyes he knew he was right.

'Okay.'

'That's what I thought.'

'No, I mean okay, you have a point. I don't mean okay, we don't have to talk about it. I want to hear it.'

'Why?' He looked her straight in the eye as he asked.

But with a flicker of her lashes she looked away and hid from him. Her naked shoulders shrugged. 'I think I need to hear some of what you do to understand it. You're telling me it was no big deal, your face tells me different and I want to know. You can't just tell me it was no big deal and then not tell me the details. All that does is let my imagination go wild and that has to be worse than "no big deal".'

She paused for breath. 'So, let me make up my own mind.'

'It's not like this every day. Most days it's just sitting around checking equipment, cleaning up and playing cards.'

'But some days it's not.'

'Some days it's not.' He nodded slowly.

'It's those days I need to hear about.'

It didn't make any sense to him. How could she be so determined that it was his job that held them apart and yet, when they finally had a moment where they could communicate, want to talk about that job? And the worst-case scenarios of that job to boot?

'Eddie must talk to you about it sometimes?'

She glanced up at him from underneath long lashes. 'Not really. He'll say things like "It was a rough one", or, "We had a bad day today", but he never goes into details. It's a firefighter thing, right?'

Shane smiled, 'Yeah, I guess it is.'

'Well, break it, then.'

'Talking about it isn't going to make you run screaming from this room?'

She thought that over for another minute, the tip of her tongue damping her lips again. 'You said it was no big deal.'

With a shake of his head he realized she had him. It was disconcerting having someone who could out-think him. Another first to add to the list of firsts he was experiencing.

Shane knew that what he told her might well enforce her fears about what he did for a living, but by not talking to her he would be closing a door on her. Which he didn't want to do.

He'd never talked to a woman about his job, not in any great detail. Maybe simply because he'd never met a woman he wanted to share that much with. The things that made him who he was. It was an intimacy he'd never felt the need to share. Well, there had to be a first time, he guessed.

'They didn't have a smoke alarm.'

Her eyes fixed on his.

He frowned. 'Anyone with a family that doesn't have a smoke alarm is a bloody fool.'

'Were there kids?'

A sharp nod. 'Yes.'

'Did they—?'

'We got them. But we had a hell of a time finding them in the smoke.'

She was blinking at him and he wondered what she was thinking, what pictures were forming in her mind. She was a smart girl, after all.

Doing his best to keep his voice calm, he rhymed off the order things had happened in. 'It was a house fire, persons reported. When we got there the bottom floor was pretty much a goner, the smoke upstairs was thick. And it's the smoke that does the damage. Everyone thinks that the fire does it but it's the smoke that's the real killer. Me and

Eddie were on one of the B.A. crews, so we put on tanks and went in.'

She continued to blink, her eyes flickering to his bruising. 'What happened?'

'There were two kids left inside at the back of the house. Callum and Mick found the first one on the floor beside his bed but we couldn't find the little girl.' He took a moment to study her face. 'You okay with this?'

She nodded. 'Go on.'

'I could hear her crying. She'd hidden in a laundry basket. Apparently she spends a load of time hiding and it's one of her favourite places. Eddie got her and I followed them down the stairs when the last three gave and I fell against the banisters. Knocked my face mask up and that was that. Everyone was okay. The parents and the boy had some smoke inhalation, the dad had some minor burns.'

'And the girl?'

Shane smiled softly. 'Not a mark. And the damp towels in the laundry basket helped her avoid the smoke.'

Finn stayed silent, her eyes locked on his. Then she asked, 'Do you get scared when you go into something like that?'

'You don't get time to get scared. It's a job. You know what you have to do and you focus on that. Then you get out.'

'Even when you felt the stairs falling?'

'I was nearly at the bottom. They'd have got me if I was hurt that bad. Relying on each other the way we all do is the most important part.'

He listened to her saying nothing at all for as long as he could stand it. 'You wanted to talk. That's a two-way thing, I've been told.'

'I just don't understand how you can do it. How you can walk into places like that and not be scared. How you can risk your life like that.'

'I told you, it's not like that every day.' She didn't look convinced so he kept talking. 'And it's not just for the people I don't know, Finn. It's for the guys I work with. I couldn't be as close to them all as I am and sit at home knowing they were doing the job without me.'

'They're like a family to you.' She stated the obvious.

'You know they are.'

She looked away from him. But not quickly enough for him not to see her eyes shimmer for the second time in one night. He wrapped an arm over her waist, held her in place so she couldn't get away from him. 'You know what I do, Finn. I know you're worried and I know you care. Or you wouldn't be lying here.'

'I've never said I didn't care.'

'Then stop trying to run away every five minutes.'

Her hand settled on his on her stomach. She focused her attention on them, on the differences in size between his and hers. It was a powerful reminder of the difference between the male and the female and she was very aware of her own femininity while she was lying against the hard length of him.

Normally she felt like Goliath most of the time. Her height and her curved figure made her stand out in a society that seemed to be made up of five-foot-six women with sylph-like figures.

But Shane was so large, so broad, so muscled, that she felt small and vulnerable beside him. It was a nice sensation. Better than nice. It would be easy to just get lost in him as she had not so long ago, to give in to her body and try and shut out her mind. She just wasn't so sure she was as brave as him.

'Tell me what you're thinking.'

The deep voice so close to her ear sent shivers of awareness over the body newly educated to what he could do.

'What do you want from me?'

She felt him go still beside her but couldn't bring herself to look at his face.

'I guess I want you to give this a try.'

'Why?'

He went silent, and then it sounded as if he had to force the words through. 'Because I care about you too.'

The simplicity of it tore a hole in her chest. 'I don't know if I can—'

'*No*, you don't know. But there's only one way to find out, isn't there?'

CHAPTER TEN

SHANE started a delicious form of torment with phone calls the next day. Phone calls that started with questions about what Finn was doing and how her day was going and then rapidly progressed to debating what underwear she was wearing.

Then he would finish the conversation by telling her where he wanted to touch her, what it would feel like to have his hands on her when she got back to the house.

By the third call she was on fire and pretty sure everyone in her workplace knew what she was thinking about while she faltered in her telesales calls.

It led her to wonder at what it was about him that had her so hot. At her age in the current millennium, it wasn't as if she were some doe-eyed virgin, but she'd never met anyone who could do the things to her imagination that he could.

Having thought that over, she smiled when she inwardly admitted that no one had ever actually phoned her at her work to talk to her the way he had. There was just something so damn sexy about that. How could the 'librarian' types that preceded him possibly hope to compete?

Not that she wasn't sure that, somewhere in the world, there was bound to be a 'librarian' type with just as dirty a mind. She just hadn't met him, was all.

Though in amongst all the sexual distraction, there were still doubts. Sex really wasn't the problem. If she hadn't known that from their first frantic encounter, then she would sure have known it from the slow deliberation of their second.

She hadn't been able to answer him with words. Having wanted to talk, she just hadn't been able to find any more words. So she'd done what she'd allowed herself to do the first time, she'd reached out for him. It seemed to be the one thing she felt she was in control of. An old-fashioned feminine thing that a woman had when she knew a man wanted her. But even that wasn't enough to take away the fear.

Surely walking away from him, even now when it would hurt so much, had to be better than having him taken from her later down the line?

By four she found herself doing something she'd never done at work before. Clock-watching.

It was just a shame her boss saw her doing it.

'You in a hurry to be somewhere?'

Heat rushed over her cheeks. 'No, I'm just mad keen to have these orders ready for the courier.'

'Well, it's as well. We have a shipment from England coming in late. So it's all hands on deck tonight.'

Finn sighed when he was out of earshot. Great. It wasn't that she wasn't used to working all the extra hours at any particular time of year; it wasn't that she didn't get paid decent overtime rates and a fairly generous Christmas bonus at the end of it—the latter two subjects things that she needed more than she ever had before.

It was just that for the first time in several years of Christmas overtime she had somewhere else she would rather be. As if her time with Shane were already on a countdown.

Her hand faltered over the phone. It would be the considerate thing to let him know she was going to be late back, right? Then why did it feel as if she was suddenly treating him like someone she was in a long-term committed relationship with? By ringing him to 'report in' would she be overstepping where they currently were? Would she be giving him the impression that she was more involved than she could let herself be?

Where were they, after all, beyond being in a very sexually charged place where none of the real problems had been resolved?

Why was she over-thinking a simple courtesy call?

With a shake of her head she picked up the phone and punched in the numbers. Reasoning with herself that it was only good manners. Though she did feel marginally better when she got the answer machine.

By half past eight the shipment still hadn't arrived. Everyone had their work cleared away and some of the next morning's work done and a lethargy had fallen over the large store rooms. And Shane hadn't called her back.

Surely it would have been equally polite of him to have called her back? Damn him.

Maybe it would be easier if he behaved like a typical thoughtless man so she would find it easier to walk away.

She was alone in the room where goods were checked in when his voice sounded behind her. 'Well, you look busy.'

The sound made her jump in her seat. Spinning around on her stool, she stared at him with wide eyes, her heart beating harder at the sight of him. 'What are you doing here? We're not supposed to have friends come visit.'

His wide shoulders shrugged. 'You have to eat.'

Her gaze fell to a bag that he lifted in front of his body and a checked rug that was thrown over his arm, 'You brought me food?'

'Have you eaten?'

'No.' Her stomach growled in response.

'Damn, guess I *should* have brought some food then.'

A quick glance at the sparkle in his eyes was

enough for her to know he was kidding. And her heart warmed; it was quite possibly one of the nicest things anyone had ever done for her. She raised her chin and blinked slowly. 'So, what did you bring me? Anything nice?'

With a small smile he walked across to her, leaned his face so close that his nose almost touched hers. Then tilted his head, his gaze focusing on her parted lips. 'Unfortunately only stuff that's decent under all your security cameras.'

'Damn again, then.'

He finally smiled. 'You're right there.'

Finn tilted her head in the opposite direction to his, her eyes narrowing slightly as a thought occurred to her. 'How did you get in here?'

'I told them I was your boyfriend.'

'Did you, now?'

'Yep.'

'And they said?'

'One of them said you were a lucky girl.'

Finn giggled. Something she hadn't done in a good fifteen years.

Shane smiled in response, his dimples creasing, 'I agreed with her.'

Quirking her eyebrows, she looked down, conscious of the fact he kept looking at her face as she did. 'So what's in the bag?'

'Uh-uh.' He waited until her chin rose again, pointing a long finger at his good cheek. 'Kiss first.'

With a slow smile and a glimpse to the flickering light on the camera in the corner, she leaned in the last couple of inches and pressed her mouth to his. His mouth was still for a moment, his body tensing, then he relaxed and moved his lips with hers in a soft, brief touch that left her wanting a lot more.

When he lifted his head back he whispered in a low grumble, 'What about the cameras?'

'You told them you're my boyfriend. They won't expect anything less.'

He smiled softly, lifted his finger again to brush it over her sensitive lips. 'Now I wish I'd told them I was your gynaecologist.'

Laughter filled the air as he stepped back and spread the checked rug on the floor behind them. Then he dug in his bag and produced packet sandwiches, crisps, a bar of her favourite chocolate, two cans of soda and a tea-light candle.

Which he lit, then raised an eyebrow as he looked up at her. 'Ta-da. Picnic à la Dwyer.'

Watching him from her stool, Finn wondered at the mystery that was Shane Dwyer. She'd thought she knew him before but apparently she'd only got half the story.

'So you do this kind of thing for all your girlfriends?'

'No, I already took take-away to the other two.'

'It's amazing you don't weigh about three hundred pounds.'

He waited until they were both sitting on the rug,

Finn hiding her eyes from him as she reached for a packet of sandwiches. 'What?'

The sandwiches refused to be opened, so Finn focused all her attention on them and avoided looking at Shane. His words had been meant as a joke, she knew that. But they had stolen away some of the glow she'd felt at him referring to himself as her boyfriend. Maybe that had just been a joke to him too.

She knew he had dated before, plenty. Though the thought of him with someone else had never affected her before. Much. Well, much that she'd admitted to herself. But it bothered her more and more on an almost daily basis now.

'I can't get these open.'

His hand reached over and took the packet from her, ripping it open in one fluid motion before he handed them back. 'What?'

'Nothing—stupid sandwiches.' She scowled down at the guilty sandwich packet that had been so easy for *him* to open. Then flashed him a quick smile before biting into one, momentarily escaping having to make any further explanation.

Shane's eyes narrowed. 'Not the kind of sandwiches you like?'

She swallowed. 'They're grand.'

He wasn't buying the smile she gave him. 'Talk to me. I can't read your mind.'

Suddenly she felt like an immature idiot. In every

other 'relationship' she'd ever had she'd known exactly
where she stood, had felt she had some semblance of
control. But just because she was reacting inside like
some nervous teenager with her first ever boyfriend
didn't mean she should act like it on the outside.

'I'm just being stupid; don't worry about it.'

His mouth quirked. 'I never have before.'

'Ha, ha.'

'So what is it?'

'Apart from the fact that this is really new territory, you mean?'

'No one else ever fed you in work before?'

'No, I can honestly say that this is a first.'

'You've been seeing the wrong guys, I told you
that already.'

'No, you said I was seeing them to avoid facing
up to the fact I fancied you.' She shrugged. 'Or something along those lines.'

Ripping open his own sandwiches, he studied her
for a long moment, then dived on in with a big one.
'And was I right?'

The question stopped her in her tracks. That would
be a big confession, now wouldn't it?

'Maybe.'

Shane let the softly spoken word hang in the air
for a while, his heart beating hard and loud. He
knew the maybe was a yes, could see it in her eyes.
And he wanted to haul her forward and kiss her
senseless for it. It was good to know he wasn't

alone. She might not have been as obsessed as he'd once tried telling himself he hadn't been. But she had been attracted and that was a big thing. Huge. It gave what was happening with them a more equal basis.

It made it potentially *serious*.

A word he had managed to avoid for most of his life.

'Even though you were so determined not to fancy a firefighter?'

'I'm still not past that part, so maybe it would be better not to talk about it right this minute.'

All right, he was happy enough with that. There was still plenty of time to persuade her that the world wasn't going to fall on his head any time soon.

His pause left an opening for her. 'How come I feel like I really don't know you all that well?'

'You know me.'

'Not that well, I don't.'

'You know me a hell of a lot better than you did twenty-four hours ago.'

Her cheeks flushed a soft pink. He loved it when she did that. There weren't too many women around who blushed any more. In fact it was only recently that he'd even managed to get Finn to blush. He loved that he had even that simple a physical effect on her.

'That goes both ways.'

Leaning towards her, he lowered his voice to the same intimate drawl he'd used on the phone. 'Tell me that camera isn't on and we can learn some more.'

Her eyes sparkled, then blinked a couple of times as she cleared her head, leaving him wondering what she'd been thinking. 'You're avoiding talking.'

'Well, we could talk about it if the camera had no sound.'

'So long as what we're talking about is sex.'

'It's one of my favourite topics of discussion with you.'

There was a small snort of laughter. 'Recently it's been pretty much the only topic of conversation with me. Try talking about something else.'

He leaned back. 'Like what?'

'Anything—you can even choose.' She leaned towards him, her eyes wide for a moment. 'I really don't know much beyond what I can see on the outside. How come I never realized that before now?'

'I could say the same thing about you.'

'No, you couldn't. You know everything there is to know about me. You know my family; you know what I do for a living—' she flung a hand out to one side '—you even know what most of my underwear looks like now!'

He couldn't help himself. 'Not while you're wearing it I don't.'

Long lashes blinked at him for a long, long time. And without her even speaking he knew he'd said the wrong thing. She really wanted to know more about him and his making with the funnies wasn't getting him out of it. 'What do you want to know?'

Her gaze softened. 'We could start with why it is I know so little?'

A shrug. 'I guess I'm not much of a talker.'

'Eddie probably knows more than me.'

'That's different.'

'Different, how?'

'We work together, we used to live in the same house—' he was almost tempted to tell her it was because Eddie was a guy, but that wouldn't really be true '—but I don't know that he knows me that much better than you do. I'm not much of a talker.'

'You already said that.'

'Well, there you go, then.' He held his hands up in surrender. 'I rest my case.'

There was a moment while thoughts crossed her expressive eyes. Then a sparkle began in their green depths and a smile teased the corners of her lips, catching his attention.

She leaned towards him, her lush breasts tilting teasingly into his line of vision. He stared at the 'V' of her plain white blouse, was tempted to raise his chin a little to see if he could catch a glimpse of lace. But her lilting voice brought his attention back to her face.

'We'll just have to see if I can find a way to *persuade* you to share information.'

'Like what, for instance?'

'I'm thinking of a reward system…'

Reward system? Damn, he'd almost tell her

anything if there were rewards of the kind he wanted involved.

In fact a list was already forming…

Finn smiled as if she knew about the list and what was on it. Her eyes sparkled with enthusiasm, her lips parted to show her even teeth. And Shane had a sudden, swift desire to keep that look on her face as long as possible. Even if it did mean breaking the habit of a lifetime and sharing personal information.

She was worth the effort.

CHAPTER ELEVEN

'I'M DEFINITELY due some of those rewards.'

'You think?' Finn laughed as Shane grabbed hold of her inside the door, spinning her around until she had her back against the solid oak. 'I've already thanked you for staying to help out.'

Raising his hands to place them, palms flat, against the door either side of her head, he then leaned the length of his body against her so that she was pinned in place.

'It was fun.'

'I think it was more fun for the girls you flirted with than it was for you.'

'It wasn't them I stayed to be with.'

Smiling up at him, she smoothed her palms down his ribcage, the taut muscles of his abdomen flexing. 'That gets a reward all right.'

Her fingers undid a button on his shirt.

Shane tilted his chin down to look at her hands as her fingers slid to another button. With his chin still down he glanced up at her from between thick dark lashes. 'A button? That's my reward for counting hundreds of CDs?'

'What was the name of the first girl you kissed?'

He smiled a slow smile as the memory entered his mind. 'Mary McCauley.'

Another button was freed. 'What age were you?'

'Six.'

'No, you weren't!' She gave him a look of outrage. 'No one has their first proper kiss at six.'

'Maybe I just started early?'

'Not that early, you didn't.'

'Okay—' he rocked his head from side to side '—she was my second cousin and after one family get-together all the grown-ups thought it would be cute if we kissed for the camera.'

Finn smiled.

'I had to stand on a telephone book to reach her and I wiped my mouth with the back of my hand after. It was very romantic.'

She laughed and slipped another button free, her fingers grazing against his warm skin. She looked down to check her progress, her voice thickening. 'First proper kiss?'

'Sinead Begley, in fourth year at high school. She was the year above me and I even tried a quick grope. Again, very romantic.'

Another button, and she smoothed the edges of the shirt back from his ribs, her eyes moving over the ridges of his abs and down to where a hint of dark hair dipped into the belt of his jeans. 'First serious relationship.'

'Define serious.'

Her eyes flickered upwards. 'Girlfriend. Someone you saw for a few months. Someone you really liked.'

His lashes blinked lazily. 'I've never dated for longer than a few months.'

'How come?'

It took a long time for him to answer. 'Just wasn't right, I s'pose.'

Unreasonably, part of her ached to have him say it was because he'd never met someone like her before. She slipped another button free. 'First time you made love?'

'Uh-uh. Not telling you that.' He started on some of her buttons, his fingers working faster than hers. 'That one can be a minefield.'

Okay, he had a point there. So she jumped into something that she had been thinking about after all his explicit phone calls. 'First time you thought about making love with me?'

His hands smoothed her blouse and jacket open while he fixed her with a sensual gaze. 'That's easy. At the shorts and shades party we threw for Eddie's thirtieth.'

Finn's eye's widened. Hang on, that had been over a year ago!

Shane smiled while his hands cupped her breasts,

caressing her through yet another lacy concoction of his own choosing. 'We were playing truths…'

It was yet another of Eddie's dumb games. It consisted of someone making a statement like, 'I've never had sex on a first date' and everyone who had had to take a drink. A game that became all the more bawdy when it was played in a large group of people who knew each other pretty damn well so that when someone didn't drink and someone else knew better a challenge ensued. And secrets were told. And the person who lied had to down a glassful.

It was why Finn had never not taken a drink when it was something she'd done. She wasn't that great a drinker to end up downing glass after glass.

His fingers found her nipples and teased them into aching peaks. 'You drank to "I've never faked an orgasm" and I told myself that would never happen when you were with me.'

Finn's fingers faltered. The irony was she remembered it too. Every woman there had silently taken a drink, not just her. Then they'd all laughed for a good ten minutes.

And she remembered looking across at Shane, thinking she'd bet no girl of his ever had to take a drink for that one.

So just how long had *she* been thinking about it?

His dimples quirked. 'After that I couldn't stop looking at you. I had all sorts of interesting fantasies.'

'You're kidding.'

'Nope.' He moved a hand round to unclasp her bra, opening it with a flick of his fingers and a wink. 'You were forbidden territory and that was erotic as hell.'

'Forbidden why?' She abandoned the shirt buttons and headed south, her fingers slipping under the edge of his jeans to slide back and forth.

With a sharp intake of breath he turned them round and backed to the stairs, his mouth descending to her neck where he mumbled, 'You're my best friend's sister. I'm going to get my ass kicked for this at some stage.'

It was an aspect she hadn't thought of in a while, wrapped up as she was in eroticism and her own warring emotions. Eddie was going to go mad when he found out. Hell, what was she thinking? They weren't going to last long enough for a problem that big to be an issue. 'What he doesn't know won't hurt him.'

Her hands were on his belt buckle as he lowered her to the stairs. When his tongue drew a line from her ear to her collar-bone her breath caught, heat pooling where she wanted him. No matter what wrongs there were in their relationship, this part was just so right. Talking on the phone had had her ready for him all day long.

Raising his head for a second, he smiled seductively at her. 'About this orgasm thing.'

Finn swallowed hard. 'Uh-huh?'

He branded her lips with a searing kiss. 'Never, ever with me. You hear?'

When his head descended to lave her breast, she

let her head drop back onto the stair and gasped in answer, 'I don't see that being a problem.'

By the time he had unbuttoned her trousers, pushed them in one confident sweep to her calves along with her panties and pushed her legs open to set his mouth to her she knew that the only orgasm problem she would ever have with Shane would possibly be dying from one.

But as she finished crying out his name and he kissed his way up her body to her mouth, his whispered words froze the blood in her heated veins. 'Now, as to the Eddie issue, I'll talk to him and sort it out.'

Her eyes flew open. 'No, you won't.'

His head rose an inch. 'I'm not having him figure this out on his own; that would be worse.'

Yes, it would. As far as Finn was concerned, Eddie not finding out and still not knowing was absolutely the best scenario. Shane wouldn't be the only one getting an ass-kicking otherwise.

But while her body still hummed and his eyes were looking into hers with unspoken questions she found she couldn't say something as honest as, 'What's the point when this won't last?'

'Wait a while.'

He continued to look at her while her fingers smoothed his thick hair back. 'You want us to just keep sneaking around?'

Finn smiled. 'There's a certain amount of fun in that, don't you think?'

'Yes—' the word came out on an almost reluctant note '—but I don't think you want to hurt someone we both care about any more than I do.'

'I don't.'

'But you still want to wait?'

'Yes.'

'Why?'

She should have known he'd ask. There were a great many things she didn't know about him, things she was loving learning, but there were just as many things she did know. And one of those things was that he not only cared for her brother, he respected him. He was an honourable man when it came to Eddie and his service mates. They all were.

She tried to smooth it over with, 'I just think it's too early.'

While she sent up a silent plea that he wouldn't push it any further, an *unlikely* miracle, he continued studying her face.

Finn could feel herself squirming inwardly. The fact that she was lying, mostly unclothed, on the stairs while he still had pretty much all of his on only added to her vulnerability.

As if he could read the thoughts in her eyes, he slowly began to put her clothing back in place, his eyes dropping to consider his progress.

He took a breath. 'You still don't get this, do you?'

Her green eyes blinked at his dark hair while she said nothing in reply.

'Yeah, that's what I thought.' Gathering the edges of her blouse together, he stood up and headed up the rest of the stairs alone.

For a few heartbeats Finn stayed where she was, stunned. She had absolutely no idea what had just happened. One minute they'd been headed for another night of endless mutual pleasure and now...

What did he mean she didn't 'get it'?

'What did you mean by that?' She stood in the open doorway of his room, still doing up the buttons on her blouse with shaky fingers.

Shane shrugged, throwing his bunched up shirt onto the end of his bed. 'You don't, that's all.'

'All I said was I thought it was too early to tell Eddie. And it is.'

'That's not what you meant, though.'

Finn was getting more frustrated by the minute. 'I have no idea what you mean and how can I if you don't say what's on your mind? Just spit it out.'

'Okay, then.' He stepped towards her with determined strides, his eyes glinting dangerously. 'It's got nothing to do with it being too early or that it's "fun" sneaking around. You don't want him to know because you think this is something that will only last until *you* say it's done.'

Finn gaped at his intuition.

His laughter was harsh. 'Yeah, that's what I figured. What I don't have figured out is how long

you're going to cling to this not-being-involved-with-
me-'cos-I'm-a-firefighter excuse.'

'Excuse?' Her voice finally reappeared and with
it her anger. 'You think I'm using it as an *excuse*?'

One dark eyebrow quirked at her in challenge.

'*Fine*.' She turned around, ready to march down
the hall and as far away from him as possible. Until
his words stopped her.

'Now there's a word I haven't heard you use in a
while. Your favourite word to use when you don't
want to talk.'

Stopping dead, she swung on him. 'As opposed to
your method of not talking at all!'

'I've done nothing but bloody talk all night!'
Leaning his face closer, he added, 'Not that you've
paid that much attention to anything else that's
been goin' on.'

Oh, she'd been paying attention. She'd listened to
every word he'd said, had watched every glance, mem-
orized every touch. As if she was making up a mental
album of memories that she could delve into when it
was all done. What amongst all of it had she missed?
Shane seemed certain she'd missed something.

And, dared she believe it, was *hurt* that she had?

'Well, why don't you try telling me now?'

His head shook again. 'You're so smart, you figure
it out. You've been so good at thinking everything
through without my help so far. You told me you
wouldn't get involved until I quit the service. Then

you said it was because if I got hurt you wouldn't be able to take it. Then when I did get a bit of a battering you threw yourself straight at me—'

'*Threw* myself at you!' It was true, but knowing that didn't make it sting any less. '*You* didn't help any?'

'You knew where I stood, Finn. It wasn't like you didn't have any warning. But you told yourself it was fine because it wouldn't last long, didn't you?'

'Because I should have expected more from the king of lasting relationships?'

The words, spat at him with such venom, seemed to halt him in his tracks. He shook his head again, ran a frustrated hand back through his hair, spiking it ridiculously while his eyes avoided hers.

Then, while the moment of silence allowed them both to take some calming breaths, he looked back into her eyes. His voice was flat. 'So this is what to you, then—some kind of itch to scratch?'

The fact that he was using the phraseology she herself had used to Mel as something *he* would do didn't pass her by unnoticed. Blinking slowly at him, she knew he was giving her the perfect opportunity to end it. Which was what she already knew she had to do, right?

So, how come she couldn't seem to bring herself to take the opportunity?

Sensing tears building at the back of her eyes, she

continued blinking to hold them back. 'You want me to build my life around someone like you, to rely on you being there for ever?'

It was Shane's turn to stay silent.

'You see that's just the thing, isn't it? You can't make me a guarantee to be around for ever, even if it was in you to do that.'

He still didn't speak.

Finn swallowed hard. 'Even if you could, Shane, there would always be a part of me I'd have to hold back. Because I *know*—' despite her best efforts, her voice cracked and she had to pause to clear her throat '—I know what it's like to lose someone who's the centre of your universe. And it hurts. It hurts way more than I ever want to hurt again. So this is it for me.'

His eyes moved to where her hand moved back and forth between them. Then back to her face again as she raised her other hand to wipe at one eye.

'Whatever this is, it's all I can give.' She pursed her lips and finished with, 'So, you can take it or leave it. It's up to you.'

When he still didn't speak, her chin dropped and she stepped back. Only to have his arm shoot out, his hand grasping hers.

Her gaze rose, looking back and forth at his eyes with unspoken questions.

He tugged, brought her back into the room, using

his free hand to close the door behind her. And still said nothing.

So with a breathy sigh she leaned forwards and communicated with him the only way she could.

CHAPTER TWELVE

Two weeks in and Shane was still asking himself why it was he found it so difficult to tell Finn how he felt. He'd known when she'd talked about building her life around someone like him, relying on him being there for ever.

He was in love with her.

Lying in the dim light of a rapidly rising dawn, watching her sleeping beside him, he knew the emotion was only getting bigger every day.

Watching her sleep was one of his favourite things to do. Sometimes he thought his body woke up so early specifically so he could watch her. So he could memorize how she looked while she slept.

The toughest thing about watching her was stopping himself from touching her. With Finn it wasn't a case of familiarity breeding boredom; he wanted her more each time he made love with her. And she didn't seem to complain.

Her breasts rose as she took a deeper breath in her

sleep and she rolled towards him, settling her head deeper into the pillow.

She was beautiful.

Even with her face devoid of make-up and her hair tumbling in untamed lengths over her shoulder and the pillow.

The first night he had watched her sleep he had been fascinated by the expressions she would make; when she would crinkle her nose or a smile would lift the edges of her mouth. Almost as if in slumber she was experiencing things he couldn't see.

The thought that some of those dreams might have him in them made the not touching her even more difficult.

But she was looking tired of late, her workload and the hours they spent making love beginning to catch up on her. So he had to make do with smiling when she smiled. Allowing himself to brush her hair back from her cheek while he wondered what it would take to get her to change her mind about what she could give him.

Because he wanted it all. For the first time in his life he wanted someone to share everything with.

They had everything going for them. Apart from the most amazing physical compatibility, they had a shared sense of humour, an ability to spend time in each other's company without having to make small talk, shared interests in things like films and books. Even the fact that there were differences in their personalities only seemed to add to the package.

It was just the lack of any honest communication that held them apart.

And Shane had no idea how to get past that, communication on something so close to the heart hardly being something he had much experience in.

When her eyes opened a couple of hours later she found him looking down at her with a soft smile on his face. She groaned and closed her eyes again. 'Please tell me I wasn't drooling.'

He laughed. 'I might be flattered if you were.'

Turning her face into the pillow, she chuckled. It was the third time she'd woken up to find him looking at her and each time she'd made a joke about what she feared she'd been doing while he watched.

And at least while they were laughing she wasn't thinking about how it felt to wake up and look straight into his eyes.

Because every morning she did it hurt a little more. And every day she had to smile her way through it, telling herself it didn't mean anything when he smiled at her the way he did. He was just a great guy. She'd always known that. She just hadn't ever thought about how it would feel to be in a relationship with him that was purely based on sex. With emotions constantly buried for survival.

She peeked out from the pillow, her voice muffled. 'How long have you been awake?'

'A while. Not long.' He smiled through the lie.

Her face gradually reappeared. She smoothed her

cheek against the pillow and blinked slowly, smiling back. 'What time does your shift start?'

'I'm filling in for Callum from one. You're on a late start today, right?'

Finn nodded. 'Just before lunchtime.'

His eyes sparkled down at her and she chuckled. So he leaned down and kissed her softly, gently nipping her bottom lip before he lifted his head again. 'How about I bring us some breakfast in bed and then we can take a shower together before you go to work?'

The suggestion woke her body up fully. Would she ever get tired of making love with him? It was a question that had been worrying her of late. Surely the thrill should have been wearing off by now?

'I'll make breakfast. It's my turn.'

'I knew I liked you for a reason.'

Grinning, she stole another quick kiss before she swung her legs off the bed and grabbed his shirt, buttoning it up as she walked barefoot into the hall.

She was still smiling as she closed the door behind her and turned.

To look straight into her brother's stunned face.

The colour drained from her face. '*Eddie*—'

He stared at her for what felt like a lifetime. Then he pointed aimlessly down the hall. 'I came to get a couple of boxes I left behind. I figured everyone was still asleep so…'

Finn swallowed hard as his words faded. 'Eddie—'

He held his palm up, shook his head. 'Don't, Finn. I don't want to hear it.'

'Eddie, wait!' She called his name softly as he turned on his heel and jogged swiftly back down the stairs.

There was really nothing else she could do but follow him, her voice rising more confidently when she was away from Shane's door. 'Damn it, Eddie, wait a minute!'

She was halfway down the stairs, could see his hand on the handle of the front door. Then he turned, glared up at her and marched into the middle of the living room.

Finn followed him, stopping when the sofa was between them. 'I didn't want you to find out like this.'

'Find out what exactly?' He crossed his arms across his chest and continued glaring. 'No, on second thought, don't bother 'cos I already get it.'

She couldn't think what to say.

Eddie's voice rose. 'Are you bloody out of your mind?'

It was certainly a pertinent question. 'Eddie—'

'I mean, how stupid are you? You know Shane! You know what he's like with women and he's a bloody firefighter, for God's sake! You said you would never get involved with one and I said that was good 'cos I'd never let you get involved with one after you explained why!'

'I remember. But this isn't what you think it is.'

Her retort raised the colour in his cheeks. 'Oh, really?'

'Yes, really.' She crossed her arms in a similar way to his and cocked a hip. 'I know what I'm doing.'

She amazed herself by not flinching at the lie.

Eddie's eyes strayed to the stairs behind her, rage flaring as he pointed upwards. 'You better stay the hell away from here while I talk to my sister. I'll deal with you later, *pal*.'

Head snapping round, she found Shane behind her. He'd managed jeans and a T-shirt, which made him less guiltily clothed than her. But the damage was already done.

His blue eyes flickered briefly to hers, then met Eddie's with a steady gaze. 'Leave her be, Eddie. You want to yell at someone, then yell at me.'

Finn managed to keep her voice calm. 'I'm fine, Shane.'

'You're not doing this alone.' He walked slowly down the last few steps.

Eddie laughed cruelly. 'Well, aren't you two just the sweetest thing?'

'I was going to talk to you abou—' Shane started.

But Finn finished, 'But I wouldn't let him.'

'Sneaking around behind my back was much better.'

'We weren't sneaking around to hurt you on purpose.' She focused her attention on Eddie as Shane reached her side. 'Eddie, this isn't some great plot. It just happened, that's all. It's no big deal.'

'Really?' They both spoke in unison.

And Finn didn't know which one of them to look at.

'I think you and me need a bit of a talk before we speak to Eddie.'

The statement made her mind up for her, her face turning towards Shane. 'No, we don't. You know what's happening here; we already talked about it.'

'That was a while ago.'

Eddie gaped. '"A while ago?" How bloody long has this been going on?'

'Nothing's changed.' She looked Shane in the eyes momentarily, then glanced at her brother. 'And not all that long.'

'It was going on when me and Kathy had the party, wasn't it? I thought I saw something then, but I told myself I was being stupid. 'Cos my sister knew better and my best friend wouldn't dare!'

She really couldn't deal with both of them at once. 'Eddie, calm yourself. I'm not a little kid and I can do whatever I want.'

She took a step back from Shane and frowned at him. 'And you needn't bother going over this with me again. We both know exactly where we stand.'

'Do we?'

The question astounded her, her voice rising in slight panic and a tint of anger. 'Yes, we do! This was never going to last long.'

'Oh, well, that's great. Now it's just a quick shag. I feel much better now.'

'Shut up, Eddie.' This time Shane and Finn spoke in unison, not even looking Eddie's way.

Eddie's arms uncrossed and he stepped round the sofa.

Immediately Shane stepped between him and Finn, his shoulders rising as he held a hand to Eddie's chest. In a flash Eddie had the hand thrown off and pushed Shane back.

Finn stepped into the fray, a hand on each of their chests. 'Would you two quit it? This is ridiculous. You're friends, for crying out loud.'

'Not any more, we're not.' Eddie stepped back as he threw the words over her shoulder.

Shane sighed. 'We'll talk about this one alone, Eddie. I know you're spitting. I knew you would be.'

'Yeah, and you know why too. You broke the rules on this, Shane; you're way outta line.'

'I know that.'

'Then why did you do it?'

Finn shook her head. 'He didn't do it alone.'

'I've seen him in action before, don't you forget. I used to live here.'

'And he's hardly the first person I've ever slept with either.'

Eddie looked as if any second he might explode and leave 'goo' on the walls. 'Why *him*, Finn? Why couldn't you just keep on dating those librarian blokes?'

'Right now I wish I had.' She sighed.

'You don't mean that and you know you don't.'

Shane had a small half-smile on his face when she looked at him.

'Don't do that.' With a small sigh she looked back at her brother. 'This has happened and that's that. I can't change it.'

'Would you change it if you could?'

It was a fair enough question. One that she might even have answered in the affirmative up until recently. But not now. Not now she had so many memories of being with him, of what it felt like being with him.

'If it hadn't happened I think I would have spent a long time wondering what it would have been like. And that wouldn't have been healthy. This way it won't screw up any future relationships I have with other librarians.'

She felt Shane tense beneath the hand she still held on his chest. So she let it drop, glancing at his face from the corner of her eye.

He, in turn, stared at her with a stony expression. 'You're planning on there being other librarians, are you?' Tilting his head, he added a sarcastic, 'So soon, my love?'

Her heart twisted painfully. 'Stop it.'

But he continued with a quirk of his eyebrows. 'Anyone in particular in mind?'

'Anyone would be preferable to her staying with you. All you'll end up doing is leaving her high and dry. It's what you know best, after all. Like father, like son, right?'

Finn's eyes widened in shock as Shane's jaw clenched, his hands bunching into fists at his sides as he glared venomously at Eddie. 'Don't go there.'

Eddie ignored the warning, hitting hurt with hurt. 'Or maybe you thought if you slept with Finn you'd be sleeping your way into a happy family?'

Shane swore viciously, took a step forward, 'I get that you're mad with me, Eddie. But you have no idea what happened with Finn and me. And it has nothing to do with my past, so leave it the hell alone.'

Eddie seemed to realize he'd overstepped the mark. His tone changed, anger giving way to coolness. 'I don't want to know what happened, Shane. The damage is done.'

'I know.' His jaw clenched again, his eyes flickering to Finn. 'In more ways than one.'

Finn watched him turn away. Watched him walk back upstairs without so much as a backwards glance. And the urge to follow him was so strong she even felt her body sway forwards.

But Eddie's firm hand on her arm stopped her. 'Leave him be, Finn.'

She turned her head to look at him, recognizing regret on his face. 'What have you just done?'

'Said something I shouldn't.'

'Oh, I got that bit.'

Eddie's gaze became more determined. 'You should never have let this happen.'

With a shaky breath she confessed the truth. 'I couldn't stop it.'

'Bloody hell, Finn.' The words came out on a sigh. 'He's the best mate I ever had.'

'It doesn't have anything to do with you and him.'

'Yes, it does. You just don't get it, do you? He broke one of the biggest rules. All the guys know it. Everyone *knows* not to break it. You don't sleep around with a sister of a mate and you don't sleep around with a mate's ex. It makes for bad feeling and that messes things up in work.'

When she frowned at his reasoning he added, 'And the brigade is all the family Shane has. It means more to him than anything else ever could.'

Finn blinked at him with wide eyes. She'd known the service was a family for all of them, but—

'And how could *you* do it, Finn? You, the one who still makes me call you after every shift? The one who, of all of us, has never got over what happened to Dad? What are you, some kind of *masochist*?' He shook his head. 'I just don't get this at all.'

Neither did Finn. That was just the problem.

CHAPTER THIRTEEN

FINN was on the end of his bed when Shane came out of the shower. She was still dressed in his shirt.

The hand that had been rubbing a towel through his hair stilled and he stared at her pale face. 'Eddie didn't throw you over his shoulder and take you off somewhere safe, then?'

'I wouldn't let him.'

He swallowed. 'Maybe you should have.'

'He's sorry about what he said, you know.'

Shane shrugged and continued rubbing his hair vigorously as he walked to his wardrobe. 'People say things when they're angry. I'll survive.'

'Why didn't you ever tell me about your father?'

'It never came up in a game of truths.' He threw the towel on the ground and yanked open the wardrobe door.

'When did he leave?'

'It doesn't matter when he left; he just did.'

'Eddie says that's the reason the brigade is so important to you.'

'Eddie needs to stop watching Oprah.'

'Is it why you've never had a serious relationship?'

'What difference does it make to you? You're the one doing the walking this time, not me.'

Finn watched as he yanked a brigade shirt from the wardrobe and draped it over his shoulders. Even before she'd heard her brother throw the new information into the argument downstairs she'd known that they had hit the end of the road. The very fact that Eddie had reacted the way he had, with both of them, and the fact that he had then pointed out all the truths to her, had pretty much been the clincher.

It had always been her who was going to walk away. She had known that from the start, even while she'd known that if she'd taken a chance and stayed Shane would eventually have been the one to walk.

By walking first, Finn had told herself she still had control over *something*. So why was it so hard to take the steps when a path opened up?

Shane glanced over his shoulder. 'If you need a few more days here I can stay at the station.'

'Kathy bought a sofa bed, apparently.'

He looked away. 'That's handy. Shame she didn't buy it a bit earlier.'

The flippant statement hurt. He didn't mean it, but he had to know it would hurt. 'Yeah, well, hindsight is a great thing.'

'Your house insurance should be through soon anyway.' Keeping his back to her, he moved to a drawer and pulled out a pair of familiar white boxers, hauling them up under his towel. Discarding the towel, he then moved back to the wardrobe. 'Eddie and Kathy won't mind you there 'til you find a new place.'

'I'm going to Mum's for Christmas soon.'

'Send her my love.'

Finn swallowed hard, nodded at his back. 'I will.'

'Tell her I'm sorry I won't be making it down there for Christmas dinner this year.'

It was a massive thing. Ever since he'd met Eddie at the brigade training centre he'd been dragged along for Christmas dinner. He only ever stayed the one day but Finn's mum loved it when he was there, heaping his plate with food and showering him with socks and ridiculous winter sweaters just as she did with her other three 'boys'.

For him not to be there would be like missing a member of the family. It wouldn't just be Finn that would feel his absence.

'Shane—' Her voice shook on his name.

'It's probably not a good idea to have me and Eddie slugging it out across the dinner table. This'll just take a wee while to blow over, is all.' He pulled on dark trousers and turned to face her as he zipped them up, tucking his shirt in. 'Maybe next year, eh?'

She didn't know what she expected to see on his

face when he turned around. Or what she hoped to see. But she didn't expect him to be so very calm.

He blinked slowly at her, his eyes giving nothing away, not a hint of emotion, before he walked back to his dresser and lifted a comb. Looking briefly at her reflection in the mirror, he stroked his spiking hair into place.

'I'm gonna head into work early. Maybe see if I can catch Eddie for a talk later before he sets the rest of the hounds on me.'

'He told me about the rule.'

'Mmm.' He nodded.

'And even when what those guys think matters to you so much you still took a chance?'

He smiled a small smile at her reflection. 'Well, you can try explainin' it to a little kid, but they don't really get that fire burns 'til they stick their hand in it. Do they?'

She suddenly had a hundred questions she wanted to ask him. A hundred things her heart wanted her to know.

But he set the comb back in place and turned to look at her face again. 'This will all blow over; don't worry about it. It just needs a bit of time. Really.'

Out of the hundred the one that jumped straight to the front of her mind was, 'Do you want me to stay?' If he'd asked her to she doubted she'd have been able to leave. Not this way anyway.

'Shane—'

'I better go. And you'll be late for work if you don't get a move on.' He smiled another small smile and turned to leave the room.

Then he stopped in the hallway, his back to her as he spoke in a husky voice. 'All the best with the next librarian, babe.'

Finn stayed on the end of his bed, still wearing the shirt that surrounded her in his scent. She sat there for a long time as the silence of the house surrounded her.

Then she dropped her head into her hands and cried until she had no more tears to shed.

The one thing she'd had right was how much it would hurt when she lost him. Not that there was much comfort in knowing she'd been right about the one thing.

The whole thing sucked. Big time.

'We'll get the spare room cleared out for you as soon as we can.' Kathy smiled as she set out bedclothes for the sofa bed. 'If I'd known you were coming I'd have got Eddie to do it sooner.'

'Don't worry about it. It's not like anyone could have seen this one coming.'

Kathy hesitated. Then she sat down on the edge of the sofa beside Finn. She seemed to wrestle with the idea of saying something and Finn felt for her. They really didn't know each other well enough to have a deep conversation.

'It's okay; you don't have to give me a shoulder to cry on. I'm fine.'

Kathy studied her face. 'Are you sure? You don't look fine to me.'

Actually she couldn't remember the last time she'd really been *fine*. She'd used the word plenty of late, but had never meant it when she'd said it.

Swallowing a thick lump in her throat, she looked down at her hands, twining her fingers in and out of each other. 'I'm just having a rough couple of months, I guess.' She smiled a weak smile. 'They say bad things come in threes don't they? I s'pose that means I've still got one to go. That's something to look forward to, right?'

'Old wives' tale. Don't you believe it.'

'You just wait and see. I'm on a roll…'

Kathy smiled. 'Look, don't worry about Eddie. He'll calm down after a bit. I think he's just annoyed he didn't see it coming. He would never have let Shane hurt you like this.'

Finn's eyes widened at the statement, her head turning to look at Kathy's face. 'You think Shane hurt me?' She blinked in surprise as Kathy nodded. 'Kathy, Shane didn't make this mess. *I* did.'

'I don't understand. Eddie says that Shane never stays with anyone, he's the love-'em-and-leave-'em type, 'cos of the way his dad was when he was growing up.'

Oh, come on! Was she the *only* one that didn't

know about Shane's past? Even Kathy, who had barely known him five minutes, seemed to know more than she did. Thanks to Eddie, no doubt.

Eddie, who could have mentioned it to his *own sister* at some point.

Finn shook her head. 'It was me that ended it. Or, more to the point, it was me that wouldn't let it be serious in the first place. I swore I wouldn't get that deeply involved with him and he knew that.'

'Well, maybe it suited him that way. No strings.'

Finn shook her head again, a frown of concentration on her face. 'I don't think so. He kept arguing with me about it, saying that I was using excuses.'

'And what *was* your excuse?'

'It wasn't an excuse!'

'I'm sorry.' Kathy looked even more uncomfortable than she had when she'd sat down. 'I didn't mean to suggest—'

'No, don't. I'm sorry.' She reached a hand across and squeezed one of Kathy's. 'I shouldn't have snapped at you; it's not your fault.'

Another hand rose to enclose Finn's as Kathy leaned her head in closer. 'Don't worry about it.'

'I'm just a bit messed up right now.' She flashed another small smile. 'Though if you didn't tell Eddie that it would be helpful.'

'You tell me not to tell him and I won't. Promise.'

'Thanks.' For the twentieth time since she'd first met her, Finn was struck by how lucky her brother had got with Kathy. She really was very lovely. And thoughtful. And she'd not only fallen for her dopey brother, she'd fallen for her dopey brother *the firefighter.*

Finn suddenly wondered how she felt about that part. Did he have to make two phone calls after every shift now? Or was his coming home enough for Kathy?

But then maybe Kathy just didn't know any better?

Finn didn't ask.

Having already messed up two relationships in one day she wasn't keen to try for a third. 'I appreciate it.'

'No problem.' And with a final squeeze of Finn's hand she stood up and walked away. 'There are more blankets in the hot press if you get cold. Those big windows to the balcony can let a bit of a chill in on cold nights.'

'Thanks, Kathy. 'Night.'

''Night.'

For a while she pondered over the question of extra blankets. Cold December nights hadn't been an issue for a couple of weeks. Because she'd had Shane's large body wrapped around hers to keep her warm. Shane's long arm around her waist to hold her close. Shane's steady breathing to lull her to sleep in the first place.

She really hadn't a hope in hell of sleeping, had she?

Which meant she had thinking time.

Easing back until she was fully supported by the sofa, she focused her gaze on the curtains and let a list of queries form.

There was a lot of new information now. Like the fact that Shane's 'love 'em and leave 'em reputation' probably did stem from his past experiences. What age had he been when his father had left? Had he felt it as deeply as she'd felt the loss of her own father? Had he ever seen him again?

Finn had always assumed that *both* his parents were dead.

But if his lack of commitment was so deeply ingrained, why had he been so determined to persuade her he wasn't going anywhere?

She'd been on the money when it came to his leaving the fire brigade. Realistically she had used it only as a delaying tactic. But although she had known he wouldn't leave, she hadn't known the full reason why.

Or had she, deep down?

She had always known the bond that existed in the service, the common memories of experiences that no one outside their group could ever understand. But she hadn't known that to Shane they were almost a substitute family, one he knew he could rely upon to always be there and so trusted himself to be bonded to. He would never, ever give that up. For any woman, would he?

But if that was the case, then why had he been prepared to risk testing that bond by breaking some stupid rule that apparently they all considered written in stone?

The man was a set of contradictions. He said so

little about the things that really mattered, but would make love to her with the skill and generosity of a lover who truly cared about pleasuring his mate before himself.

And as for the times when she had woken up and found him staring at her with that gentle smile on his face and softness in his eyes that practically said—

Finn sat bolt upright on the sofa, her eyes wide and her heart thumping so loudly in her chest that she could hear it in her ears.

He couldn't, could he?

Not Shane Dwyer, the love-'em-and-leave-'em guy! And it would be so much better if he didn't really, right? Because that wasn't what she wanted, was it?

Finn's breathing sped up.

No. It wasn't as if she would want him to be. Because, well, if he was, then that meant that when she left him she'd have really hurt him.

He hadn't looked hurt. He'd looked resigned.

Yes, that was it, calm and resigned. He hadn't looked as if she'd just stomped all over his heart with her size six feet.

Her breathing continued to come in quick, ragged breaths, and suddenly the room really wasn't all that cold. She flapped a hand in front of her face.

But if he really was hurting *would* he have shown her? After all, she'd made it plain from the start that she wasn't interested in getting that involved. And she'd meant it.

Yes, she had!

She'd meant it because she couldn't face the possibility of losing him. And she'd been right about that. Because she really couldn't. Even though she'd just, well, let him *be* lost to her.

But at least that had been her choice, *right*? She couldn't change her own past any more than she could change his. That was just the way things were.

The way she felt was deeply ingrained, was an imprint on her that had been present for most of her life. She really couldn't wait at home for him every day and eat herself up inside. *Waiting*.

She wasn't strong enough for that. Much as she'd like to be. But with her luck—

She'd just set her own house on fire, for crying out loud!

And if she wasn't strong enough to get over the fear of losing him, to take a chance on caring about someone *that* much…

Well, then realistically she didn't deserve him.

He deserved more than her just letting him go without a full explanation, though. He deserved an understanding of how she felt and why it was better for them to leave it be. Because if he *felt*—

Well, if he felt anything and she'd hurt him then he deserved to know that it wasn't just him that felt that way and it wasn't just him that was hurting.

They both needed a better form of closure than she'd left them with.

With the decision made, she moved swiftly, hauling on clothes over the top of her pyjamas and slipping trainers onto her feet.

She needed to see him.

CHAPTER FOURTEEN

SHANE had never actually been in his own house on his own before. Funny how he'd never thought about it.

It was only when the place was empty and he hadn't even the energy to switch on the TV for background noise that he noticed.

It was silent.

For someone who worked in an environment full of noise and people it was a shock to the system. And, worse still, it meant his mind had peace and quiet to think in.

But when all thinking did was lead him round and round in circles and back to the same damn subject every time, he had enough of silence.

So he marched to the stereo and put on some good, old-fashioned, angry rock music.

Which meant, coming back out of the kitchen with a beer, he was caught off guard to find Finn standing at the doorway staring at him. Off guard because he hadn't expected to see her and off guard because, quite simply, he hadn't heard her come in.

She looked nervous as hell.

What was she doing back?

For a brief second he was so pleased to see her he didn't care what had brought her back. But he'd been walking round with an ache in his chest all afternoon and the fact that seeing her reminded him of it made him angry.

So he scowled at her. 'You leave some stuff behind?'

Finn had to raise her voice to the same yell level as his, 'No. I came to talk to you.'

'We don't have anything to talk about.'

'Yes!' With a sigh she stepped over to the stereo and turned the volume down, adjusting her voice level to something more civilized. '*We do*. We can't just leave this the way it is.'

'As in over, you mean?'

'As in, the *way* that it ended. I need you to talk to me, really talk to me.'

Shane could see the plea in her eyes from way across the room. 'To make you feel better about it?' He waved a nonchalant hand in the air. 'Forget about it.'

'I can't.'

'Oh, no, you don't.' He suddenly got what she was doing. 'You're here to do some female "understanding what happened thing", right? You were the one who always said it wouldn't last, remember?'

'I remember. And I remember you being the one to push for me to try. Why did you do that?'

'Nope.' He shook his head. 'You're not sucking me into a post-mortem, Finn. Leave it be.'

Still watching her with a cold gaze, he saw how her throat convulsed as she swallowed, saw how she blinked hard while she thought what to say next.

So he saved her the bother. 'What do you want me to say to you? That I'm sorry it ended like this? I'm sorry. It's messy right now and we both know it.'

'But why—?'

'Leave it be. I mean it.' Looking at her was getting to be tough, so he let his eyes stray to the sofa. 'I've done plenty of post-mortems before this and they don't make a blind bit of difference.'

She waited until he was sitting down, his back to her as he put his long legs up on the coffee-table.

'You're angry at me.'

'What does it matter now whether I am or not?'

A frustrated sound escaped her throat and she walked round so she could see his face. 'It matters to me.'

'Why?'

'Because I can't live with knowing I hurt you by not trying more.'

His laughter was bitter. 'Oh, good. This is a sympathy visit, then.'

'Don't be ridiculous!'

'I'm not being ridiculous. You've come over here

to make sure that poor wee Shane, the commitment-
phobic bloke, isn't all torn up that the first relationship he fancied having a go at went pear-shaped.
And took a big chunk of the rest of his life with it.'

He was tired of sitting, and tired of trying to
pretend that everything he'd just said wasn't true. So
he stood up, thumped his beer bottle down on the
coffee-table and towered over her, leaning his face
close to hers. 'Go home, Finn.'

Finn merely raised her chin and looked at him
with glittering eyes.

And Shane's heart cracked open in his chest.

'Maybe you didn't come over here to talk at all.'
He seized hold of her arm and tilted his face closer,
his mouth hovering over hers. 'Maybe you came for
a different goodbye.'

'You son-of-a—'

His mouth silenced her with a hard, angry kiss.
Finn struggled, tried to pull back from his searing
lips, but he merely raised his other hand to the back
of her head and held her in place. She tried using her
free hand to push him away, but he pulled her closer.

It was only when she met anger with anger, kissed
him back with equal force, that he tore his mouth
from hers, his blue eyes glinting dangerously as he
spoke in a hoarse whisper.

''Cos this is what we do best, isn't it? This is the only
time that you forget what I am and let yourself go.'

'There's more to it than this.'

'But not enough for you to stay.'

Her breasts heaving against his chest, her eyes fixed on his, she let the confession of a lifetime out. Because there was only one truth left really. Now that she'd seen him again, kissed him again. 'I love you, Shane. That's why I can't stay.'

His breath caught. Staring for a long, silent while, he eventually answered her. 'If you loved me you wouldn't want to leave.'

'If I stayed I'd end up hating you.' She fought her way through tears. She was *so* not going to let herself cry. 'I'd try to be strong; I would. But every time you went out that door I'd be scared stupid. And even if you came home every time I'd have eaten a little piece of myself away worrying. Until I was so eaten up that I didn't feel anything any more. And I'd hate you for that one day.'

Untwisting her arm from behind her back, he asked her in a low voice, 'Was it that bad? When your dad died?'

'Yes.' A harsh sob caught in her throat as she looked away from the softness in his eyes.

She found herself studying the epaulette on his shirt, then her eyes dropped down to the 'Dublin City Fire Brigade' emblazoned in red letters on one side of his chest. 'He was my hero when I was a kid. A big giant of a man who came home every day in a shirt the same as the one you're wearing right now. And everything about him just seemed so big and brave to me.'

The hand on the back of her head eased, began a soothing caress on her scalp, and he felt her lean back into it.

'It was my mum who was the strict one, the one who laid down the law and forced us to do the things we didn't want to do. But when my dad came home the house changed. It got filled up with laughter and fun.' She smiled through the tears that streaked down her face.

'He used to lift me up and swing me. Every time he came home. He would lift me up and swing me round and round 'til I was dizzy and squealing. So I used to wait by the front door when I knew he was coming home, so I was the first one that saw him.'

Shane watched as her hand rose and her forefinger traced the lettering on his shirt.

'I was at the door when the men came in their dress uniforms. I can remember looking past them for my daddy. But he wasn't there. And when my mum came to the front door she started to cry before they even spoke.'

When her voice broke on the last words Shane couldn't bear it. He hauled her into his arms and held her close, feeling her pain as if it were his own. Hurting simply because she hurt.

'I didn't know what was happening. I remember Conor trying to take me out of the room. But I wouldn't go. And the men said all these things like how great a firefighter he was and how he'd been very brave and what a loss it was for everyone. And I still didn't understand. Then there were people all over the house, making cups of tea and talking in low voices. And I still didn't get it.' She let large tears soak his chest, her chin resting against the lettering.

'And I waited by the door. I waited by the door for him to come home and swing me. And he never came.'

Shane felt his breathing growing ragged beneath her cheek. He was glad she was telling him all of it. That she cared enough about him to want him to hear it. But while she shook against his body and the emotion was so raw in her voice it brought back memories of his own.

Made him think about the feelings he'd never shared with anyone else. Not so openly and honestly.

'I watched my mum disappear for a long while. I guess I was too young for her to talk to, but I wasn't so young that I didn't notice how she would cry when she didn't think we could hear her. Then she stopped crying and she went quiet and that was worse. It took a long time for the house to stop being quiet.'

Her breathing steadied and Shane felt her fighting for control.

'As I got older I understood better what she'd lost. And hurting the way I did I could only imagine how bad it was for her. I just *can't,* I just can't do that. Not when I already know what it will feel like. I'm not strong enough. And you deserve better than that.'

Then she stopped talking.

Shane held her for a long while, blinking as he stared into the middle distance. It would be easy to let the words out and tell her how he felt about her in that moment. But while he held her he knew that loving her as he did meant wanting what was best for her. He couldn't give her a written guarantee that nothing bad would ever happen to him, could he?

And knowing now how much she had been hurt he couldn't put her through the same thing again. It would be selfish, wouldn't it?

He cleared his throat. 'You're strong Finn McNeill. If you weren't you wouldn't have come over here to tell me all this so that I understood.'

'I couldn't let go without you knowing.'

Long arms squeezed around her. 'Knowing doesn't make it any easier to let you go.' He leaned his head down against hers, buried his face in her hair to mumble, 'I can't change who I am.'

'I wouldn't let you try.' It wouldn't be who he was. And if he wasn't who he was she might not love him so much.

Pressing a kiss against her hair, he rested his cheek against her head for a moment before she tilted it back to look up at him.

Summoning every ounce of self-control he had, he smiled at her. 'So, here we are, then.'

She smiled a sad smile in response to the low words.

Loosening his arms, he leaned back to make enough room to bring his hands up. He framed her face, his thumbs touching the edges of her swollen lips. Then he leaned closer, looking into her eyes.

'I'm not good with words, Finn, you know that. Not the important kind anyway. So I'll just do this my way.'

Finn held her breath while his head descended, his eyes not closing as his mouth settled on hers. Unlike the previous angry kiss that had been searing and possessive, this one started out like a whisper.

And it tore at her aching heart.

She moaned softly, brought her hands to his face in a mirror of his, with her thumbs touching the corners of his mouth. And she kissed him back equally softly, tracing the shape of his mouth from thumb to thumb and back again.

His thumbs moved, joining his fingertips in a slow, sensual tracing of the contours of her face. Up to her temples, over the curves of her eyebrows, sweeping over her eyelids to close them. Down over her cheekbones, lingering again on the edges of her mouth and then over the line of her jaw where it tilted up towards his face.

She let her hands move from his face to his chest, where she flattened her palms so she could feel his heart beating. She sighed against his lips, her head tilting back as he moved from her mouth to her jaw, from her jaw to the length of her neck, lingering on the pulse that beat at its base.

'*Shane.*'

'Yes.' The word was a whisper against her skin.

'Make love to me.'

His head lifted and he took her hand without saying a word, led her towards the stairs.

In his room he took his time, kissing every inch of skin he uncovered as he undressed her while he allowed her to take her time undressing him. Then, clothes in two piles on the wooden floor, he eased her back on the bed so slowly it was almost as if she were floating.

Of all the times they'd made love before, to Finn it was the most agonizing. Every touch, every kiss, every caress was a goodbye.

And happening so slowly it was excruciatingly painful to her heart.

He hadn't said the words to her. But skilful as she'd already known he was before, he'd never made love to her with such sweetness. He spent what felt like hours on her breasts, tracing their shape with gentle fingers, suckling on her turgid nipples until they ached.

When she tried to give the same attention to him, he merely pushed her back into the soft mattress and continued to caress her.

When she tried to reach between their bodies for the hard length of him, he tilted his hips and pressed himself closer to her side.

And all the while he kissed and licked and suckled so that by the time he pressed a long finger between her thighs she was wet and ready.

In the brief second it took for him to reach for protection she fixed her eyes on his. As she had when they'd made love for the first time. And she kept them fixed when he came back to her, when his fingers coaxed her legs wide and he settled into her body with deliberate slowness.

Finn knew in the moment that his pelvis hit hers, when he was buried as deep as he could go, that she would never make love with anyone else and feel such a soul-deep connection.

She loved him that much.

By the time he was moving with her, her hips rising to meet each thrust, tears were seeping from the corners of her eyes and onto the pillow. And when her body had clamped around his and she could hear her blood roaring in her ears she was weeping.

His body went tight, the muscles in his back bunching beneath her hands and he groaned, long and loud. Then he dropped onto her, his body spent.

And with his head buried in the curve of her neck he held onto her, whispering words she couldn't hear. But she didn't need to hear them to know what he was saying.

CHAPTER FIFTEEN

SHANE'S first meeting with Eddie was every bit as rough as he'd expected it would be. It took a few days with their shift pattern, and he had been hoping it would happen before the first shift they had together. Because it wouldn't make for much of a working relationship otherwise, and he really didn't want the pair of them hauled in front of the O.I.C. to explain the problem.

So when he finished a fifteen-hour night shift he wasn't completely surprised to see Eddie in the locker room.

But, prepared as he'd thought he would be, he hesitated nevertheless.

He had wanted his wits about him when they talked. And truth be told, he was wrecked. He hadn't slept much the last few nights and it had been a long shift.

Eddie's head rose and their eyes clashed across the room.

When he didn't get up off the bench Shane braved a few steps closer. 'We need to talk, mate.'

'I have nothing to say to you.'

'Well, you can listen, then.'

He laughed harshly. 'The hell I will.'

Shane watched as he stood up, shoved his trainers into his locker and slammed the door shut with more force than necessary.

'You'll listen, Eddie. 'Cos at the end of the day we have to work together and we need to talk about this to be able to do that.'

'I can make sure I'm never on a shift with you again.'

'Don't be daft. It'll happen some time.'

Eddie glared at him, seeming to wrestle with what he was saying, and then leaned his face closer to Shane's to spit out, 'You should never have touched her!'

'Eddie—'

'There are dozens of women out there you could have had, and have done!'

Shane sighed. 'Nice and all as it would be for me to be the stud you *think* I am, it's not actually all that many. And it hasn't been *any* for a long while.'

'So in a drought you decided to sleep with my sister?'

He scowled at Eddie's reasoning. 'Don't be so ridiculous! You think if all it was was a quick roll that I'd have picked *Finn* to have it with?'

Two firefighters for the morning shift froze in the doorway at the sound of raised voices. 'What's going on?'

Eddie pointed at them. 'Get out.'

Shane glanced over at them and said in a calmer voice, 'Give us a minute, would you, lads?'

When they were gone he turned back to Eddie, just as Eddie swung for him. Shane dodged, grabbed his arm and shoved him back against the lockers. 'Damn it, Eddie, knock it off! I'm not gonna have a fight with you.'

Eddie swore viciously and fought to get off the lockers.

With them pretty much of equal height and build it took a few minutes of ungraceful struggling before Shane had him stilled, his forearm over Eddie's shoulders to hold him still.

'Bloody hell, Eddie, stop a minute and listen. This wasn't just some quick shag! I *love* her.'

Eyes wide, Eddie froze. 'You *what*?'

Shane's hold loosened, his voice flat. 'You heard me.'

It took a long, tense moment of determined staring before Eddie realized he was telling the truth. And Shane knew him well enough to know when he knew.

So he let go and stepped back, sitting down on the bench facing him.

Eddie straightened his uniform, his eyes still on Shane's face, 'You love her?'

Shane nodded slowly, his tongue pushing against the inside of his bottom lip.

'This is serious, then?' Eddie shook his head, running both hands over his hair while he looked around the small room. 'What am I saying? This is you. It's serious if *you're* saying *that*.'

'It *was* serious. It's over. I just couldn't have you not knowing it meant something.'

All too familiar green eyes settled back on his face, 'It's over? For sure?'

Another slow nod.

Quirking his brows in surprise, Eddie turned round and sat down beside him. In a synchronicity borne of familiarity they both leaned forward and rested their forearms on their thighs.

Eddie took a breath. 'What happened?'

Shane shrugged. 'She didn't want to be involved with a firefighter. It was too much for her after your dad.'

'Yeah, I know about that. I have to call her every time I finish a shift so she knows I'm in one piece. That's a lot of calls over the years.'

Shane glanced at him in surprise. He'd just thought it was something they did because they were close. 'You never told me that.'

'Yeah, well, we don't talk about it that much. She broke down not long after I told her I was going in for the training. We talked all night and the only thing I could do was promise her the calls if she promised to remember what a charmed life I lead. I've never so much as broken a bone and that was a miracle itself in our house. Conor and Niall could be right so-and-so's. And as for Finn. Well, you've seen the running disaster her life can be.'

'Phone calls won't do it this time.'

'I don't think they would. It's a real big deal for her, you know, especially with her luck.'

'I know.' He looked down at the floor. 'Now.'

Eddie studied the top of his head. 'It would have to be equally as big a deal for her to get involved with you.'

'Yeah.'

'And you just let her go?'

He didn't answer.

'Well, then you're a fool.'

Shane's face turned in his direction. 'You don't want me involved with her. It wasn't my style, re-member? Like father like son…'

Eddie grimaced. 'Okay, that one was uncalled for. I'm sorry about that. If you'd just sat down and talked to me I might not have been such a nutter about it when I found out. It was the fact the two of you did it all Secret Service style that I had the biggest problem with.' He sighed, thought for a moment.

'But that was before I knew all this stuff. If Finn got that involved with you knowing what you do for a living, then it's as serious for her as it is for you. And that's a whole other story.'

'Was.'

He glanced at Shane from the corner of his eye. 'I have to say I'm disappointed in you, Shane.'

Shane sighed. 'Great. I think I liked it better when you hated my guts.'

'No, c'mon, now. You've gone all this time without a serious relationship and now that you go and fall for my *sister*, you just let her wander off?' He made little walking legs in the air with his fingers. 'I thought you had more fight than that.'

Shane stared in disgust as the walking fingers came back to dangle off Eddie's knees. Then he sighed and rubbed his hands over his face. 'I need more sleep before I have the rest of this talk.'

'Tough.'

'Look, Eddie, I've had a really rubbish couple of days and the only way I've got through them is by telling myself I'll find a way round this. I just haven't found it yet.'

'Well, then, tell your uncle Eddie what you've come up with so far and with my insider info we'll work it out between us.'

Shane smiled a lopsided smile. 'Not this time.'

'Aw, c'mon. How many choices have you come up with on your own?'

'How about a choice between Finn and the fire brigade?'

Eddie swore again.

'Exactly. I understand why she feels the way she does, the history behind it. And I can't give her up, Eddie. But I just don't know that I can give this up either. It's not like I'm built for a desk job.'

'You'd look like you were sittin' at one of those wee desks you get in primary school.'

Shane laughed.

'So, what you gonna do?'

He dropped his head again. 'Dunno yet. But I'll figure something out.'

They sat in silence for a while. Then Shane turned his head and asked, 'So, are we good again, you and me?'

Eddie pursed his mouth. 'I still owe you a good swing for going behind my back. That stung, pal.'

Shane mimicked the pursing. Waiting.

'But we've been friends a long while. Longer than you've been in love with my sister, and I guess that counts for something.' He took a long breath. 'Tell you what: just sort it out with her, do it right, and we'll forget about the way it happened. Okay?'

'Okay with me.'

It was the second worst Christmas she'd ever had. She'd made it through the couple of days running up to it by working every hour that had needed work done and had consequently been so exhausted she had almost fallen onto Kathy's sofa bed at night.

But that hadn't stopped her bad dream from coming back with monotonous regularity. It occurred to her that she hadn't had it the entire time she'd been sharing a bed with Shane. Which was a tad ironic.

She truly resented everything about that dream

now. All right, so a shrink could probably have made money out of interpreting it for her, but it didn't really take a genius.

All it was was her obsession with firefighters getting hurt. Her subconscious mind's way of keeping her on track.

While her conscious mind spent every waking moment obsessing about the one firefighter she missed so much it was like having had a limb removed. Without an anaesthetic.

The only saving grace had been that she'd managed to avoid her brother while she'd been so busy with everything else.

Unfortunately that meant she ended up with him staring at her all the way through Christmas dinner. Which annoyed her so much that by the time the heavy fruit pudding was being handed around she lifted her eyebrows and challenged him outright to say something.

'Quiet round here without Shane, isn't it, Mam?'

Finn wanted to kill him.

'It's a shame he couldn't make it. I'll have to send him up a plate.'

'Finn could drop it in when she gets back to Dublin, couldn't you, Finn?'

Finn glared.

'Take his presents as well, pet.' Her mother patted her shoulder on the way past. 'I got him a lovely Aran sweater this year and big long thermal socks.'

She took a deep breath and prayed for Easter to come.

There was no point in trying to leave the table to hide in her old room, because her mother would come and find her. And there was no point in arguing with Eddie because her mother would want to know what it was about.

So she just sat still and said nothing.

Somehow she got through the rest of the day. She even told herself she'd done a pretty good job of smiling when she was supposed to smile and talking when she was spoken to. Though for the first time in her life she was deeply relieved when her brothers and their partners started to leave.

She stood in the hallway, swept along in the madness of them all going. Then Eddie stood in front of her with the same studious look on his face.

With a bright smile pinned to her face she said a cheery, 'Bye, Eddie.'

Because she really *was* glad he was going.

He blinked a couple of times and then kissed her on the cheek. 'Tell Shane I said hello.'

Finn sighed as he left.

Her mother closed the door after she'd finished waving and smiled, 'Right, then. You can help me clean up and you can tell me what's wrong.'

'There's nothing wrong.'

'Aye, and I'm the Queen of England.' She linked her arm with her daughter's and steered them into the kitchen. 'You've been quiet as the grave all day long and your brother has been staring at you like you have two heads.'

Sitting at the breakfast bar Finn poured two glasses of wine and gave in to the inevitable with a deep breath. 'Can I ask you a question first?'

'Of course you can.' She smiled encouragingly as she lifted a glass and perched on a matching stool.

'It's about Dad.'

Her face transformed into the wistful smile that she always wore when she talked about her husband. 'Ask away.'

'How did you cope?'

'I coped like everyone copes. I let myself grieve. Then I kept going until it didn't hurt so much any more. It doesn't go away, you know. You just learn to live with it, is all.'

Finn watched as her mother's hands automatically reached for a roll of cling film while she talked. Without breaking her speech, she began wrapping plates of leftovers for the fridge.

So Finn continued, 'I didn't mean after it happened. I meant when he was going to work every day. Weren't you scared for him?'

'Oh, Lord, every day.' She laughed softly. 'I used to drive your dad mad asking about every call they were on.'

Finn blinked at her in silent amazement. 'But how did you not end up torturing yourself over it?'

Her mother's shoulders shrugged. 'I had all of you. You kept me busy most of the time, and the rest of the time I was just happy that he kept coming home. If I'd have let myself think he wasn't coming back every time I couldn't have got through the day.'

'But then he didn't.'

'No.' Her hands stilled. 'No, he didn't and no amount of worrying can prepare you for how that feels. But I had my time with him, sweetheart, and I wouldn't have missed out on that.'

If Finn hadn't been there to witness the aftermath she wouldn't have known just how devastating it was from her mother's synopsis of it. She shook her head slightly in wonder.

'But what about if you'd known what it would feel like beforehand? Would you still have put yourself through it?'

Moira McNeill's astute hazel eyes focused firmly on her daughter's face. 'Now what on earth has you asking something like that?'

She shrugged and looked down at her wineglass. 'We've never talked about it.'

'We've talked about your dad lots before. But you've never asked me that. You know I loved your dad more than life. I still love him.'

'I know.' She aimed a small smile at her, her eyes shimmering. 'Me too. I just need to know, Mum. It's important. If you could go back and do it all again, knowing what you do now, how could you have coped with it?'

'Well, for goodness' sake. If we all worried about the bad things that might happen and forgot about the good we might find we'd never leave the house, would we?'

The reasoning made her feel vaguely infantile. 'It's not as simple as that. If you know the chances of experiencing that much pain exist then it's only natural you would do something to protect yourself against it.'

There was a brief pause. 'Has this got something to do with Shane Dwyer?'

Finn's eyes widened, then narrowed. 'Did Eddie say something to you?'

'No, but if it's something to do with Shane, then it explains why he's not here and why you and Eddie were glaring all the way through dinner.'

Caught. 'All right, it's something to do with Shane.'

Her mother's face transformed. 'Oh, I am pleased! He's such a dish. I had hoped when he was looking at you the way he did last Christmas…'

'Mum!'

'If I was twenty years younger…' She fanned her face with her hand.

'*Mum!*'

'And it must be serious for him to go getting involved with you, what with his family history and all.'

'Oh, for crying out loud! Am I the *only* one that didn't know that about him?'

'He's not much of a talker, that boy.'

'He talked to *you*.' She tilted her head and raised her eyebrows sarcastically.

'Well, yes, but that's different. I'm like an adoptive mother to him. I think it was his third or fourth Christmas here when we got to talking about his mother. And I managed to coax the rest out of him.'

Which was more than Finn had managed. Why was it so very difficult for him to communicate with her on any level other than—?

'I think he carries a lot of that around with him still. It's not easy when your father has another family and ignores his first child completely. Made him wary of getting close to people, I think. But everyone has something they carry about these days, don't they?' She paused.

'Are you telling me you're worried about getting involved with him because of what happened with your dad?'

Finn paused, swallowed down a bubble of emotion and then managed a nod.

'Auch, sweetheart!' Her mother was around the breakfast bar in a flash and had an arm around her shoulders before the first tear had escaped her eyes. 'You can't let what happened to your dad ruin your chance at being happy. Your dad would hate that!'

'I just don't know how to stop it. If anything happened to Shane—'

'Nothing might ever happen to him. And you're a firefighter's girl!' She squeezed her shoulders tight. 'You're made of sterner stuff than that.'

'No, I'm not. There's still a part of me standing by that front door and hoping Dad will come back through it.'

'Oh, goodness, I'd forgotten how you used to do that. He used to swing you so high that sometimes I thought he'd hit your head off the ceiling.' She smiled down at her daughter.

'You were his little girl. He loved his boys, but you were different. I think all men are that way with their wee girls. You wait and see, your Shane will be the same. And unless I'm mistaken, all the more determined to be a good father after what he went through himself.'

The thought of Shane swinging a little dark-haired girl in the air made her catch her breath. It was an achingly beautiful image. Especially for someone who hadn't even considered having children until her biological clock was ticking *really* loudly.

Her shoulders were squeezed again.

Then her mother reached across for a piece of kitchen roll and handed it to her before she sat down on a stool beside her. 'Wait'll I tell you something my darlin'. Your dad would kick you from here to next week if he saw you making yourself sad when you didn't have to. He lived every day the way he wanted to. He loved me, he loved his kids, he loved the men he worked with and what he did. And that made him a very happy man while he was here. You can't ask much more than that.'

Finn blew her nose loudly into the kitchen roll.

'When you love someone it's a risk. It always is. But that's just life. You're the one that has to make the choice to live it.'

She crumpled. She wanted to make that choice, she really, really did. Just how much of a self-destructive idiot was she?

'We should have had a talk like this a long time ago.'

'Yes, we should.'

The arm snaked around her shoulders again. 'That boy needs someone like you in his life as much as you need him. Maybe more. Because he never knew love growing up like you did. If you love him, then you have to take a chance. That's all there is to it.'

Finn sat on the stool in her mother's embrace as the tears dried and she blew her nose again. Why was it that, even as a fully grown independent woman, it still took wise words and a hug from her mother for her to find the courage to believe in herself enough to admit the truth?

It wasn't just losing Shane that scared her. It was her own ability to love someone that much and allow herself to trust the emotion.

She'd probably been in love with him for years. It wasn't him she'd been fighting. It had been herself. Maybe part of loving was letting go of fear and trusting in whatever came next.

CHAPTER SIXTEEN

AFTER three days at her mum's Finn felt as if she'd done months of therapy. She'd always known she had things from her dad's death that she hadn't ever dealt with, or talked through with her mum.

And, ironically, she had the love for another fire-fighter to thank for that breakthrough.

Now all she had to do was figure out what to do about that firefighter.

Because if she was going to try and work on doing away with half a lifetime of being scared, then she was going to need some help. And having convinced him so thoroughly that she wasn't strong enough to stay with him, she was going to have quite a job convincing him that she wasn't strong enough to be without him.

But what she was going to say completely escaped her already exhausted mind. She had to get it right this time. She couldn't keep running to him and then running away. And realistically *he* wasn't one that was good with words either so *one* of them had to get it right when it mattered most.

Maybe she should just make an effort to show him in the way he was good at showing her? Every day. Every day and at least a couple of times a night.

Until he believed her need for him was greater than her fear of losing him.

It was a stinker of a day to make the trip back to Dublin. Of the varying different types of rain available to the connoisseur in Ireland she was driving through the sideways variety. The sideways, hit-the-ground-and-bounce-up-to-get-you-a-second-time variety.

The traffic picked up as she paid through the toll-bridge, dozens of cars vying to get ahead as they streamed back into the lanes of the motorway. And it was getting dark, the heavy rain clouds and sideways rain obscuring any light from the evening sky.

Finn had just allowed her thoughts to stray from Shane long enough to wish she'd left a couple of hours earlier when a car veered in front of her from the fast lane.

She swore, stood on the brakes and felt her car slide on the wet surface.

Her heart caught as the nutcase in front then pulled back out into the fast lane. Right in front of another car.

And after that everything moved into slow motion. Until her ears were filled with the sickening sound of metal hitting metal.

Slow motion could only have been a few minutes.
And then there was silence.

She knew there was silence so that meant, technically, she was aware it was silent. Which meant she
was okay. And after a tentative check on her wriggling
toes and fingers she knew she was still in one piece.

So she looked around her.

She could see headlights pointed the wrong way,
one car on its side. And her immediate instinct was
to get out and help. To try and do what she could for
anyone else who might be hurt. It was an instinctive,
automatic reaction.

Which might have struck her as ironic for someone
who had spent half their life trying to persuade others
to give up doing the same thing, if around about that
moment she hadn't realized she was stuck.

'Oh, gimme a *break* here!'

Shane was on the second appliance called to the
scene. Eddie had been on the first crew and was the
first person he met when they parked up and got out.

'Where do they need us?'

'The paramedics have everyone that needs to be
stabilized looked at.' Eddie's face was grim below his
yellow helmet. 'We're cutting one out down the
bottom now. No fatalities.'

Shane nodded and started forwards only to be
stopped by a gloved hand. He looked back at
Eddie. 'What?'

'Don't panic, okay?'

He felt a bubble of panic. '*Why*?'

'Finn—' It was as far as he got before he had to grip harder. 'She's okay. I've already been over there and she's been checked out.'

Shane yanked his arm again.

'Wait a minute!' Eddie's voice rose above approaching sirens. 'Seriously, *she's fine*! She's a bit bumped up but she's fine. When I got over there the paramedic was trying to chat her up.'

A thunderous look was aimed his way.

Releasing the braced arm, he held his hands up in surrender. 'Not my fault.'

'Where is she?'

'Over by the bridge. Her car is stuck against the pillar. She won't be cut out for a bit 'cos the others take priority.'

But the words were already fading into the distance as Shane took off at the run.

His heart thundered as his eyes found the familiar sight of her car. There were lights set up and in the rain he could see the upward bend in the car's roof, but it was still in one piece and didn't look to be in as bad shape as the one the other crew were working on.

For the first time in his career, Shane ignored those in worse shape, knowing they were being taken care of by others.

He was only concerned with one person.

As he got closer a tall paramedic was stepping

back from the passenger door. Shane's fists bunched as he approached him.

The paramedic stepped towards him, took one look at his face and smiled. 'I guess you're Shane.'

Shane nodded, his eyes on the front of the car.

The man's voice lowered. 'The other firefighter said you might appear. He also said it would be good if I wasn't chatting up your girl when you got here.'

'He was right.' Shane's eyes strayed to him. He gave him the once-over and just as quickly dismissed him. 'How's she doing?'

'She's great—bit bruised, I'd say. Leg is stuck but it's not broken or cut. Her vitals are all fine and she has a sense of humour about her predicament, so I'd say that was a good sign. Just waiting for your guys to get her out now and I'll check her over again to be sure before she goes to the hospital.' He grinned. 'She's a real trooper.'

Shane smiled a small, warmer smile. 'I know. You're sure she's okay?'

'Yep.'

He took a deep breath to steady himself.

Okay. Calm, Shane. She's fine. She's fine and she's stuck there.

Right then. In that case she was getting a talking to. Enough was enough.

Finn had accepted the fact that she wasn't going anywhere. Had finished watching raindrops drifting down her cracked windscreen and was contemplating what other disasters could possibly come her way when there was movement at her passenger door.

Large boots were followed by long legs and finally a huge fluorescent striped jacket appeared beside her.

It couldn't be Eddie, as he'd already been over for a wee visit, so that could only mean…

She looked upwards as the helmet turned her way.

Shane smiled. 'Well, hello.'

With a small, resigned burst of laughter, she shook her head and leaned it back against the head rest. 'Hello.'

'Glad you drive a Volvo now, aren't you?'

'Yes, I most definitely am.'

'You're on a roll at the minute.'

'I did tell Kathy these things come in threes, but she wouldn't listen.'

He turned his head and looked out of her cracked windscreen. 'That's them done now then. You'll be safe to leave the house for another while.'

Finn chanced a glimpse at his profile, so ridiculously glad to see him that everything else seemed to fade into the background against it.

'Hope so. But then seein' as I don't have a house or a car now I might be forced to live on the street for a while.'

'Mmm.'

She watched him purse his mouth in thought, frus-

trated that he seemed so calm. Well, wasn't he just
Mr Professional? She was about to open her mouth
and say as much when—

'You scared me, Finn.' He turned his head and
looked her straight in the eye, his voice stern.
'Locked indoors where I can keep an eye on you
would be the best place for you.'

'I didn't do this on purpose. I was driving along
minding my own business when some moron decided to play dodgems on the motorway!' She had
lifted her head to give out to him, but flumped it
back in frustration, wriggling the toes on her trapped
leg as the paramedic had told her to.

'And now I'm stuck. Just stuck, that's all. In the
words of someone I know: "It's no big deal".'

'Do you hurt anywhere?'

The question stopped her sarcasm dead. And she
blinked a small look of reassurance in his direction,
'The nice paramedic already checked me out.'

'Oh, I *heard*.'

The look on his face made her smile. He was
jealous. Jealous was good. Jealous was fantastically
good. Almost worth getting her car crumpled for.

Though it was an extreme method of getting his
attention.

Shane considered her face for a moment, then
seemed to make a decision. He turned around on the
seat, settling himself so his large body was facing
hers in the intimate space.

'Right, well, if you're fine and you're stuck here for a while, then we're having a bit of a talk.'

Finn's eyes widened. 'You're going to take advantage of my predicament to talk to me? *You*, the amazing talking man who—'

'Finn, *shut up.*'

He said it so firmly, she shut up. Her mouth was a silent 'oh' of surprise.

'I've been working on what I was going to say to you when you got back to Dublin for days now and since you're stuck here you're gonna get it all in one go. So you need to shut up and listen.'

She snapped her mouth shut.

He pulled a glove off one hand and fished in a pocket under his jacket. Then he produced a folded piece of paper and waved it in front of her.

'I did some research to begin with, but it's useless now you're in here.' So he scrumpled it up and threw it out of the open door behind him. Then, pulling his glove back on, he tilted his helmet back on his head. 'So thanks for that. I'll just have to start with this…'

Head still resting on the head rest, but her face turned towards his, her eyes widened as he leaned in and placed a gentle, lingering kiss on her mouth.

Then, his face back a little from hers, he continued. Warm breath fanning her cheeks, he simply said, 'I love you, Finn McNeill.'

In a husky voice that said he meant it.

The world went still. Well, it did for Finn. He'd

said it. He loved her. It was the most amazingly wonderful thing. So this was what it felt like to love and be loved in return. God, it felt *good*.

She blinked hard.

He waggled a gloved finger at her as he leaned back, 'You needn't think for one minute that I'm all that easy to get rid of. That paper—' the glove transformed from a waggling finger into a thumb that jerked back over his shoulder '—had firefighter fatality stats for the last fifty years on it. And they were a pain in the ass to get just so you know. I figured I needed the stats to show you the likelihood of anything happening to me was slim. But seeing as you're here in an R.T.A. it doesn't matter a damn what they say. 'Cos statistically you're more likely to get killed on the roads in this country than I am doing what I do. 'Cos I prepare for my job, every day, and there's no way anyone can prepare for this.'

He paused. 'Now, if I thought for one second you were going to get into this kind of trouble every time you drove a car then there would be no way I'd let you out of the house for the next sixty years. But you know what?'

He didn't wait for an answer. 'A plane could fall on either of our heads tomorrow or a bus could run over us or any of a dozen things. The thing is, the way I see it, you don't spend your whole life waiting for something bad to happen when something as good as us comes along.'

Her blinking got harder.

The gloved finger waggled at her again as he frowned. 'Nah, and don't you dare go lookin' at me like you're gonna cry, 'cos I'm not done.'

'Shane, 'bout ten minutes, okay?'

He yelled back over his shoulder, 'Grand. We're fine in here.'

Finn blinked through moist eyes as he looked back at her.

'Now, where was I? Oh, yeah.' He leaned in again. 'I know that you're scared babe, I do. And I know why. What happened to your dad was the thing that every firefighter hopes will never happen to them. But doing this job isn't just doing a job, it's what I am and if I stopped doing it I'd be selling the both of us short. And, yes, it's probably a bigger deal for me than most, 'cos 'til I had the service I didn't know what it was like to be part of a family like that. A bunch of people who care about you even when you don't ask them to and who take your caring about them in return as a given. *For life.* I've never once felt in the service that I was less important because new family members came along.'

He thought for a split second. 'There *is* some stuff about my family for you to know, and I'll tell you about that as we go along, but I'm on the clock here. It's just a load of stuff about my dad skipping off to a new family and forgetting he had me.'

Finn watched in silence as he shrugged it off, literally. She wouldn't tell him she already knew, she wanted him to tell her in his own words, to share it so that she could hold him as he'd held her when she'd shared painful private memories.

'*So*. Anyway. Here's how I see it. I can't quit the job 'cos it would kill a part of me, and you're getting it all whether you want it or not. Hell, you've already got it. What I can do is make a promise to you to never do anything dumb, which I don't do anyway. I can't stop the very low percentage of accidents that do happen, but then, *obviously*—' the glove rose and waved in the air in front of his body '—neither can you.'

Finn found herself smiling.

He was actually making perfect sense in the same region of perfect sense that had been talked to her by her mother for the last few days. Bless him.

'I can promise you that we'll make every day count. That even when we row we'll have so much fun making up that we'll forget what we rowed about in the first place. That you'll never doubt for a minute that you're it for me, 'cos you are. When you get scared you're gonna say so and I'll hold onto you. And when I get scared—' his dimples flashed '—I'll pretty much do the same thing.'

When her eyebrows rose in disbelief he laughed. 'I have my moments. Five minutes ago being a good example.'

She laughed with him.

Then his voice dropped to a husky level that reminded her of tangled sheets and bodies wrapped around each other. 'No one has any guarantees these days. All I can do is tell you, you'll never have any regrets. I'll make bloody sure of that, trust me.'

There was the sound of voices getting closer to the car.

Shane aimed a glance out the back window. 'They're coming to get you out now, so I'll be quick.'

Finn chuckled.

His blue eyes were almost black again in the dim light but Finn didn't need to see to know there was infinite softness there; she could hear it in his voice. 'Thing is. You've got this impression that I'm some hero type 'cos of what I do. But it's you that's the hero. You got me to believe in something I never knew could happen for me. And now that you've rescued me from a string of useless relationships you're stuck with me. Full stop.'

She could feel her eyes filling again as he looked at her. Could honestly feel as if any second her heart would explode out of her chest.

That would be what happiness felt like, then.

It was like having someone lift her up and swing her round and round, endlessly.

'Say something.'

She waited a long moment. 'For someone who claims they're not much of a talker, you had a lot to say, didn't you?'

He shrugged. 'I've been thinking for a while.'

'Yeah.' She nodded. 'I got that impression.'

'We're gonna take the roof off, Shane.' Callum appeared at the passenger door with a fireproof sheet. Handing it in, he winked at Finn. 'Hey, Finn, how ya doin'? Long time no see.'

'Hi, Callum, you're looking well.'

'Ah, y'see now, nothing quite like a man in uniform.'

Shane shook his head. 'Mind your fingers on that big tin opener, won't you, Callum?'

Finn giggled as he spread the sheet over their heads. 'Aren't you going to get out?'

'Nah. Already told you. You're stuck with me.' He smiled before it went dim under the sheet. As the compressor started up, he raised his voice. 'So, you get all that?'

She moved her head closer and yelled back, 'I got that you love me and sixty years indoors and after that it went a wee bit blurry.'

'Well, so long as you got the important stuff.'

There was a loud creaking as they cut the roof off. Then another, followed by an equally loud sound of metal being bent.

All of which Shane distracted her from by kissing her with a kiss that spoke of heartfelt promises and lost time to be made up for.

When they came out of the sheet, rain was falling on their heads.

The compressor went silent as several firefighters

gathered around to figure out where to safely free the steering column and Finn looked at Shane again.

He turned slowly, silhouetted by emergency lighting, rain falling off his helmet. And he took her breath away.

But not because of the way he looked in his work gear. Because he was Shane, and she loved him. She'd be an idiot not to want to make the most of her time with him. No matter how long that time was. And after everything he'd said, she felt stronger, had more faith in herself and her ability to love and be loved.

As if by loving her he had given her the faith she needed to get past her demons.

Or at least to give them a pretty good run for their money…

He smiled. 'So?'

'So?' She smiled back.

'What's your answer?'

'I wasn't aware you'd asked me a question.'

'I'm sure it was in there somewhere.'

She laughed. 'Maybe you should try asking me again.'

'Now, *babe*, you know I'm not good with words.' His eyes sparkled in the rain. 'Just say yes.'

Reaching out, she took a gloved hand in hers and squeezed. 'I love you.'

'Yeah.' His voice was seduction itself. 'I know.'

They sat and smiled at each other for a while.

Then Shane looked up at the faces around them. 'Right, then—' his voice rose '—any chance of you losers getting my fiancée outta this wreck so I can take her home?'

'Aw, Finn, what you marrying him for?'

'Ah, sure, some women will do anything to get themselves out of a car when they're stuck.'

Shane freed her hand, and pushed himself upright with a curse.

'Do I have to do everything round here? You lot need to read the manual when we get back to the station. I know there's one with pictures somewhere.'

Finn laughed as he stepped onto the bonnet as if he were taking a walk in the park, pushing Callum out of the way. She looked round at the faces that surrounded her while they tossed insults at each other. And finally noticed her brother's face amongst them.

Grinning at her.

Then, with a nod, he winked and handed up some equipment to Shane. 'Get a move on, then, *brother-in-law.*'

For Finn it was the first memory she could store in her heart from the beginning of the rest of her life. She'd taken up enough of her life obsessed with the worst.

And what better way to start all the good stuff than surrounded by the family she'd been born into? She had a feeling her dad would approve…

Though what he'd have had to say about the underwear incident would have been more than her ears would have stood.

Funny how fires had been the one thing she had hated all her life. And yet, in the end, had been the one thing that had given back to her what she'd been missing for half her life.

A great big lump of a firefighter as the centre of her world.

Finn had a feeling she'd definitely come to the end of her run of bad luck. She should have burnt those big pants much, much earlier.

* * * *

Be swept off your feet in California with
Trish Wylie's His L.A. Cinderella.
Available this month from
Mills & Boon® Romance.

The Brazilian's Blackmail Bargain

ABBY GREEN

Abby Green got hooked on Mills & Boon®
romances while still in her teens, when she stumbled across one belonging to her grandmother in
the west of Ireland. After many years of reading
them voraciously, she sat down one day and gave
it a go herself. Happily, after a few failed attempts,
Mills & Boon bought her first manuscript. Abby
works freelance in the film and TV industry, but
thankfully the four a.m. starts and the stresses of
dealing with recalcitrant actors are becoming
more and more infrequent – leaving more time to
write! She loves to hear from readers, and you can
contact her through her website at www.abby-
green.com. She lives and works in Dublin.

Dear Reader,

I first discovered Mills & Boon® romances in a travelling library while spending summer holidays with my grandmother in the west of Ireland. It was the start of a lifelong passion for the rose-emblemed books, culminating very happily in my first sale to the company in 2006.

Reading the books transported me away from my own rain-swept home to exotic locales: hot and tropical jungles; desert islands with white sandy beaches; glamorous buzzing cities. And yet, some of my favourite stories were set in England or Scotland. Mills & Boon managed to incorporate both worlds and make them equally fantastic.

I fell in love with hot-blooded Mediterranean heroes and darkly mysterious sheikhs, and haven't been quite the same since.

It's been an absolute thrill to be able to introduce my own Irish heroines to this heady mix; I hope you enjoy Caleb and Maggie's story.

Best regards,

Abby

PROLOGUE

London, November

MAGGIE HOLLAND stood just on the other side of the revolving door, the late November darkness throwing the glittering lights of the exclusive London hotel into sharp relief. Her heart was in her mouth, legs shaking, hands clammy and a trickle of sweat ran down her back. Her head ached where pins held the thick mass of curls on top of her head and, with a visibly trembling hand, she pulled the too short mac more tightly around her body. The cold wind whistled around her exposed legs but couldn't shock her out of the stupor that seemed to have taken control of her body.

A couple clambered out of a cab on the street just behind her and, in a flurry of doormen, luggage and broken German on the cuttingly cold breeze, she knew she had to move into the lobby just behind the glass or move aside and let them pass.

The stupor passed; reality rushed in. Taking a deep breath, she didn't move aside, much as she wanted to, but pushed the revolving door and stepped into the warm foyer.

She saw him as soon as she walked in. Impossible to miss him; he would draw the eye of anyone with a pulse.

He was standing facing away from her, talking to someone,

so hadn't noted her arrival and she was glad of the respite. A
chance, however flimsy, to gather herself and her exposed
nerves. And a chance to observe him for a moment.

He stood with hands in his pockets, making the material
of his tailored trousers run taut over his behind, drawing attention to a powerful physique that was more like that of an
athlete in his prime than a corporate tycoon worth millions...
some even said billions. A tycoon who had a fearsome reputation as one of the most innovative and powerful in Europe.

Caleb Cameron hadn't existed in her world until two weeks
ago, when she'd met him at her stepfather's house for the first
time. Never an enthusiastic visitor unless requested by her
mother, that had been one of those times when Maggie's mother
had begged her for some support. He had been one of a few
assorted businessmen who in the last two weeks had conducted
intense meetings with her stepfather. And having been there
nearly every day to help her mother hostess, Maggie's every
waking and sleeping thought had quickly become filled with
this dynamic man, and still the disbelief that he could possibly
be interested in *her*. Proof of which was this date tonight.

Her mouth compressed. A date which had been hijacked
for other ends.

Maggie swallowed with difficulty. She couldn't escape what
she had to do. She knew that with an awful fatality. But...surely
he would see through her in a second? She almost hoped he
would. He had a rapier-sharp intellect. And yet *she* was
somehow expected to...no, had been *ordered* to be the one to...
Her mind shut down; she felt sick again and shut her eyes briefly.

All she wanted to do was turn around and walk back out
of the door. But she couldn't. If she didn't go through with
this, the consequences didn't bear thinking about and affected
the one person dearest to her. She had no choice.

'Maggie.'

Her eyes snapped open. How had she not heard him approach? An impression struck her of a large, lethal, graceful jungle cat. She strove for calm, straightening her spine.

'Caleb, I'm sorry. I hope you weren't waiting for too long.'

He skimmed a look up and down, leaving her a little breathless, a broad shoulder lifted negligently. 'A few minutes is a pleasant surprise. I've been kept waiting for longer.'

Somehow Maggie knew *that* was a lie. No woman would keep this man waiting. His penetrating blue gaze held hers captive. She couldn't look away and that familiar boneless feeling permeated her, making her blood slow and throb through her veins. This was the effect he had had on her ever since she'd laid eyes on him. When she'd been innocent of the part she was being primed to play in her stepfather's Machiavellian plans. When she'd been aware of nothing more than Caleb…as a man…not someone who had to be betrayed, ruined…plundered for his wealth.

And now…seduced.

Looking up at him, her mind was scrambled. For a second she could almost fool herself into thinking that what was outside didn't exist. Maybe this really could just be the simple date he'd asked her on…with no agenda. That thought made her breathless with a dangerous excitement. She wasn't aware of the slight ironic smile that touched her lips at her wishful thinking. After tonight she'd never see him again and that made her insides feel hollow.

An icy gleam lit Caleb's eyes for a split second, but then it was gone, replaced with benign politeness. 'Shall we? The dinner table is ready…'

Maggie's heart plummeted. *This was it…no turning back.* 'Fine.'

On wooden legs she preceded him through the foyer to the doors at the other end. She felt as though she was walking to the guillotine. And then, to compound it, the heavy room key in her pocket brushed against her leg. Nausea clawed her stomach again. The key to the room upstairs that had been booked by her stepfather. The scene where the seduction was to take place. He even had his man there somewhere, in the shadows, watching, monitoring proceedings…to make sure one or the other didn't leave too soon. Before the damage could be done.

Dear God. How could she do this?

At the door to the dining room she felt Caleb's fingers on her shoulders. She half turned, acutely aware of the bare scrap of lace she was wearing. The excuse for a dress that *he* had bought for her to wear. She wanted to halt the inevitable slide of the coat from her shoulders even as the *maître d'* came forward to take it. Panic rose. She couldn't do this…she couldn't look. Couldn't bear to see the reaction on Caleb's face when he saw her outfit.

She was wearing a slip. That was all. He'd seen more clothes on a lap dancer. It didn't suit her pale colouring. The rich red hair was pinned up, making his fingers itch to take it down. A curious burning disappointment licked through his veins as he realised that, even in the cheapest outfit, she still had the power to ignite forceful desire in his body. The tingling awareness of which was making itself very apparent. And something else licked through him too. Self-derision. For a brief moment, before he had found out who she was, or what was going on, he had thought… He tried to stop his thoughts going in that direction. But his mind refused to obey.

When he had first met her, something deep and hidden and *unknown* had been touched. He had been shaken out of his usual cynical inertia. She had looked at him that first time with such sweet shyness and had then smiled. That smile had captured self-deprecation at her response, the current of sexual awareness running between them and something so intangible...but so innocently feminine, that he'd felt a lurch of surprise. He was used to women smiling at him, but usually with such blatant calculation that his blood ran cold.

His mouth thinned as he followed her through the dining room; he was aware of the openly admiring glances she was getting, the sexy sway of her hips, and his eyes, like theirs, were drawn to the scrap of lace and silk that was barely decent. To see her tonight, with her intentions so disappointingly *obvious*, he wondered again how he could ever have thought he'd been surprised...or that she wasn't exactly the same as every other woman.

He knew with confident arrogance that she wanted him. She had felt the same immediate impact on first sight—he knew *that*. But she probably turned it on for everyone, no distinction being made.

She was nothing more than a mediocre actress, but yet...and he hated the admission, she'd almost fooled him, got under his guard. He'd never had a lapse in his attention before now, keeping corporations going in every major city from Tokyo to London. He knew the minutiae of every single one of them, his control legendary and fear-inducing among his competition. A skill that would not let *her* or her family undermine that control, even now, when they thought they had him. The fools.

He focused on the facts.

She was here to take him to bed, to seduce him and distract him. To act as the honey trap. One of the oldest tricks in the book. If he wasn't mistaken, he was sure he'd seen the distinctive shape of a key in her pocket as he'd taken her coat. Was it a key to a hotel room there? The disgust rose like bile.

But two could play at that game; he was here to seduce her too. A little luxury he was affording himself, the spoils of war. Because this was war. Since he'd felt that punch to his gut on first sight, had then discovered what their little game was, the way she'd so blatantly been put on display for him…he'd been determined to sample what was on offer.

They reached the table.

Maggie walked to the other side and faced him with a look of almost, for a fleeting moment…*unbelievable* trepidation on her face. He mentally shook his head. Hell, she was good. He'd never seen anything like the level of her guile. He reasserted his cool mental clarity, ignored the ache in his loins. The slow burning fire that *would* be sated.

She would soon know just how dismally their machinations had failed. Then he would take his revenge on her family. And then he would be free of this all-consuming desire that held him in its grip.

By the end of the night she would never…*ever* forget him or want to cross his path again.

CHAPTER ONE

Dublin, six months later…

'WE JUST have to meet with Mr Murphy and then it's all over.' In the back of the car as they left the graveyard, Maggie took her mother's hand in hers, concerned by her ashen pallor.

Her mother drew in a shaky breath. 'Love, I don't think I can sit through it…I really don't—'

Maggie tightened her hand in comfort as her mother's eyes filled and her mouth trembled.

She turned stricken eyes to her daughter. 'I'm not sad… Is that terrible? I'm so relieved that he's finally gone; when I think of what I put you through all these years, how I could have—'

'Shh, Mum. Don't think about it now. It's over. He'll never harm either of us again. We're free.'

Her heart ached at the desolation in her mother's eyes, the lines on her face, the lifeless hair scraped back. She had once been a beautiful, vibrant woman. The reason why Tom Holland had wanted her for himself after her father's untimely death. He'd been pathologically jealous of his cousin.

In those days, as a young widow in Ireland with nothing but the house left to her and a small child, Maggie's mother had been vulnerable. When Tom had promised to look after her if she married him, she had thought she was doing the best thing for her and her daughter. It was only after the wedding that his vicious cruelty had become apparent and, in a noto-riously conservative society where divorce hadn't been allowed until relatively recently, her mother had effectively been trapped. Until now.

'Look, you don't have to sit in on the reading of the will; it's going to be a matter of routine anyway. Mr Murphy knows us well enough not to insist on your being there and Tom left everything to you. It's the least he could have done.' Maggie's voice couldn't hide its bitter edge.

'Oh, really love, do you think so? If I could just take a rest…'

'Of course, everything is going to be fine.' Maggie tried to inject upbeat energy into her voice when all she felt was drained beyond belief.

A short time later the car pulled off the main road in the small village outside Dublin and swept through the gates of a large, welcoming country house. Maggie took a deep com-forting breath. The first glimpse of the house through the trees that lined the short drive never failed to lift her spirits. It had been their own family home—her father and mother's. It was the one thing her stepfather hadn't got his hands on. A link back to happier days, the memories of which she knew had helped her mother get through the worst times. It was here she and her mother had moved back to six months ago, after that… Even now she couldn't bring herself to think of that night. The pain in her heart was still acute, despite her attempts to ignore it, deny it. The awful humiliation was still vivid.

Luckily her mother had listened to her and they'd left London almost immediately. By the time Tom had realised that his plan hadn't worked he'd been too caught up with his business to come after them. And now he was gone for good.

Dead. She brought her mother up to her bedroom and was almost at the door when she called her back.

'What is it, Mum?' Maggie walked over and sat down.

Her mother's eyes were suddenly bright and serious. 'Promise me you'll never speak of what happened to us… what Tom did to us…I couldn't bear the shame.'

She was used to this recurring plea of her mother's. 'Of course not…you know I never have; why would I now?'

Her mother grabbed her hand with surprising strength. 'Promise me, Margaret.'

'I promise.' She pressed a kiss to her mother's forehead and left again. It was a promise she wouldn't find hard to keep; she had no intention of talking or thinking about Tom Holland ever again if she could help it. Maggie went back downstairs and heard the sound of a car. The solicitor. After hanging up her coat, she quickly smoothed back her hair, opening the door with a smile as the bell sounded. She had always liked the small man with twinkling eyes. Unlike the rest of Tom Holland's coterie of hangers-on and staff, his local Dublin solicitor had also been her father's solicitor.

She showed the older gentleman into the front room. 'I hope you'll excuse my mother; she's not feeling the best.'

He turned to face Maggie, 'Nothing serious, I hope?'

'No,' she quickly assured him, knowing of his genuine concern. 'She's just tired and drained from the past few days. But if you need her here—'

He put up a hand. 'Actually, maybe it's better if she doesn't hear what I have to say.' Suddenly he couldn't meet Maggie's eyes and shifted uncomfortably on his feet. A sliver of fear made her stop breathing for a second. It was too good to be true that Tom Holland was gone. She knew it.

'What do you mean?'

'Maggie let's sit down. I'm afraid I've got some bad news.'

She moved numbly to a chair and watched as the solicitor sat down near a table and put down his briefcase. He didn't take out any papers. She struggled to stay calm, despite his bleak face.

'What…what is it?'

He looked up at her finally, his hands stretching out, palms up, empty. 'I'm afraid that you and your mother have been left with nothing.'

Her heart started to beat normally again, as she relaxed. It wasn't too bad. She and her mother hadn't ever received much from Tom and she had been supporting herself for years since college and was building a modest income from her paintings.

'Well, that's not the end of the world, is it? But…but where did it all go?'

They were talking about millions of pounds after all. Mr Murphy sighed; he hated being the bearer of bad news. 'It would appear that one of his adversaries finally brought him down, lock stock and barrel—the timing is most unfortunate. A tycoon in the UK that your stepfather attempted to take over some time ago has been steadily buying up stock, taking over his companies and on the day Tom had the heart attack the last of his businesses crumbled—a freak coincidence.'

That would explain his absence, why he hadn't followed them home, demanded her mother return to London, *punished them*. Despite the dire news, Maggie couldn't help the spike of satisfaction that rushed through her; she only wished she could have seen his reaction when he had found out.

'Well, there's nothing to be done now; at least we have our house.'

The words fell into the space between them and Maggie watched with growing dread as she saw Mr Murphy's eyes flicker away guiltily and his hand went to his collar as if he needed air.

'Mr Murphy, we do have this house, don't we? It's my mother's.'

He shook his head slowly, as if he couldn't even bring himself to articulate the words. At Maggie's desperate look he had to. He cleared his throat and it sounded harsh in the silence of the room.

'My dear…nearly a year ago in London your stepfather persuaded your mother to sign over this house in his name as collateral. God knows how he persuaded her; maybe she didn't understand what she was doing…I'm afraid it was tied up with all of his other assets. It now belongs to—'

Just then the sound of a car outside the window stopped his words. Maggie couldn't move; she was in shock. She couldn't even begin to figure how her mother had done such a thing; this house was sacrosanct. Rage and disbelief warred inside her as the information sank in.

Mr Murphy was looking out of the window. 'That's him. The head of the corporation. He came to see me personally and insisted on coming here today to see you and your mother. I'm so sorry, but he refused to be dissuaded.'

When the doorbell rang and Maggie didn't move, Mr Murphy finally got up to answer it. She was numb, barely aware of the sound of the door opening, footsteps approaching, the deep timbre of a voice answering something the solicitor had said. Maggie looked up and suddenly her world stopped turning. She felt herself standing slowly as if moving through treacle, her limbs sluggish and unwieldy.

Caleb Cameron. Larger than life, his huge frame filling the doorway. He cocked his head slightly and a mocking smile touched his lips. His eyes captured Maggie's and she couldn't look away. They were glacial, moving over her, stripping her. The man who had turned her world upside down that night six months ago was back…apparently to turn it upside down again. She fought strenuously against the shocking pull she could feel in every cell as she reacted to his commanding aura. The room seemed to tilt slightly on its axis as she unconsciously sucked in a breath, her need for oxygen necessary but secondary to the shock after shock that she was reeling from.

Unable to tear her eyes away from his in morbid fascination, she didn't notice the solicitor precede Caleb into the room and gesture towards her. 'This is Margaret Holland. Maggie, this is Caleb Cameron, he's the man who has taken over all of your stepfather's holdings…including this—'

Before he could say it, she cut in through bloodless lips, 'I know Mr Cameron; we met in London.'

She sank back down on to the chair behind her because her legs were trembling so much they wouldn't hold her up any more and looked up, stricken, as Caleb advanced into the room and sat in the chair just vacated by Mr Murphy.

Despite the urbane, debonair exterior, his body clothed in an exquisite suit, he still exuded that untamed potent maleness she remembered all too well. The virile essence of the man couldn't be contained or disguised by a mere suit. It had bowled her over the first time she had seen him and was having the same effect now, except this time she had the experience of their explosive night together to make seeing him three thousand times worse. And, even though months had passed in the interim, she could feel a hot tide of colour rise up from her chest as countless familiar disturbing images flooded her head.

Caleb exercised iron-willed self-control as he looked her over dispassionately. But despite that effort he couldn't dismiss the heady rush at seeing her in the flesh again. Her face had paled dramatically on seeing him, almond-shaped green eyes huge in her small oval face, the rich abundant hair pulled back severely. The plain black top and straight black skirt couldn't hide the curves he remembered all too well— curves she had flaunted for him…yet now she looked thinner. Somehow fragile. And a protective instinct took him unawares.

A vivid memory struck him just then of seeing her for the first time, her hair falling in a mass of vibrant red curls down her back, like some vision from a medieval painting. Freckles stood out starkly against the paleness of her smooth skin as he subjected her to an exacting inspection. He noticed with satisfaction that her cheeks flooded with hectic colour. If he hadn't known better six months ago, he could have imagined she wore her heart on her sleeve, at the mercy of every reaction showing on that translucent skin. He could have succumbed to a dangerous fantasy. But he hadn't. Because he had known, almost from the very start, exactly what she was.

Maggie Holland was a mercenary bitch who had tried, with her stepfather, to play him for a fool. Never again.

He could see her throat work as she tried to speak.

'You…you've taken over everything.' Her voice was faint. *She was so transparent…*

It gave him such pleasure to know that he was pulling the rug of wealth from under her deceitful feet. He brought his glance, which had shifted to take in the room, back to her face.

'Yes, Ms Holland.'

The implied insult in his use of her surname was obvious and a part of her shrank back.

'As of now, I own every single business interest of your

stepfather's, including this very house. Naturally I declined to take on board his more dubious holdings; the Inland Revenue here and in the UK are currently investigating those and you might find that you're due to receive some hefty tax bills; they have a surprisingly low regard for offshore accounts that haven't been declared.'

Maggie stood up, galvanized into action by the explicit threat in his voice. For the first time since she had seen him again, she tore her gaze away and looked at Mr Murphy, who was near the door.

'Is this true? Can it be possible?'

The older man just nodded his head miserably. She looked back to Caleb, a wild panic rising up. He was utterly unconcerned, as if watching a fly on its back struggling to right itself.

'But…but *how* is this possible? I mean, how can we not have known?' She feverishly went over everything in her pounding head. Even though they hadn't seen Tom in months…how had they somehow missed noticing the dire straits he was leading them to? And how, for the love of God, was it possible that even now he was reaching out from the grave to ruin them…as if he hadn't done enough already?

Because he tried to ruin this man in front of you, with your help…

She shut out the voice with difficulty. She couldn't dwell on that now.

'Mr Murphy…' she implored, incapable of saying another word. Her eyes said it all. The solicitor took her arm and led her to sit down on a couch. She was glad of his protection from facing Caleb alone. She refused to acknowledge him, just feet away, willing him to be gone with all of his threatening words and devastating presence.

'I'm sorry, Maggie, but it is true. Your mother is potentially in debt to the Revenue if they find that Tom was hiding funds in offshore accounts, as they suspect. I can fight the case for you if it comes up, but…' He shrugged.

It was getting worse and worse. Maggie pressed a hand to her forehead.

Caleb stood up with lithe grace and rearranged his cuffs negligently. Maggie looked at him warily from beneath dark lashes, her heart still hammering painfully. 'Murphy, I'll leave the rest to you. Ms Holland, I have nothing more to say to you. I'll expect you and your mother to be out of this house within two weeks; I trust that will give you time to sort yourselves out.' He smiled cruelly. 'I could have exercised my right to take the house today, but would rather you be gone should I decide to move in.'

'Move in…' Maggie repeated dumbly.

'Yes. I'm doing some business in Dublin for a couple of months and need a bolt-hole from the city. This place would serve nicely…' he flicked a dismissive glance around the room '…after I've had it redecorated, of course.'

Maggie stood up again, every inch of her body quivering in anger and reaction, this intrusion into their private sanctuary too much. 'How dare you come in here and speak to me like this, on the very day of a funeral…have you no decency?'

'Decency?' He laughed mirthlessly. They had both forgotten the presence of the other man. Standing close to him, Maggie's head bent back to look up, her throat exposed. She could feel the pulse beat rapidly at her neck. His eyes roved her face contemptuously, his lips curling in obvious distaste at what he saw. 'You have a nerve to talk about decency…or should I inform our friend here exactly what role you played in your own downfall?'

So this was his revenge. He had gone after her stepfather

with ruthless precision and now it was her turn. She looked at him, aghast at his capacity to take vengeance to the very last degree. In his mind she had been just as complicit as Tom Holland and deserved everything she was getting.

Without a backward glance, he strode from the room. It felt curiously flat and drained of colour after his explosive energy had left. She heard the doors close, the car start up, the gravel spurt from under the wheels as he sped away, taking their lives with him. After he was gone, Mr Murphy stood too. Maggie looked at him blankly, still stunned.

'As you can see, your stepfather bit off a little more than he could chew with Cameron. He's never been known to suffer fools gladly and when your stepfather made a second bid to topple Cameron's empire he unleashed the tiger.'

'The second bid…'

'Well, actually, it was the third or fourth… Your stepfather really had a bee in his bonnet about Cameron, saw him as the ultimate prize to win. I know you and your mother weren't aware of most of Tom's dealings. After he tried to take over the Cameron Corporation by legitimate means and failed, he then went underground…and used other tactics, but still couldn't do it.'

Maggie felt sick. She remembered all too well her unwitting role in those tactics. It had been she who had been used in the effort to divert his attention for a crucial moment in time. Thank God Mr Murphy didn't seem to know too much and, after all, it had been in London, not Dublin.

The solicitor continued with a touch of awe in his voice, oblivious to Maggie's turmoil. 'Cameron systematically went through every one of Tom's interests and with a lot more finesse managed to bring him to his knees, which was unusual really; Cameron isn't known for going after his enemies so arbitrarily and mercilessly—he's usually happy to cripple their defences, render them impotent.' He shook his head. 'Tom must have really pushed his buttons…'

Maggie flushed guiltily. 'Well, he's finished us too, it would seem.'

'Yes.' He sighed heavily. 'I've looked at it every which way and he really does have it all sewn up. About the Revenue—I'm hoping if it comes to it that we can make a case…I can try to prove that your mother, while being named in the will, had no other part in her husband's affairs.'

Maggie turned worried eyes to his. 'But we don't have anything any more, no money… How could we afford…?'

He patted her hand. 'Don't worry about that now. I know how hard it's been for your mother. I won't let that man make her life worse than it's already been if I can help it.'

Maggie felt tears threaten at his kindness. 'Thank you.'

With a few more comforting words he got up to leave and, after Maggie had closed the front door, she sagged against it. How on earth was she going to tell her mother? She knew this news would devastate her. For Maggie, her worst nightmare had just happened—coming face to face with Caleb Cameron again. She went back into the front room and, for the first time in her life, with a shaking hand, poured herself a shot of brandy and swallowed it back in one gulp.

As Caleb came to a halt in traffic, he struck the steering wheel with such force that drivers around him looked over, but the light of sudden interest in one woman's eyes went unnoticed. When the lights went green he pulled away sharply, castigating himself. What had he been thinking? He'd always known he was going to ruin Tom Holland after his regular repeated takeover bids—the last one being the closest call. Far too close. The one that had involved *her*. But the takeover wasn't what occupied his thoughts.

He'd told Maggie Holland he never wanted to see her again six months ago and yet, within hours of landing in the country, he had to come and see for himself…stand over his final piece of revenge. He could have left it in the solicitor's hands. So why had he gone all the way out there? To confirm for himself that she couldn't possibly still hold him in thrall?

But it had backfired spectacularly.

To his utter and complete self-disgust, his body had told him in no uncertain terms that she did indeed have the same intoxicating effect. The minute he'd seen her. And yet now he'd made them all pay. So why didn't he feel satisfied? Why was her image burned on to his retina? And how the hell did he think he was going to survive in Dublin for two months, knowing she was in the same city?

As if to dampen the desire, he thought back to that night, when she had done everything exactly as he had suspected. Even down to having a room booked at the hotel. She'd brought him up there and seduced him. Exactly as he'd known she would.

But yet she didn't sleep with you…a small voice reminded him mockingly.

Maybe that was it? He'd never walked away from a woman he desired before and yet he'd walked away from her that night. He still wasn't sure why he'd left, when he knew he could have had her…without force. Her attraction had been undeniable, it was in every breathless gasp, every eye-dilating look she'd given him. But when she'd refused him herself at the last moment…somehow he couldn't… He cursed and halted uncomfortable memories. All he knew now was that the unsatisfied ache he remembered had taken up residence again. The ache that had never really gone away if he was brutally honest with himself.

He would have to take a mistress. And soon. He'd been without a woman for too long and that was just what he needed to redirect his wandering attention. And erase Maggie Holland from his thoughts once and for all.

CHAPTER TWO

THAT evening Maggie prepared a light supper and woke her
mother up. When they were sitting in the kitchen afterwards
she finally asked the question Maggie had been dreading.
'How did it go with Michael?'

She steeled herself. 'Not great. I'm afraid I have some bad
news.'

Her mother's fingers clenched around the mug, her
knuckles white. 'What is it?'

Maggie could have wept at the familiar stoic look in her
eyes. She drove down the lump. 'Mum...someone took over
Tom's business... Just the day after he died it became apparent
that he had lost everything. Effectively we're bankrupt. It
was...' she quashed the potent image of Caleb from her
mind's eye '...someone who he had tried to take over.'

'I always knew a lot of people had grievances against
him... There was bound to be someone... So what does it
mean?' her mother asked.

'Well...' Maggie desperately fought against saying *the house*
just yet '...it means that we don't get anything; it's all gone.'

Her mother gave much the same reaction as Maggie had
earlier. 'Well, that's not the worst thing, is it? I mean, what
have we ever had?' She smiled a watery smile at her daughter

and looked around the kitchen. 'At least we have the house…
Honestly, love, I don't know what I'd do if we didn't have this;
it's all I have left of your father and now I'll be able to live
here in peace.' Maggie's mother reached across the table and
took her daughter's hand, 'Don't look so worried, pet, everything will work out. I'll get a job…you've got your painting;
we'll be okay.'

She hadn't figured it out yet, Maggie knew with a sick
horror. Somehow, her mother hadn't equated signing over the
house as collateral with Tom losing everything.

'Mum…you don't realise. We've lost *everything*…'

Her mother still looked at her blankly.

'Mr Murphy said you signed the house over to Tom before
we left London…'

'Yes, love, but that was just…he just said it was…that it
was only to…' She stopped talking.

'Oh, dear God, what did I do?'

Maggie held her hand. 'It's gone too. It was included in
the rest of his assets.'

Her mother didn't move for some time and then pulled her
hand away slowly and got up to rinse out her cup. Maggie
followed her, worried about her lack of reaction.

When her mother turned to face her she felt real fear, her
eyes were dead, any sign of life or spark gone.

'Mum…'

'Margaret, I can't…don't make me think about this…I
can't bear it.'

She watched helplessly as the bowed woman walked out
of the kitchen and knew that she was struggling with all of
her might to keep herself together. That night she heard the
muted sobs through her wall and knew that her proud
mother would hate her to witness the awful grief. She

couldn't bear to hear her pain. What could she do? There had to be some way out…some solution.

The next morning, as the weak dawn light filtered through the curtains, Maggie lay with eyes wide open after a sleepless night. A night where demons had invaded every thought. Demons that had a familiar severely handsome face. She knew with a fatal certainty what she had to do. What the only option was.

When she walked into the kitchen a short while later any doubts in her head about her plan fled. Her mother was sitting there listlessly. She looked up briefly with shadowed eyes, her face a grey mask of disappointment and weariness. Maggie went and sat down beside her. 'Mum, look at me.' She waited until her mother brought her head around, slowly, as if it were a heavy weight.

'I'm going to go into town for a while…I have something to do, but I'll be back later or first thing in the morning.'

Hopefully with good news…

She didn't want to say too much in case she got her mother's hopes up, but right then and there Maggie vowed with everything in her heart that she would do whatever it took to get the house back in her mother's name. She cooked a light breakfast and forced her mother to have some, relieved to see a slight bloom return to her cheeks before she left.

Once in her small, battered Mini, she stopped by Michael Murphy's office in the main street to find out where Caleb's offices were. He didn't ask any questions, just said as he handed her the address, 'He's not going to be easy to see; everyone in Dublin is begging an audience…'

'I know, but I'll camp outside his door if I have to,' Maggie replied grimly.

She hit the rush hour traffic on the way into town and the

journey, which might normally take thirty minutes, took three times as long.

Finally she was in the city centre and parked near the building in the financial district where Caleb's offices had been set up. She was dressed smartly in her one and only suit. She wanted to look as businesslike as possible. It was dark blue—a skirt and short jacket with a matching cream silk shirt. She wore sheer stockings and high heels and had tied her unruly hair back in a severe bun. She wanted to feel armoured against Caleb's scathing looks and condemnation. Even if she was shaking like a leaf on the inside.

The spring air was deceptively mild, yet she shivered. At reception they directed her up to the top floor, which Caleb had taken over in its entirety for his sole use. Her stomach churned as she ascended in the lift, the thought of seeing him face to face again more daunting than she had thought possible.

Any illusion of ease in getting to see him was swiftly dashed on her arrival on to the opulently designed floor. A veritable bulldog of a secretary was guarding the main foyer and looked Maggie up and down when she requested to see Caleb.

'Do you have an appointment?'

'Well…not exactly, but when he hears who it is he might have a couple of minutes to spare. I won't take up much of his time.'

'I'll let him know, but he has meetings back to back all day. You might be waiting for some time.'

'That's fine.' She'd wait until midnight if she had to. She made a quick call on her mobile to a friend of her mother's in the village, asking her to look in and make sure she was okay. With that done, she settled in for the wait.

Some eight hours later Maggie had run the gamut of emotions: irritation, boredom, anger, despair, disbelief and

now she was just exhausted. Her suit was crumpled, her
shoes were off and her hair was unravelling. Any make-up
that had been there had long slid off. She hadn't left for
anything except a crucial toilet visit in case she missed him.
All day long men in suits had come and gone. She'd seen
lunch being delivered and then taken away again, prompting
her own stomach to rumble. The first secretary had been and
gone and had been replaced by another similarly bad-
tempered one.

Caleb's door opened again and Maggie resigned herself to
seeing yet more faceless suits departing and thought dimly
that the man's stamina was unbelievable. She didn't register
for a minute that it was Caleb himself walking out, his tall,
powerful build unmistakable. When her sluggish brain finally
clicked into gear, she jumped up, her body protesting at the
sudden movement after sitting for so long. He was striding
towards the lift, not looking left or right; he hadn't even seen
her as she was partially tucked away behind a plant.

'Caleb…' she cursed her impulse to call him by his first
name '…Mr Cameron—wait!'

He had just pressed the button for the lift and turned around
slowly, his brows snapping together when he saw her. Maggie
forced herself to stand tall, only realising then that she was
in stockinged feet, her shoes abandoned somewhere near the
chair. She hitched up her chin.

'Mr Cameron, I've been waiting all day to see you. I know
you're busy, but I'd appreciate just a few minutes of your time.'

'Ivy told me you were here earlier, but she knew I was tied
up all day.'

'I insisted on staying…I hoped you might have a window
somewhere…'

'Well, as you can see, I didn't. And now, if you'll excuse

me… Call tomorrow and maybe there will be a free appointment.'

He couldn't leave. Maggie stood, open-mouthed. She'd been waiting for hours without food or water to see him. The look on his face said he couldn't have cared less if she'd been bleeding and begging at his feet. He turned away dismissively.

She looked at his broad back, the doors of the lift opening silently; she had to stop him. She ran forward and put her hands in to stop the closing doors, looking up into his forbiddingly expressionless face.

'Please, Mr Cameron, I'm begging you to just listen to what I have to say for five minutes. I've been waiting here since half ten this morning. I know that's my own fault, but I have to talk to you.'

He stood back against the wall of the lift, casually looking Maggie up and down as if he were used to women flinging themselves in his path. Which he more than likely was, she thought bitterly. He regarded her for a long moment. She fought against squirming under his look.

'Very well. Five minutes.'

'Thank you,' Maggie let out on a sigh of relief.

He stepped back out of the lift and, with a flick of his hand, instructed the gaping secretary to go for the night. Without looking back to see if Maggie was following, he went into his office. She found her shoes and scrambled to put them on and follow him in before he changed his mind.

When she walked in warily he was pouring himself a shot of some dark liquid and sat down at his desk, one large hand clamped around the glass. Maggie stood nervously, taking in the dominantly masculine aura of the room. One low lamp cast a pool of light. The shadows in the room made him look even darker than he normally did, which, she remembered, came from his Brazilian mother. His father was the quintessential Englishman and the two sides—one tempestuous and passionate, the other sophisticated—proved to be a heady combination. As Maggie remembered all too well.

'Well?' he asked softly, with more than a hint of steel in his tone.

She took a deep breath. 'It's about our house.'

'You mean my house.'

She nodded slightly, feeling a surge of anger at his proprietary arrogance. 'That house belonged to my father…my birth father,' she qualified. 'It's always been my mother's, the one thing that Tom didn't own.'

'And…?' he asked in a bored tone, vaguely remembering a plain, nervous woman who had hovered around the edges of the meetings in Holland's house.

Maggie moved closer behind the chair opposite his, her hands curling unconsciously around the top, knuckles white. 'Tom made her sign the house over to him. It's always been in her name. I…I don't know how he managed it; she always vowed she'd never—' Maggie stopped herself. He didn't need to know the gory details. 'By taking the house, the only person you're punishing is my mother, and she's got nothing to do with what happened… She's suffered enough—'

'As the wife of a multi-millionaire?' he sneered, his lip curling in disbelief. 'You must be joking if you expect me to believe that. You just want to salvage something and you've concocted some lame sob story—'

'It's not!' Maggie said fiercely. 'Please. You have to believe me.'

'Believe you?' He stood up and advanced around the desk to her side. She stood rooted to the spot. 'You don't have a truthful bone in your body… Tell me, how many other men have you teased for Tom Holland in the last few months… Ten? Twenty? Or maybe you gave them the delectable fruits of your body that you denied me?'

His crude words shocked her into action, wide green eyes stared up and, without thinking about what she was doing, somehow she had moved closer and her hand lifted up, trembling, but before it could reach its target, her wrist was caught. She *abhorred* violence and yet, here she was, about to strike him.

'Now, now… Sheath your claws, you little cat. I don't think you really want to do that, do you?'

With the shock of the near violence and Caleb's hand like a steel clamp around her wrist, Maggie felt her pulse speeding up to triple time. Her eyes drank him in despite herself, taking in the hard jaw, the dark hair swept back off his forehead. The sensuous lips pulled into a grim line. But it was the eyes she remembered the most. Piercing blue—a blue that she'd fancied herself drowning in once…she shut her eyes at the memories…eyes which sliced through her when she opened her own again.

'You can give up the act.' He dropped her hand as though it was infectious and Maggie stepped back; she had to put space between them. She rubbed her wrist absently where he had gripped it, knowing that she'd have a bruise in the morning. She forced herself to look at him again.

'The simple fact is that if you take the house it will kill my mother. It's all she's ever counted on, all that she has to remind her of my father. She didn't get anything from Tom Holland except—'

Maggie belatedly remembered her mother's desperate plea not to reveal the reality of her marriage.

'Yes? Except what?'

This man would never understand. Too much had happened for her to count on any level of trust.

She steeled herself against his overpowering presence, the condemnation in his cold, implacable gaze. She ignored his prompt. 'I know my word means nothing to you, but please just hear me out. She never had anything to do with any of his business concerns and certainly nothing to do with trying to take you down…'

Caleb's eyes narrowed and Maggie seized on a chink in the armour. 'You can ask anyone who knew him,' she said in a rush, 'Ask Mr Murphy; he knows. This isn't for me; it's for her. I'm asking you to put the house back into her name…for *her* sake.'

He just watched her with those hard eyes, his face shuttered. Then he said slowly, 'And all the time your mother was supposedly blithely unaware, you were in league with your stepfather, doing your seductive routine, conning innocent men…and now what? You have a fit of conscience and want to make it up to her? I don't buy it.'

Maggie couldn't fight his opinion of her; it was so low that it may as well have been in the gutter.

She answered with a brittle smile. 'Yes, you could say that's what it is. I'm trying to mend my ways, starting with my mother.' She felt silly tears smart at the back of her eyes. The truth of what she too had suffered at the hands of that man burned like a brand and that someone like Caleb, especially Caleb, would never believe her.

'If I were to do as you ask, how can I be sure you're being altruistic—and what will make it worth my while?'

'I'll do anything you want…anything! Wash floors…' she said wildly, the brittleness gone, sensing a chance, however flimsy. '*Anything*. Just please give my mother back her house; she doesn't deserve this punishment.'

Caleb lounged back nonchalantly against the desk, arms folded across his broad chest, the material of his shirt straining. Maggie couldn't believe that in the midst of all this she could be so aware of him. His gaze was uncomfortably assessing.

He'd already decided he was going to take a mistress, but why go to the tiresome bother of having to go through the motions just to get someone into his bed? When what…*who* he really wanted was conveniently within his grasp. One thing he knew for certain as she stood in front of him, her whole petite frame quivering so lightly that it was barely perceptible—was that he wanted her. Badly. More than he'd ever wanted a woman in his life. And he always got what he wanted…

'You'd sell your soul to the devil?'

'Yes.' She answered simply, without hesitation. 'If I had to.'

'You'd sell yourself to me?' he asked softly.

It took slow seconds for his words to sink in; she wasn't sure if she had heard him correctly. 'I'm sorry—what…?'

'You heard me.'

'Sell myself like…like some kind of—'

'Mistress. You…' He looked her up and down thoroughly, his eyes resting for long seconds on her breasts, which rose and fell, her distress evident. 'Your body to me in exchange for the house.'

Maggie stepped back, blanching at his stark words, his intent, but Caleb stood and advanced a step for every one that she took back. As if she could have ever hoped that she could appeal to just his mercy. Men like him exacted payment for everything.

'I couldn't do that… How…how could you even suggest such a thing?'

'Because, you see, I can. Believe me, I don't want to want you…but I do. And you owe me…ever since you seduced me up in that hotel room six months ago and then turned on the ice maiden act. Tell me, did it turn you on? Was it part of the plan? Did you feel powerful, knowing that you could bring a man to the brink—'

'Stop! It wasn't… I didn't…' she denied automatically, wanting to halt his words, the tide of burning humiliation that threatened to overwhelm her, as she remembered just how awfully wanton she had been, the shock of her response to him. It had been *that*, along with the crushing burden of guilt, that had stunned her into frozen immobility at the time. Everything else had been forgotten. Even her mother. Even the threat. And it had scared the life out of her.

But it had been too late for her to laugh it off or feign nonchalance and then he had dropped the bombshell…revealing just how much he had known all along. Far more than her. Any nebulous desire she might have had to confide in him had died a death right there. He had set out to seduce her as cold-bloodedly as he'd believed she had done. She shivered. And yet there'd been nothing cold-blooded about their lovemaking.

'You tricked me, Maggie. Can you deny that you met me that night with seduction and betrayal in mind?' he asked, making her focus again on the present conversation. A stillness came into the air around them.

'No…' she replied faintly. Because that was exactly what she had done. Albeit against her will. But if he knew that… He could never know how much she had wanted it to be for real. Finding out the extent of his own deceit when hers had been unintended had exposed a wound that was still far too raw… He'd annihilate her *and* it would bring up all the emotions she'd buried in London, thinking she'd never see him again. She desperately tried another tack. 'But you hate me… How can you want me?'

'I think that you aren't so naïve as to imagine that love or even friendship needs to be involved in the act of sex. I want you—you want the house. It's a simple equation.'

His words flayed her somewhere inside and her hands were clenched tight into fists by her sides. 'But how? I mean, for how long or when?'

'Until I leave Dublin.'

She backed away again, the house, her mother, forgotten. All she could see was the menacing threat in front of her. The dispassionate way he was talking reached down to some-where deep inside her and she knew that he had the power to rip away the very fabric of herself if she allowed him to do this. She summoned up some last reserve of strength. 'But that's two months… I can't…I won't sleep with you. I couldn't…' she sought feverishly for something to make him back off '…I don't want you.'

'Liar.'

Before she could emit a sound of protest, with lightning speed his arms reached out and he hauled her against his chest, his head descending so quickly that she didn't have time to twist her own away. A hand snaked around to hold it in place, his mouth covering hers, crushing her lips to his. She could taste blood on the tender inner skin of her mouth. Despite the obvious cruelty of the kiss, Maggie could feel an intense ex-citement explode in her belly, every cell straining to get closer, acutely aware of his absolute maleness and strength.

Then, with a subtle and expert change in tempo, his lips softened, the hand on the back of her head became caressing. His fingers loosening the already unravelling bun, she felt her hair tumble down her back. Her fists, crushed against his chest, could feel his heart beating, the warm skin under the shirt, and they wanted to stretch out, feel, take in the exquisite breadth of it. She shook with the effort it took not to allow that to happen.

With the long wait and no food all day, she was already light-headed; Caleb's potent sexuality effortlessly swept away any resistance. Her eyes closed, Maggie was soon lost in sensation, unaware of anything but the feel of his mouth on hers, hard yet soft. When his tongue sought entry, her mouth opened on a defeated sigh and his tongue touching hers ignited a fire between her legs.

Being in his arms again, with the intensely sensual memories that had never abated...she didn't stand a chance. His mouth moved away and Maggie sucked in a betraying breath until she felt his lips blaze a hot trail down her neck, down to where the pulse beat erratically against her skin. The hand on her back moved lower and pulled her bottom up and into him where she could feel the hard evidence of his desire. She felt every part of her pulsating with the need for him to take her.

That desire transported her back in time and was as effective as a cold douche. She used all her strength to break free. If he hadn't kept his hands on her shoulders she would have collapsed at his feet. Her eyes were glazed, wide and dark green with unmistakable arousal. Her lips were swollen and moist.

The look on his face was triumphant, derision in his eyes at what he thought of her paltry attempt to stop his lovemaking. 'As I said...you're a liar.' He cupped one hand around her chin, tilting her head up inexorably. 'The honey of the honey trap still tastes surprisingly sweet.'

Maggie breathed out on a shuddering breath. She pulled herself away and tried to disguise the trembling in her legs.

'You should be thankful that I still desire you...or you'd have nothing to bargain with.'

His stark words forced Maggie's stricken mind back to why she was there. How could she have forgotten? She focused on them—anything to take her mind off her awful weakness. 'Are you saying you'll give my mother back her house?'

He inclined his head slowly. 'If you give me what I want.'

'Me.'

'Yes.'

Maggie suddenly thought of something and seized on it. 'But…don't you have a girlfriend?'

'What?' he asked sharply.

She flushed at her quick words and the realisation that it might be obvious she'd scoured the papers for news of him—where it was common knowledge that he was never without a beautiful companion. 'The papers…' Her voice trailed off, her cheeks pink.

'Girlfriend!' He laughed mockingly. 'How quaint. I don't think I've had a girlfriend since I was six and living in Rio de Janeiro with my mother. I don't *do* girlfriends, and no, there's no one at the moment, not that you should care, since you have the morals of an alley cat.'

That's handy, Maggie thought slightly hysterically, not even registering his insulting words—plenty of room for the sacrificial lamb to enter stage left. And he was right—how could she be so naïve? This man moved in rarefied circles where the most beautiful and socially acceptable women would be available. Men like him took mistresses until they grew bored or until they needed to marry. And then it would be to the right person, groomed for the job.

Knowing she sounded strangely calm, and knowing it was shock, she asked, 'How would this work?'

'If I'm going to sign the house back to your mother, then be here at two p.m. tomorrow with your bags packed.'

A numbness seeped into her bones. 'You'd expect me to move in with you?'

'Yes. I'll need an escort, companion…and a *willing* lover.'

The word *lover*, never mind *willing*, made shivers of treacherous anticipation skitter down Maggie's spine. She stood stock-still, her hair and clothes in disarray, legs still trembling slightly, her mouth feeling bruised and sensitised.

How had he done this to her? How had she let him?

He had been as guilty as her stepfather six months ago, as far as she was concerned. Both had used her like a pawn in their game of domination. And yet she couldn't help this awful, craving desire that wiped all logic from her brain. That made her weak to him. She hated herself for it. Self-contempt laced her voice. 'What, then?'

'You'll sign a contract that makes sure you get nothing from the deal. The house goes into your mother's name solely, not even to pass to you as inheritance. One condition will be that she can't sell it…just in case that was what you were planning.'

She felt sick. 'God…what they say about you is true; you've already sized up every way I could possibly use this for my own ends. You have no heart.'

A flash of something crossed his face for a split second; if Maggie had been less biased at that moment she could almost have said it was hurt. But *him*? No way. The man wasn't capable of such a feeling. As if to confirm her opinion, his face was like a mask again—it must have been her imagination.

He ignored her words. 'And this will happen when you've given me what I want.'

'When I've slept with you.'

'For two months or as long as I desire you.'

'What if that's only one night?' she said defiantly.

He stepped closer again and stopped just short of her. His

scent enveloped her. She froze. 'Oh, but it won't be, Maggie. I can tell you that much.'

Turning her back for a moment, she sought some respite from his laser-like gaze. Her hands twisted as her mind raced. Their house was worth millions by now… She hadn't a hope of raising that kind of money, and it wasn't about the money. That house was where her mother should be able to live out her days. In peace at last. For Maggie's whole life she had protected her mother. Sometimes more successfully than others. Ever since the first time she'd tried ineffectually to come between Tom's fists and her mother's body. She'd been just six years old and she still bore the scar of that day.

But Tom was gone. This was her mother's last chance of happiness and if she could make sure it happened, undo the wrong that had been done, then she had to. Somehow…and she couldn't think now, not when he was so close…she would have to do this. She turned around again and faced Caleb unflinchingly, determined not to let him see how she had crumbled inside. She hitched her chin. 'And if I'm not here tomorrow?'

At the look on her face Caleb felt a bizarre lurch somewhere in his chest. For a split second he actually wasn't sure if she would do this…and didn't like how that felt. At all. Not after having decided that he would take her as his mistress. He quashed the doubt and the feeling ruthlessly. She was just playing him, probably already trying to figure out how much she could walk away with, which he vowed would be nothing more than he was prepared to give. He stood to his full intimidating height and glanced at the heavy platinum watch that encircled one brown wrist. 'You would now have one week and six days to move out of that house before I move in.'

She watched as Caleb started to walk away, no hint of the

passionate kiss they'd just shared in evidence anywhere. He wasn't tousled and shaking like her. He was cool and almost…bored. As if he did this sort of thing every day. He turned, closing his top button, straightening his tie.

'It's up to you, Maggie. Be here tomorrow or say goodbye to the house. You can let yourself out.'

And then he walked out the door.

CHAPTER THREE

THE next day at half past one, Maggie sat in her car outside Caleb's offices, feeling hot and cold and clammy all at the same time. Her mind lurched from one dead end to another. Going home last night, she'd almost convinced herself that she could persuade her mother that they could start afresh somewhere, let the house go…anything so she wouldn't have to become Caleb's…chattel.

But when she'd arrived home she'd met the doctor on his way out. Panic had seized her, Caleb forgotten. The doctor had been grim. Things were not good. He'd said that he was afraid for her mother's long-term health…her mental health in particular. That he hadn't seen such acute grief in a long time. Miserably, Maggie knew exactly what was wrong.

The house being taken was just the straw breaking the camel's back. And if anything placed her in a position of no going back, this was it. Even though she'd known deep down she'd never have had the heart to deny her mother this anyway. Not when she could do something about it. Not when she'd been partly responsible, however coerced she'd been at the time. She knew with that thought she wasn't really being fair on herself, but the truth was…she *was* responsible. Tom had sucked her into an awful complicity with him. And, however misplaced, she still felt the guilt.

The absolute point of no return had been that morning when she'd informed her mother that, amazingly, Caleb had been merciful enough to leave her the house. But on the condition that Maggie start work for him immediately in recompense.

Maggie had explained that he'd agreed to sign the house back over once she'd started work and moved into the city to be closer. Her mother had been too stunned and ecstatic to question Maggie too deeply. And the difference in her, in the space of even those few minutes, had been nothing short of miraculous, driving the nail into the coffin of Maggie's hopes for escaping her fate.

And now here she was. About to embark on the longest, most treacherous two months of her life. But in the end, if it bought *her* freedom too…then she would cope. Somehow. And she thought she knew how. Caleb thought she was a conniving, mercenary woman of the world…so that was what she would be. He would never see inside the protective shell she was going to erect around herself. Would never see the part of her that was so vulnerable to him. The part that had stupidly believed six months ago…for a brief moment…that he might actually be interested in her. Her mouth compressed. *Oh, he had been*…just not in the way her silly, foolish heart had believed, or hoped. She looked at her watch. Two o'clock. She took a deep breath and opened the car door.

Lifting a hand to knock on Caleb's office door, having been directed there by the unsmiling Ivy, Maggie jumped when it opened suddenly. Caleb stood on the other side, his shirt unbuttoned, showing a few crisp hairs and the smooth brown column of his throat. His rolled-up sleeves revealed muscular forearms and his hair looked as though he'd just run an impatient hand through it.

'You're late,' he bit out.

Maggie made a herculean effort to appear blasé and looked at her watch. 'Two minutes late, Mr Cameron.'

'I take it you're accepting the offer.'

She nodded jerkily. 'If you'll keep your end of the bargain.'

'Of course.' He ran a heated look up and down her body, then focused on her face; freckles descended all the way down to the cleavage just exposed by the V-necked cardigan she wore. His body tightened. 'Don't be late again.'

'I'll do my best.'

They bristled at each other from either side of the door for a few seconds. A muscle twitched at Caleb's jaw. Maggie could feel a light sweat break out on her brow. He reached out and, taking her arm, pulled her into his office, the bizarre moment gone. Once inside, she pulled free and walked to one corner. Caleb went and propped a hip on the side of his desk.

For a moment Maggie was simply stunned by the view that had been obscured by last night's darkness. Windows on all sides gave a breathtaking vista of the bustling city, all the way to the Dublin mountains in the distance. She would have loved to go and study it but kept the awe from her face and resolutely fixed her gaze on him.

'I think we can progress from Mr Cameron to Caleb from now on…I don't like formality in the bedroom.'

'We're not in the bedroom yet,' she snapped.

He stood and was automatically dangerous. Maggie fought against backing away. How was she going to convince him she was a world-weary socialite if she jumped every time he moved? He strolled indolently towards her, coming to a halt just inches away. He was so close that she could see darker flecks of blue in his eyes. 'Oh…we will be. Soon enough. Now, say my name. I want to hear it.'

What? She frowned up at him, opened her mouth to speak and, for the life of her…just couldn't. For some reason, even though she'd called him by his first name only the day before, right now, she couldn't conceive of saying it out loud. It felt as if it had become loaded with some kind of meaning…an endearment of sorts. She shook her head, confusion in the depths of her eyes, a red tide creeping up her face.

He moved closer, bringing a hand to the back of her neck, caressing, finding the delicate spot just below her hairline. 'Maggie…'

Paralysis gripped her. 'I…can't.'

'Maggie. Say it.'

She felt as though she'd been drugged, her limbs heavy, blood flowing thick and slow through her veins. His head was bending, drawing closer…he was going to kiss her. Weakly, she brought her hands up between them.

'Caleb.' It came out huskily, much like a lover would say it. And, in saying it, she knew why it had been so hard. She'd stepped over the line completely. She was his now. How could such an innocuous moment feel so full of meaning?

He stopped and straightened slowly. 'There…now, that wasn't so hard, was it?'

God. She had only been in his office less than five minutes and already she was being reduced to a gibbering wreck. She had to get a grip. Had to play the part she'd planned. The only way she knew how to protect herself.

She moved briskly away, dislodging his hand, and searched her mind for something, anything, to deflect his intense focus. She seized on the first thing and whirled around, a bright forced smile on her face. 'Clothes!'

'What about them?' Caleb was very watchful, arms crossed. He couldn't figure it; in the space of a split second she'd gone from blushing just saying his name to *clothes*? One thing he knew for certain—he couldn't trust her an inch. She was up to something. And, from what he knew of women, that something always amounted to something financial.

Maggie twirled a lock of hair around one finger, something she normally did out of unconscious habit but this time contrived to look as coquettish as possible. 'Well, I expect you'll want me to look my best…and I've left all those sorts of clothes in London…so unless you like this casual look…' She gestured disdainfully at her chain store outfit. She hated this. It went against every sensibility she had to ask for anything, but she wanted him to think the worst.

Her abrupt volte-face jarred with him but then a world-weariness seeped into his bones. She was just like all the others. No different. But then he'd hardly expected her to be different, had he? And he didn't want her in some other man's cast-offs. The very thought made his fists curl. She was his now. She would dress for his pleasure—no one else's.

'Just tell me where and I'll set up an account—you can go this afternoon. I have to go to Monte Carlo for two days tomorrow—something that's just come up—so you can come too. I presume your passport is in order?'

Maggie blanched, her sham of confidence abruptly shaken, and nodded dumbly, taking in the rapid-fire delivery. Monte Carlo? She really was in another world now…

Caleb had moved back to his desk and was picking up the phone, looking at her expectantly, impatiently. Maggie furiously tried to remember his question and mentioned the double-barrelled name of an exclusive store nearby—somewhere she'd never normally go.

After a quick, brusque conversation it was done. Caleb stood and came around to Maggie, tilting her face to his with long fingers. 'Stay away from the cheap tarty stuff, if you can. I don't want a repeat performance of that dinner, where I had to endure every man in the room tripping over himself to get a look at your…' he flicked a glance down to her chest '…assets.'

She burned with humiliation at his mention of the dress her stepfather had forced her to wear. A memory rushed back. Tom Holland's mottled, angry red face in hers.

'You can wear this or go naked. If you don't…you'll be responsible for what's going to happen to your mother.'

Maggie willed the image away and clenched her jaw against Caleb's hand.

'I'll do my best. But I still have the dress, so I might just surprise you.'

The look on his face was chilling. 'Do that and I'll rip it off and dress you myself. Don't play games with me. You won't win.'

A finger of fear clutched at her throat. She didn't know what had made her want to provoke him just then. Of course she didn't still have the dress; it had been relegated to a bin that awful night. She would have burned it if she could.

Finally he released her. She went on wobbly legs to the door. Just as she was about to leave, he called her name. She turned around reluctantly.

'I can use my own car later, so my driver will pick you up when you're done with shopping and bring you to the apartment. Where's your luggage?'

'It…it's in my car. I'll have to pick it up anyway so I can drive to the apartment.'

He shrugged and gave her the address, which she committed to memory. She knew where it was, an exclusive building
nearby in the city centre. Then she fled.

Early that evening Maggie pulled into the only parking space
left outside the apartment building. The back of her tiny car
was piled high with bags. Despite having had a wicked desire
to buy nothing but trashy clothes or exorbitant designer
outfits…she just couldn't. She was hardwired a certain way
and had ended up getting exactly what she thought she needed
and might be required to wear to various functions. She had
enough knowledge of Caleb's world from her days in London
and the various social occasions Tom had forced her to
attend—again all in the name of his precious bogus family
solidarity.

The concierge had been informed of her arrival and gave
her a key before telling her he'd follow her up with the bags.
Maggie couldn't stop the unwelcome train of her thoughts as
she rode up in the lift—Caleb's catastrophic arrival back into
her life was a bitter catalyst precipitating unhappy memories.

She had grown up seeing Tom Holland do his worst to
everyone around him—wheeling, dealing, wrecking lives.
She had come to hate that world and what it represented. In
a way she knew that was one reason why she'd chosen art
college—apart from having a unique gift inherited from her
father, it had made Tom apoplectic with rage.

She had always avoided him and his cronies like the
plague…until those two weeks six months ago. It was only
for her mother, otherwise she wouldn't have had anything to
do with helping Holland host two weeks of intense meetings
and negotiations in his own house. Caleb Cameron had been
the guest of honour, invited under the guise of sharing infor-

mation with some of the world's best financial minds. When all along Tom had planned it in order to get Caleb close... close enough to bring him down.

Maggie had walked straight into the lion's den when she'd seen Caleb for the first time and had fallen head over heels. Not like Tom's usual associates, he'd stood out immediately. Physically and intellectually. And, she'd thought—morally. But how wrong that naïve notion had been. He'd been the same as Tom all along, the same beast in different clothes. But that hadn't stopped the intense attraction flaring.

Unfortunately, Tom had also been aware of the spark that had erupted between them and, with evil cunning, had manipulated events to make sure they were thrown together at every opportunity, all designed to culminate in that night.

The lift doors opened abruptly, ending her intense reverie. She shook herself out of dwelling on the past. She had to think of the future now, surviving for the next eight weeks and then putting as much space between her and Caleb Cameron as possible. She entered the apartment cautiously, walking in and out of the rooms as though they might bite. Nothing but the best, of course, for the city's most venerated guest.

Maggie had read all about this building, this apartment, which had been designed by a world-renowned architect. It stood on a hill opposite the main cathedral and had invited controversy because it represented, some people thought, a jarring juxtaposition to the ancient cathedral across the road. Personally, Maggie loved it. The old facing the new.

She left one room till last, then took a deep breath and opened the door. Much like his office, Caleb's bedroom had wall-to-wall, ceiling-to-floor windows, affording what was truly a millionaire's view of the city. There weren't any personal effects that she could see; a few of Caleb's things were neatly hung in a walk-in dressing room and there were toiletries in the bathroom, but she guessed he hadn't had much time to move in.

Just enough time to take a mistress...

She tried to avoid looking at the focal point, but couldn't. A huge king-size bed dominated the room. Dressed in dark, luxurious linen, it looked crisp and inviting, yet very, very scary. Suddenly an image formed of her with Caleb, limbs entangled, the sheets cast aside, covering her whole body with his own, dark against pale.

What would it be like? Skin to skin...Caleb pressing down on her with his aroused body...

A sound at the door nearly made her jump out of her skin. She whirled around, her hand going to her throat in fright. It was the concierge. The relief that pulsed through her body made her feel weak.

'This is the last of the bags.'

'Thank you so much; you shouldn't have...' She followed the man out and, when he was gone, leant back against the front door, her heart still hammering. Shaking her head, she pushed herself away and set about exploring more thoroughly and putting the clothes in the dressing room.

By nine o'clock that night Maggie's nerves were wound to a stretching point she hadn't known they'd possessed. Every time a noise sounded she held her breath, only relaxing once it had gone away. She'd rung her mother to check in, being as vague as possible about her situation. To her utter relief, she sounded so much improved that Maggie knew she could relax for the first time in a long time. With a friend from the village checking in every day, she knew she'd get a call immediately if anything was wrong.

The phone rang, startling her out of her thoughts. Warily she picked it up.

'Maggie…' A pulse between her legs throbbed just at the sound of his voice; why did it have to come down the line like a caress? She pressed her legs together fiercely.

'Caleb. I was just hoping you weren't in a hospital somewhere.'

She could have sworn she almost heard a chuckle, disconcerting her for a moment. 'I just bet you were. I meant to ring earlier but I've been held up waiting for a call from Los Angeles. With the time difference, I won't get in till after midnight. You should go to bed.'

She remembered how late it had been last night when he'd left the office and bizarrely couldn't stop a rush of concern, which she rapidly dampened. She was disconcerted and flummoxed by his having the courtesy to call.

'I'll go ahead and eat, then.' The minute the words were out, she cursed silently. The last thing she wanted was to appear in any way concerned. Or that she'd been waiting for him.

'Don't tell me you cooked us a romantic meal?'

'No such luck,' she said sweetly, mentally crossing her fingers for the white lie. 'I've been known to burn water.' She had actually prepared a simple casserole, but wasn't going to tell him that.

'I assume you've settled in.'

'Yes.'

'Good. I'll try not to wake you when I get in…or you could always wait up…?'

Maggie faked a yawn, her stomach cramping with panic. 'Much as I'd love to, I can't stay awake. All the excitement… Goodbye, then.'

She was about to put the phone down when she heard her

name; she lifted it back up. His voice was low and lethally silky in her ear. 'If you're not in my bed when I get in, Maggie…you will be by morning.'

The phone clicked down. Maggie thought of the furthest guest room she'd already picked in some futile attempt to deny what was expected of her. She knew he would do exactly as he said. He would carry her bodily out of that bed, into his own.

Knowing she had no choice, she packed away her comfy nightshirt and closed the door on that room. She went into the dressing room, where she'd laid out all the new clothes. She'd placed the underwear and negligées in a drawer. They'd not been her choice to buy, but the shop assistant who'd helped her had been so enthusiastic she hadn't had the heart to curtail her, or deny her the commission. And she thought of a couple of dresses that the girl had picked out. Dresses Maggie would never normally choose…but, she'd guessed at the time, they were dresses that would be suitable for Caleb's mistress to wear. So she had taken them also.

And, if she was honest, a part of her had thought, *Hang Caleb, he can pay for all this ten times over, and more.* She resolutely refused to look too deeply into the possibility that she had in fact bought them because she *wanted* to…for him. She had to remember she was playing a part. And what he would expect was a mistress, dressed suitably, in his bed. That thought made her shiver as she prepared.

Later, while waiting for sleep to claim her, as she lay on the very edge of the huge bed, Maggie reflected uncomfortably that their phone conversation earlier had been almost…too easy, with a hint of warmth even. And that was dangerous. Because it reminded her of the heady days when she'd first got to know him in London, when she'd seen that other side to him. She turned over and rested her head on her hand. If he was to turn on the charm she'd be lost, for certain. She knew because she'd been lost before. Despite everything that had transpired, she was very much afraid that she was still lost.

The drama of the last few days caught up with her finally, the sleepless nights. She gave in to a deep dreamless sleep.

Caleb woke early. He was aware of the heat of another body close to his. Turning so that he was on one side, he looked to see Maggie nestling close, curled towards him. Vibrant red hair fanned out around her head. He'd been dimly aware of her shape on the far side of the bed the previous night and had been too exhausted to investigate further. But they'd obviously gravitated towards each other during the night.

Now, however, he could study her at leisure. She looked younger, innocent…oddly vulnerable. His face took on a hardness as he dismissed the notion, his eyes travelling down. With the cover drawn back, she was revealed in a creamy negligée, the delicate lace just disguising the mounds of her breasts, which rose and fell with even breaths. Caleb felt his body respond forcefully. He shifted uncomfortably and Maggie shifted too, as if they were linked by an invisible thread. He stilled.

In repose, her lips went into what looked almost like a petulant moue. He wanted to bend his head and kiss her soft mouth. He wanted to have her wake and look at him with sleepy eyes, smile and turn into him, giving herself to him. But he didn't. Because he knew that if he was to wake her with a kiss, she'd look at him first with surprise, but then with censure…and, without wanting to question why, he knew he didn't want that. When he made love to her he wanted her eyes to be open, aware of every moment and darkened with passion—when he took her for the first time.

In a split second she had shifted and moved even closer, a hand reaching out, finding his chest and resting there. As if to test him. Small and pale against the darkness of his skin. Fingers curling softly. His jaw clenched with the effort not to give in to temptation and very gently and slowly he extricated himself and went to take a shower. A cold one. On the bed behind him Maggie stirred but did not wake.

CHAPTER FOUR

WHEN Maggie did wake it took a minute to figure out where she was. She felt completely refreshed, as though she'd had the most restorative sleep in her life. Stretching under the covers, she smiled to herself and then stopped. The feel of the slinky silk material on her body was all too alien.

She remembered exactly where she was.

Sitting up slightly, she realised that she was practically on the other side of the bed to the one she'd taken last night and the evidence of a head imprint very close to hers told her that Caleb had joined her at some stage, but he was gone now. From where she was, she must have been on top of him...or maybe he had pulled her over? No, she would have woken. And how had she had such a good sleep with him in the bed beside her? She was a finicky sleeper at the best of times and yet, her first night in a new place, sharing her bed with the most disturbing person she'd ever met, she'd slept like a baby for the first time in years.

The door opened to reveal a clean-shaven, impeccably dressed Caleb. Maggie sank back down and pulled the covers to her chin, unbelievably relieved to see him fully clothed.

'Morning.' He put a cup of coffee on the bedside table. She looked at him very warily.

'You know you're quite the wriggler when you're asleep. All over me when I woke up. You'd think a king-size bed would be big enough…'

Just after the way her own thoughts had been going, it was too much. She would not let him goad her and stifled a defensive retort, but then had to say something.

'Well, maybe this has been a mistake after all, if I slept through the magnitude of sharing your bed without my clothes inadvertently dropping off…'

He came down on the bed beside her and suddenly she couldn't breathe, the air trapped in her throat. Two strong, sinewy arms came either side of her. The sheet slipped down to reveal her upper body, hardly concealed by the lace and satin. His eyes made a leisurely inspection from her face downwards, until his eyes rested on her breasts. Just under his look, she could feel them swell, her nipples tightening into small hard peaks, pouting flagrantly forward, as if begging for his touch. Almost carelessly, he lifted the back of his hand and brushed knuckles over one sensitive peak, causing her to swallow a moan, before he tipped up her chin, forcing her to meet his gaze.

'Mistake…? I don't think so, my love.'

Her insides quivered, her lower body on fire with need. He had proved with little more than a look just how, if he'd wanted to, he could have had her last night, over and over. He knew it and she knew it.

In one fluid movement he stood up from the bed, his expression unreadable. 'I'll be back for you at eleven to go to Monte Carlo, so be ready.'

And he was gone.

Maggie shut her eyes fiercely. She *would* do this. She *had* to. How hard could it be?

* * *

At the designated time Maggie was waiting with a bag, ready to go. She'd rung her mother, had explained that as Caleb's 'assistant' she had to accompany him on a short trip. Having packed away all of her own clothes and dressed in the new ones, she felt a little more like the actress she was trying to be. A simple linen skirt, silk camisole and matching jacket. Her hair twisted back and up in a smart chignon. The phone rang. It was Caleb informing her that he was downstairs in the car. This was it.

Outside, Maggie stood on the steps for a moment. Caleb was watching from the shadows in the back of the car. When she appeared at the door, looking fresh and bright and so sweetly sexy, he had to restrain himself from jumping out to go over and touch her. Almost to see if she was real.

With her bag deposited in the boot seconds later, about to get in Maggie suddenly remembered something and stepped back.

Caleb's voice from the interior was terse. 'What's wrong?'

'I just want to make sure my car is locked…' She hurried over to the car, which was close by, and checked quickly. When she turned to go back, Caleb was standing by the car, shades on against the sun.

'*That* thing is your car?'

'Yes,' she replied defensively.

'It's a health hazard.'

Maggie fought against the protective urge that kicked in. She'd bought that car with her first savings, from the family gardener. She'd learnt to drive in it, lovingly cared for it. She realised then that Caleb, of course, would have expected her to be driving something much more ostentatious. She picked her words carefully, hoping she sounded breezy and uncon-cerned. 'Oh…it's just something I borrow from the house when I'm home. It used to belong to the gardener. It gets me from A to B.'

She slid into his car and hoped he'd forget about it. The driver turned around in his seat to face Maggie, introducing himself as John. She was surprised to hear an English accent. 'Great cars, aren't they? My first was a Mini too. I know how attached you can get to them.' He winked back at her and, with the first genuine human warmth in days, Maggie smiled effervescently back. Then flicked a glance to where Caleb was lounging on the other side of the car.

He was looking at her with a strange expression on his face. She hurriedly schooled her features and looked out of the window. She could see from the corner of her eye when he buried himself in a paper. Without his eyes on her, Maggie breathed slowly and her thoughts for the first time flew ahead to where they were going.

Somewhere warm…and glamorous…and exotic…and foreign. Where the inevitable would happen. Within hours. By the time they got back to Dublin, they were going to be lovers. Her loose top felt constrictive all of a sudden. Could she make love to him and cut herself off from her emotions?

She'd have to.

Maggie lifted her face to the sun. Bliss. If you didn't count the fact that she was here more or less under duress, for which she only had herself to blame, and that her stomach was in a constant knot since Caleb had walked back into her life just three days ago. Her mind reeled at that thought. Three days…and now she was about to start the life of a kept woman with someone who despised her…yet desired her enough to look past it.

She opened her eyes and shaded them against the sun. She was sitting out on the terrace of their hotel suite, on a balcony that overlooked a small idyllic square. Flowers everywhere burst in a colourful profusion so bright that it almost hurt the eye. She got up and leant against the wall. The sea glinted and sparkled in the distance. How many other women had had this treatment? Whisked away at a moment's notice to luxurious hotels, fantastic locations… there purely for *his* pleasure. The thought hurt like a knife edge in her heart and she angrily pushed herself away from the wall.

She gave a startled gasp when she saw Caleb lounging against the French window that led back into the suite. His eyes were shaded.

'How long have you been there…? What happened to your meeting?' She felt absurdly exposed, as though he'd known exactly what she'd been thinking about.

He pushed himself away from the door and walked over. 'You should be careful…you'll burn in this sun.' He could already see that more freckles had appeared on her face and shoulders, making her look ridiculously young.

She stiffened under his finger as it trailed over the smooth skin of her shoulder, hoping he wouldn't see how she was responding to the light touch. 'Don't worry,' she said breezily, belying her tense body. 'Many painful past experiences have made sure that I never go out unless I've got factor thirty on. I gave up trying to tan years ago.'

He was still caressing her hot skin. 'Still…you should watch out.'

'If you're not careful, I might think you are concerned for my welfare,' she mocked.

Caleb's mouth thinned. 'Hardly. You come with an expensive price tag. And I don't intend waiting for you to recover from sunstroke tonight.'

Her mouth went dry. Despite his blatant insult, she couldn't halt the images that invaded her head at the thought of *tonight*. She searched for words, something to negate the awful liquid heat that was winding its way through her blood, glad that his eyes were covered so she couldn't see into the blue depths, where she could well imagine his contempt laid bare.

He spoke before she could articulate a word. 'My first meeting was quicker than I thought. I haven't eaten yet; have you?'

She shook her head.

'I've got a table in a bistro just around the corner; let's get something light, I have another meeting in about an hour.'

'Okay…' Maggie picked up her bag and followed him out of the suite. A short stroll from the hotel and tucked down a small cobbled side street, Caleb gestured to a restaurant artfully hidden by plants and flowering baskets. Inside, it was cool and airy. The waiter led them to an intimate table in the corner beside an open window.

It was romantic and glamorous beyond belief. Heady stuff, with Caleb across the small table, long legs stretched out alongside hers. When she realised that, she tucked hers primly under her chair. He noted her movement with a mocking lift of one brow. She ignored it.

He handed her a menu. The waiter came back and they gave their order, Caleb asking for some sparkling water. When the waiter left the water and had gone again, Caleb lifted his glass. 'In the absence of wine…can we drink to a truce, Maggie?'

A fluttery feeling hit her belly. She couldn't avoid his eyes, the blue hypnotising her. She lifted her glass too, dampening the feeling ruthlessly. He was doing this just to make things easier for himself. No one wanted a reluctant mistress. And she *had* to stop her wayward thoughts… 'To a truce, then…'

He smiled. She took a sip and the rogue fluttery feeling came back a thousandfold. When he trained that smile on her…she couldn't think straight. Danger.

He's turning on the charm, just to get what he wants— you…a little sing-song voice warned. Maggie ignored it. She knew exactly what he was doing.

'Let's not forget why we're here though…'

'Enlighten me, Maggie, please.' A hard glitter entered his eyes.

'The house, of course.'

'Ah, yes. The house. I was attempting, however hopelessly, to give us the chance to perhaps ignore the ugly reality. You don't need to remind me of how you're bartering yourself for a house worth millions. The fact is you are. And I'm the fool who thinks you're worth it.' His words rang with bitterness and she could see a pulse beat at his temple. He obviously regretted saying too much.

She flushed a dull red. Well, she'd asked for it. And why did she feel in the wrong? Just because he was the one who had held out the tentative olive branch?

She took a gulp of water.

He leant forward. 'But Maggie, there's no reason why we can't come to some mutual accord.'

She had to be careful; she was letting her vulnerable emotions run away with her. The type of woman he was used to wouldn't bat an eyelid at what they were doing. She strove for that cool insouciance. Albeit slightly after the fact.

'Yes. You're right. Let's drink to that truce again.' She held up her glass. With narrowed, calculating eyes he clinked hers again. She smiled brilliantly, hiding the hurt. She willed the awkward feeling away and, with more aplomb and skill than she'd thought she could possibly possess, she managed to steer them into a light conversation.

As Caleb seemed to disregard her little outburst, as they talked of inconsequential matters, like a bittersweet pain, she remembered all too well how much they'd had in common, or so she had thought. How much she'd loved talking to him once. Without knowing how it happened, somehow they'd gravitated to more personal matters.

'Do you go back to Rio much?' The plates had been cleared and Maggie was cradling her coffee cup in one hand, feeling deliciously full. Even though they hadn't had wine, she felt a mellow feeling snake through her bones, relaxing her. And it surprised her, how easily she'd let herself become this relaxed.

Caleb looked away for a second and something flashed over his face. 'Not that much. Although my mother is still there, she's busy with her new husband...'

'You mentioned him before, didn't you? Isn't he—'

'The same age as me.' He gave a harsh laugh. 'Yes. And he has lots of money for her to be kept in the style to which she's accustomed.'

Maggie tried desperately to keep things light. 'Well, you have to admit, for feminists out there, it's a nice reversal. Usually it's the other way around, an old man with a woman no older than his own daughter.'

There was tension for a second and then Caleb smiled. 'You're right. You'd probably like her, you know. She's very forthright, very outspoken.'

She felt suddenly shy at the thought of meeting his mother, but knew he hadn't meant it like that, literally. If anything, it was more likely to be a cloaked insult.

'Is...is your father still in England?'

He nodded as he took a sip of coffee, 'Yes. He's in Brighton, so I get down there whenever I can.' There was none of the tension in his voice when talking about his father. Maggie guessed he had a very fraught relationship with his mother and remembered him telling her before about how his parents had fought over him as a boy, having divorced when he'd been only three or four. He'd been shunted back and forth between Brazil and the UK for years.

'But you're living in London? Or you were...' She couldn't say the words, *six months ago*.

He nodded briefly. 'I have an apartment there and one in Rio, New York, Paris...but I'm never in one place long enough to call it home...'

At that moment he caught her eyes and they were clouded with some indefinable emotion; it reached out across the table and made him suddenly feel the need for something he'd never felt before. Maggie cut into his disturbing thoughts, echoing them.

'I can't imagine that. All the years we lived in London, Ireland was always our home. Somewhere to come back to...'

A refuge from terror. Dublin had always been too boring for Tom. He'd never stayed long and her happiest times had been during her Irish boarding school years whenever he'd let her mother stay...which had usually been when he was off on a holiday with one of his many mistresses.

'Is that where you'll stay now?'

She dragged her attention back and nodded. 'I'd like to. We've been home for six months—'

'Six months?' He was sharp. Maggie coloured guiltily and wondered frantically if she'd let her guard down too much. But what could that possibly tell him?

She picked her words carefully. 'Mum wanted to come home, so I came back with her to settle her in…'

His eyes were narrowed on her face. Intense. 'So you left London six months ago?'

Maggie nodded.

Caleb studied her. There was a kernel of something there; he was sure of it. But he couldn't figure what it was. Tom must have sent her away, fearing that Caleb might somehow come after her. Protection. The thought made him feel that impotent rage again. At her betrayal, at his own weakness for her. He made a huge effort to put it out of his mind. They'd agreed to a truce. 'You're close to your mother?'

Maggie, relieved that he'd let the London focus go, nodded emphatically. She was unaware of the protective gleam that lit her eyes, making them almost luminous. Caleb's breath stopped; she looked radiant. The sun had already given her pale skin a warm glow, freckles that made him want to reach out and touch. Her top hinted at the valley between her breasts. A tendril of red-gold hair had drifted over one shoulder and curled tantalisingly close to her breast. This was crazy; he felt jealous…of some hair? He shifted on his seat, his body throbbing. Tonight, he vowed, a steady pulse of anticipation and desire beating through his blood…

A short while later, making their way back to the hotel, Caleb casually took Maggie's hand in his. She felt tiny and feminine next to his much larger build. He threaded his fingers through hers and she was on very shaky legs by the time they returned. He turned to face her. She looked up, meeting his eyes. The sun was behind him, dazzling her.

He was going to kiss her and there was nothing she could do to stop it. If she tried…he'd wonder why and that would lead them down a dangerous path. Their mutual attraction was undeniable—always had been. He wouldn't understand her fear… He had her pegged as someone far more sophisticated in these matters. This was a simple transaction for him and no doubt he imagined it was the same for her. She couldn't afford to appear anything less than willing from now on. For as long as he desired her. And she knew that as terrified as she was of the response he evoked in her physically, it was the emotional minefield at the other end that worried her most.

He pulled her close into his body with one arm, his other hand cradling her head and threading through the silky strands of her hair. His mouth touched hers.

With flames of desire licking along every vein, Maggie finally gave in and, for the first time since seeing him again, even though they'd already kissed, she kissed him back. With full consciousness. Because, despite everything, she wanted to. Because she couldn't *not*. This was as necessary to her as breathing. Her mind fought a pathetic battle for a few seconds; it must be the surroundings…the feeling that somehow they were not in the real world, that was making her behave like this… She just couldn't help it.

With a moan of approval, he felt her tacit acquiescence and tightened the embrace. His tongue sought hers and sweetly stroked and explored and plundered. Maggie gave into powerful desire and slid her hands up his arms. She could feel the bunched muscle under the thin material of his shirt and desperately wanted to be able to feel the silky skin, explore the texture of his muscles, feel how they shifted…changed contours as he held her.

When he finally lifted his head, he pressed another quick kiss to her mouth as though he was loath to let her go. Maggie felt dizzy and light-headed. The only thing holding her upright was his arm anchoring her to him. She hated herself for this; he had her exactly where he wanted her. Acquiescent and pliant, in his arms. And there was nothing she could do except…comply.

'I won't have much time later so I'll have my tux delivered to me and meet you in the hotel bar before the function.' He let her go and pushed her gently in the direction of the hotel. Before she could be completely humiliated, she turned and briskly walked into the hotel, without a backward glance.

CHAPTER FIVE

DISMISSING the car and deciding to walk back to his meeting, which was just a few minutes away, Caleb's mind raced. That kiss…and Maggie filled his senses so much that the thought of work was a thorn in his side. His step became more brisk, as if he could put distance between himself and his uncomfortable thoughts. He'd had other mistresses, lots…what was the problem now? Maggie was just another one. Then he remembered reluctantly that, walking down a street in London some weeks before and seeing the back of a petite redhead, his pulse had quickened through his body with such force that he'd been shaking by the time he'd caught up with her, only to find that she was nothing like Maggie. The force of need that had ripped through him had disturbed him more than he'd cared to admit at the time.

Was that what had spurred him to see her again? To wreak the final, devastating revenge? Because he hated the pull she still had over him?

He berated himself inwardly for giving rein to such thoughts. Applied the stern logic he was famed for. He desired her and she'd offered him the key he'd needed to make her his mistress, *that was all*. She was just the next in line, however she'd come to him. Reluctantly or not. And the jury was still out on whether or not she had manipulated events from the word go. She had, after all, been instrumental in a bid to see him crushed. He could never afford to forget that. Could never trust her.

But now, after just hours in Maggie's company—a woman who didn't even pretend to like him—for the first time ever he was suddenly wishing for an afternoon off. Why on earth was he suddenly questioning the control he wielded that didn't make it easy for him to walk away on a whim? It was desire pure and simple. Even if it was a more powerful desire than he'd ever experienced, still, that's all it was. Nothing else. Yet…

Yet nothing…

He hated the thought that he could very well be dancing to her tune…still.

As she waited that evening for the lift to arrive, Maggie's reflection stared back from the mirrored door. She felt a little unrecognisable. Having always rebelled at Tom's attempts to get her to 'dress up', she had never normally made much of an effort.

And yet now…she suddenly felt the urge? a small mocking voice jeered in her ear. Still, she was glad she'd made the effort, she told herself defiantly, pressing the button again with undue force, a quiver of butterflies taking flight in her belly when the bell pinged loudly, announcing the lift's arrival.

Caleb nursed a whiskey in the dark bar as he waited. He drew admiring, openly covetous looks from every woman there. He knew it, could feel it, was always aware of it, but let it roll off him like droplets of water off a duck's back. The only gaze he sought right now was a green-eyed one. Except it was more likely to be combative than covetous, despite her acquiescence earlier.

He was steeled to see her again. All defences raised. She'd

invaded his thoughts all afternoon, had made him lose his concentration, his focus. He'd found himself on the verge of agreeing to a merger that would have cost him millions until he'd woken up at the last moment. This is what she'd done before. And, after the call he'd just taken from his assistant in Dublin, he knew she was up to a lot more than wanting her house back for her poor, *supposedly* innocent, mother. She was up to a whole lot more.

A distinct hush fell over the already muted tones of conversation in the bar. The hairs stood up on the back of Caleb's neck as he looked up slowly from his glass. Maggie stood in the doorway. His chest grew tight and his breathing constricted as he drank in the sight of her. She looked…stunning.

He could see her eyes dart around the room and knew she wouldn't see him straight away as he was partially hidden, a force of habit. She wore a dark olive-coloured dress, the flowing folds meeting in a deep V over an empire-line that rested just under her bosom, the pale voluptuous swells hinting at other hidden curves. Her hair was held back from one side and swept over her other shoulder in a thick russet wave. She stood out from every other woman there, with their overdone, overtight bodies and faces. Like a glowing pearl against dark coral.

His hand tightened reflexively on the glass when her gaze caught his and an immediate flush of colour entered her cheeks. She moved towards him and for a split second he had the strongest urge to leave, run…get away. As if he was on a collision course with a very definite yet unknown danger.

And then she stopped in front of him and he was still there. She looked up at him, the almond shape of her eyes accentuated with kohl and a clean, fresh scent which intoxicated his nostrils. He summoned all of his skill and experience to bring the guard down over his conflicting emotions. He stood. 'If you're ready, let's go.'

Maggie searched his face for some clue of what he was thinking but could see nothing. He hadn't even said if he thought she looked okay. He took her hand possessively and led her out to the foyer entrance, where a sleek car pulled up and he guided her into the back before following. Back in the bar he'd been so brusque she hadn't had a chance to get her breath, since it had been taken by the sight of him. But now she took him in surreptitiously. He was even more handsome in the tuxedo, his hair smoothed back, highlighting the strong forehead, the aquiline line of his nose.

But he didn't look happy. After hesitating for a moment, she couldn't help asking, 'Is…is everything okay?'

He shot her a brooding look.

'You just seem a little preoccupied…is it work?'

'What's this?' he sneered. 'The nice, caring, considerate Maggie? Trying to lull me into a false sense of security… charm me?'

'What are you talking about?'

Caleb knew he was being irrational and that he was re-acting to something he wasn't even aware of, but couldn't stop. He wanted to push Maggie back to a safe distance.

'You must have known I was close to bringing Holland to his knees—he certainly did. I don't trust you for a second. I know you're up to something more than trying to secure the house.'

Maggie quailed at the contempt stamped into his features and a sharp pain filled her chest because she had known no such thing and she trembled with the effort not to cry tears of frustration. 'It's not bad enough that you believe me to have betrayed you once—now you're trying to accuse me of more?'

'Absolutely.' His tone rang with conviction. 'And if you

think that by taking you as my mistress it will afford you that opportunity, then you'd better wise up fast.'

Maggie was genuinely aghast. Where had this come from? As if reading her thoughts, he answered her question. He leaned over and took her hands, dragging her close to his chest. His scent enveloped her and Maggie closed her eyes in a futile attempt to avoid his sensual threat.

'You think you're smart, do you? To spend such a small amount of money on the clothes…then making sure I see the ancient car, as though you wouldn't normally be driving something much more expensive.'

Her eyes snapped open. Wide. 'What?'

Had he lost his mind?

'All designed, no doubt, to make me think that perhaps I've judged you too harshly…'

'That's crazy…' His words cut her to the quick. Too close to the bone. Of course he would have checked up on her. She thought of the amount of money she'd put on his account; it had taken a lot of nerve to walk away with her head high. What on earth was he used to? She shook her head. 'Maybe I'm just different to your other—'

'Different? I don't think so, Maggie; they're always upfront about what they want. Honest. You're conniving and deceitful.'

His words were hurting her in a place she didn't want to look at. She fought back.

'And maybe you're just too cynical.'

He smiled grimly, still in possession of her hands, 'You could say that. My mother taught me that all women appreciate the spoils of being a rich man's plaything and I've yet to meet a woman to persuade me otherwise… Perhaps it's your mother who has taken on Tom's legacy, thinking you can both manipulate me, using you as the bait again. Is that why she couldn't meet me that day at the house…? You were laying the ground work for the sympathy vote even then, getting Murphy to tell me she was weakened by everything…'

At the mention of her mother, Maggie stiffened against his hands, her face paling dramatically. Her voice shook with emotion. 'Don't you ever mention my mother like that again. This is between you and me. That's all you need to know; keep her out of this.'

Caleb took in her passionate response. She seemed genuinely angry. He kept holding her, his eyes trying to assess the expressions flitting across her face. But then the moment was gone… He saw her face close up again.

Maggie couldn't take back the words and knew she'd given far too much away. But she couldn't bear to think of her mother being so slighted. It made her sick that he could even think that for a second. Miserably she knew she couldn't say anything, make him listen to her. She couldn't defend herself anyway—that way lay exposure to ridicule and betraying her mother's secret pain.

So instead she pasted a brilliant smile on her face and tossed her head, praying that he wouldn't dwell on her careless words. She had to be more careful.

'As for the clothes, I only got what I needed for now…and what's wrong with hoping for a few spoils…after all, I am your plaything for the next two months, am I not? Unless, of course, you want to let me go? If what I am is too distasteful to you—'

With a sudden harsh breath that was expelled heavily, Caleb silenced her words with his mouth. And, as much as Maggie's own self-respect screamed at her to pull away, shout out her innocence, she felt herself moulding into Caleb's chest, her soft curves pressing into rock-hard muscle. Her senses quickly became drunk on him, but suddenly the car came to a smooth halt, not that she would have even noticed if Caleb hadn't pulled back at that moment. His eyes glittered fiercely in the dim light as they waited for the door to be opened.

'Just don't forget that that's all you are, Maggie. My plaything.'

The heat of the ballroom was stifling, even with all the doors thrown open to the fragrant night outside. Maggie's cheeks ached and the balls of her feet were burning in the high heels. She was moving from foot to foot in an effort to ease the pain. Caleb, at her side, looked down sharply.

'What's wrong with you?'

She refused to look at him, staring at a point to his left. 'Nothing.' She'd barely communicated with him since they'd arrived, still stung and hurt and dismayed by the level of his distrust.

He hadn't seemed to even notice. For what seemed like hours now, she'd endured conversations of inane small talk, being relegated to the sidelines while Caleb had entertained a never ending stream of sycophantic admirers. And she'd endured none too friendly speculative glances from every other woman in the room. When a crush of people had moved forward, Maggie had got separated from Caleb and found herself surrounded by three or four women. They were all dressed in what she knew to be haute couture, totally over the top, but a clear statement of their wealth and status. They had looked her up and down as if she were a specimen in a glass box. She couldn't believe how rude they were being and tried not to look as intimidated as she felt. One of them spoke.

'*Vous êtes ici avec Monsieur Cameron?*'

Without even thinking, Maggie immediately slipped into her schoolgirl French, trying to be polite, wondering who they were and why they wanted to know. *'Oui...'*

'Ah, bon. Mais juste pour ce soir, n'est ce pas?'

Maggie was trying to figure out what the woman was saying... Was she actually suggesting that she was here with Caleb just for tonight, like some kind of...call girl? A mortified blush rushed through her; they were hemming her in and their overdone faces, lacquered hair and cloying perfume was making her feel sick.

'I'm sorry...excuse me.' She tried to push her way out, but couldn't. She was feeling more and more desperate.

Caleb swivelled his head. Where had she gone? She'd been at his side only two minutes before. He'd got caught in a conversation with a property investor from France and hadn't been able to extricate himself. He felt mildly guilty that he hadn't been more attentive to Maggie, but he was still feeling the uncomfortable sensation of being somehow open, foolish in his desire for her... He had to be careful around her.

Then he saw her. She was surrounded by the doyennes of Monte Carlo—he knew them well. His mouth tightened. They were responsible for many matchmaking attempts with one or other of their invariably too young, spoilt and petulant daughters. And he suddenly realised that Maggie looked terrified. Without stopping to think, and knowing that it surprised him as he would have imagined her to be a match for them, he strode over and reached through the women to take Maggie's arm.

She looked up and the flash of sheer relief and something else that crossed her face made something flip flop in his chest. But then it was gone, as if it had never happened, and now her eyes flashed veritable sparks at him. He smiled his excuses to the ladies and led Maggie away.

'Are you okay?' He slanted a look down at her.

She glared up at him. 'No thanks to you. Those women are…unbelievable.' She shook her head. 'You could have warned me I'd need a flak jacket to come here.'

He couldn't help the unbidden smile. He doubted the women would last again in Maggie's company; they'd obviously just caught her off guard. He could well imagine what they'd said. And again he wondered at how she hadn't been better able to handle them. He would have cast her as one herself—well used to the poison-talon-tipped women of society who were more akin to social climbing piranhas.

He refused to dwell on that now. He was thinking ahead and wondering how long he could suffer to be polite before he could get out of there and take Maggie with him. Take her to bed.

'Ah Cameron, there you are…'

Not just yet, anyway. He pulled Maggie into his side, swallowed a grimace and smiled as yet another colleague bore down on him.

Maggie flicked the object of everyone's fascination a reluctant look, anger still bubbling through her. She had to admit that he *was* the most handsome man in the room. He stood head and shoulders above everyone and with that physique…again her insides cramped with nerves and anticipation. Finally, after what seemed like more torturous hours, he leant down, his mouth close to her ear, sending a little shock wave through her.

'Let's get out of here.'

She nodded mutely. Time was up, no more waiting. Tonight he would demand payment…take her body and, she was afraid, her soul too. And she couldn't say a thing.

She suddenly felt absurdly vulnerable and alone, her anger dissolving. What *could* she say, anyway? As she followed him through the crowd, stopping every two seconds for people to say goodbye, she thought a little hysterically of what she might say if given a chance: how six months ago, on the day of their date, Tom, her beloved stepfather had informed her of his plans to take Caleb over and ruin him. And how, if Maggie didn't co-operate with his plans to keep Caleb *occupied*, he would beat Maggie's mother so comprehensively that—in Tom's succinct, devastating words, 'I'll put her in hospital'.

She could tell him how she'd racked her brains for a way out…but had known, no matter what she did, even if she'd gone to the police, that he'd still make her mother pay. Because, you see, he'd been doing it for years. Once, in her youthful naïvety, Maggie *had* gone to the police. Tom hadn't punished *her*… No, it had been her mother who'd suffered, even though she'd claimed a random mugging to protect Tom. Classic bullying, abusive tactics. He had been very cunning—you could never see the bruises. They had always been well hidden.

She could tell him of how, before Tom's bombshell, she'd been ridiculously excited at the thought of going on the date with him, had even bought a new outfit. But then…that was when Tom had forced her to go to that shop, had bought that excuse for a dress instead. And had informed her of her role in his awful macabre play.

She could tell him how she'd been so filled with guilt that she couldn't go through with sleeping with him, that was why she'd stopped… She'd been on the verge of actually telling him everything, somehow trusting that, maybe for once, her mother could be protected.

Maggie was not in Monte Carlo any more; she was back in that hotel room, the memories rushing back with sickening clarity, and she was powerless to escape them. She was on that bed, the sheet pulled around her shaking, half naked body as Caleb stood in front of her, pulling on his clothes. 'Maggie, you're a fool. You think I didn't know exactly what you had planned?' He gave a harsh laugh as he pulled on his shirt. Maggie felt an icy stream washing through her, the defensive words of explanation dying on her lips.

'I heard your stepfather. His exact words were, "That stepdaughter of mine will do anything and she wants Cameron; she's with us". So you see, Maggie, I've known for days now that you've been cooking up this little plan…very hammy, though. And the outfit? I've seen classier ones on women who tout for business on the streets.'

Maggie could feel her insides contracting, pulling inward as if to protect herself from the cruel blows. Her voice was dry and raspy when it came out. 'But…I never knew…I—'

'Save it, Maggie. You knew all right. I even have the evidence.'

And she watched as he found his jacket and took out a small envelope, throwing the contents at her. Photos. Lots of them—of Tom and her on Oxford Street, going into the shop, emerging with the bag. Getting into his car. And from these deceptive angles it looked to all the world as though she were the eager accomplice…

She looked up with huge wounded eyes, 'But when, how…?'

He was almost dressed, not even looking at her any more. 'I had you followed for the day, just to see for myself. And what a pretty picture those photos paint, don't you think?'

'But…you've known…you knew all along, for the past—'

'Yes, Maggie, I've known since practically the first day we met. So all those shy, innocent glances, the blushes, were for nothing. Entertaining, but for nothing.'

'But how could you, I mean, why did you…do it?' She

didn't know why she was still speaking, couldn't understand what protective part of her hadn't kicked in yet.

He came close to the bed and she had to look up. His face was coldly impassive. Shut. 'Because, Maggie, I desired you. I wanted you. And I knew I could have you. You were offering yourself on a plate, for God's sake…' He came down close to her, hands on either side of her body, where she could see the utter disgust and contempt in his eyes. 'We both know I could still have you now…' he flicked a derisory glance up and down '…but I can't be bothered. Because, believe me, I never want to see your face again.'

And he walked out of the room without a backward glance. Maggie sat on the bed for a long time, the cold seeping into her bones as she felt something within her shrivel up and die.

By now they were at the entrance to the function room but Maggie wasn't even aware. She was locked in her own private hell of memories. Caleb looked abstractedly at her hand in his—it was icy cold. Then he looked at her face. She was so pale that he felt a jolt go through him. When he called her name she didn't respond. Something was very wrong. He lifted her into his arms and strode out of the building. In the car he held her close to his body. He knew that, whatever it was, she wasn't faking it. No one could fake that.

Back at the hotel, he carried her again, all the way from the car up to the suite. Once inside he poured a glass of brandy and sat her down, making her swallow it. He could see the effect of the alcohol hitting her system; her eyes flared and she coughed. And then she started to shake uncontrollably. He pulled her into his body, waiting until the shaking subsided. Finally he could feel her pull away slightly and he let her go. She looked at him as though seeing him for the first time.

'What…what happened?'

She could see a light of rare concern in his eyes and wondered faintly what had put it there, while also having the wits to wish desperately that he was *really* concerned for her.

He brushed her hair back with a gesture that was almost tender, confusing her even more. 'I think you fainted…without fainting. I've seen it before. It's like a state of shock.'

Maggie dimly remembered following him out of the function room but for the life of her couldn't remember anything else. She shook her head. 'I don't know why… I'm sorry…'

'Don't be,' he said abruptly. 'Why don't you get ready for bed? You should sleep.'

She nodded her head and went into the bathroom. She felt exhausted, as if she'd run a marathon.

Caleb went out to the balcony and stood leaning on the same wall that Maggie had earlier. He shook his head. How could she be feeling such grief for that odious man? For that was what it was, *must be*. Yet, for all that she was, all that her stepfather had been, he shouldn't have underestimated the fact that she was bound to be in mourning. They had been family, after all. His cynical brain kicked into gear. Perhaps it was also the delayed shock of finding out that Tom's millions weren't going to be hers after all. That thought made something cold settle into his chest.

He went to the door of the suite and looked in. Maggie lay curled up on the bed, already asleep.

CHAPTER SIX

WHEN she woke the next morning Maggie's head throbbed. She was alone in the bed. A note on the pillow next to her caught her eye:

I'm at a meeting but will come and meet you for lunch on the terrace at twelve-thirty. Caleb.

She checked the bedside clock. It was ten a.m. Sinking back on to the pillows, fragments of the previous night came back. Like water dripping into a well, she began to recall what had made her have that bizarre, terrifying reaction. She remembered the crowds, the heat of the room and then how her thoughts had begun to circulate sickeningly on the events of all those months before.

She had to concede that it was possible for a kind of delayed shock to set in. She'd been shouldering the burden for so long…even her mother didn't know what had happened in London, the extent of Maggie's involvement. The threat that only Maggie had been aware of.

And her mother wasn't even aware of the plans Maggie had made for them to flee and hide in case Tom came after them. How relieved she'd been when she'd managed to persuade her mother to return home. Because she'd known that Tom would soon find out that Caleb had been aware all along, had prepared for the crude takeover bid. And when he found out, she knew he'd have blamed her…she worried her lower lip…but what had obviously happened then was that Caleb had immediately launched his own retaliation, thereby keeping Tom occupied. In a sick, twisted way, she recognised now that he had inadvertently saved her and her mother from Tom's wrath.

It had to be seeing Caleb again, all the intense emotions he was provoking…that had led to a mini meltdown of sorts. She managed to smile ruefully at herself as she went on to the terrace to soak up the morning sun; she'd never seen herself as a drama queen.

Then she remembered how gentle Caleb had been, how he'd held her tight against his body. A warmth invaded her limbs; she could still recall the feeling of safety. The yearning that had overwhelmed her with its sweetness. The wish that it could be for real… She was very much afraid of being sucked into the same dangerous dream as before. A dream of Caleb *loving* her. She blocked the thought ruthlessly and went inside to have a shower. She didn't love him…she didn't. She didn't even like him.

But you thought you did once… Can you just switch that off?

She ignored the prompt; if she repeated the words enough to herself like a mantra, she might just believe it.

At twelve-thirty Maggie was feeling back to normal. A table had just been delivered with a mouth-watering array of food—fresh fish, salad and crusty bread and a bottle of champagne on ice. She heard the door in the suite open and close and stood slightly awkwardly on the terrace when Caleb emerged. Her heart tripped predictably, the way it did every time she saw him, whether it had been seconds or hours in the interim.

'How are you this morning?' he asked coolly.

'Fine. Much better. About last night, I'm so sorry, that's never happened before.'

He lifted a hand. 'It's fine.'

'Okay…' Maggie trailed off. He clearly didn't want to discuss it. Maybe he *was* angry that they hadn't slept together. Maybe he thought it was an elaborate attempt on her part to avoid it? She suddenly hated the thought he might suspect that of her. She moved closer and put an impulsive hand on his arm. 'You don't think that I… Well, that I did it on purpose to…' She stopped, her face crimson with awkwardness and a cold horror struck her… *Had* her body somehow shut down because of that too?

'No, of course not.' And he genuinely didn't. That thought had never even entered his head and it surprised him now.

The residue of her disturbing thoughts still lingered and she answered absently, 'Good.'

'Let's eat.'

'All right.'

They sat down at the table that had been erected, complete with a pristine tablecloth and gleaming cutlery. With only the faint sounds of a few cars down in the square, someone calling to someone else, it was unbelievably intimate and private on their little terrace. The scent of the flowers hung heavy in the air.

Caleb busied himself opening the champagne and poured Maggie a glass before tending to himself. She murmured thanks and tried to appear cool, as though this happened every day for her.

'So what's on the cards for later? Another dinner?'

Caleb inclined his head. 'Yes, I'm afraid so. But you don't have to come if you think you're not up to it.'

His consideration touched her, despite the wall of ice she was trying to pack around her heart as she looked at him. She shook her head. 'No, I'll be fine. I'm not normally the fainting type. It's really never happened before.' She even felt guilty now because she knew what had brought it on. Not that she could tell him. She had to make an effort to appear unconcerned. As if he didn't hold her world in his hands.

She flashed him a rare smile. 'I can't wait to fend off more women, listen to people talk about the royal family as though they're intimate friends and try to decipher your financial jargon…'

A sharp burst of empathy made him suck in a breath. He caught himself and grimaced, unable to help a rueful smile that transformed his face and took Maggie's breath away; he seemed to have taken her unspoken cue to be light too. It made him look years younger.

'I'm sorry; I know how boring they can be. As for fending off the women, you saw the worst of the bunch last night. They don't see me, they see dollar signs, no ring and a potential husband for their daughters.'

She was thrown by his apology. He seemed for once not to be lumping her into that category and he was wrong—they saw far more than that. He was all the more attractive because of his youth, virility *and* his wallet. She couldn't help asking, 'Don't you want to get married some day?'

She could feel herself holding her breath as she saw the expressions flit over his face and the shutters came back down. A muscle twitched at his jaw. His voice was unbearably harsh. 'With what I've seen? Hardly. If I do marry, it'll be purely a business arrangement…and for children.'

She couldn't help the shiver that seemed to invade her very bones at his words. In a way, from the brief experience she'd had of the circles he moved in, she couldn't blame him. She remembered the looks of pure vitriol that had come her way from those women and could only imagine the conversations in the bathroom. There was a melancholic ring to his words too that made Maggie want to question him, find out what had put it there, find out more about his life, parents…but she couldn't.

In an effort to avoid talking about anything too personal, she started chattering about anything and everything. Caleb sat back and studied her. She was casual in a sleeveless cross-over top and linen trousers. And something niggled him about that, but before he could figure out what it was, he was distracted. Her face was animated, telling a story, but he was captivated by her movements, the way her eyes widened in emphasising a point. They'd spent two nights sharing the same bed…and still not slept together. That was a first for him. And he knew he couldn't bear to wait much longer. He'd woken several times during the previous night and even had to take a cold shower at one stage. Again.

'…and that was it, really.' Maggie stopped awkwardly; she knew he hadn't really been listening to her. Was she that boring?

Caleb sat forward. 'Sorry, I was miles away.'

'That's okay.' She smiled tightly.

Suddenly he felt like kicking himself. He'd hurt her, by not listening to her. And he was perplexed by her reaction. Shouldn't she be cajoling him now? Making him pay for his lack of attention, sliding on to his lap, trying to entice him to go to bed for the afternoon?

He shook his head. Her act of innocence was so ingrained that it was second nature. He shook his head at himself. She was reeling him in *again*.

'What is it?' Maggie had a look of almost concern on her face.

'Nothing,' he said harshly. He stood and pushed back his chair; it sounded shrill on the stone ground. Maggie flinched, a tiny movement. 'You should take it easy this afternoon.'

She could be cool too. 'I'm fine, Caleb, really. It won't happen again. I'm going to do some sightseeing this afternoon.' She shrugged lightly. 'I might never be back here again…'

His eyes narrowed. She really hadn't said that with any guile. Had she? His mouth quirked dryly. 'Oh, I'm sure you could persuade someone to bring you here again…'

She fought off the urge to defend herself from the obvious implication that he meant another lover…if she could even call him that. Right now, when he was being cynical and hateful, it was very easy to forget nonsensical, fantastical notions of being in love. She clung on to it like a shield around her heart.

'I'm sure you're right.' And she smiled up at him sunnily. 'I'll see you this evening. We go out at half seven.'

She nodded her head and watched as he walked away, sagging back into the chair once he'd gone, only aware then how much tension she'd been holding in.

Maggie was determined that Caleb would not affect her equilibrium, not with thoughts of the evening ahead or his tart barbs. So much for their short-lived truce.

She was doing a bus top sightseeing tour. But…try as she might, she couldn't block out the fantasy that hovered annoyingly like a wispy mist on the periphery of her mind. That if they'd met under different circumstances, he could perhaps feel something for her—beyond the mild contempt, distrust, all wrapped up in overwhelming desire, which was the reality.

She flipped her sunglasses back down on to her nose and

grimaced. That was the problem; even if she could indulge herself for one second that Caleb didn't have an axe to grind with her…then that would only put her in the same category as his usual mistresses. Which meant, she knew well, a bit of fun for a while, being indulged, cosseted, then…he'd walk away. That was what he'd meant last night, when he'd alluded to the fact that they always knew where they stood with him. And, even if that was the case, that wouldn't be enough. Not for her.

Maybe they had thicker skins? She valiantly ignored the absurd desire to line all of them up in front of a firing range. In a way, she reassured herself, she was better off; because she and Caleb had such a tangled history, it meant that he would never allow her to get too close.

Or you him…

Of course! she thought angrily, answering herself, it worked in her favour too. It did. She just wasn't entirely sure how…yet.

She spotted something on the street and got off at the next stop. Without questioning why, she found herself walking into the beautician's she'd seen. It was *not* because she wanted to make an effort. It was *not* giving into this fantasy. It was just female pride.

That night at another glittering function, it was like a carbon copy of the previous night. The same people, the same conversations. And yet…what was going on between them was subtly different. Maggie was tucked into Caleb's side, a possessive arm around her waist. He was including her in conversations, making it very clear she was with him. His woman. She could remember the look he'd given her earlier when she'd emerged from the dressing room in the suite. Her whole body still tingled from it.

At the beauticians she'd been waxed, plucked, buffed.

Nothing that he would notice…but she knew. That somehow made it erotic. She berated herself. Indulging herself like this would only end in pain. She knew it. But she couldn't help it. Couldn't help the devilish, rogue desire within her that had chosen the dress she had. It was one of the ones the sales girl had picked out, something Maggie would never normally have the nerve to wear. But something she guessed would be *suitable*.

With her hair piled in a loose knot on top of her head, the black dress was deceptively simple. A cowl neckline at the front didn't reveal too much but then, behind, it fell away, revealing her whole back. She'd always been self-conscious of her freckles everywhere but somehow now, here with Caleb, with his possessive arm around her, she felt…something close to beautiful for the first time in her life.

Without her realising it, the crowd had dispersed somewhat and Caleb led Maggie out to the terrace. The balmy air drifted around them on a light scented breeze and she breathed in deeply. There was a secluded gazebo at one end and Caleb took her hand, bringing her over.

'What…what are we doing here?'

Under the trellis roof that had flowers hanging down in a mass of twisting vines and leaves, he turned her to face him. 'Something I've been wanting to do all evening.' He dipped his head to her ear, making a delicious shiver skate up and down her spine. 'Your back has been driving me crazy.'

He pulled her even closer and she gasped when she felt the hardness of his arousal pressing into her belly. It called to her, made her damp with anticipation. She was breathless, waiting for the kiss, the embrace which was inevitable. His mouth hovered infuriatingly over her neck, lips barely skimming her skin. She wound her hands up and around his neck, craving an even closer embrace. Not thinking, not capable, just feeling.

Then his hands were on her bare back and a tremor shot through her. And in that moment his mouth covered hers and she was lost. He traced the outline of her lips, before his tongue delved in and met hers in an intoxicating dance. She was helpless but to succumb, matching his thrusts with her own, shyly allowing him to teach her, guide her.

His hands moulded, traced her waist, her spine, the smooth silky skin. Then one hand moved down and down until it rested just over the material of the dress that lay over her buttocks. She drew back, eyes dark and wide. Breath coming in short gasps. Watching her as he did, his hand went under the material, down until he felt the curve of her bottom, sheathed in silk panties. Her hands tightened on his shoulders.

His eyes were on her flushed face; they glittered with intent as he bent his head and took her mouth again with passionate bruising force, just as his hand went beneath the silk and caressed, smoothed, explored the voluptuous curves. Then his hand dipped all the way down, fingers seeking, underneath, all the way until…

Maggie gasped against his lips as his fingers found the moist evidence of her desire. Stroking back and forth, seeking the most sensitive part. When she would have pulled away, he held her to him fast and it was the most exquisite torture. She couldn't do anything, couldn't move. He was relentless. And then he was there…at that part… A spasm passed through her in response and still she was held captive. Unable to escape a pleasure that was almost too much. Too intense.

With his head bent, pressing fiery kisses against her neck, her head fell back. One hand held her like a vise against his body and with his other hand he was fast bringing her whole body upwards on a spiral of some devilish, overwhelming sensation, the like of which she'd never experienced. She could feel the subtle rhythm of his hard body as it pressed against her, she knew she'd widened her legs to tacitly give him access and their movements became more and more urgent, she didn't know what she was seeking, it was something that lay tantalisingly just out of reach and then… suddenly something gripped her that was so devastating…she stopped breathing for a minute.

Slow seconds later, as if she'd been transported to some other place, she slowly returned and felt her whole being throbbing, pulsating in the aftermath of what felt like an earthquake on her senses. As reality trickled back into her fuzzy mind, as Caleb straightened and loosened his hold slightly, she knew with astounding clarity that she'd just had her first orgasm. She looked up at Caleb, knew that she must have a dazed expression on her face and couldn't even begin to disguise it. She had lost her virginity to her one boyfriend in college, but he'd never ever made her feel anything beyond mild discomfort. This…this, however, was in another league. She heard the murmur of low voices nearby, a tinkle of laughter coming from the ballroom just yards away.

She had come apart in his arms, on little more than the strength of a kiss, had allowed him full access without so much as a murmur of dissent. Without thinking, she just reacted, had to get away. 'Excuse me…I need to go to the bathroom.'

Caleb let her go and she went, hoping she didn't look as devastated by what had just happened as she felt.

He watched her go, sitting back on the seat behind him in a sprawl. His own heart rate was just beginning to return to normal and the unsatisfied ache was acute.

He shook his head grimly; he'd only planned on kissing her. Hadn't planned on the sudden need to maul her senseless. What was wrong with him? The last time he'd caressed a woman so comprehensively in a public place was when he'd been a gauche teenager. And it had been a girl, not a woman. He cursed himself; he wouldn't be surprised if she had a love bite on her neck.

But she had been so responsive... That subtle touch of feigned innocence was fast pushing him over the edge whenever he came near her. With just his hands on her back! He could still feel the tremor that had run through her, pushing her breasts against him, igniting a fire in his belly...in his loins. And that had intoxicated him beyond the point of reason. She'd been the same that night in London, which he remembered all too well...and yet she'd stopped just when...just when he'd been able to stop. Maybe she was doing it again? Giving him a taste of nirvana, only to bring him to his knees, expose him.

She would not do that to him again. No way. And this time he wouldn't stop. He knew her response wasn't fake. He was arrogantly sure of that. She wouldn't be able to stop herself this time. With a determined lithe push to stand, he was hidden in the shadows for a moment before going in search of Maggie. It was time to claim his prize.

Back in the hotel room, Maggie heard the door click ominously shut behind Caleb. She felt skittish and on edge. She wasn't ready for this. She needed time to process what had happened, had to be in control of her emotions when she gave herself to him. She was still stunned, shocked by the depth of her response to him in the gazebo. As soon as she'd emerged back into the ballroom she'd caught his eye immediately. She'd stood there, fighting the urge to run in the opposite direction as he'd strode towards her, the people melting away either side of him. Without saying a word, he'd halted in front of her, taken her hand and led her out. Not one word. To anyone. And now here they were, back in the hotel. The huge bed just there, in her field of vision.

Maggie turned to face him, not even knowing what to say, but before she could speak, unaware of the turmoil of her thoughts, he went towards the bathroom, shedding his jacket as he did so.

'I'm going to have a shower…'

'Okay…' Panic gripped her voice, making it sound shrill to her ears. 'I'll have one after you.'

He turned at the door, raising one black brow. 'Unless you want to share?'

'No…' she said hastily—too hastily. 'I'll wait.'

He shrugged.

Maggie went out to the balcony and paced up and down with arms wrapped around her body. She couldn't even think coherently. This was happening too fast—way too fast. She was still in pieces after little more than a bout of heavy petting. How would she cope when Caleb…took her completely? Her belly flooded with liquid fire just at the thought and she sat on a chair weakly. She wasn't the woman of the world that he was used to. She was just plain, simple Maggie Holland. The girl with the red hair and freckles who bruised easily and still had scars from falling off trees when she was small. And other scars that he could never know about. She needed time, space. To fight off the inevitable for just a little longer.

The bathroom door opened. She sprang up. He was finished already? Caleb emerged with an indecently small towel around his waist. Hair wet, sleek against his head. Maggie's stricken gaze couldn't escape the wide, broad, muscled chest, a light sprinkling of hair that tapered down to his lean waist. Her eyes skipped over the towel and down over long, long, strong, shapely legs. She gulped. He was shameless under her gaze and indicated the door. 'Bathroom's all yours... Don't be long, Maggie.'

Once inside, she sagged against the door. The mist enveloped her—the heat of his body, the musky scent still in the air. It brought her whole body back into tingling awareness. She had to do something. She couldn't face her ultimate capitulation tonight. Tomorrow, maybe...but not now, not after that...explosive experience.

She kicked off her shoes and went to the mirror, looking at her reflection. Two bright spots of colour highlighted her cheeks; her eyes were too wide and bright. She ran the bath in a desperate attempt to buy some more time to think.

Finally. After waiting for as long as she thought she could, Maggie cautiously opened the bathroom door. Caleb lay on the bed against the pillows with his eyes closed. She emerged slowly. Maybe he was asleep? His eyes snapped open. No such luck. He came up on one arm, a frown appearing when he noticed that she hadn't changed out of the dress. Then a gleam of appreciation lit them.

'Good. I was just fantasising about taking it off you. Come here.'

He thought she'd left it on, on purpose...

Little did he know the terror in her chest—how could he not see it? She moved forward one foot and stopped.

He frowned again. She looked too serious. 'Maggie...' he said warningly.

'Caleb. Wait.' She put up a hand and prayed for courage. 'I'm not going to sleep with you until I've signed the contract.'

He sprang from the bed and Maggie fled back into the bathroom, slamming the door and locking it just as she heard

Caleb's fist make a connection. Her heart hammered against her ribs. The door knob jiggled. She jumped back.

'Maggie… Open up or, so help me God, I will break this door down.'

Desperation made her voice weak. 'You said I'd sign a contract guaranteeing that the house would go back into my mother's name. I want to do that before anything…happens between us.'

'It's already happened, sweetheart.'

She burned on the other side of the door. But at least he wasn't threatening to break it down any more, although he did sound as though he wanted to throttle her.

'Maggie, come out…'

'No way.'

She could hear a muffled oath.

'Not unless you promise not to touch me.'

There was a very long silence. So long that Maggie was afraid he'd left without telling her and now she'd be stuck in the bathroom all night. Then she heard a very low, 'Fine.'

She turned the lock and opened the door. She was relieved when she saw Caleb on the other side of the room in his trousers, arms folded across his chest. His face like thunder. She quivered inwardly but strove for confidence on the outside.

'Do you want to tell me what this is all about?' he asked tightly.

'I want to sign that contract. Once I know for sure you're going to keep your word, then you can…have…make me yours.' Those words alone sent a spiral of heat through her body.

He came a little closer. She backed away slightly. 'If I remember correctly, I made no such assurance; the agreement was that you would move in, become my mistress and then…I would sign the house back to your mother.'

Damn him, he was right. Her shoulders sagged. For a moment Caleb felt something move through him…almost concern. She looked unbelievably vulnerable.

The only thing stopping him from doing what he wanted, going over and shaking her, then kissing her thoroughly was the knowledge that he wanted to do it so badly it scared him. And he would control himself around her, although the gazebo and the passion she had incited still held him in its grip.

Remembering something, he looked and, sure enough, he could see a faint red mark on her neck. It firmed his resolve not to let her see how close he was to losing it. He, Caleb Cameron, one of the wealthiest tycoons in the world, his expertise worth millions, had given a grown woman a love bite. So he stood back. Maybe he needed some time, a little space to make sure he was in control the next time.

Maggie lifted her head and looked at him, those huge green eyes pinning him to the spot.

'Look. You have me. I'm not going to deny you what you want…'

'You want me too, Maggie…'

More than anything.

Her eyes flared for a second, telling him of her agreement even though she didn't say it. 'My dignity and self-respect are pretty much in the gutter right now. All I'm asking is that when we get back you let me sign the contract and then… then…'

There would be no more excuses to avoid the inevitable…

'Okay.'

Maggie thought she hadn't heard him correctly it was so quick. 'Okay?'

'Yes. Fine.' He walked past her, his face expressionless, and started to dress again.

'What…where are you going?'

'Well, Maggie, as you're not willing to share my bed yet…I'm going to go out. You'd better hope to be asleep by the time I return.'

And with that he was gone. Maggie had got what she wanted, so why didn't she feel happy? Why did she want to run out of the door after him and say, Stop! I'm sorry, please come back, take me to bed? She cursed herself, she was only prolonging the pain, the anticipation, the misery. What had she done? Her brain was scrambled beyond all comprehension with him around. But the minute he was gone it was clear again. She had pushed him too far. And now he was gone, back to the function. It was the only place. Or maybe he'd go to a small smoky bar, seek out a kindred soul.

She sat down on a chair. He could have his pick of any number of the beauties who had been vying for his attention the past two evenings. Any number of the beauties in this place. He had gone, to take his pick. He was letting her know that she wouldn't hold him back. But even with that knowledge, her weak body burned for his, ached for a deeper fulfilment than she'd experienced earlier. She changed, washed and climbed into bed, letting sleep obliterate her tortured imaginings.

The next morning Maggie woke and felt safe and secure. A cocoon of warmth surrounded her. She moved experimentally to try and keep it, deepen it, and then froze as she realised where she was. She was comprehensively tucked into the warm embrace of Caleb's arms. Their bodies touched from head to toe. His chest against her back, his long legs spooning hers effortlessly, one almost thrown over her thigh. And he was completely naked. She realized that with burning alarm.

Arms held her an easy captive, one hand spread over her breasts, which she could feel coming to life, becoming engorged with rushing blood, her nipples becoming hard, pushing against the warm skin of his hand. If he was to move, just even slightly, curl that hand... She swallowed. Torture. She tried to move but his arms were like steel bands and, when she made a bigger movement, they tightened.

A sleep-rough voice growled in her ear, 'Going somewhere?'

She froze. Again.

'Too late for that. I know you're awake.'

And so was her body. Spectacularly. Betraying her with its eager response to his proximity.

The hand at her breast left and made lazy progress down to her belly, feeling the soft swell under the satin of her negligée, then back up. Maggie's breath came quicker as his hand hovered over the full mounds, the lace of her top chafing unbearably, and then let out a ragged sigh and closed her eyes tightly as it cupped, moulded and caught one taut peak, thumb and forefinger pinching gently, making it even harder until it was like a knife-edge of sensation running all the way down her body to between her legs.

And then, while his hand was busy stimulating one erogenous zone, she became aware of how her negligée had ridden up. He was sliding a hair-roughened thigh between her legs, opening her up, nudging past her resistance, and then she could feel the blatant hardness of his arousal *there*, against her, only a mere breath away from being inside, where she longed for fulfilment. She moved her bottom against him. 'Caleb...'

'What...what is it?' His breath was driving her insane. She wanted...she wanted...

'What do you want? This?'

He moved upwards and she could feel the head of him

nudge against her moistness. Her muscles quivered and contracted in anticipation. This was going so fast but, in the heady half sleep limbo land, it was all Maggie could do not to turn and give herself completely.

'Yes…oh, yes.' She bit her lip in an effort not to plead any more.

And then, in a moment so quick and brutal she didn't know which way was up, Caleb was out of the bed and standing there with a towel slung around his waist, hiding the extent of his erection, though she could still feel the size of it, imagine the length of it. His face was stamped with the lines that told her how hard it had been for him to stop. Waves of censure reached out to envelop her.

Confusion showed on her face. Her voice breathless, she said, 'What's wrong?'

'Nothing, Maggie, that a signed contract won't solve.'

He came down and rested on his hands over her, taking in her flushed face, dilated pupils, her still aroused body. 'When we come together it'll be like this, Maggie, so I can watch your face as you give yourself to me.'

So much for her grand announcements last night. Within moments she'd been ready to forget everything—her precious vulnerability swept aside by the burning ache that still pounded in her blood.

She shrank back against the pillows, more humiliated than she had been even that night in London. For at least that time she hadn't tasted the total bliss he could evoke. They hadn't gone so far that she couldn't stop herself. But…he, she remembered uncomfortably, had been in a similar state to now. This time, however, *he* was the one calling a halt. Demonstrating her lack of control over him.

He was binding a silken thread around her, so tight that she knew she'd never be free of it. Even after he was finished with her. Pain made her lash out, her words clumsily inarticulate. 'Wasn't whoever's bed you warmed last night not enough?'

He stopped in the act of straightening up from the bed, his body lithe and supple and heart-stoppingly beautiful. The thought of him with another woman was making her insides fizz with anger. Along with the ache that permeated every bone, betraying how much she wanted him.

He looked at her coldly. 'I, unlike you, have a moral code. I don't share myself around. Aren't you lucky, Maggie?' He gave a short, mirthless laugh. 'I'm all yours. For now. And I won't be made to wait again or, trust me, the agreement will be revoked and I will take a new mistress.'

A rush of elation surged through her—so he hadn't slept with another woman. She was heedless to the incongruity of how happy that made her feel—despite the evidence of their shaky truce in tatters around them, despite the ache, the humiliation, Maggie was suddenly absurdly happy. He flicked her a dismissive glance before turning away. 'We leave for Dublin in an hour.'

CHAPTER SEVEN

JOHN, Caleb's driver, was waiting with the car at the small private airport. Maggie was glad of the distraction of having someone else to talk to as Caleb stood outside the car taking a phone call for a few minutes. In the course of their conversation, Maggie discovered that John had lost his entire family in a tragic accident some ten years previously. He had been working for someone else in the company, but when Caleb had heard the news he'd made John his own driver and now brought him everywhere.

'To tell the truth, love, I don't know what I would have done. He kept me going and there were times…' He stopped and his eyes grew moist. Maggie stretched a hand out to his shoulder in sympathy.

'Sorry, love, it's still…' He recovered and cast a glance out of the car. 'He's a good man. He'll look after you. Loyal to a fault, I'd say. Far too easy on some of them that's tried to put one over on him…'

Caleb slipped back into the car at that moment and John winked at Maggie, lightening the atmosphere, before turning around to drive them into town. She went over his words. Well, Caleb certainly had a fan there. She couldn't fault his behaviour with the man. But she didn't want to know nice things about him; she wanted pettishly for everyone to hate him, to confirm that he was cynical and ruthless.

His voice broke into her thoughts. 'John, drop me off at the office—I have some meetings lined up for the afternoon—then bring Maggie home.'

In the car outside his offices, he turned to Maggie. 'I'll be back about seven and I'll bring the contract. So why don't you burn some water and we can celebrate later?'

Maggie flushed under his pointed gaze that wouldn't let her escape, knowing John could hear their conversation. 'Fine.'

When he was gone, she sat back and breathed properly for the first time that day. Her mind and stomach churned. At least she had a few hours to get control of herself. When they pulled up outside the apartment building, Maggie took her bag from John and watched as he drove away with a cheery wave.

She took a spin out to see her mother that afternoon, to confirm for herself that she was all right. She was so ecstatic and happy and relaxed that Maggie felt real relief for the first time. She was almost a changed woman; she even looked different from the last time Maggie had seen her. Younger. This was her proof, her motivation. She *was* doing the right thing. She knew it. She was heartened for the first time in days as she drove back into town.

Back in the apartment, she decided she couldn't be bothered lying about her ability to cook and made a wild mushroom risotto. Cooking always relaxed her and she needed all the help she could get. Having reluctantly skipped over an old pair of comfy jeans and plain shirt, she figured she'd better dress as he'd expect. So she stood now in the kitchen and felt ridiculously uncomfortable in a silk shirt and light tweed trousers. Her hair, despite her having tried to tame it back into a tidy bun, was already tousled at the nape of her neck. When Caleb walked in, the carpet muffling his entrance, that was what he saw.

Maggie was stirring something in a pot, bending low to smell, a small frown on her face. Then she straightened and started chopping spring onions for a salad. The dexterity with which she chopped told him, as a keen cook himself, that she was no novice. He ignored the strange ache in his chest just from looking at her.

'The burnt water smells surprisingly appetising,' he drawled dryly.

She jumped and whirled around. But quickly regained her composure. He could see that there was tension in the lines of her body that hadn't been there seconds before and bizarrely hated the fact that he had done that.

'Yes…well, I didn't want to give you the satisfaction of thinking you had a live-in cook as well as a mistress. But, as it happens, I can cook quite well.'

'Good. Because I'm starving. I'll have a shower and join you.'

Maggie shrugged negligently, as if she didn't care, but since he'd surprised her at the door her pulse had been thumping out of control.

When he'd gone she ran her wrists under the cold tap to try and calm her pulse. She lifted her hands to her hot cheeks. She was a wreck. Images, fantasies, erotic pictures were taking control of every corner of her brain. She was a walking hormone. She set out the cutlery and a bottle of wine because she knew he'd expect it, but vowed only to have a little herself so that she was in complete control.

And then he was there. He'd dressed down as she would have preferred to, in faded jeans and a T-shirt that was taut across his muscled chest. Wet hair curling just above the collar. His potency, the raw sexuality, reached across the room and called to her, made her want to walk over, sink into him.

'What can I do?'

She shut her eyes for a split second at the lurid images that jumped into her mind's eye at his question. Her voice, when it came, was husky. 'You could bring the salad through; everything else is here.'

Her appetite had just disappeared.

He brought it in and they sat down. Caleb poured them both a glass of wine and lifted his glass high. 'To tonight.'

Maggie blanched and took a deep breath. She just nodded in response. And took a big gulp of wine. So much for her good intentions.

He took a mouthful of the risotto and a look of disbelief came over his face. 'Maggie, this is really good. Where did you learn to do this? Do you know how hard it is to get this right?'

She blushed with acute pleasure and couldn't stop a grin. 'Really?'

'Really. I've eaten in some of the best restaurants in Italy and they certainly haven't done risotto as well as this.'

With pleasure fizzing through her at his rare approval, she explained, 'I worked as a chef's assistant when I was working my way through college. In return for portraits of his family, he gave me extra lessons.'

'Worked your way through college?' Those eyes were narrowed speculatively on hers. She thought quickly. Tom had had millions. Money shouldn't have been an object. Maggie had always refused it, though, seeing it as tantamount to blood money, despite her mother's pleas to let him help her.

She shrugged lightly. 'I thought I wanted to prove to Tom that I could do it on my own, but I soon got bored...' The next words killed her when she thought of the awful bedsit she'd lived in, cockroaches everywhere. 'But of course I didn't last long. Why take the hard way?'

'Why, indeed?' Caleb seemed happy to let it drop. As if she'd jumped out of the box he had her in, but was now safely back inside. They both took another sip of wine.

She had to try and keep him off personal subjects. She was too inclined to speak quickly and openly. He was far too easy to talk to. Like the lunch they'd had in Monte Carlo, they slipped into a light conversation, skating across several subjects. When Caleb poured the last of the wine into her glass she wondered how they'd drunk the whole bottle. She could feel the mellow aftermath through her bones and wanted to wake up. Stay alert.

'I'll make some coffee.' She went to get up and Caleb stayed her with a hand.

'No. You made dinner; I'll do the coffee. Sit on the couch and I'll bring it in.'

His easy courtesy unsettled her. She watched as he proceeded to clear the table and then she heard him moving around the kitchen. She did as he'd said and sat on the couch. That was when she saw it on the table, low down near her feet. The contract. That sobered her up more quickly than any coffee could. She picked it up warily and flicked through it. There, in stark black and white, were the hideous words…

Margaret Holland…become the mistress of Caleb Cameron for two months only…from this date…and the house in question at the following address…revert to the name of Fidelma Holland…but only when said relations have…

Nausea rose. Now that it was in front of her in black and white, she couldn't actually believe that he'd had the gall to draw this up…with the advice of a solicitor? With witnesses? And there were the lines for their signatures. As bold and impersonal and dry as the way her mouth felt right now. Even if she was the one that had begged for their house…had created this situation…this was too much.

He came into the room and Maggie carefully placed it back on the table. He followed her movements as he put down the coffee cups. She picked hers up and placed chilled hands around it, feeling a shudder go through her system.

'So you've seen it.' His voice came low and implacable from her right.

'Yes. Which is, no doubt, what you expected when you directed me over here.'

She could feel him tense beside her. 'I didn't, actually. I'd forgotten I'd put it down. But what's the problem, Maggie? Isn't this what you wanted?'

She put down the coffee jerkily and sprang up away from the couch, willing herself desperately not to cry. 'No! It's not what I wanted. I never wanted any of this. None of it. And certainly not for my private details to be pored over by complete strangers.'

He stood too. She spun away, oblivious to the spectacular backdrop of the city lights starting to come on outside. He came and whirled her round to face him.

'I'm sorry, Maggie, but this is a direct result of your actions. Six months ago you played with fire and now you're getting burnt.'

She was burning up all right.

He captured her close, two harsh hands on her arms. 'You want me, Maggie, as much as I want you. Can you deny it?'

Miserable, intoxicated by his closeness, the contract fading into the background, she couldn't move. He shifted subtly so that she was pressed tight up against the length of him. He brought his hands down her arms and then her two hands were captured behind her back with one of his.

'You want me, don't you?' With his other hand he brushed back a tendril of hair from her face, then threaded through it to cradle her head. She had to fight against wanting to let it sink, fall into his hand. Her body flamed into life everywhere it connected with his…but she wanted to make sure he knew she was fighting it all the way. Had to. It was her only defence.

After seeing that contract, she had a bare thread of dignity left and this was it.

'Yes…' The word was wrung harshly from her. 'I may want you on the outside, but know that on the inside I'm hating you with every breath I take.'

A tension and stillness came into his body. A savage look passed over his face so quickly she might have imagined it. Then his look narrowed and, with his eyes so intensely blue on hers that it hurt, he said, 'Then it's just as well it's not your heart I'm after. Just your body. It's time to finish what you started that night, Maggie.'

His cruelly stark words seared her alive. An ache closed the back of her throat as he bent and took her mouth in a possessive, punishing kiss. And while her foolish, weak body rejoiced in the contact, her heart made a lie of her words— every beat telling her what she didn't want to know, what she didn't want to face up to. What she couldn't face up to yet. His mouth finally gentled and he freed her hands at last, where she hesitated for one weak, desperate moment before giving in under his sensual onslaught and the inevitability of her situation, which meant she couldn't walk away again. She had no choice. She was on a course that was destined to come to its conclusion. A course that she had put them on. A course Tom had put them on six months ago.

As much as they conversely wanted to punch against him for making her feel like this, those treacherous hands climbed up over his chest, up again…until they were around his neck, fingers tangling in the silky strands of hair that brushed his T-shirt. Knowing that somewhere within her all was lost, she gave into what she had for now. And what she had was him— kissing her, making love to her. She pressed close, as close as she could, and wound her arms even tighter round his neck, her kisses matching his, passion for passion. This was all she'd have. His contempt and his passion. So she'd take it.

Caleb pulled back for a moment; he could feel Maggie trembling violently in his arms, had felt something run through her. 'Hey…slow down.' He felt as though he should be comforting her. The light of something very guarded in her eyes caught him and held him; she reminded him of a cornered animal, fighting to protect itself. But that was crazy…

'I'm sorry, I just…I…'

With a finger to her lips, he silenced her. If he didn't know better he'd say she was overwhelmed, inexperienced…but then dismissed that notion. An act. It *had* to be. For some reason it was vitally important.

Her uneven breaths were pushing her breasts against him. He trailed one finger down her heated cheek, around the delicate line of her jaw and down, over her collar-bone, to where the first button held her shirt together. Not allowing her to pull away, he flipped it open, then the next, then the next. He could feel her breath growing more ragged but at least that awful desperation seemed to have gone. That enigmatic light in her eyes had now been replaced by something much more recognisable. Desire.

The shirt fell open to reveal a simple plain sheer bra. He could see the pink aureoles of her nipples, beading, puckering around the tight tips. He brought up his hand and traced the line of her breast, staying away from the sensitive centre, down into the valley, over the mound that spilled from the top, and then finally, slowly, down to where the nipples had grown even harder, tighter.

Maggie was biting into her bottom lip, a shudder running through her, a faint sign of perspiration on her brow as one thumb rotated around that aureole, before finally coming to the centre of where all of her nerve-endings were screaming for release. With a thumb and forefinger, he pinched gently and Maggie felt her legs buckle. Caleb caught her and, just feet away from them, brought her over and lowered her on to the couch. Her response was testing his control to the limit. She lay back and watched as he pulled his T-shirt impatiently over his head, revealing his perfect torso.

He put his hands over hers at her sides and pressed a quick kiss to her mouth, before moving down, lips over her neck, the thumping pulse and down, into the valley, before closing in a kiss over one aching peak. Her arms held captive, Maggie writhed with the pleasure as his mouth moved to the other side and the onslaught started all over again. She couldn't think, couldn't speak. All she was blissfully aware of was the heaven of sensations Caleb was taking her to as his mouth sucked, teeth nipped.

With a graceful movement he pulled her up and pushed the shirt from her shoulders, unhooked her bra and pulled it off. He set her back and looked his fill.

'So beautiful.'

He traced the curves of her waist, her soft belly, and his fingers halted at the button on her trousers. He pressed her back down and came over her, his chest rubbing deliciously against her breasts. His mouth covered hers, her arms wound around his neck and their tongues met in a dance that took her breath away. The hand at her trousers undid the button. She felt constricted and wanted them off, lifting her hips to help him pull them down, kicking them free, their lips still clinging together.

He stopped and looked down, saw her plain white knickers, her slender, shapely legs. He ran a hand upwards over one silken flank and hovered close to where he wanted nothing more than to feel the evidence of her desire. He heard, felt her breath stop.

She was so beguiling, in nothing but the knickers, her whole body covered in a dusting of freckles, and he wanted her more desperately than he'd ever wanted anyone. His jeans contained his arousal…just.

In the next instant he lifted her into his arms and brought her into the bedroom. She felt curiously vulnerable to him, naked in his arms against his chest, her arms tight around his neck. Maggie marvelled dimly that she had thought that when they got to this stage she'd be paralysed with nerves…but there was a fever in her blood that drowned out anything other than Caleb…and her. It felt right. And good. As if how they had got here didn't matter—what mattered was that they were here.

Once in the bedroom, he put her down on unsteady feet. Her eyes were dark and fathomless. He reached around and undid the pins holding her hair back and it fell in a curtain of waves and curls around her shoulders and down her back. Without taking his eyes off hers, he undid his jeans and pulled them down, stepping out of them.

He was naked. Maggie's hot gaze moved down and took him in. He was magnificent. Having been with only one man before, she felt out of her depth…and yet, conversely…*knew* what to do. It was something she couldn't even begin to figure—it was just an innate knowing. Something between *her* and this man. A knowing that made every cell in her body ache to have him inside her, filling her. She shook with the force of the emotion running through her and yet, to her surprise, it didn't scare her.

She looked up for a brief moment and the expression in Caleb's eyes set her pulse on fire. Filled with a sense of sensual adventure, emboldened by his dark look, his obvious arousal for her, she reached out, dimly wondering how on earth she had the nerve, and closed one small hand around the length of him. She could feel it pulse, jump slightly, the satin smooth skin moving against the hard shaft. Her hand looked tiny and pale around it, barely able to encircle it. She felt a liquid coil of desire within her.

She looked up into Caleb's face and his eyes were slits; there were slashes of dark colour on each cheek bone and he struggled with his breath. The thought that she was doing this to him made her feel exultant in her sexuality.

He was gone beyond the place of reason or coherence. The intoxicating mix of her wide-eyed innocence and her obvious know-how was too much. He shook with the need to be inside her, filling her…this woman, no one else. He wouldn't, couldn't think of all the other men she'd done this for. It would kill him. He vowed to take her so completely that she'd never want another man again. He stopped her hand with his, his voice was guttural, hoarse. 'Maggie…stop unless you want this to be over very quickly.'

He moved her back to the bed, tumbling her down. She watched as he came over her on two strong arms. She moved back to allow him room and then he was running his hands down, over the peaks and hollows, lingering, sometimes tracing with his mouth where his hands had been and then his mouth hovered over her belly button, his tongue flicking out to taste.

His hands reached her knickers and slowly but surely started to pull them down. They dropped on to the floor. Now she was bared completely and she felt Caleb nudge her legs open with his body. She felt a breath *there*, where the molten core of her was. She couldn't look and flung an arm over her face in a fit of shyness. His hands came under her buttocks, tilting her slightly, and then she felt his tongue exploring, leaving a wet, hot trail as it crept up one inner thigh, then the other, before spreading her even further, opening her up so that his mouth…and tongue could seek and find that rock-hard small piece of flesh that no other man had ever touched with such intimacy.

When his tongue found it, circled it, sucked…she thought she'd die…and then his tongue moved down…and entered her. She tensed and arched her back. Her other hand gripped the sheets. Her breathing was so fractured and tortured she thought she might pass out. How could he do this…make her feel like this…so liquid and wanton and…? She couldn't stop herself—the spiral was building, like a coil tightening; his tongue was harder, thrusting deeper, until finally she was pushed to the point of no return and she came, her whole body bucking in the aftershock. Her arm was still over her face; she was too mortified to look and felt tears under her eyelids at the intensity of emotion she was feeling. She could feel Caleb move up over her sensitive body and he brought her arm down. She blinked away the tears before he could see them.

He kissed her so deeply that she could taste herself on him. He was drunk on the scent of her, the taste of her, the feel of her and couldn't wait any longer. After slipping on protection, he fought the urge to thrust in so deep and far that he'd have immediate relief. She was looking at him now, an intense look of concentration on her face which made him feel a fierce tenderness, but he was in the grip of something so powerful that he couldn't dwell on it…or question it.

'Don't close your eyes, Maggie.'

She shook her head. She couldn't look away even if she wanted to. She felt him push against her slick folds and lifted her hips to him. He brought a hand under her back, arching her to him, and pushed in further. And further. Her eyes opened wide at the exquisite sensation. He was so big…but she could feel her muscles taking him in, and then he thrust again. The entire hard length of him was within her tight embrace. She still had that look of concentration on her face, as though it was all she wanted to do—give him this pleasure. The force of how it made him feel rippled through his body.

Her legs instinctively came around his buttocks, her hands on his shoulders as he pulled out before filling her again. Her eyes on his, their gazes locked, with steady thrusts Caleb brought Maggie into another universe. Where she forgot time and space, her name, everything. He waited until her body convulsed around his and then, with beads of sweat on his brow, gave in to his own earth-shattering capitulation.

As he curled his body around Maggie's, Caleb felt for the first time in his life as if he'd finally come home.

What a ridiculous thought…

But, more importantly, finally…she was his.

Maggie took the cup of tea she'd just made and walked over to the huge window in the sitting room. Hardly seeing the view, her thoughts inward, she felt…curiously still…and empty. As if something monumental had shifted within her. She was very much afraid she'd never be the same. And she knew she'd compartmentalised it somehow, put it into some corner where she wouldn't have to deal with it...just yet. Her whole body ached, muscles protesting if she moved too quickly, and when she'd looked in the mirror earlier she'd been shocked at the bruises on her skin. She blushed then as she remembered raking Caleb's back with her nails and wondered if she'd left him with marks too.

She took a sip of tea, feeling the hot liquid go down, warming her insides, which felt curiously cold. Maybe this was just her defence mechanism kicking in. All she *was* willing to acknowledge was that he had made her take leave of her senses and that the two of them had ignited a passion that scared her with its intensity. And it had started a craving ache that she knew wouldn't be sated until she saw Caleb again.

The phone rang, piercing the air, and she jumped. Little fiery shivers of sensation raced along her nerve-endings as she already anticipated his voice on the other end. Images of last night flooded her head. Thank God he couldn't see her.

'Hello?'

'There's a courier on the way around for—'

'Okay, fine.'

'See you later, then.'

'Fine.'

She cut him off. Didn't want him to say it. She knew exactly what he was talking about. Their conversation couldn't have been more sterile. He was talking about the contract. In the headiness of last night, when he'd swept her so effortlessly into that vortex of need and want and pleasure, she'd forgotten all about it. Only to wake this morning to an empty bed and the contract beside her. She smiled grimly—that just about summed up what was going on. He'd signed his part and left a curt note:

Countersign and I'll send over a courier. Consider it done.

So it was done. Her mother had her house back…and, in seven weeks and a bit, Maggie would be free to walk away. Curiously, the thought didn't fill her with the elation she'd thought it would. Was she really so pathetic? She jerked away from the phone and the window and went to rinse out the cup. She found a pen, signed the contract and put it in an envelope Caleb had left behind. Then she waited for the courier downstairs. She almost thrust it at him when he arrived, more distraught than she would have imagined or thought she'd be.

CHAPTER EIGHT

OVER the following days the packages started to arrive. Velvet boxes that held stunning jewels. Usually with a note, nothing endearing, something curt like: *For tonight* or *This'll go with something black.* Maggie stopped being stunned and saying thank you because Caleb didn't seem to like it. He told her he expected her to wear them…much like she'd wear a designer dress. As if he were just kitting her out. And with each piece, whether it was a bracelet or a necklace or earrings, she felt cheaper and cheaper. More and more humiliated.

As much as she tried, she just found it so hard to put on all those jewels and parade around like some gilded lily. It made her uncomfortable…uneasy. Went against all her moral and political sensibilities. If he were giving them to her from a place of genuine pleasure, *in her*, then that would be different. But that fantasy belonged in a world that didn't exist.

She had to realise, now that she was sharing his bed…this was his usual *modus operandi*. She was no different and she'd be a fool to dream otherwise. On the fifth day, after the fourth night in his bed, when she received a priceless diamond bracelet, it finally drove her from the apartment, the sense of rising panic too much. She walked…for hours, for miles. And eventually ducked into an old cinema in an effort to block out the thoughts that hounded her brain like whirling dervishes.

'Where the hell have you been?'

Maggie tried not to quail at the anger stamped into Caleb's features, but she could feel an old familiar panic rise up.

Caleb is not Tom…

She closed the front door behind her. 'I went to the cinema, Caleb. You can't lock me in here every day—'

'Oh, can't I?' he said threateningly as he advanced on her. The colour leached from her face, stopping him in his tracks. Her eyes were huge. He forced himself to calm down. She was back. She was here. Had he really thought she'd try and leave once the contract was signed? But he had…for a moment.

He thrust a hand through his hair. 'Maggie, look… Of course I can't lock you in here. I got back and you were gone…I don't know, I guess I thought…' He shook his head. 'It doesn't matter. Just call me next time…'

Maggie couldn't believe it, slowly allowing herself to calm again. He actually looked…almost shaken. Had he really thought she'd run away? As if! She had no doubt that if she had even tried anything like that, he'd have reneged on the agreement, contract or no.

'I don't actually have your mobile number,' she said dryly.

'Well, let's remedy that now.' He took her bag with proprietary ease and fished out her phone. She looked on, bemused, as he punched in his number and handed it back.

'You don't need mine?'

He looked addled. 'Yes, I do.'

He handed her his phone and she put in her number and handed it back. Somehow, she felt a twitch at the corner of her mouth. Was it hysteria? Who cared? Suddenly a lightness was bubbling up and she couldn't hold it in. Caleb caught her rapidly contorting face and frowned for a second. 'What—?'

She couldn't stop it; laughter bubbled out and she gasped with the effort to control it. 'I'm sorry…it's…just…a bit…'

'After the fact?' he asked with a twitch on his mouth too. He watched as she tried to control herself, felt her lightness reach out to touch him. She gasped in big breaths and wiped at the tears that had sprung from her eyes. He reached out a finger and trailed it over one cheek, saying almost wonderingly, 'You're even more beautiful when you laugh… You should do it more often.'

Her belly quivered at his touch, then she hiccuped, 'Well, I haven't had much cause lately.'

Or ever…

Something dark crossed Caleb's face and she could see him close up again. No! she wanted to say. Stay with me. He dropped his finger; she felt bereft. She controlled herself again. They were still standing just inside the door.

'I've put on some chicken…how does that sound?'

'You cook?' she asked inanely.

His mouth quirked. 'Apparently quite well.'

She shrugged, trying not to look too impressed, finding herself inordinately relieved to be eating in. They'd eaten out every other night so far, each restaurant more glittering and exclusive than the last, and Maggie was tired. 'The proof will be in the eating,' she quipped quickly, not wanting him to see her relief.

'Ouch.' He winced and started to head back towards the kitchen. 'Not all of us were trained by chefs; some of us had to learn the hard way.'

She followed him into the sparkling, brand new kitchen, curious. 'So where did you learn, then?'

As she watched, he seemed to know what he was doing, tossing a salad with fluid ease. It would be just like the man to be able to do everything perfectly.

'My mother can't cook to save her life, or my father, and in lean times, when Dad became bankrupt and when Mother left to tout for her next rich ticket, I had to cook for them or we'd all have gone hungry.'

Maggie gasped, 'But you were only a child!'

He shrugged negligently. 'Once my mother married again in Brazil, we had a housekeeper, but I still used to cook for Dad in England. I enjoyed it, even if I was one of the only boys doing home economics when I went to school there in my teens.'

She shook her head; something flipped over in her at this more human side to him. 'Wow, that was pretty brave! I remember the ribbing we used to give the boys in our school.'

She thought of his words then and remembered something that Michael Murphy had said that day of the funeral. 'You said your dad became bankrupt…was…is that why you don't go after your enemies with total ruthlessness?'

He looked up, his eyes narrowed sharply on hers. She flushed—what was she doing? They'd been actually getting along.

He wouldn't let her escape, lifting a brow.

'What I mean is…Mr Murphy said something about you not being known for being…so merciless,' she finished lamely.

He stopped what he was doing and leant both hands on the counter top. 'And yet I was merciless to you and your family…?'

She nodded miserably, desperately wishing she hadn't opened her mouth.

'I only fight back when provoked beyond reason…and you and your stepfather did that, Maggie. You can spare me the armchair psychoanalysis.'

He had retreated back behind the cool front. She backed away from the door. 'I'll just have a quick shower.'

He looked at the empty doorway for a long time. For a few moments there, they'd shared a lightness he rarely encountered with anyone. And then, with that one comment…she'd actually pinpointed something that was so fundamental about the way he lived, did business, something that no one else had ever picked up on. Not the broadsheets, tabloids, reporters…and they had done their best over the years to figure out the Cameron phenomenon. The way he'd built his fortune from next to nothing, first in Rio and London, then encompassing the world. All by the age of thirty-six.

The truth was, the way he conducted his business life *was* inextricably bound up with his past experiences. Seeing his father comprehensively ruined, become a shell of a man, only to be deserted by his tempestuous wife as soon as the money was gone, had left deep wounds. Somewhere deep down, he'd vowed that would never happen to him. His hands had curled to fists and he just noticed them now, consciously uncurling them. He willed the dark memories away. Maggie was just trying to push his buttons…and he wouldn't let her.

'What can I do?' Maggie's chin was tilted, her voice almost defiant as she spoke from the doorway. She was determined not to let Caleb see how his shut-down had affected her. His face was still grim. He flicked her a glance, taking in the damp hair that coiled down past her shoulders, a soft V-neck cashmere sweater that clung to her curves. Couldn't help but notice the shadow of something—was it hurt?—that lit her eyes an intense green. Distracted by that and how it made him feel, he listed off abstractedly, 'Set the table, get some cutlery, glasses…'

'Yes, sir,' she muttered under her breath and started

opening cupboards. She would not let him see how hurt she was but it was still there, just under her skin like a wound. What had she expected, after all? She shook her head at herself and stretched up to look for plates.

Suddenly she felt her waist grabbed and she was whirled around and into Caleb's chest so fast that the breath left her body. He brought two hands around her face, caressing her jaw. Immediately she could feel her body responding, sinking, craving... She looked up helplessly.

'Maggie...just...don't try to figure me out. I don't need that. All I need is you...' he looked to her mouth '...this.'

He bent his head and met her lips with his, kissing, drawing in her full bottom lip, tugging and teasing before sliding his tongue in to delve deep and stroke hers. Her arms moved around his waist and clung, hands moving unconsciously over his shirt. She guessed it was an apology of sorts. But he was also saying that he didn't need anything from her, not her opinions, not her thoughts, not her concern...certainly not her heart. And, while he kissed her, she could forget that...but when he stopped, she knew the pain would filter through. So, in an effort to avoid that, she kissed him back, hoping, wishing that he'd never stop. She craved the contact that would obliterate her churning thoughts.

He pulled back. Looking down, he could see Maggie's eyes still closed and her lips full and pouting. He groaned. She opened her eyes. They looked slumberous. She looked down to his mouth.

'Don't stop...' There was something desperate in her voice.

Reaching up on tiptoe, she brought Caleb's head down again; she couldn't reach, she was so much smaller and her mouth hovered inches away, like a succulent fruit. When she said again, 'Please...don't stop,' it lit a flame of desire so strong that he couldn't resist and he lifted her up, sitting her on the island in the kitchen.

Coming between her legs, he cupped her face again, kissing her long and deeply. He could feel her hands resting on his chest, then the fingers move to open the buttons of his shirt, slipping inside to caress his skin. It made a tremor of intense longing surge through him.

He pulled up her sweater, taking it off completely, and her breasts were bare, pert and pink with arousal; he cupped one and ran a thumb over and back over the peak. Her head fell back with the sensation and then he took it into his hot mouth, rolling it, sucking. Maggie was gasping, her hair damp against her back. When he lifted his head finally, she tried to open his shirt the rest of the way but her hands were shaking too much. Caleb's hands took hers away. 'Let me…'

He opened his shirt and Maggie felt the ache growing between her legs. She wriggled on the island and Caleb threw his shirt aside, pulling her against him and running his hands over her back, his mouth on her neck, her shoulder. Her blood was thumping, pumping out of control. She wanted him… now. She wasn't aware that she'd even said the words out loud until she heard, 'Really? You want me here? Now?'

She couldn't believe they were still in the kitchen, that she'd been so bold, that she'd *begged* him to kiss her, take her, but it was too late. And she knew she was blocking out something…some hurt.

Coward.

She nodded jerkily, glad to see that, despite his cool, rational words, he was breathing fast too, his eyes dark and pupils dilated. His hand went to her jeans and she lifted her hips so he could pull them off.

Her eyes followed his hands as they undid his belt and it

snaked through the loops on his trousers just below his taut stomach. She breathed in, her stomach tight with desire, slid off the island and opened the button on his trousers herself, pressing kisses to his chest, finding a nipple, biting gently.

His hand captured her head and she heard a whistle of breath escape through his teeth. 'Maggie, Maggie, what are you doing to me?'

He stilled her hand and picked her up, carrying her into the bedroom. He placed her down on the bed and stripped off his trousers and briefs. Then he pulled her panties down, over her hips and off. Invaded by a wanton, hitherto unexplored need, she instinctively arched her back, her hips rising to meet him as he spread her legs with his thigh. He leant back for a second and, getting protection, rolled it on, then he pressed down, close over her whole body and thrust in, so completely and deeply that she cried out. The spiral of ecstasy finally obliterated all coherent, troubling thoughts. Just as she'd wished and hoped for.

'More wine?'

Maggie shook her head and placed a hand over her glass. She was still finding it hard to meet Caleb's eyes. An hour after dinner had been ready, they were eating.

And all because…all because…

Maggie wished the ground would just open up and let her disappear. *She* had begged him to kiss her, not to stop. *She* had practically ripped his clothes off him. *She* had initiated an act of lovemaking that had combusted around them like a white-hot flame. She'd been half naked in the *kitchen*. An awful mortification twisted her insides.

He'd taken her hard and fast and so totally that she still felt dizzy. And she knew it had been motivated purely by her desire to avoid being faced with his indifference to her feelings—feelings she wasn't ready to acknowledge. That was a route to self-destruction if ever there was one.

'Maggie?'

Reluctantly, she forced herself to meet his gaze.

'Do you want to tell me what's causing that pained expression on your face? Or will I just assume it was my cooking?'

Her gaze slipped away, then back. Of course he'd be used to his mistresses taking the initiative; they'd no doubt be far more experienced than her in the ways of lovemaking to keep a man like Caleb happy. In contrast to her inner agitation, he seemed to think nothing out of the ordinary had just happened. She forced a bland, cool look and smiled. 'Nothing, and your chicken was…delicious.'

It had been sublime, cooked to perfection. And would have been even better had they eaten it when it had been ready. That thought made her cringe inwardly again.

'Flattery?' he mocked with a raised brow. 'Trying to throw me off the scent of something, Maggie?'

She couldn't be that transparent, could she? She could feel a red tide ascending.

'Your blushes make you as easy to read as a book.'

A sudden pain gripped her. Thank God he thought he had her so well sized up that every time she blushed it meant the opposite to what she was really feeling. But the pain struck sharp. She got up to clear away the plates. When she came back in, he grabbed her wrist and pulled her down into his lap.

'What?' Why did she have to sound so breathless? And why was her body coming to vibrant life so easily? Traitor.

'I've got a surprise for you… You didn't spot anything outside when you came back?'

Maggie shook her head. Where was this going?

'I wanted to show you earlier, but then you were so late… and we got distracted.'

He felt Maggie tense against his body. She was such a mass of contradictions. Making love to him with an intensity and passion he'd never encountered, only to spend the next hour avoiding his eyes. He was used to having to firmly extricate himself from cloying embraces after making love and with Maggie…she was the complete opposite, couldn't wait to get away from him. And, for the first time, he actually felt a little…piqued.

But then she was nothing but a heartless, mercenary…he wanted to say *bitch*, but it felt wrong. He couldn't actually say the word, even in his head. In an effort to avoid thinking about it, he stood abruptly, taking Maggie with him. Her serious eyes were focused on his face; he could feel a responding heat unfurl just under her look.

'Come downstairs; I'll show you.'

He took her hand and led her out of the apartment. Down the lift, to the door and out into the rapidly darkening night. They were on the street.

'Well?' he asked a little impatiently after a few minutes' silence.

Maggie looked up and down, more and more bemused. 'Caleb, I don't know what you want me to—' She stopped suddenly and he felt her hand tighten on his. 'My car…my car is gone… It was just here…' She pulled free and stepped closer to the road. 'Where…? I mean, I parked it just here. I know I did.' She could feel panic start to rise and turned to face him. 'Maybe it's been towed. I paid the meter earlier, though; no one could possibly want to take it—'

'Maggie, stop.' Caleb came and turned her back round to face the cars parked on the street. He brought his arms around her body and pointed at a gleaming brand-new Mini Cooper, sitting in exactly the same spot as her car had been.

'No…my one was old, remember?' she said, slightly bitterly in light of his recent opinion on why she might own a car like it.

'I got it towed away, Maggie. It was an accident waiting to happen, believe me. This is your new car.' He dangled a key in front of her face.

What? Just like that?

'But…I… Where…what did you do with mine?'

'It's probably the size of a tin can by now.'

As Maggie was still held in the circle of his arms, her back to him, she couldn't stop the wobble in her lip. She felt inexplicably as though Caleb had just pulled her soul out, wrung it dry and handed it back. She knew it was just a car, but it had been *hers*, the first thing she'd bought. A symbol of her independence from Tom. She'd taught her mother how to drive in it. And now, without so much as a by your leave, Caleb had thrown it away.

She bit down furiously on her lip to stop the tremble. There was no way he could know how much this hurt her—he'd probably think she was just acting again. He was still dangling the key. She picked it out of his hand—still hadn't said anything, couldn't trust herself. He let her go and she walked over. It was so silly, she knew, to be this upset. And she was angry. She blinked her eyes, ignored the ache in her heart, took a deep breath and turned around with a huge smile on her face. 'It's beautiful. Sorry, I was just stunned…I've never…I mean it's been so long since anyone gave me a gift so generous…'

The anger and pain galvanised her actions; she came back and reached up to kiss him and pouted prettily. 'I presume it'll be mine after the two months are up? After all, I do need a car…' here she trailed a finger down his front and the gesture jarred uncomfortably with him '…and the jewels too…?'

She looked up coquettishly from under long lashes and could see the hoped for reaction set in, the hardening of his jaw, that harsh glitter in his eyes. She was acting true to the form he expected. And it made her sick inside. But also, bizarrely, for some reason, protected.

'Of course.' As much as he detested her behaviour, he could feel a sense of relief flood through him. Had he actually for one moment thought that she was anything other than *this*? What a fool! It somehow helped to justify giving her priceless gems, even the car.

It was no less than he'd given any other mistress.

You're just giving into her mercenary little heart. It's what she wanted all along…and more…

He furiously reasoned with himself—her car, if it had been hers, which he seriously doubted, had been a liability…and, as for the jewels…he *wanted* to adorn her luminous skin in fiery rubies and flashing emeralds. It was purely for his pleasure alone. Their collective worth was chicken-feed to him. He took her hand and led her back inside. Maggie shut out the image of the sparkly new car that she would have traded any day of the week to have her own again.

She took the car for a drive the next day, on a visit to her mother. When they came out of the house a few hours later, her mother sounded suspicious.

'He's a very generous employer, giving you a car just like that…'

Maggie tried to avoid the scrutiny of her mother's gaze. 'Yes, well, the other thing was a rattle trap and you were the one always telling me to get rid of it.'

'I know, but I also know how much you loved it.'

'Yes, well…' Maggie said airily. 'As Caleb's assistant now, I have to look a certain way, maintain a certain… image.'

Her mother had that all too familiar worried frown again. 'Maggie…are you sure everything is all right? I remember that you and Caleb had that—'

Maggie cut her off rapidly. 'Mum, that was dinner—once. I'm not in his league—don't worry.'

She leant in to kiss her. She longed to give in and lean on her mother…but years of being the support had ingrained her sense of responsibility too deep.

'And what about your painting?'

Maggie pulled back. 'That'll just have to wait for a few weeks.'

She didn't look convinced but let Maggie sit in the small car before saying innocently, 'I've invited Caleb for lunch next week, to say thank you for being so kind—I'm still so embarrassed that Tom tried his best to ruin him.'

Maggie looked up wildly. Caleb *here*? At the house? With her mother gushing about how wonderful he was?

'He's far too busy. He can't possibly make time—' She went cold. 'Hang on a second, did you say *invited*?'

'Yes, dear. I asked Michael Murphy to call him and extend the invitation; he said yes immediately. You'll come too, of course.'

Her words were still reverberating in Maggie's head as she arrived back at the apartment. Disaster. Her mother was likely to give everything away with just a few words. Yet she knew if she tried to dissuade Caleb from going, he'd suspect something immediately and be even more determined to go. No doubt he was wondering what on earth Tom's widow wanted with him. Maggie would have to watch her mother like a hawk and just make sure she said nothing incriminating. Her head was throbbing.

The phone was ringing as she got in, but stopped before she could reach it. She knew it was Caleb, could feel his impatience as, sure enough, her mobile started to shrill.

'Where were you?'

'Out…I went for a drive; is that okay?'

He grunted.

She had to check, to confirm for herself. 'I believe my mother has asked you for lunch…?'

Please say no, laugh, say you won't be able to go…

'Yes and I'm looking forward to it… I'm even intrigued, you could say. I was calling to say I'll be back at eight.'

Maggie felt sick as the phone went dead.

That night and for the next few days they seemed to settle into an uneasy truce. Uneasy because Maggie had to guard her tongue all the time. Especially when Caleb was relaxed and charming. Which, she hated to admit, was more often than not. Unless something from the past reared its ugly head. Then he shut down. By day she stocked up on some art supplies, explored the outdoor terrace of the apartment, even tried to do a little painting, and by night…by night, she and Caleb entered another realm, where no words were spoken, no words were blessedly needed as he took her to height after height of pleasure.

As the day of the lunch approached, Maggie was hoping against hope that Caleb had forgotten about it, but her wishes were dashed when he emerged from the shower on the Sunday morning.

'What time is lunch?'

He'd remembered.

Maggie sat up in the bed, pulling the sheet up, still absurdly shy in front of Caleb, even though just minutes before he'd wrought a response from her that still had her pulse beating fast. She willed down the tell-tale heat with monumental effort.

'One o'clock.'

As if she didn't already know that his mind was as sharp as a sword. She fled into the bathroom so she wouldn't have to watch him dress and, when she emerged, she could hear him whistling merrily in the kitchen. As if he didn't have a care in the world. She envied him his cool ability to ride roughshod over people's lives and ignored the traitorous tingle in her body and the voice that whispered to her how much she enjoyed *certain* aspects of being with him.

On the way out of the city she asked him to stop by a newsagents so she could get some papers. He looked at her with a strange expression.

'What?'

'Nothing…' He lifted his brows innocently.

'I can read, you know. And I do like to keep up with current affairs. I'm sorry if your usual…' The word stuck in her craw.

'Girlfriends?' he supplied with a quirk on his lips.

'Mistresses…are more intellectually challenged.'

He lifted a hand and ticked off on his fingers. 'Actually, the last one was a human rights lawyer; the one before that was a hedge fund manager; the one before that—'

'Okay, okay, I get the point. So I'm your dumbest mistress—'

He'd parked the car and leant over suddenly, thinking of how dry and sterile and *boring* those women had been. 'Dumb? That's not a word I'd use to describe you, Maggie.' And he was suddenly surprised to know that he really meant it. In the last few days he'd had more stimulating conversations with her than he'd had with anyone in a long time. And he was uncomfortably aware of how much he'd come to look forward to walking in that door every day…as much as he might deny it to himself.

When he looked at her the way he was now, with that heated expression in his eyes, Maggie just wanted to drown in the blue depths. She willed herself back to sanity and felt for the door handle, not even able to break away, much as she wanted to. Finally she found it and practically fell out of the car, fled into the shop…and then came back.

'Sorry, I should have asked, did you want anything?'

Caleb just shook his head and watched her leave. That something was niggling him again. Like a constant barely-there buzzing in his head, he couldn't put his finger on it, it was so elusive. And he had to acknowledge the dark part of him that didn't want to investigate what it was.

By the time they reached the house he'd put it from his mind. Maggie turned around to face him in the car when they pulled in, something urgent in her movements.

'My mother thinks I'm working for you as an assistant, so please don't disabuse her of that, and Caleb…'

He faced her properly, momentarily stunned by the serious expression on her face, the unmistakable protective light in her eyes. He'd seen it before, in Monte Carlo.

'If you do or say *anything* to upset her…the deal will be off—we'll cope somehow, but I will walk away and you can have the house.'

'How on earth could I upset your mother, Maggie?'

'She had nothing to do with anything, Caleb, nothing. Just remember it's me you're punishing, not her.'

And she got out of the car.

For a second Caleb sat there. Punishing her? As he watched her walk to the door, the soft folds of the dress she wore flowing round her hips and legs, as he felt the familiar surge of desire that wasn't abating one tiny bit, the thought that she felt he was punishing her was not a comfortable one. And he didn't know why. Because that was what he'd set out to do all along, wasn't it?

He stepped out, meeting Maggie at the door just as it opened. He almost didn't recognise the woman who stood there. She certainly looked different from how he remembered her—as almost grey, fading into the background. This woman looked…vibrant. Although he could see something in her eyes, some light that had been diminished, and there was a distinct wariness, a jumpiness there. He could see traces of the beauty she'd once been. A different beauty from Maggie's, but there all the same. Maggie was hugging her and re-introducing them, as they'd met in London. He could feel the waves of warning emanate from her tightly held body and suddenly wanted to reassure her. He fought down the urge, telling himself he must be getting soft.

Maggie's mother showed them into the front room, the same one that he'd been in before, where he'd seen Maggie again for the first time since they met in London. When they had drinks in their hands, she sat nervously on the edge of a chair.

'Mr Cameron—'

He smiled urbanely. 'Caleb, please.'

She smiled. 'Very well, Caleb. I just wanted to say…thank you so much for being so generous. I don't know how we can ever repay you. You have no idea how much this house meant, means to us…me and Maggie.' She took Maggie's hand beside her. 'After my beloved Brendan died, it was all I had to remind me of him…'

'Mrs Holland, I had no intention of making you suffer. Once Maggie explained the situation to me, I couldn't have taken your house too…'

'But…I know what this house is worth, Mr Cameron—'

Caleb could see tears come into her eyes. Then, he just *knew*. Maggie had told him the truth. This woman had had nothing to do with Tom's plans.

'Mrs Holland, I'm making full use of Maggie while I'm here in Dublin. When I leave, I'll be more than satisfied to leave the house to you. Believe me, it's enough.'

He looked at Maggie. She was burning up and he could see the pulse thumping erratically against her neck. She finally managed to get out a strangled, 'Mum…shouldn't we check the lunch?'

CHAPTER NINE

BY THE time they were eating their desserts, Maggie was relatively relaxed. Caleb had been charm personified, her mother suitably impressed and Maggie had kept quiet. She had just made coffee and was bringing it on a tray into the dining room.

'And how on earth did you manage to persuade her to get rid of that car? Believe me, I've been trying for years; you would have thought it was like some kind of family pet. The only reason she didn't drive it over to London was because she knew it'd never survive the journey...'

Maggie stood, stunned into immobility by her mother's chatter, and then spoke quickly, putting down the tray, giving out the cups, trying not to slop the coffee everywhere with her shaking hands.

'Mum...I'm sure Mr Cameron doesn't want to hear about my banger. He did me a favour. I grew out of that long ago.'

'But Maggie, only a few weeks ago you told me—'

'More dessert, Mum? More coffee?'

'We haven't drunk it yet, Maggie,' Caleb said dryly, an assessing gleam in his eyes as he took in Maggie's all too obvious discomfiture.

She managed to distract her mother with something else

and prayed that Caleb wouldn't have taken too much notice. A short while later they stood up.

'Mr—I mean, Caleb…' Maggie's mother laughed almost girlishly—the effect of a couple of glasses of wine. Maggie cringed; she was practically flirting with the man. And while she loved nothing more than seeing this more relaxed, peaceful side to her mother, she wished it could have been with anyone else. Not the all too dangerous Caleb, who would be sizing up every word.

'I'll give you the guided tour…'

'Mum, we should really be going.'

Caleb smiled dangerously, confirming her fears. 'Nonsense, Maggie, there's nothing pressing and I'd love to see the house.'

He extended a gallant arm to Mrs Holland, who looked at Maggie triumphantly.

'See? Now, why don't you get started on the washing-up and let me show Caleb around?'

They were gone for what felt like ages. Maggie's brain was working overtime when she thought of her bedroom, which hadn't been redecorated since her teens, with all her teen idol posters still up and the flowery bedspread. With the move to London for college and only intermittent visits since, she hadn't had the time. Or inclination, after returning from London.

Then Caleb walked into her line of vision in the garden. Alone. He stood there with hands in his pockets, surveying the view. Spectacular in a black sweater and dark trousers that hugged every bit of his tall, lean length. She sighed. And jumped when her mother appeared.

'Well, love. Now there's a man.'

I'll say…

She joined Maggie at the sink and started to help dry the

dishes. Caleb disappeared from view and Maggie felt scared suddenly, imagining when he'd be gone for good.

Her mother put an arm around her shoulders and Maggie leant into her, taking refuge for a moment.

'We're okay, love. Thanks to that man, we're going to be fine.'

Maggie nodded and leant her head on her mother's shoulder so she wouldn't see the bright glitter of her tears. Her mother would be fine and that was all that mattered, but she…she knew she wouldn't be fine at all. And it was thanks to that man.

Caleb came back through the house, his footsteps muffled on the carpet, and halted in his stride when he saw through the open kitchen door. Maggie had her head on her mother's shoulder, their arms were around each other. There was something in the scene that was so primal and private that he couldn't intrude. He walked away and waited for a few minutes before coming back, coughing as he did so to make them aware of his presence. He could have sworn he hadn't just seen what he had when Maggie turned around to face him with a bright smile on her face.

'We'd better get going.'

'Fine, dear. I've held you young people up long enough.'

They said their goodbyes and finally left.

As the car pulled out of the drive, Maggie turned to Caleb. 'That day—the day you came to the house—you said you wanted to use it as a bolt-hole… Would you really have moved in?'

Caleb had the grace to look sheepish for a moment. It threw Maggie.

'I never really had any intention of using it. Most likely I would have sold it…I think I wanted to get a rise out of you.'

He shrugged. 'What can I say, Maggie? You bring out the worst in me.'

After that she was tight-lipped and distant. He'd never had any intention of moving in, redecorating. And she'd risen to the bait beautifully.

He cut into her thoughts after a while. 'Maggie...I believe you about your mother.'

'Good.' She just felt weary when he said that. She could feel him flick her a probing glance, could feel it heat her skin. Why did she have to be so *aware* of him?

'What's up?'

She took a deep breath and looked at him. 'Nothing, I'm just a little tired...'

And drained and heart sore...

'There's a ball we're meant to attend tonight, but if—'

'No,' she said quickly. 'I'm absolutely fine. We'll go.'

The rest of the journey was made in silence as Maggie fell asleep and Caleb wrestled with countless disturbing thoughts and feelings. Something just didn't...fit. When he'd walked around the house with her mother, all she'd talked about was her first husband, as if he were the one who had just died...and not Tom Holland. Maybe it was some form of self-protection? But he didn't think so. He'd mentioned Tom Holland once and she'd gone pale and changed the subject immediately. All in all, she seemed far too...happy...for someone who'd just been bereaved and not only that. She was far too happy for someone who'd just been disinherited of millions of pounds.

He shook his head grimly. Felt as if he was in new territory, somewhere he'd never wanted to be. The boundaries were shifting. He took in Maggie's sleeping form and stretched out a hand to tuck some errant hair back behind one delicate ear. She moved slightly against his hand and smiled a tiny smile. Something didn't fit...at all. But did he really want to find out what that was?

When they returned to the apartment that night after the ball Maggie kicked her shoes off just inside the door—her feet were aching. Her nerves were on a knife-edge. All evening Caleb had been watching her, scrutinising her. It was making her nervous. She went into the kitchen to put on the kettle. She sensed Caleb come in and lean against the door frame. Finally she couldn't stand it any more and whirled around. 'What...what is it? You've been staring at me all night.'

His eyes ran up and down her body, leisurely and explicit, and she felt a hot flush invade her skin.

'I don't like it.'

'Yes, Maggie, you do.'

He strolled towards her. She couldn't go anywhere. She was backed against the counter and suddenly remembered that other night in the kitchen when she'd practically ravished him. She went even redder.

'My, what blushes. What could possibly be going through that head of yours?'

He was almost touching her. His hand lifted and cupped her jaw, caressing, moulding, his fingers tracing the line.

He fixated on her mouth for long seconds and Maggie's breathing felt far too loud. Her heart was hammering. Her nerves were screaming.

Just do it...kiss me!

Instead, he seemed to wage some inner struggle and met her eyes. He saw the pulse beating at her temple, under the translucent skin.

'Are you going to tell me what that was all about earlier?'

'What…earlier?' She was genuinely mystified and had trouble concentrating when he was so close.

'Your car, Maggie. The whole song and dance to get your mother off the subject.'

She stiffened. He could sense her distancing herself even though she couldn't physically get away. He had that sensation of her feeling cornered again.

'What do you mean? There was nothing going on.'

'Please. Spare me.'

He brought his arms either side of her body. They brushed against the sides of her breasts. She closed her eyes for a split second. It was so unfair of him to question her like this, when she felt so…weak.

He could see her struggle.

Could see the shutters descend over those lovely eyes, which now flashed a stormy green.

'It was nothing, Caleb. She thinks I have some adolescent attachment to the car, but I outgrew it years ago. Believe me, I hated it, couldn't wait to get rid of it.' She shrugged lightly. 'When she saw the new one…she just wouldn't let it drop. That's all.'

He hadn't made millions from not being able to read people and, right now, he knew Maggie was lying through her teeth. But why? And what did it mean if she was? A door slammed in his head. He did *not* want to go there.

He let his gaze wander down. She looked sexily prim and proper tonight. Her hair had been straightened and pulled back into a low chignon. The high-necked designer gown hugged every curve, hiding far too much and conversely revealing everything. He slipped an arm around her waist and pulled her into him. She melted against him, a tinge of pink along each cheek bone. He told himself he didn't care. Why was he even bothering to question her about it, anyway? All he wanted from her was right here in his arms. She was warm and willing and oh, so ready.

'Fine, Maggie, whatever you say...' and he bent his head and moulded her every curve to his hard length, took her soft lips and kissed her until he felt her legs weaken. Then he led her into the bedroom, opened every button on her dress, kissing each piece of flesh as he did so, by which time she was boneless with want and need. As Caleb came over her, dark and powerful, Maggie had one last coherent thought of thanks that he hadn't felt the need to pursue the matter. And lost herself in him. Again.

Caleb woke early. A misty dawn light illuminated the bedroom. Maggie was tucked into his side, nestled close, one leg thrown over his, disturbingly close to a part of him that was already responding to her proximity. An arm was flung over his belly and her head rested on his chest. Her hair streamed out like a silken caress over his other arm, which held her in this close embrace. He wanted to pull Maggie even closer. Breathe in the scent of her hair, stroke that thigh that hovered so close, have her move her hand down until she could feel for herself what she was doing to him. She felt so good—every soft curve and smooth, silky bit of skin. Her breasts were pressing into his side. He was growing harder. He never wanted to let her go.

What?

He tensed. Wide awake now. Violently awake. Without thinking about what he was doing, he slowly and stealthily managed to extricate himself from her embrace and didn't wake her. His body hummed with arousal. She tossed for a second and he held his breath but then she curled away on the other side and he could hear her breaths deepen again. With her back bared, he could see faint bruises. He had done that? Then something caught his eye—on the back of her thigh, he could see a very pink puckering of the skin, a scar of some kind. It looked as if it had been very angry at some stage, but he guessed it was years old. He wanted to reach out and touch it.

That thought galvanised him into action.

Enough!

He was mooning over his mistress as she lay sleeping. His mistress—that was all she was; he had to remember that.

CHAPTER TEN

'MR CAMERON, you're leaving early…*again*?'

Caleb looked up as he shrugged on his jacket to see Ivy at the door of his office.

'Yes. I presume, as the CEO of the Cameron Corporation, I'm allowed that distinction?' Something in her voice had him sharply on the defensive and he regretted it straight away when he saw an embarrassed flush stain the older woman's cheeks.

'Well…of course, Mr Cameron, I never meant to imply for a second—'

'Ivy, I'm sorry. It's me. I'm just tired, that's all.'

'Of course. This deal with New York is trying all of our patience.'

Yes, it was. And all Caleb wanted to do was go home, walk through that door and see Maggie. Two words had him halt mentally. *Home* and *Maggie*. Since when was that designer apartment home and since when did he long to see Maggie?

Since she'd made it a home…since her toiletries nestled alongside yours…since the smell of home cooking greeted you almost every night…since you've been happy to sit in and watch movies…

He cut off his thoughts with a ruthless effort.

'Do you have everything you need for the flight tomorrow?'

'Yes…' he answered Ivy with relief. He hadn't told Maggie about the trip to New York, which he had to leave for in the morning. And why did that make him feel so damn guilty now? He'd never felt the need to answer to anyone before, tell them his whereabouts.

Just then a younger colleague stopped by the door. He hovered nervously at the threshold. 'Mr Cameron, a few of us are going for a drink around the corner…if you want to join us?'

Caleb picked up his briefcase. 'There's nothing I'd like more.' He was oblivious to the smile that lit up the younger man's face.

Much later, when he let himself in, the apartment was still and quiet. Maggie's light floral fragrance hung on the air and Caleb breathed it in. He'd lasted in the bar for as long as he could, but he'd soon become bored with the youthful conversation, the young men trying to impress him, the women brushing past him suggestively.

He dropped his things, shed his coat and walked to the bedroom, already imagining Maggie curled up, warm and soft and silky. He imagined slipping in behind her, moulding her pliant form to his and waking her, making her body come to life… He walked in the door and the bed…was empty. A crushing feeling resounded in his chest. Where was she?

He retraced his steps and looked in every room. A panicky sensation was rising and he fought to keep it down. Maybe she'd just gone to see a movie again…and he suddenly wished he'd been here—they could have gone together. A snide voice whispered that maybe she was out in a bar, looking for company…

About to pick up the phone, he spotted a light coming from the huge glass doors that led on to the terrace. They'd started using it more and more as the weather got better. Morning coffee, breakfast at the weekend. He'd found it far more relaxing than he would have thought. The idea of such domesticity before would have made him come out in a rash, but somehow with Maggie it didn't feel like that. When he thought about it now, despite having other mistresses in the past, he'd never invited them to live with him. Maggie was the first woman he'd spent so much time with. Which was ironic.

He opened the doors and they made no sound. The cool night breeze swirled around him; the sounds of traffic came up from the streets. Lights twinkled across the city. And there was Maggie. Curled up on a deckchair, in an old comfy tracksuit, a shawl wrapped over her. A mug of something beside her. She'd fallen asleep.

And in a flash Caleb knew exactly what had been bothering him from the start. Maggie had never once dressed like she had that night of the seduction in London. In fact, she displayed an effortless, timeless style and everything she wore complemented her unique colouring and figure exactly. So why had she come to him dressed so cheaply that night? Yet more questions rushed in and he couldn't halt the onslaught. Why didn't she ever want to go clubbing? Which he personally abhorred, but still, usually had to indulge in. Why didn't she call ten times a day just to be reassured that he still desired her? Why, when he offered to take her to the newest, most exclusive restaurant, had she screwed up her nose? And why was she so content just to stay in...and read...or watch TV?

It didn't make sense. But, as these questions begged for his attention, he brutally used the desire rushing through his body to drown them out. He walked over and pressed a light kiss to Maggie's lips. Her eyes opened—dark and greenly mysterious against the black night.

'Caleb...'

'Maggie…'

'Where were you?'

'I had to go out…' And why did he feel like such a heel when he said that?

She just put her arms around his neck and allowed him to lift her against his chest. He carried her into the bedroom, where she buried her hurt and allowed him to undress her. He was back so late. Where had he really been? He'd never say and she'd never ask because he didn't have to tell her. He owed her nothing. She meant nothing to him.

'I have to go to New York for a few days.'

Maggie looked at Caleb reluctantly from over her morning coffee cup in the kitchen. She felt tousled and unkempt in her dressing gown next to his pristinely suited, clean-shaven appearance.

'You're going…alone?' She held her breath.

'Yes.' He was terse. He needed to get away—from here, from her…from too many questions, making his head sore.

She suddenly felt a weight lift off her shoulders; the thought of a few days' respite from the bitter-sweet ache of seeing him, sleeping with him every night, was like an oasis in the desert. Her eyes gleamed with relief and he couldn't fail to notice it.

'You don't have to look so pleased, Maggie.'

She rapidly schooled her features, saying flippantly, 'I'm missing you already.'

'Maybe you should come with me…' he taunted, but he knew she couldn't. This deal was important and she'd be far too much of a distraction. But he'd never tell her that and didn't like the way she tensed at those words. 'Relax, Maggie, you can't.'

He drained his cup and left it in the sink, picked up his coat. Despite the feeling of relief that had invaded her, now as she watched him walk away, about to go out the door, she felt a huge well of loneliness surround her. This was ridiculous. They didn't even get on.

But…they did when they forgot themselves for a moment and had something approximating a normal, easy conversation. At times, they did have a remarkable accord, an easiness in each other's company—something she'd never felt with anyone else. But yet, each time it seemed they might actually get close, one or the other would say something and the past would rear its ugly head. Then bed would conveniently take the need to talk further out of the equation. And she knew she couldn't bear to see him walking away because she knew that one day very soon he'd be doing it for good.

'Caleb.'

He stopped at the door and she walked up and pulled his head down to hers. She pressed her mouth to his and kissed him with desperate fervour. With a groan she felt him drop his case, wrap his arms around her back and pull her up, off her feet and into him. He kissed her back with a raw hunger, almost as though they'd been separated for days already.

Shakily he lowered her back down his body and put her away from him. 'Is that so I don't forget you?'

'You'd better go.'

He stepped out and the door closed. Maggie leaned against it but couldn't hold in the shaking that took hold of her body. She would not cry. She could not cry. She went over to the couch and sat down, hugging her arms around herself.

Just another few weeks, that's all…

She was useless, pathetic. She thought back to when Caleb had come home last night and found her asleep, in a tracksuit. She'd meant to change… She was doing so well at maintaining that all-important front…she hoped. But last night, when he hadn't shown, hadn't called, she'd been so weary. She had felt the fight leaving her. And in a way she hadn't cared. He'd never know the full truth and he didn't seem to mind enough to question her. He hadn't even cared enough to tell her he was going away…

She stood resolutely and vowed to enjoy the few days of freedom. Even as she realised that she *was* already missing him. So much for her facetious mocking words. She may as well have been mocking herself.

For the next few days Maggie painted herself into a frenzy, trying her best to block all thoughts of Caleb. He rang every night but the calls were quick, brusque and she felt as though he was just checking up on her. One night she went to bed in one of his T-shirts, breathing his scent in deeply, ashamed of how badly she missed him.

By the weekend it didn't look as if he was going to make it back. The time stretched ahead of her, yawning, empty. Her feeling of giddy relief at having some time alone had long gone. By the time Monday rolled around, missing him was an ache in her chest. Tuesday came and went. At one stage Maggie thought hysterically that perhaps this was it. She'd get a call from Ivy one day to say that Mr Cameron had shipped everything back to England and could she please vacate the apartment by noon.

The phone rang late on Wednesday night. She nearly dropped it, her heart was beating so fast. Her hands were slippy.

'It's me.'

'Hi.' Why did she have to sound so shy?

'I'll be back tomorrow.' He sounded deathly tired. His voice raw.

'Okay. See you then.'

The phones clicked down. Not another word. No *I miss you* or *Can't wait to see you.* Even so, Maggie couldn't help springing up and wrapping her arms around her body, her blood fizzing with treacherous happiness. He was coming back. He wasn't leaving just yet.

The following morning she answered a knock at the door; it could hardly be Caleb already? Her pulse speeded up anyway and promptly slowed when she saw John, his driver. He looked terrible and his skin was grey. Her concern was immediate and washed away any thoughts of Caleb.

'John…? What is it?'

'I'm sorry to bother you, Maggie. It's my heart…I was on my way to the airport but had to stop… It's a stupid angina thing and I need a doctor…I don't think I can pick Mr Cameron up later.'

Maggie led him into the room and took control. She'd have to collect Caleb from the airport. She'd take John's car—she could hardly turn up to meet him in the Mini! She slid her feet into flip flops.

'We're going straight to the hospital. We'll take your car; you can show me the ropes on the way and I'll pick Caleb up.'

'But…'

'No buts, John; you could have had an accident… You did the right thing coming here.'

He let her lead him downstairs, into the car. At the great age of twenty-seven Maggie had, unbelievably, never driven anything bigger than the Mini and took a few minutes to feel the much bigger car. She squashed the nervous feeling and trepidation, not wanting to give John anything else to worry about. With a bright smile that hid her nerves and sweaty hands, she pulled out into the manic rush hour traffic.

Some time later, after making sure John was stable and

settled into a bed in the hospital, she left. She'd have just enough time to make it to the airport. The car seemed even more daunting now when she got in, not having John by her side to point things out.

Through sheer guts and determination, Maggie managed to navigate it out of the city and on to the main airport road. Finally she managed to loosen her white-knuckle grip on the wheel.

Miraculously she found a parking space, managed not to hit anything and sat there for a few minutes taking deep breaths. She smiled wryly at herself; this was certainly one way to take her mind off Caleb, driving a car worth at least a hundred thousand and three times the size of her own. In the VIP airport arrivals area, John had told her where to wait, as Caleb was due in on a private jet. She stood and waited, her nerves coming back a thousandfold. Would he be surprised? Pleased? Angry?

He was tired. God, he was tired. He'd never felt so tired in all his life. His eyes were gritty behind his lids as he waited for his luggage to be delivered to him. And all he could see was Maggie. He cursed himself again. He could have brought her with him. It wouldn't have made the slightest bit of difference to his concentration levels and might have actually helped them. She'd managed to invade his every waking thought, every sleeping moment. He'd hoped that the trip might prove to him that she was losing her hold on him, on his desire. If anything it was even stronger. One night he'd had to endure a dinner party where he'd been presented with woman after woman, available for his pleasure. They'd been stunning, the *crème de la crème* of New York society, models, actresses. And they'd done nothing for him. All he'd wanted was... Maggie. And it tore him up inside to admit it.

Finally his luggage arrived and he walked out, looking to

the usual spot for John. And then he saw *her*. The joy that ripped through him nearly threw him off balance. He felt dizzy for a second. Was he conjuring her up? She was looking away; he saw her in profile. Her hair a shock of red against her light green cardigan, wrapped around a short shift dress. Bare legs, flip flops.

And then she turned and looked straight at him with those huge green eyes, ringed with the longest black lashes. He saw her eyes widen; she slightly lifted a hand awkwardly and it dropped slowly.

Why was he looking at her so angrily? She steeled her heart, which had somersaulted on seeing him, and hitched her chin.

He came over, face shuttered. Stern. 'Where's John?'

She blocked the hurt that he'd asked for John first and remembered him guiltily. 'He's in hospital—'

'What?'

She put a hand on his arm. 'He's fine. It's an ongoing angina problem and it flared up. I brought him in and insisted on coming to collect you; he was so worried…' She took her hand away awkwardly.

He rubbed a weary hand over his eyes and Maggie noticed how tired he was.

'Really, he's going to be fine. He just needs to be observed for twenty-four hours.'

'Okay.' He looked at her then, blue eyes pinning her to the spot. A hand reached out and he trailed a finger down one cheek. 'And you?'

She gulped for a breath and just shrugged, nodding. She couldn't even speak. She was useless.

'Thank you for looking after John.'

She shrugged again. 'It's fine. I was hardly going to insist he pick you up or leave him there. The car is parked nearby.'

'You drove his car?'

'Yes, Caleb.' Her dry tone belied the turmoil it had taken to drive there.

When they reached it, she couldn't resist saying cheekily, 'I was going to bring the Mini but was afraid your ego wouldn't fit…'

He smiled a rare smile and felt a burst of pleasure at her irreverence; it was something he never encountered. 'Ha, ha.'

He automatically went to the driver's side and Maggie could see him pass a hand over his eyes. He looked pale with exhaustion.

He gestured for the keys. She shook her head. 'You're not driving; you're half asleep.'

'Maggie—'

She was so firm, she surprised him. 'No way.'

She promptly got into the driver's seat and, short of pulling her back out, Caleb had no choice. Frankly he was too tired to argue. He sat in the passenger seat. He could feel his eyes drift shut; couldn't keep them open. His last waking thoughts were that he'd never ever been met by a woman at the airport before, how much he'd liked it…and that he couldn't remember the last time a woman had driven him. And yet, of all women, Maggie had done these two things. And he knew in his exhausted, vulnerable state, before his mind could jump in and deny it, that he wouldn't have wanted to see anyone else there. The darkness enfolded him.

That night, after dinner, Maggie was preparing for bed. In the bathroom, she took her hair out of the clip and it fell around her shoulders and down her back. She couldn't mistake the light in her eyes. For *him*. Because he was back. A flush stained her cheeks. The silk peignoir felt almost painfully sensuous against her heated skin.

This was so dangerous. She knew it. Like being in a car going a hundred miles an hour, hurtling towards a brick wall with no brakes.

She resolutely turned off the light and went into the bedroom. Her heart turned over when she saw the scene in front of her. Caleb, asleep on the bed, sheets pulled up to his waist, chest bare. A lock of hair had fallen forward and he looked so achingly handsome that Maggie couldn't breathe for a moment.

He sleeps...

As if in a dream, she walked over and sat down beside him on the edge of the bed. He didn't move. She reached out a hand and smoothed his hair back and brought her finger to her lip and kissed it before pressing it lightly against his mouth.

Without opening his eyes, he grabbed her wrist lightly. He pressed a kiss against the pulse fluttering against the delicate inner skin. He opened slumberous eyes and Maggie was trapped. He brought her inexorably forward until she was lying against his chest, her breasts crushed against him. He made a slow, thorough study of her face and then down, to where he could see the voluptuous V of her cleavage.

'Caleb...we don't...you're too tired...'

He shook his head. 'Not too tired for this, ever...'

And with a fluid, graceful movement he rolled her over until she was on her back and he hovered over her. With a hand caressing her face, he bent and met her mouth with his, in a sensual onslaught that washed away any resistance. She was as incapable of stopping him as he seemed to be incapable of wanting to stop.

That hand drifted down and over her silk-covered breast,

teasing the aching peak that jutted out against the material. Maggie groaned hungrily, her hands searching and finding his chest, moving, exploring, down, under the sheet where she came in contact with the heated evidence of his desire.

He pulled up her slip, baring her to his hungry gaze. 'God, Maggie…I've missed you… You're like a fever in my blood.'

An answering cry deep within her had her pull her slip up and off completely and they kissed hungrily, passionately, bodies straining together. With uncustomary clumsiness, Caleb found and rolled on protection. And then, finally, he was home…entering her satin flesh. And she was reaching up to meet him. All tiredness and fatigue gone. A distant memory.

That control that he valued so much was slipping again. His aching hardness sheathed in her warmth made him suck in a rasping breath. He opened his eyes and looked down and sank into green depths. As deep as the ocean. Her cheeks were flushed with arousal; he could feel her body start to tense around him.

He tried to hold on…tried to regain some sense of control and couldn't. Her body tautened and arched against his, her arms wrapped around his back. He could feel her hard nipples pushing against his chest and, giving in to the wild surge building through him, he felt himself being pushed to the brink on the wave of her orgasm and for a moment was poised…about to fall down, into the abyss. But, just before he did, before he crashed, he had the most overwhelming desire to experience this, skin to skin. Without protection. He'd never before felt the lack of that contact with anyone and yet here, now…with *her*, the protective barrier felt… somehow *wrong*.

As the carnal pleasure rippled through him and he felt himself explode, he wanted with a fierce primal desire to be spilling deep into her...to brand her, mark her. Seconds later, when the world had righted itself again, when the realisation hit...of what had just gone through his mind, what it meant, his whole body tensed and stilled over hers. Dear God. He wanted to make her pregnant?

That devastating thought drove him to pull free abruptly from her body and he heard her whimper. Their bodies were still painfully sensitive, his own protesting when he moved away—every cell, every inch of him wanting to pull her close and meld her to him again. His body was still hard but now he had to get away...from her...from himself. Was he just going mad with exhaustion? That was all it was. Feeling sudden wry humour at his crazy ramblings, he pushed himself up from the bed and, without looking back at Maggie, went into the bathroom and stepped into the shower.

Behind him, bereft on the bed, tears stung the back of Maggie's eyes but she would not let them fall. She knew how it was possible to make love and want to cry with a broken heart at the same time. Because she couldn't deny it any longer, couldn't deny the certain knowledge that he had her heart, for ever. Every beat was for him. And it would kill her in the end.

CHAPTER ELEVEN

'MORNING.'

'Morning…' Maggie was sleepily shy. Last night came rushing back. The desolation she'd felt when he'd practically run from the bed after making love. She woke up fast. Erected the barriers.

Caleb was propped on one arm, watching her. He took in all the expressions flitting across her face like clouds passing over a sunny day; he felt something dark pass between them. It was the first time she'd woken in the bed to find him there, watching her like this. Even on weekends, he would invariably go into the office for a few hours in the morning, or else he was out jogging, or just…up.

It made her heart speed up. Despite her best efforts to be cool.

'Don't you have to go to work?'

He quirked a brow. 'Trying to get rid of me?'

She shook her head and her glance jumped down to his bare chest. She could feel the heat starting to invade her blood, could feel her pulse jump. She looked back up and Caleb was smiling. She scowled. Damn him and his arrogance. Damn him and his insufferable coolness.

'As it happens, I do have to go…much as I'm enjoying watching you wake…'

He pressed a kiss to her startled mouth and swung out of bed. She watched him walk away into the bathroom and sighed deeply, pulling the covers up. She'd never get tired of looking at his body. When he emerged a short while later Maggie pretended to be asleep. She felt him come close to the bed and willed him away. In the cold light of morning, if he took her, she'd never be able to hide her feelings.

'Maggie, I know you're awake. I'll be home at seven. We're going out tonight.'

And she felt, rather than heard, him leave the room. She opened her eyes and looked out on a cityscape. They were back to normal. Back to the routine. Functions…balls…and this apartment which was becoming a prison.

Only two more weeks…

The words jumped into her head and she sat up, stunned. Only two more weeks, then…freedom. She couldn't believe it. Where had the time gone? She counted back the weeks and yes, sure enough, Caleb only had another ten to fourteen days here, then he'd be due back in London. He'd even mentioned going back. Had she just shut it out of her head? She sank back down. Her mind couldn't contemplate it right now or what it meant.

That evening, she had just showered and was dressed in a towelling robe when Caleb walked into the bedroom. Her heart lurched crazily. She noticed lines and shadows under his eyes and longed to go over and smooth them, tell him they didn't need to go out. But she couldn't because she didn't have that jurisdiction in his life.

His gaze raked her up and down hungrily; she stood in front of him, a clean scent perfuming the air, her skin still pink from the shower. God, he'd missed her today; his body had ached for her in a way that made him very, very nervous. Yet he couldn't think about that now. It was only the fact that he was running late that had him walk past, shedding clothes.

'We need to be ready to leave in fifteen minutes…'

'I'll be ready,' she answered tightly, stung by his lack of greeting, his brusque voice.

He came out into the hall a short while later, arranging the cuffs of his tuxedo. Maggie stood with her back to him, looking out the window.

She'd arranged her hair so it fell in a coiled rope down her back. The dark grey dress was some kind of jersey material and clung to every curve. It was tantalisingly see-through, giving heady glimpses of a pale curve here, a dark hollow there. She sensed him, tensed and turned around. It dipped in a dark V at the front, between her cleavage. Yet…it lacked…something. Why wouldn't she wear the jewels he gave her?

Despite that first impression she'd given him when she'd cockily asked if she could keep them…he had to make her wear them. She never chose to wear them—it was just another facet to her *act*, no doubt. But, a little voice crowed, *yet another anomaly*… Usually women were begging him for more and more. Bigger, glitzier, gaudier. He ignored the voice.

He strolled forward with indolent grace, making Maggie's breath catch in her throat. She'd seen him in a tux many times by now but somehow, tonight, he was more devastating than ever. Was it because she knew his body intimately? Was it because of the way his gaze drifted up and down her body, stopping, lingering…

He presented her with a long velvet box. Her heart fell. She took it hesitantly, opening it with a stunned gasp she couldn't keep in. It revealed an antique earring and necklace set made entirely out of green diamonds, set in platinum. The faintly yellow-green hue caught the light and dazzled her. She felt herself closing inwards.

She looked up, distant. 'More trinkets for your mistress?'

She was used to this. That was it. She was bored by it. Bizarrely, as much as it pained him, it also comforted him.

He took the necklace out of the box and proceeded to place it around her neck, deftly fastening it. The jewel hung just above the valley of her breasts. He took out the earrings and handed them to her.

'Yes…'

With shaking fingers she took them and put them in her ears. She could feel them sway and move against her neck and hair. He stood back. Cold eyes flicked up and down. She felt a chill.

'Beautiful.'

She felt like a brood mare. She was there purely for his pleasure and if he wanted her dripping in jewels then she would just have to put up with the discomfort. But everytime she'd move and feel them sway against her skin, she'd be reminded that, all too soon, he'd be walking away, out of her life and moving on to the next in line, with whom he'd be saying exactly the same words. Placing jewels around *their* necks in the same dispassionate way…or maybe not so dispassionate. Maybe one of them would break through that austere exterior…find the beating heart of the man, unlock his mysteries. Claim him. Her heart felt like a stone.

'Let's go.'

She followed him out, mute and stung. His revenge was already total. Complete. And he didn't even know it.

This function was similar to every other, in that everyone was beating a steady path to bask in the commanding, phenomenally successful aura of Caleb Cameron. As if by merely being near him some kind of Midas touch would rub off. Maggie was enduring the same unfriendly glances from the Dublin socialites, who wondered how she'd suddenly appeared on their scene. And with the temerity to turn up on *his* arm, not even giving them a fair chance.

She'd hardly ever socialised with Tom or her mother in Dublin. But yet, it was a relatively small city and already she'd caught glimpses of some of Tom's old colleagues, making a shudder of revulsion run through her. One of them in particular, who had been as nasty, if not even worse than her stepfather. She prayed that he hadn't seen her, but it was hard, with everyone's focus on Caleb and him clamping her to his side. She endured the dinner, the small talk, people's curiosity when they found out she came from Dublin herself, yet they were too polite to ask how she'd managed to inveigle her way into Caleb's life.

She could feel him loop a casual arm around the back of her chair, close to his, his hand caressing, toying with her neck. Her breath became ragged. She could feel her body respond and crossed her arms to cover the evidence. He turned to look at her; the sheer weight of his gaze made her turn. Everyone around them, the muted music, chatter of cutlery, raucous laughter, faded. A dense, heavy electric energy hummed between them. He caught her hand and lifted it to his mouth, kissing the delicate underside of her wrist. Maggie's breath stopped. Her eyes flared.

Why had he done that?

He let her hand go and turned back to the person on the other side of him. She was confused and muddled and very much afraid of the seething emotions he was responsible for in her breast.

'And where did you say you were from, dear?'

Maggie turned gratefully into conversation with the old woman on her right.

After dinner the guests were free to mingle and dance in the stunning ballroom. Maggie murmured her excuses and went to look for the bathroom. On her way back, just feet from the door, a voice halted her in her tracks. A definite, hard slap of unease hit her between the shoulder blades.

'Well, well, little Maggie Holland. I thought it was you, but my, haven't you turned into a sexy lady?'

Against her will, she turned slowly to face the man behind the unctuous voice.

'Patrick Deveney.'

The small, squat man had bulging eyes that were looking her up and down with such crawling impunity that it held Maggie immobile. He'd been one of her stepfather's closest friends. And for years he'd slimed around Maggie, but she'd always escaped his advances—just.

He moved closer when someone passed by. She was desperate not to show how scared she was or draw attention. She craned her neck to look for Caleb. She couldn't see him anywhere.

'Looking for your…date?'

'Yes…it's nice to see you again, Mr Deveney, but I really must be—'

Suddenly her arm was grabbed in an intensely brutal grip. She gasped as he pulled her into a nearby corner.

'What do you think you're—?'

He looked her up and down again with obvious lascivious intent. 'I haven't had a chance to offer my condolences,

Maggie, dear. You must be so devastated at the loss of Tom…
We didn't even get a chance to mourn him ourselves. Your
mother had him back here and buried so quickly we couldn't
even pay our respects. That's hardly fair, is it? But now I can
offer them to you personally.'

Maggie stared in disgust, unable to move from the explicit
threat in Deveney's voice. His hand on her arm was stopping
the blood flow; the pain was intense. 'Let me go,' she bit out
through the pain, knowing she'd have an almighty bruise.

'You know, Tom would have come after you if Cameron
hadn't been so quick to take revenge; he knew you blabbed
everything. You and that stupid wife of his. *You* caused his
heart attack; you messed it up for all of us.'

She was transported back in time, her skin going clammy
in remembered fear. She stood stock still, knowing that if she
made a move she'd enrage him further and there would be
more pain. Past and present were tangled; the pain wouldn't
be meant for her, never her, it was always her mother. She only
ever suffered if she got in the way. Yet why was she in pain
now? The mist cleared and Maggie came to.

This was *not* Tom. He was gone. She could handle this
bully. He wasn't going to hurt her. With a swift move she
caught him off guard, extricated herself from his grip and delivered an elbow blow to his fleshy solar plexus. He was
gasping and red-faced, but still far too close.

'I was just wondering where you'd got to.'

Caleb. A wild rush of relief rushed through her, but when
she turned, her heart fell. He was glowering, taking in her
flushed face, close proximity to Deveney and the other man's
obvious breathlessness. And jumped to entirely the wrong
conclusion.

Trying desperately to save face, Deveney slid away, saying

nastily, 'You're welcome to her, Cameron, she always was a little wildcat.'

Caleb's temper ratcheted up a few notches. He grabbed Maggie's arm and she had to stifle her moan of pain as his hand clamped around exactly where Deveney's had been.

'Who is he and how does he know me?'

Without giving her time to speak and in so much pain that she couldn't, Caleb was marching her out and away from the building. The driver who was standing in for John materialised with the car in seconds. They got in. Maggie was still shaken— couldn't believe that Caleb had misread the situation so badly.

'He was a friend of Tom's…and everyone in there knows who you are.' She rubbed her arm distractedly.

He was fighting to keep his mouth shut but wouldn't say anything here in the car. Within minutes they were back at the apartment. The front door closed behind him; Maggie circled slowly to face him. A wary look on her face—a guilty look? He couldn't tell but he was willing to bet it was guilt. What could she possibly see in that creep?

He came in and lounged against a wall, hands deep in his pockets. In the dim light of the room, he looked magnificent. Dark and brooding, the blue glitter of his eyes brilliant against she snowy white shirt and black tuxedo.

'So…do you want to tell me what that was? Already lining up my replacement…going for someone you know? Who works the way you're used to?'

'You're sick. I don't have to listen to this…'

She went to walk from the room, but Caleb took her arm again in exactly the same spot. This time she couldn't disguise her pain.

'What is it?' he asked sharply, taking in the way her face had paled and she looked green. As if she was about to throw up.

'Nothing,' she muttered thickly, but couldn't disguise the tears smarting.

He saw the brightness. 'Maggie what the hell is it?'

'Nothing, Caleb,' she lashed out fiercely. 'If you can't see something that's as plain as the nose on your face, then you don't deserve an explanation.' She pulled free and fled for the bedroom, uncaring of where she went, just wanting sanctuary.

He followed her in. 'What is it? You're angry because I guessed right? How could you, Maggie? That man is odious… Tell me, did you kiss him?' He let out a harsh breath, a jealous red mist descending on his vision, his judgement. 'Of course you did. God! Does he really do it for you? He looks to me to be the type who likes it rough…'

The only thing that halted his tirade was the awful stillness that invaded Maggie's limbs. Her eyes were huge pools of un-mistakable hurt, her mouth open in horror. He knew immediately he'd gone too far and stepped closer. She backed away so jerkily that she tripped over the bed and fell backwards. In a second Caleb was there, bending over, picking her up. His hand on her arm was too much; Maggie felt faint with the pain.

'What is it…?' he asked urgently.

'My…arm…you're hurting my arm…'

He let go immediately and sat her down on the bed. 'Maggie, did I hurt you? Show me…'

She shook her head—it was swimming. 'Not you…him…'

He cursed volubly. Very carefully, he pulled the shoulder of the dress down and uttered an oath fit for a sailor when he saw the livid bruise of finger marks that was lurid against her skin. 'Why didn't you tell me…?'

'Well, you didn't give me much opportunity.'

No, he hadn't. Had he really misjudged the situation that badly? All he knew was that he'd taken one look and seen red. He wasn't used to misreading anything. Never mind a woman being mauled by some jerk. And it was this woman. Maggie. He wanted to go straight out and find Deveney and beat him to a pulp.

'What happened, Maggie?'

She avoided the question. 'I need to put some arnica on this or it'll get worse.'

He jumped up. 'I'll get it.'

She directed him to find it in her wash bag and he came back. With infinite tenderness he gently massaged it into her skin. She could feel the tears start again. Couldn't stop them slipping down her cheeks. She was suddenly very tired of being on the receiving end of Caleb's cynical mistrust. Tired of having to maintain a façade. And didn't know if she could go on with the whole charade.

But then…when he caught her face and brought it round to his, and his hands cupped her jaw, his thumbs wiping her tears away, and whispered *sorry* against her mouth, she felt herself melt inside. Yes, she could tell him the truth. Yes, she could tell him exactly what had happened. And if she did…she might not have to face his censure any more. But that would be it—the end. For the one thing he'd despise even more than what he perceived her to be right now, would be the certain knowledge that she'd fallen for him.

And now, when he was being so gentle, so tender, kissing her with such sweet, restrained passion, the tiredness slipped away and all she wanted was to cling on to this…for a little longer.

That night they didn't make love. Caleb just tucked her against him, careful to make her lie on her good arm, and held her within the circle of his embrace. When he acted like this, it made it even harder to maintain a distance. Tomorrow— she'd think about it tomorrow, think about building back up her wall of defence. But for now…for now she'd sink deep into the dream…and she did.

A week later Maggie was painting on the terrace; it was a beautiful summer's day. Her thoughts were on that night, almost a week ago. Since then, she'd caught Caleb looking at her a couple of times with something…some light she couldn't define. And when he'd caught her eye, invariably the shutters would come down. But something had definitely changed between them. There was some kind of stillness. A kind of reverence when they made love…*or maybe it was just her ridiculous imagination.*

She furiously stroked her brush back and forth over the canvas, as if to blot out her wayward thoughts. When she heard the phone ring she went in with relief, glad of the distraction. She picked it up. When she put it down she had a frown on her face.

Caleb wanted to see her in his office. For some reason an icy trickle of foreboding skittered down her back. She changed out of her paint-spattered overalls and into simple trousers and a light V-neck sweater. Her hair swung in a plait down her back.

When she arrived on the top floor of his offices, the unsmiling Ivy had morphed into smiling Ivy. 'Maggie, isn't it? Please come through. Mr Cameron is expecting you.'

Maggie hid her bemusement as she followed the older lady to Caleb's office. She knocked and ushered Maggie through the door.

Caleb was standing at the window, looking out over the city. He turned when she came in and Maggie was struck by how serious he looked.

The door closed behind Ivy. Caleb raked a glance over her. 'What is it?' She laughed a little nervously. 'Caleb, you're scaring me…' She thought of something. 'Is it John; is it his heart again?'

He lifted a hand. 'No…it's not John. He's fine and he said to say thank you again for looking after him so well; he was a lot more frightened than he let on. I've sent him home to London to recuperate.'

She shrugged, a little embarrassed. 'It was nothing.'

He walked around the desk and came close. 'You have paint on your cheek.'

She flushed and lifted a hand to wipe it away. 'I never looked in the mirror.'

She couldn't read the expression on his face.

'Maggie, I've finished my work here. I'm going back to London tomorrow.'

Oh, my God…this is it…he's leaving.

Everything felt woolly and fuzzy, as if it were coming from far away. There was a seat behind Maggie and she sat in it, hoping that it didn't look as if she'd fallen into it, which was what she had done. She tried to maintain an iron grip on her emotions. This was exactly what she wanted. Exactly what she'd been waiting for. She looked up and met Caleb's eyes. They were shadowed. God. Was he looking at her with pity? Did he suspect for one second how much this was killing her?

He couldn't.

She feigned the best look of delayed surprised comprehension that she could. 'Oh! So this is it? You're letting me go…'

His mouth tightened. 'Well, technically, I could insist that you come to London with me; you've got one week to work out the contract.'

Maggie stood, galvanised by shock, the bile rising in her

throat. He saw the way she paled, remembered her reaction on seeing the contract for the first time. 'As far as I recall, the contract stated two months or the duration of your stay in Dublin…so technically, if your stay is up tomorrow, then we're out of contract.'

He looked at her steadily for a long moment. A muscle twitched in his jaw. He couldn't deceive her. 'Actually, I have to confess something. That contract was a bogus document…'

Her mouth opened, her jaw dropped.

'When you reminded me about it in Monte Carlo, I drew something up myself on the computer. It was only to reassure you that I was going to keep my word.'

And he had. Her mother had signed papers already, so the house was legally back in her name. This made something drop out of Maggie's chest.

'So…no one ever looked at it? No one witnessed it?'

He shook his head.

She wasn't sure how to take this, how to react. 'Well… thank you.' She backed away behind the chair. The same chair she'd stood behind that night, when she'd come to beg for the house. 'But then…if there's no contract…then there's nothing to stop me just leaving…walking away.'

'I guess not,' he said heavily.

'You're leaving tomorrow…'

'Yes.'

He looked at her. She was biting her lip. He wanted to go over and take her in his arms, slip his tongue between those soft lips, feel her response as he delved in deep and stroked, enticed…but, for some reason, he couldn't. They'd gone over a line. He was letting her go. So why did it feel as though his heart was being ripped from his chest? Why did it feel as if this woman standing in front of him was the only woman on the planet who he'd ever desire again?

She shrugged her shoulders. 'This is it…'

'Maggie.'

She met his eyes warily.

'You could come to London with me… This doesn't have to end here. Now that your mother has the house…we could go on…you could move in with me…'

She backed away, shaking her head. 'Never,' she said in a thin voice. 'Never. You'll never trust me, Caleb. You'll never respect me. And I won't warm your bed until the next woman comes along. I've paid my dues.'

He stiffened. Damned if he'd let her see what her words were doing to him. He shrugged nonchalantly. 'Whatever you want, Maggie.'

Something lit her eyes, a desperation. 'What I want is to go today. I'm going to go and pack now. When you get back, I'll be gone. I can't stay another night.' Then she said, 'Please, don't make me…'

She wanted to get away from him that badly? He felt a granite block weigh him down in his chest. His face closed, eyes shuttered. His mouth was a grim line.

'If you could be gone by the time I get back, I'd prefer it.'

Maggie walked to the door, her legs having bypassed shaking, had gone straight to wooden shock. She turned back for the last time and faced him.

'I never want to see you again.'

And she went out the door.

Caleb's heart was thumping when he let himself into the apartment. He'd seen the Mini Cooper parked outside… She hadn't gone… Did that mean she'd decided to stay on, as his mistress? But as soon as he walked in the door he knew she was gone. Even though her scent lingered on the air, the place felt flat, devoid of energy.

He saw the car key on the hall table. And a note.

I can't accept the car…or anything else. All the best in your future, Caleb. Maggie.

It fluttered to the floor out of his fingers. Sure enough, when he walked into the bedroom, all the clothes were neatly laid out in bags, labelled up for the relevant shops. And all the jewellery was on the dressing table in each individual box. She hadn't kept one thing.

Why?

Inexplicably, this made him sick. If she'd taken everything, as he'd expected her to, it would have made him feel… somehow justified. But wasn't this typical of her? He sat down heavily on the bed. Every step along the way, she had consistently surprised him by not acting the way he'd thought she would. He got up and went out to the terrace. For the first time in his life, he felt at a loss, didn't know what to do…felt impotent. He wanted Maggie. So badly he could taste it.

As he looked out over the city, felt the ache spreading through his limbs, he knew it. And had to acknowledge it. She'd got so far and so deep under his skin…that he'd fallen for her. He slammed a hand down on the railing. Who was he kidding? He'd fallen for her back in London. And, despite everything she'd done…he was so far in love with her now… that he knew he'd never find a way back.

And she never wanted to see him again. Karma. Revenge.

He left the view and went back in, slamming the door shut behind him so forcefully that the windows shuddered. And the next day, when he got on the plane to go back to London, his face was so grim and stern that no one dared speak to him.

CHAPTER TWELVE

'AND the stock shares went through the roof; they just didn't know how to handle the ramifications…'

Caleb tuned out the conversation. His mind couldn't settle and the heavy weight lodged in his chest was threatening to choke him. All he could see, all he could think about, was Maggie. She was everywhere he looked, but only in his mind's eye. He took in the glittering London crowd that surrounded him. The women were beautiful, stunning, bedecked in jewels. Hair perfectly teased, too thin bodies poured into the latest fashions. And it all seemed so vacuous. Meaningless.

He felt cold when he looked at them and studiously avoided their none too subtle glances from right under the noses of their partners. Several times he'd had to catch himself when he'd turned to his side as if to get Maggie's attention, touch her, have her look up at him with those luminous, wide eyes that said so much and yet held back so much. A sense of panic rose and he couldn't contain it as he imagined never finding out what she'd hidden in those unfathomable depths or never seeing her again. Never waking up beside her, never holding her, talking to her. Seeing her face light up. And yet…how could he have these feelings for someone who had done…what she had, for someone who patently didn't feel the same way?

'…Holland…'

'What?' Caleb said sharply as his focus zoomed in on the man looking at him expectantly. Had he just conjured up her name from his pathetic imaginings?

'Holland. Not wanting to speak ill of the dead or anything, but he was one nasty piece of work; it's only a pity he didn't live to see you in control of everything. That really was some coup, Cameron.'

Caleb smiled tightly; he'd never have wished Holland's ultimate fate on him, no matter what kind of a man he'd been and disliked the inference, but before he could cut in his associate was continuing.

'Now that he's gone and can't keep mouths shut, the truth is out. Did you hear—?'

'Spencer, I've really no interest—'

But the other man took no heed, his drink sloshing over the side of his glass in his obviously inebriated state. '…apparently the man had mistresses in every city and he was a violent bastard—'

Caleb had turned to walk away, but stopped in his tracks.

'…terrorised his poor wife for years. The police were called once but of course it all got hushed up…he greased their palms to keep it quiet. Didn't he have a daughter too? I think they said she was the one who called the cops…never saw her but heard she was a little siren—'

Caleb had the other man up against a wall so fast his drink smashed to the ground.

'What did you say…?'

'Cameron, what the devil is wrong with you?' the other man blustered.

Caleb let him go abruptly and strode out of the room, cutting a swathe through the crowd, who watched in stunned silence.

On the basis of those few words, which rang so true it hurt, Caleb knew that he'd just made the biggest mistake of his life. And he couldn't stop the rising tide of panic that gripped him.

His heart rate was doing triple time.

It couldn't be possible. She could have told me... Why wouldn't she have told me?

The world seemed to tilt crazily as he stood on the steps outside. The past two months ran in his head like a bad horror movie. The signs and clues had been there every step of the way, so obvious...and he had ignored them all. How had he been such a fool? How had he been so blind? Had he really let himself become so cynical and jaded and downright mistrustful that he didn't even recognise a true gem when it was right in front of him?

Like a rock hitting a still, perfect lake and the ripples spreading outwards, everything was so clear in his head now that he felt sick to his stomach. And more terrified than he'd ever felt in his life. *This was it.* And he'd thrown it away. He'd thrown Maggie away. Her words came back into his head with sickening clarity. He could even remember the look on her face. She had wanted nothing more than to get away from him so fast...

I never want to see you again.

Harsh lines transformed his face into a mask of haunted pain as he grabbed his car keys from the valet stepping out and took off as though he had a death wish.

Maggie stood at the edge of the water and watched how the spray came in and rushed back, taking the imprint of her feet with it. They sank a little more. She wished she could sink all the way, her whole body submerged in dark bliss where she wouldn't ever have to think or feel again. She gave herself a mental shake and stepped back out of the oncoming waves.

She looked around. Sheer isolation. A huge beach with acres of empty sand. Bordered by green cliffs on all sides, it was in the furthermost reaches of western Ireland. And it was empty because of a freak summer storm that had blown in for the last two days. The crowds hadn't yet returned but already she could see a figure in the distance, way ahead, near the tiny cottage a family friend had lent her for a few days. Her blessed peace would be gone soon.

She looked back out to the sea and breathed in deeply. She was free. Really free for the first time in her life. So why did she feel as though she were still in prison? It was her heart—her heart was in the prison, not her. And she would just have to learn to live with it. In time…she knew the pain would fade, become less.

She turned and walked back in the direction she'd come, hands in the pockets of a light fleece zipped up against the strong breeze, her jeans rolled up to her knees. There was still just that one figure in the distance, far too far away for Maggie to be able to make out if it were a man or a woman. She emptied her mind and looked down, stopping to pick up shells or stones along the way.

After walking for quite a bit, she could make out that it was a man. A tall man. With dark hair. In a T-shirt and jeans. Even from here, she could see a well-built physique. Her heart twisted painfully. What demon god was sending her a look-alike to test her heart? She drew nearer and nearer—could make out more detail. Thick, dark hair—swept off a high forehead, by the looks of it. Broad shoulders. He was looking out to sea and then he turned around. Maggie stopped. Blood rushed to her head, pounded in her ears, drowning out the crashing waves. It *couldn't* be.

But it was. Every cell in her body told her that it was. Caleb. Just metres away. She shook her head as if to clear the image, but he didn't disappear. He was coming towards her. That struck her into action. She could see the cottage on the bluff just behind him and made a diagonal path away from where he was walking, towards home. She could see from the corner of her eye that he too had changed direction, heading straight for her. She couldn't think. Couldn't feel. One foot in front of the other, until she was behind the door. And safe.

'Maggie.'

She ignored his call, walking faster, desperation making it hard to breathe.

'Maggie.' He was much closer, his long strides effortlessly catching up with hers.

She started a small jog and then felt herself caught and whirled around. She looked up, stunned, into Caleb's face. The shells and stones dropped unnoticed on to the sand.

'Maggie. Please don't run away from me. We have to talk.'

She laughed. 'Talk? Caleb, I told you I never wanted to see you again, and I certainly don't now.' She pulled away and started to walk up the hill. Focus on the house, focus on the house.

'Maggie. Please.' He was close behind her. 'You once came to me to beg me to listen to you for five minutes. That's all I'm asking now. Please.'

She stopped and had to shut her eyes at the memories. Pain lancing through her. This would kill her. But damned if he'd know it. She didn't turn around. 'Five minutes.'

She went into the house through the back door. Not even bothering to hold it open for him.

In the small kitchen she turned around to face him, crossing her arms over her chest. Her heart was beating way too fast for what she had just done. Her hair was windblown, face pink from the wind. And she looked more beautiful than he'd ever seen her. And never more distant.

She was pointedly focusing on a point over his shoulder. 'Well? The clock is ticking.'

'Maggie…I'm sorry…'

She looked at him aghast, her mouth dropping open. 'Sorry? What on earth do you have to be sorry for, Caleb? I got what I wanted; you got what you wanted…'

He smiled but it didn't reach his eyes and she noticed lines around his mouth, smudges of dark colour under his eyes. 'I didn't get you, Maggie, not really. And I still want you.'

She frowned, suddenly feeling a little adrift, wanting to know what he meant but not wanting to ask.

He raked a hand through his hair and looked out to the tumultuous Atlantic for a minute.

'Caleb—'

He looked back, blue eyes vivid. 'I know, I know—the time… God, this is hard.'

Her heart squeezed crazily and she tightened her arms as if to stop it.

'I think I know what happened…that night, eight months ago. Someone said something in London and everything dropped into place…'

Maggie felt a sudden fear. 'Did you go to my mother to find out where I was?'

He nodded.

'Did you say anything to her…?' Her breasts rose and fell in her agitation. 'Did you—?'

Caleb put out a hand, coming a step closer. Maggie moved

away. 'No! No, Maggie…I could have asked her, but I didn't need to. I *know*. I just want to hear it from you.'

'Know what, Caleb? Time is really running out—'

He took a deep breath. 'Eight months ago you seduced me that night against your will, didn't you?'

The room went fuzzy for a second and Maggie could feel her legs wanting to buckle but somehow she managed to stay upright. 'Don't be ridiculous,' she said faintly.

But Caleb had taken in her reaction, the ashen tinge to her skin. It made something joyous erupt in his chest. Even as it was just confirming his worst fears. That she'd never really felt anything for him. Just physical desire.

'Your stepfather saw the attraction between us and made the most of it, didn't he?'

She shook her head numbly.

'He made you flirt with me…made you pretend to show an interest…made you come to the hotel that night dressed like a—'

'Stop!' Her mind worked feverishly. He still didn't know that she hadn't been aware until that day. Her heart was still safe. Her arms dropped to her sides unconsciously. 'How… how do you know this?'

'Just something someone said. I didn't need to hear any more…I knew immediately. I can't believe I didn't see it at the time…but I was blinded.'

She tried to figure out what she could say to keep him happy and send him on his way. Looking at him, having him so close, was quickly becoming unbearable. 'He threatened me with something…too huge for me to fight alone.'

'Your mother?'

She sucked in a breath. 'How do you…?'

'You have a bond that goes beyond anything I've ever seen.

And you're like a mother bear with a cub whenever she's mentioned...plus she's inordinately happy for a recently widowed woman who had been left with nothing.' His voice softened. 'Maggie, I heard...that he was violent... Did he ever—?'

'Never me. Unless I got in the way,' she said bitterly. 'Always her, though. And I could never protect her. Nothing could. Not even the police. He was too powerful.'

A vivid image came into his head, a sick feeling. 'That scar...on your thigh...'

Maggie went paler. 'I got in the way one day...when he was...when I tried to...he knocked me out of the way and I fell into the ironing board, the iron...'

Rage filled him. He opened his mouth but Maggie had had enough. She held up a hand. 'Please, Caleb. You know now. Thank you for giving us back the house and for paying off the tax debts... My mother told me. You didn't have to do that—'

His hand slashed the air. 'Of course I did. It was my fault your mother was put in that situation; it was the least I could do.'

Maggie continued; she wanted him gone. 'I'm sorry I deceived you too eight months ago, but it's over. Please, just go.'

For a second he half turned as if he was going to go. Maggie held her breath, a hollow feeling spreading throughout her body, but then, abruptly, he came back. She was rooted to the spot.

'No...Maggie, I won't go. Because I want to know—once Holland had died and there was no threat any more, why didn't you try to defend yourself?'

'Would you have believed me?'

'Perhaps not at first,' he conceded. 'But it wouldn't have taken much to convince me. I'm not such an ogre and I would never have taken the house if I'd known.'

'I know...' she said quietly.

'So…why?'

Her brain had become mush. *Why, indeed?*

When he said it like that now, so simply, she could have cursed herself. It had simply never occurred to her. Her main priority had been self-protection, but hadn't she ironically gone the most self-destructive route? Since she'd seen him again…her brain had become so scrambled that she'd happily sabotaged herself. In an effort to block out reality and to have him on any terms. His terms. She was pathetic.

'Because I thought you wouldn't believe me…' It sounded weak to her ears.

'So you allowed me to use you, take you as my mistress, let me make love to you almost every night…put on the not very successful pretence of someone who was the complete opposite to what you really are?'

'But it was…' she breathed, not realising that she was giving herself away spectacularly.

He felt triumphant. He lifted a brow. 'Then why leave everything behind? The clothes, the jewels, the *car*?'

'Because they weren't mine,' she answered simply.

'Exactly.' He looked smug. 'Any other woman would have cleaned out the lot. And more. Believe me.'

She felt as though she was being wrung out on a rack; he was stretching her and stretching her to breaking-point. Her voice came out brittle and harsh. 'Look, Caleb; what do you want? I can't tell you any more…'

But he was relentless. 'I bet you made it all up, just to keep up the front… College? You put yourself through it and never took a penny from Holland, am I right? Probably lived in a bedsit with mice rather than take his money. Lovers? I know you weren't a virgin, but you weren't far off it, Maggie.'

She went even more ashen at his uncannily accurate assessment. He noted it with something close to fury rising in his chest—fury at himself.

He was immovable, implacable. She knew instantly the only thing that would move him would be the one thing that would kill her. But if it meant she'd get rid of him then she had no choice. Before he guessed the full truth, if she could protect herself from at least that…

She squared her shoulders. 'It was cockroaches, actually, and you want the truth?' She tossed her head. 'Here it is. The truth is that I had one lover before I met you, in college. And I didn't know what Tom had planned until…until…' She couldn't do it.

A stillness entered Caleb's body. He came closer and Maggie could feel the heat from his body reach out to caress her, touch her. He had to go…*now*. She had to be strong.

'That day.'

'The day of the date?' he queried sharply. Too sharply.

Maggie turned away in agitation, arms around her body. 'Yes, damn you, yes!' She turned around again. 'There! Are you happy now? I didn't know until that day, so in case it's not completely obvious, let me spell it out for you. I had a crush on you, Caleb, a monumental crush. I believed that you possibly felt something for me too and I *stupidly* believed that you *wanted* to take me on that date, to get to know me.'

'Maggie…'

She could see a flare of something in his eyes. Her voice shook. 'Don't you *dare* pity me, Caleb Cameron. I don't need your pity. It was a crush, that's all. Desire. Tom followed me to Oxford Street that day and made me buy that…that dress…' a shudder of revulsion went through her '…then he told me what he'd do to my mother if I didn't comply. I had no choice.' The fight went out of her; she looked away. 'But then…I just…'

'Couldn't go through with it.'

She looked back quickly and a shiver of something inde-finable ran through her. He was looking at her with…not pity…something else and it made her silly heart speed up. He came close, too close, and only then she became aware of the fat tear sliding down her cheek. She didn't even know she'd been crying. He reached out a hand and she jerked away.

'You've been minding her for a long time. And you came back to Dublin to escape, didn't you?'

Why did he have to say that so gently, as though he really cared? She nodded slowly, more tears slipping hotly down. His hand came out again. This time she couldn't move as he wiped his thumb back and forth. The contact was too much. A broken sob escaped and, with a curse, Caleb closed the distance, pulled her forward and into his arms. He held her for a long time. Until the sobbing had stopped. Rubbing her back as though she were ten years old.

But then she didn't feel ten any more. She felt like a grown woman whose body was springing into life, pressed as she was, tight against the length of him.

She tried to pull back but he wouldn't let her go.

'Caleb…let me go, I'm okay now…'

She was sure she looked awful; as a freckled redhead, she didn't do pretty crying.

'I can't let you go.'

She looked up. 'What?'

She felt rather than saw him shrug. His eyes bored down into hers. 'I can't let you go. I'm afraid that if I do…I'll wake up and have dreamt all this and that I'll never see you again.'

A taut, pregnant stillness seemed to surround them.

'But…you can go now. Leave. You don't want to see me again.'

'No. *You* don't want to see *me*.'

Maggie's brow creased as she took in a vulnerable light in the depths of Caleb's eyes. It couldn't be. She shook her head. 'Caleb, stop confusing me. Let me go.' She tried to pull away again, a little desperately. There was no give.

'Just tell me one thing, Maggie… Was it really just a crush?'

She felt him stop breathing. Nodded her head slowly. And inexplicably, started to drown in his eyes. She just…couldn't do it. Couldn't lie. Feeling the last vestiges of her defence and fight fall away, leaving her limp and defeated, she stopped nodding and slowly shook her head.

A surge of mounting hope moved through him. 'So…if it wasn't just a crush…was it something more?'

She was feeling boneless. All that existed were those mesmerising eyes. She nodded again, barely aware of what she was saying yes to, only aware that she wanted Caleb to keep holding her. For ever.

Caleb tried to contain himself but could feel the tremor building all the way upwards from his feet. 'For the past two months…and now…is it still there?'

She broke out of the seductive trance. She could feel the tears well again. 'Please Caleb…don't tease…don't make me say it.'

He lifted his hands and framed her face and she could feel them trembling. 'You don't have to…I will. Maggie Holland, I love you. I love you so much that if you can't tell me you love me too then I'm going to walk straight into the Atlantic and never come back because my life would not be worth living.'

A hard shell seemed to crack open around her. She clung on to his eyes, searching, seeking…and could see nothing but pure love shining back. Could she trust?

She had to trust.

With a very shaky voice she said huskily, 'That'd be an awful waste because I love you too…I've loved you since the moment I set eyes on you.'

'Oh, Maggie…' He groaned and lowered his lips to hers, taking her mouth in a sweet kiss, hunger barely checked, but there. He stopped and pulled back. 'When I saw you that first time…I fell so hard and then when I overheard Holland talking about using you…I cynically assumed you were in on it too. It was easier to see you as an accomplice than face up to my true feelings…I'm so, so sorry; when you tried to stop and tell me—'

Maggie just shook her head, putting a finger to his lips. 'It *was* pretty damning and we'd only just met. You had no idea who I was…'

She wound her arms tightly around his neck and, stretching up, pressed her mouth to his and urged him to kiss her deeper, harder. They pulled apart after a few seconds, breathing harshly. She touched his face wonderingly.

'Are you here? Is this real?'

He laughed shakily. 'I hope so because I'm about to get down on one knee and propose.'

'Caleb…' She watched, open-mouthed, as he knelt down before her. Tears blurred her vision again. They just wouldn't stop.

He took her hand. 'Margaret Holland. Will you please become my wife? So that I can spend my life loving you, minding you, protecting you…'

'But…but you never stay in one place for long…your work…'

His voice was raw and husky, pulling at her heart. 'Maggie, I'm so tired. I'm tired of living under the shadow of my parents' disastrous marriage. I'm tired of working so hard. It's time I delegated. I want to settle down, have babies…with you. Wherever you are, or want to be…this house…we could buy this, live here, *anywhere*, just as long as I'm with you. I never believed this could happen to me, but…' he shrugged with endearing vulnerability '…you're my home…and I want to come home, so much.'

She shook her head, her lip wobbling, tears still streaming, and got down on her knees to meet him. 'Oh, Caleb…you're my home too. I love you so much it scares me…'

They looked at each other for an intense moment and he cradled her head before kissing her again. Her eyes were closed and she was breathless when he pulled away finally, both blissfully unaware of the hard floor under their knees. Then Caleb stood and pulled her with him. 'I have something for you.'

She was incapable of speech, touching her lips, feeling them tingle from the kiss, wanting to pinch herself to see if she was really awake. She wiped at her cheeks as he led her out to the front door and there, parked in front of the house, was her battered Mini. Exactly as it always had been.

She clapped a shocked hand to her mouth. Wide-eyed, she looked at Caleb, shaking her head. 'But…how…I mean, it was a tin can…'

He grimaced. 'Just seconds away from it. I started tracking it down after that day your mother spilled the beans, even though you professed not to care, somehow, I knew.'

'But that was…weeks ago.'

He shrugged. 'I was fighting a losing battle even then, trying to keep you in the little box I'd built around you, but more and more I was beginning to suspect things weren't as they seemed, but it was still easier to mistrust you than look at my real feelings…'

She looked away reluctantly from the intense emotion blazing from his eyes.

'Is that how you came down here? That's at least five hours…in a car that doesn't go over forty miles an hour…'

He rolled his shoulders. 'Don't I know it and it was more like eight hours.'

He brought her round to the back of the car. 'This was Plan *B* in case you weren't going to listen to me.'

There at the back of the car were tin cans tied on pieces of string hanging off the bumper, trailing on the ground, and a huge sign, which read:

I love you, Maggie. Please marry me?

'Believe me,' he said dryly, 'it's the only thing that convinced your mother to tell me where you were.'

The laughter bubbled up out of her and she gripped his hand. He brought her round in front of him and she could feel the slight tremor still evident in his hands as they smoothed back her hair. The awe on his face, as if he couldn't really believe he'd found her. It made her heart soar and flip over.

She wrapped her arms tightly around his waist. 'The answer is yes, yes, yes…'

She gave him a shyly coy look. 'About those knots in your shoulders…'

He relaxed visibly and Maggie exulted in the gift he was giving her, that she was giving him. After so much heartache. Perhaps now, she could finally be safe…and happy.

He bent low to whisper in her ear with husky promise, 'We have so much to talk about, catch up on…but first let's see about making those babies…'

With one graceful movement, he lifted his most treasured possession and carried her over the threshold of the tiny cottage that clung to the edge of a beautiful beach, with the waves pounding just metres away, and into their new lives.

* * * *

Ruthlessly Bedded, Forcibly Wedded
by Abby Green is available this month from
Modern™ romance.

THE ROYAL HOUSE OF KAREDES

Two crowns, two islands, one legacy

Volume 1 – April 2009
BILLIONAIRE PRINCE, PREGNANT MISTRESS
by Sandra Marton

Volume 2 – May 2009
THE SHEIKH'S VIRGIN STABLE-GIRL
by Sharon Kendrick

Volume 3 – June 2009
THE PRINCE'S CAPTIVE WIFE
by Marion Lennox

Volume 4 – July 2009
THE SHEIKH'S FORBIDDEN VIRGIN
by Kate Hewitt

8 VOLUMES IN ALL TO COLLECT!

THE ROYAL HOUSE OF KAREDES

Two crowns, two islands, one legacy

Volume 5 – August 2009
THE GREEK BILLIONAIRE'S INNOCENT PRINCESS
by Chantelle Shaw

Volume 6 – September 2009
THE FUTURE KING'S LOVE-CHILD
by Melanie Milburne

Volume 7 – October 2009
RUTHLESS BOSS, ROYAL MISTRESS
by Natalie Anderson

Volume 8 – November 2009
THE DESERT KING'S HOUSEKEEPER BRIDE
by Carol Marinelli

8 VOLUMES IN ALL TO COLLECT!